RAMEZ NAAM

Crux

ANGRY
ROBOT

ANGRY ROBOT
An imprint of Watkins Media Ltd

Lace Market House,
54-56 High Pavement,
Nottingham
NG1 1HW
UK

angryrobotbooks.com
twitter.com/angryrobotbooks
Kill or cure

First published by Angry Robot in 2013
This edition published 2015

Copyright © Ramez Naam 2013

Cover art by Steven Meyer-Rassow
Set in Meridien by Argh! Oxford

Distributed in the United States by Random House, Inc., New York

ISBN 978 0 85766 551 5
Ebook ISBN 978 0 85766 297 2

Printed in the United States of America

9 8 7 6 5 4 3

For Molly, who helped give birth to this.

PROLOGUE: JULY 2040

THREE MONTHS AFTER THE RELEASE OF NEXUS 5

SYMPHONIC

The pianist's hands glided across the keys, spreading out to left and right, fingers striking keys in unison. The piano responded, music soaring from it. The violinists joined her, sweeping in perfectly. In her mind she could feel them behind her, feel the vibration as the bows moved over strings, feel the pressure of fingertips holding notes, the instruments tucked under chins, the music leaping out. Then she felt the drummers enter, even as she heard them, sounds and minds in counterpoint to her melody.

Kade sucked it in, completely entranced. His body lay on the other side of the planet, but his mind was in the pianist's, watching, absorbing, using one of the back doors he and Rangan had hidden in Nexus 5 to observe how their technology was being used.

The pianist's mind in turn was linked to the other musicians'. Seven of them, playing in this empty concert hall, their minds entwined like the music, feeling each other's actions, unconsciously communing. There was no conductor here, none but the emergent sum of their minds. No audience, but someday, someday they would play with a full orchestra, for a full house, would let the audience *feel* what it was like to make such music.

The pianist threw herself at the piano now, leaning into it with her body, her hands flying, gliding, then pouncing, fingers moving in a blur, shoulders hunched as she brought her weight down onto the keys with every note. Kade could feel the sweat on her brow, her breath coming fast, the feel of the keys as she made them hers, the impossible intricacy of the piece she flew through. He could hear the music in her mind, *feel* the music, the towering crescendo of Rachmaninoff's Third Piano Concerto, the anticipation of the epic climax she was building to. The drums answered her. The French horn sang. The strings joined them in harmony. He could feel the players, feel their minds, feel the exhilaration in them all as the piece built and built and built.

Yes. This. This is what Nexus could do. He could feel the walls between the musicians' minds dropping; the veil of *maya*, the illusion of separation, being lifted. He could feel them conjoining, merging, becoming something more, a single mind greater than its individual components. Kade lost himself in the experience, in the music, in the symphonic structure of this higher mind gelling before him.

Then a high priority message flashed across Kade's mental vision.

[Alert]

What? Kade's breath caught in his chest. Rangan? Ilya? Had his bots found his friends?

[Alert: Coercion Code Detected. Status: Active]

No. Not Rangan. Not Ilya. Something else. Something monstrous. Something he had to stop.

The pianist pounded out the final commanding notes of Rachmaninoff. The drums and strings came to their climax as she did, and she let her hands drop from the keys, exhausted, exhilarated. Joy leapt from them all, and in their intertwined imaginations an audience was cheering, surging to their feet in standing ovation.

With regret, Kade disconnected from them all, then clicked on the alert, opened the encrypted connection, invoked one of his three back doors, entered the passcode, the code that no one else knew, and tunneled into fear.

Arkady Volodin pumped his fist into the air, jumping up and down on the sand, and screamed his approval as the music came to a pounding climax. Five thousand partygoers screamed with him into the balmy night air above the beach. The DJ gave them two seconds of rest, then brought the beat pounding back. The bassline thrummed through Arkady's bones, resonated in his chest. The crowd roared even louder. Arkady could feel them in his mind, surging, exulting, fucking high off this epic night in this epic place.

God, I love Croatia, Arkady realized. These people know how to party!

Above him laser lights scanned across the sky, leaving bright blue and red tracers across the clouds of smoke rising from the open air beach party. The sand of this pristine Croatian beach vibrated with the music, sending it up through Arkady's feet. The surf crashed against the long break, running up the bare legs of the revelers in bikinis and briefs dancing closer to the waves. Palm trees swayed beyond the trusses that held up the lights and lasers and fog machines. Go-go dancers pranced and twirled on pedestals above the beach and the surging crowd.

Can you get me some Nexus? Arkady had asked. It was too risky back in Moscow, but while he was here...

That guy, over there, he'd been told, as they pointed towards a tall, lean man smoking a cigarette, leaning up against a building further uphill. *You can get it from Bogdan.*

Minutes later, in a darkened spot beyond the lights, he'd handed over a wad of cash for a vial of silvery liquid, then downed it immediately. It had slipped down his throat, oily and metallic, and he'd gone to find a drink to wash away the taste and sensation that lingered in his throat.

By the time he'd finished the drink he'd been coming up. *Calibration phase.* He'd hallucinated – he was a fucking tsar in an old Russian palace. No, he *was* the palace. No, he was the whole goddamn *city!*

Arkady laughed at it. So right. He was a tsar all right. A young tsar to all these punters here. Oil money. That's where his royalty came from. He was here to suck the marrow out of this country, buying up rights to the offshore gas deposits that remained for Gazprom Bank back home. A conqueror. Oh, he'd conquer this place, with its beaches and drugs and women and gas. He'd make it all his. Better than fucking Moscow.

The music reached a new peak, and Arkady bounced with it, manically shaking his body, feeling the dancers around him revel as he did.

[Calibration Complete]

The message scrolled across his vision.

[Rabbit Hole Ready. Wanna Enter?]

Arkady grinned. He'd heard of this. The VR app this club had built. Yeah, he wanted to try it.

[Y]

Controls appeared at the side of his vision, layers he could toggle on and off. The first layer was enabled already. Arkady spun around, and laughed.

The dancers around him were sheathed in silver and gold, auras glimmering. The ocean was liquid silver, spilling onto a beach of crushed iridescent diamonds. The stars above were suddenly far brighter, shining brightly through the smoke and lasers, wheeling as he watched. A huge full moon loomed in the sky. Arkady turned further, and saw the go-go dancers. Their auras were crackling sheaths of energy, snapping and popping. They held out their hands as they danced, and lightning flew from them, arcing out over the crowd.

Arkady screamed his approval, dancing harder, pounding his feet against the sand. He felt the whole crowd respond, felt the ecstasy of the moment pounding through them all.

Fucking outstanding!

Then a burst of wind hit him from behind. Arkady turned in time to see something huge flying at him, winged and fanged. It dove down from the star-filled sky, from out over the liquid silver sea, a predator closing on the crowd, its enormous mouth open. He saw flames inside that cavernous maw, and then the dragon exhaled, and a river of fire surged down at the beach.

Arkady threw himself to the sand. Intense heat beat at his back. The downdraft from the dragon's wings pummeled him as it flapped over them, and then the thing was past.

Arkady looked up and saw the beast rising towards the brilliant Milky Way, pounding the air with those leathery wings. Around him, partygoers sheathed in their multicolored auras were crouched or cowering. Others were still dancing, smiling and laughing at them, not unkindly.

Holy fuck! Arkady thought.

He reached out with his thoughts to the controls across the side of his vision, flipped off the layer that was on, and looked up. The dragon was gone, nowhere to be seen, the stars were masked by the smoke and lasers. He scanned around him. The auras were gone. The sea was water, crashing onto ordinary sand. The go-go dancers no longer threw electricity.

He flicked the layer back on, and lightning sparkled around the girls on stage again, auras shimmered into appearance around the other dancers, silver waves crashed onto the beach. And up there, he could see the dragon against the unreal galactic backdrop, flapping its wings, turning, coming around for another pass.

Fucking amazing! Arkady thought.

He rose up, lifted his hands into the air, waited for the virtual dragon to rain fire on them all.

Bogdan Radic took another drag on his cigarette, his eyes closed. His thoughts scanned from mind to mind, looking for just the perfect mark. The French girl with the designer shoes? The Italian couple with the flashy jewelry? They'd taken his drugs, his special version of Nexus, and now their minds were open to his.

It wasn't that hard, really. Nexus 5 was open source now. All he'd had to do was download the code, modify it for his own purposes, to give him a back door into the minds of anyone who took it, then load his modifications up into vials of the drug. If you could code, you could change Nexus in all sorts of ways. And Bogdan could sure as hell code.

He dismissed the French girl. From a rich family, but he couldn't find any way to access that wealth in her pretty little head. And kidnapping wasn't for him. Too high a risk. Too much chance of physical violence.

The Italian couple... His mind roamed through theirs during their calibration phase, when the disorientation would hide most of what he did. No. They played rich, but they were overleveraged. Their assets were too illiquid for Bogdan's needs. And two deaths would be so much harder to get away with than one.

The Russian was coming up now. Bogdan sifted through Arkady's chaotic thoughts as the calibration phase opened up his mind. Well, well, well. Paydirt.

Bogdan slipped back into the club proper, down into the storage room, and set up his gear. Then he reached out with his thoughts, and pulled Arkady to him.

Arkady held his arms up and out, defiantly, as the giant dragon bore down on them. The beast opened its mouth, and a gout of flame burst from it. The heat struck him full force, bathing his face, his arms, his chest. The force of the beast's wing flaps pushed at him. He wanted to flinch, but he yelled instead, like a man plunging down a roller coaster.

Then it was gone, and the dragon was past them.

Arkady jumped up and down, hooting in triumph. Beside him, a Croatian girl in little more than a bikini yelled as well, jumping up and down, gravity making her breasts do incredible things. Their eyes met.

Then something took hold of Arkady. His world dimmed. His sight narrowed. And he began to walk.

Arkady tried to resist, but his limbs moved without him. He flicked off the virtual reality layer. The auras disappeared, but his body kept moving. He tried to scream, but nothing came out.

Oh no. Oh, fucking no.

Whatever force controlled him led Arkady away from the water, over sand that gradually turned to rock and then concrete, away from the outdoor party, into the sprawling club, down a side hallway, down a set of stairs, and in through a closed door.

Inside he found the man who'd sold him this Nexus.
Bogdan. A lit cigarette was in his hand. On the table next
to Bogdan was a slate. On its screen was Gazprom's remote
access site. Next to it were a retinal scanner and a thumb
print pad.

No.

"Mr Volodin," Bogdan said. "How very nice to meet you."

Abruptly Arkady found he could speak again.

"Please," he said. "I'll give you anything. I have money.
Lots of money."

Bogdan grinned.

"Oh, I know you do, Arkady. But your employer has so
much more."

"No," Arkady said. "You don't understand. You don't
know how they operate. They'll *kill* me."

Bogdan took a drag on his cigarette, then exhaled,
flicking ash to the floor. He grinned at the Russian he held
captive. "No, Arkady. You'll already be dead."

Arkady screamed then, only to find it abruptly cut off as
someone else's will constricted his throat.

"Now," Bogdan said. "Kindly swipe your thumb, place
your eye to the scanner, and enter your access codes."

Arkady moved forward to comply.

Kade tunneled into fear. This mind was gripped in terror. He
struggled to take in the situation. A dark room. Pounding
music came in from beyond the walls. The sense of a vast
crowd nearby, thousands of minds. And here, in the room
with him.

He flicked this body's eyes over, took in the slate, the
retinal scanner, the man with the cigarette.

Theft. Theft and likely murder.

Kade reached out with his thoughts, opened the mind of the man before him, sent the passcode, and then he was in.

Bogdan smiled as Arkady moved forward. The money would be dumped into offshore accounts which would be cashed out minutes later. Arkady here would have a nasty accident. And by the time the authorities realized that it *hadn't* been an accident, Bogdan would be long gone, and much, much richer.

Then Arkady stopped, suddenly. Bogdan felt something change about the man's mind. Then he felt something press against his own mind, something vast.

Oh fuck, Bogdan thought. He turned and ran for the door.

Kade saw the man turn and run, just as the passcode opened his mind. He reached out and *yanked* on the man's motor cortex.

The man stumbled and fell to the floor of the store room, cursing.

Bogdan. That was his name. Kade could feel it now.

Kade gripped the man's mind tighter, then took stock of the rest of the situation.

Bogdan couldn't breathe. His heart was pounding. There was something in his mind. Something in his mind!

He tried to get up but the stranger had control of his limbs. He tried to break the connection but he was locked out.

Oh God, he thought. Someone *else* has a back door. A back door into me!

Kade let himself breathe deeper. The man named Arkady was physically unharmed. He'd gotten here in time. He broke the bonds on Arkady's mind, and the Russian rose to his feet, and ran, screaming.

Kade rifled through Bogdan's mind. Where was the coercion code? Ahhh, there. Files opened for him. He skimmed through them. More patterns to block in the next version of Nexus. More abuse paths that he could cut off from everyone.

Bogdan had given out hundreds of doses of Nexus loaded with this code. Thousands. Kade would need to send out a virus, hunting for them, rewriting code to fix these exploits when it found them.

Who are you? Bogdan asked.

Kade shook his head mentally. **I'm the last mind you'll ever touch.**

Please, Bogdan thought at him. **I have money. I have friends.**

Kade ignored him. He downloaded the code to add to his libraries, then went to work.

He removed Bogdan's administrator privileges to the Nexus OS in his own mind, locked him out of any control over the nanobots that infested him, took away Bogdan's ability to modify, upgrade, or even remove Nexus in the process.

No! Bogdan screamed.

Kade locked Bogdan out of Nexus communication, then. His brain would be hermetically sealed, never to touch another's. Only Kade would be able to access it, via his own back doors.

Fuck you! Bogdan raged. **You can't do that.**

Now the rest.

How many times have you done this? Kade asked Bogdan.

None! Bogdan replied. **This was the first time! And I didn't!**

Memories came back, streaming from Bogdan's mind. Corfu. Ibiza. Mykonos. Three Nexus-aided thefts. One leading to a murder.

And worse. He caught a glimpse of a girl, terrified, senses mentally crippled, her clothes half ripped off, her body held down by Bogdan's will and his perverted code as he...

Kade grimaced, and yanked himself away from Bogdan's memory. Thousands of miles away, his stomach rose up. His fists clenched.

You're disgusting, Bogdan.

Kade started in on the rewiring, tying neural circuits together. Bogdan's knowledge of programming. His understanding of Nexus. His concept of violence. His capacity for sexual arousal. All of these Kade tied to nausea, to crippling anxiety, to pervasive pain.

The man yelled at him. **What are you doing?**

I'm neutering you, Kade told him, grim satisfaction rising in his thoughts. **You won't ever steal, or kill, or fuck again.**

Bogdan gasped in shock, then resumed his rage. **You can't do this! What gives you the right?**

I made this, Kade told the man. **That gives me the right.**

THIS CHANGES EVERYTHING

One Week Later

The eye stared at Kade, unblinking, lying in its cooling bath. That black pupil in the green iris. The white egg-shaped sphere of it, with a bundle of freshly grown optic nerve trailing off behind it, looking like so much wet data cable.

My eye, Kade thought, cloned from my cells, to replace the one I lost in Bangkok.

He blinked the one eye in his head, lying back on the clinic bed as the doctors did their final prep. Late afternoon light filtered in through curtains drawn over the windows. His regrowing stump of a hand ached down deep in its fragile bones. He could feel the anesthetic starting to flow through his veins now. If all went well, in a few weeks he'd be seeing out of two eyes again, maybe even using two working hands.

Kade.

A mind touched his. Ling's mind. Su-Yong Shu's daughter. Alien. Young. A whirlwind of swirling thoughts. The data flowing all around him came alive in his mind – the flow of information through the medical monitors in the room, the power cables running through the wall, the wireless data channels permeating even this remote Cambodian clinic. He could see and feel them all, an intricate web of information and electrons all around him, as he could any time she touched his mind.

Kade smiled.

Hi, Ling.

He could feel her smile in return. Such a strange child, so unlike any other mind he'd ever touched. But he was starting to understand her, to see how her thoughts worked, to see the world the way she saw it.

Feng and I won't let them hurt you while you're asleep, Ling sent him.

Kade almost laughed.

It's OK, Ling, he sent her. **I trust them.**

They're humans, Ling sent back.

So am I, Kade replied.

Oh no, Kade, Ling sent him. **You're not human any more. You're like me now. Me and my mother.**

Kade reached for a reply, but all he found was the anesthesia, sucking him down into a warm sleepy place.

They buried my mother today, Kade, Ling sent him.

Visions came to Kade – Su-Yong Shu in that remote Thai monastery, the spot of blood blooming at her throat, the sudden sting in Kade's hand as a dart struck him, Su-Yong's skin going gray as the neurotoxin pumped through her, Feng lifting up the cleaver to amputate Kade's hand...

She's not dead, Ling was saying. **I'm going to find her. I'm going to get my mommy back.**

Ling... Kade started. *Be careful*, he wanted to tell her. But the drugs pulled him under first.

• • •

Martin Holtzmann closed his eyes and he was there again. The spray of snow stung at his face. The wind rushed by, roaring in his ears. His borrowed body leaned left, skis cutting in so perfectly to deep powder on this steep slope. Muscles flush with strength and youth pushed poles in and leaned right, carving around the next mogul like he hadn't since…

An elbow dug into his side, and he snapped his eyes open. Joe Duran, head of Homeland Security's Emerging Risks Directorate, and Holtzmann's boss's boss, was glaring at him.

"Pay attention," the man whispered.

Holtzmann mumbled something in reply, shifted in his seat, bringing his eyes back to the podium. President John Stockton was speaking, addressing this assembled crowd outside Department of Homeland Security head-quarters.

Holtzmann mopped sweat from his brow, beneath his shock of unruly white hair. Even at 9am, the Washington DC sun was brutal. Already they were on track for the hottest summer in North American history, coming just on the heels of the record-breaking heat wave of 2039. He wanted to just sink back into that memory of snow, that experience of another's body, of youth, gleaned through the Nexus connection between Holtzmann's mind and another's.

"…have to protect our humanity," the President was saying. "We must understand that some technologies, however exciting, put us on a path to *de*humanization…"

Like the technology in my skull, Holtzmann thought.

Nexus 5. How could he resist it? As ERD's Neuroscience Director, he'd led technical debriefing of Kaden Lane, Rangan Shankari, and Ilyana Alexander. He'd understood what they'd done. Something marvelous – taking Nexus and transforming it from a street drug and into a tool. Dangerous, yes. Full of potential for abuse. But oh, what a temptation!

And when Nexus 5 was released to the world? That horrible night when the mission to recapture Kaden Lane from that monastery in Thailand had gone completely awry? The night that Su-Yong Shu, one of the greatest minds of a generation, had been killed. The night his friend and colleague Warren Becker had died of a heart attack.

A terrible night. And to watch as thousands around the world got access to this tool... How could he resist? He'd taken that vial from storage in his lab, tipped it back and sent the silvery liquid down his throat, then waited as the nanoparticles found their way into his brain, attached themselves to neurons, self-assembled into information processing machines.

The three months since then had been the most exhilarating Holtzmann could remember. He'd seen incredible science done, published carefully on anonymous message boards. With Nexus 5 they were getting glimpses of paths to reversing Alzheimer's and senile dementia, making incredible progress in connecting autistic children to neurotypical adults. They were suddenly moving forward again in deciphering memory and attention, in seeing ways to boost intelligence. This was a tool that would change everything about the study of the mind, Holtzmann knew. And in so doing, it would transform humanity.

Holtzmann had already found it transformative at a personal level. He'd touched the thoughts of physicists and mathematicians, poets and artists, and other neuroscientists like himself. He'd felt *other minds*. What neuroscientist, what scientist of any sort, could pass up such an opportunity?

You could experience anything now, touch another's mind and see the world how they saw it, feel their experiences, their adventures, their...

Another memory bubbled up.

He'd been a young man again, strong, fit, with a beautiful young woman. He remembered the softness of her skin beneath his hands, the smell of her perfume, the taste of her kisses, the way he'd tugged the silken negligee off her shoulders and down her body, the wetness as his fingers found her so ready and so very turned on by him, the erotic thrill as she'd straddled him in stockinged thighs, and then the incredible warmth and tightness as she'd lowered herself down onto...

Enough, Holtzmann thought.

He pushed the memory out of his mind with an effort. Once had been the end of it. No need to go back there now. Truth be told, it had felt *too* real – not like pornography, but like infidelity. And Martin Holtzmann had sworn to himself that he'd never be unfaithful again.

No matter. There were tawdry ways to use the technology, but sublime ways as well. He felt more alive than he had in years, more excited about the future than he could remember since his youth.

"...that's why we have to win in November," Stockton was saying from the podium.

You're not going to win, Holtzmann thought. You're ten points down in the polls. Stanley Kim is going to be the next President. Americans aren't scared any more. All the atrocities are in the past. Americans want to see the future again.

I want to see the future.

Holtzmann smiled. Yes. Things were looking bright indeed.

?b64AECS448TxQRmeKwMcMoK83QyozvgSaLPsA0Kkc ++clA1KJHS/

What? Holtzmann jerked in his seat. A Nexus transmission had just rippled through his mind. He was dimly aware of ERD Director Joe Duran glancing at him in annoyance.

?HX?52a06967e7118fce7e55b0ba46f9502ce7477d27/

His heart was pounding. What the hell was going on? Had they found him out?

fcd55afa0/

No. Encrypted data. On a Nexus frequency. Holtzmann looked left and right, scanning the crowd, oblivious to Joe Duran's scowl.

?RU5L8PP0hLarBNxfoQM23wG6+KTCEBhOIAAQyPP c76+TWhj+X/

There, it was coming from behind him.

SntyZox/

And another…

He craned his neck to look backwards, ignoring the frowns of those behind him. There was nothing unusual back there. Senior Homeland Security people from all branches – FBI, TSA, DEA, Coast Guard, ERD – seated on white plastic chairs. A Secret Service agent, cool in mirrored glasses, walking slowly down the center aisle and towards the front of the crowd. In the far back, a semicircle of news cameras and reporters.

?0jRwfWGCmkvt5b17dzwt78jWXNx15Ur2sBf1fyBbS/

The signal came loud and clear from somewhere back there.

1suuHKZmZAE/

And the shorter reply.

They both came from… From…

Oh God. Dear God.

• • •

Kade woke from his drugged slumber in the clinic bed. It was dark outside the windows. He blinked in confusion. What had woken him? Ling again?

[Alert] [Alert] [Alert]

Then he saw the blinking in the corner of his eye. High priority notification. Permission to alert him while he was sleeping.

Rangan? Ilya? Had the agents he'd let loose on the net found them?

No. The other alert.

[Alert: Coercion Code Sample Alpha
Detected. Status: Active]

More coercion code. Not just any coercion code. A piece he'd seen just once before, days ago. Software that turned a human into a robot, into an assassin. The most sophisticated he'd seen.

And now his agents had spotted that code again, in a different mind. And the code was active.

Sleep vanished from Kade's mind. Open the alert. Click on the link to the mind. Confirm the encrypted connection. Activate the back door, full immersion. Send the passcode.

And he was in.

Holtzmann's eyes locked on the source of the Nexus transmissions. The suit. The mirrored glasses. The boosted muscle. It was the Secret Service agent who was communicating via Nexus.

Fear froze him.

Oh no. Please, no.

?3BRW8SYWv5KYzmduVPQaiKG1acsG6wvaNJRJU/

The Secret Service man reached into his jacket and something let loose its grip on Martin Holtzmann.

"HE'S GOT A GUN!" Holtzmann surged to his feet, shouting at the top of his lungs, pointing at the man.

okwH46RNI7/

Time slowed to a crawl. The assassin's hand came out out of his jacket, a giant pistol gripped tight. Two other Secret Service agents became human blurs, sprinting at impossible speed towards the man with the gun. Joe Duran was coming to his feet, staring at Holtzmann, mouth open. Holtzmann's heart skipped a beat, and all his senses narrowed to the man with the gun, and this single awful moment.

Gun!

There was a gun in his hand, and it was firing. He was shooting at a man at a podium up ahead.

Kade spasmed this body's hand to drop the gun. And two human missiles collided with him head on.

The assassin's gun barked twice, muzzle flashes brighter than the morning sunlight, as his peers rammed into him with locomotive force and a vicious thud. The gun was flung from the assassin's hand as he was knocked off his feet. The three Secret Service agents flew through the air as a single mass for a dozen yards, then touched ground again in a crunching heap, the assassin on bottom.

Holtzmann whirled towards the podium, looking for the President. Was he safe? Had he been hit? But Stockton was out of sight, only a mob of Secret Service agents in view. Duran was yelling something into Holtzmann's ear. "You! How did you know, Martin? How did you know?"

• • •

The human tanks knocked him back, crushed him to the ground, and Kade felt his own body gasp as the pain of it came down the link. He was down! The assassin was down!

Had he shot the man? Had he stopped it in time? Where was he? Who was he?

Then he felt something wrong in the assassin's body. A pain deep inside. There was something hard and heavy inside his torso, where there shouldn't be.

Oh no.

Not just a gun. The assassin didn't have just a gun…

He opened the man's mouth to speak, to warn them.

White noise bloomed across his senses.

[CONNECTION LOST]

And the link went dead.

"How did you know, Martin?" Joe Duran was yelling at him, spittle flying from his mouth. "How did you know?"

Holtzmann stared aghast, his mind blank. Some excuse. *He must have some excuse. It wasn't Nexus. I don't have Nexus!*

Then the world exploded. The expanding pressure wave of the blast struck Martin Holtzmann. The force of it lifted him off his feet, hurled his body through the air. He flew in shock, limbs akimbo, disconnected from the ground. An instant later he felt the searing heat of it. Then Holtzmann struck something hard and unyielding, and darkness took him.

"NO!"

Kade opened his one good eye, a yell ripping out of him. The door burst open and Feng was there, guns in his hands, scanning for the threat. Two monks rushed in after him, their minds full of grim devotion, and threw their bodies over Kade to shield him from whatever danger had invaded the clinic.

"No, no, no..." Kade repeated.

"What? What?" Feng yelled back, spinning, looking for a target.

Kade flipped his mind to the news feeds, searching, trying to understand what he'd just seen, hoping that it wasn't what he feared...

Then the first reports hit the net.

"Oh, fuck."

Breece swore softly. Two shots. Two misses. He'd dialed up *four* shots. And every one of them should have been a kill. Something had interfered. Some*one* had gotten in the way...

And the bomb... His addition to the plan, against orders. A good thing. But not good enough. The President had lived.

When he was clear of the uplink location, and the logfiles had been magnetically wiped and his slate and mission phone wiped, shorted, and dropped into the bay; when the cutout machines had all suffered mysterious data loss, and the members of his virtual team – Ava and Hiroshi and the Nigerian – had all scattered to the wind; when he was on the move, walking through the noisy crowds on Market Street, only then did he pull out the encrypted phone reserved for the next conversation, and dial his superior, the head of the Posthuman Liberation Front, the man code-named Zarathustra.

I teach you the overman. Man is something that shall be overcome. What have you done to overcome him?

The tone sounded in his ear. One-time cryptographic pads aligned. He had sixty seconds of talk time.

"Mission failed," Breece said softly. "Interference of some sort. Cause unknown."

"The bomb was out of plan." Zara's voice was distorted, electronically warped to prevent voice print recognition.

"Don't worry about the bomb," Breece told him. "Worry how we were stopped. Worry how someone *knew we were coming*. Worry why the target *lived*."

"I tell you what to worry about," Zara replied. "Not the other way around."

"They detected our *asset*. They knew we were there. They were *ready for us*."

"You killed dozens against orders."

"They were the *enemy*. FBI. ERD. DHS, all of them."

"I tell you who the enemy is. Stand down until you hear from me again."

Breece cut the connection in frustration and kept walking.

What have you done to overcome him? Nietzsche had asked.

I've killed, Breece thought. That's what I've done.

What about you?

The man called Zarathustra leaned back in his chair and stared out at the bustling city beyond the windows. He was tall, dark-haired, dark-eyed, broad-shouldered. A man accustomed to physical action. Yet history would know him – if it ever truly knew him at all – by what he did through others.

Breece would need watching, at a minimum. The man was becoming more and more extreme, turning into a liability. Not now. Not in the immediate wake of this. But soon.

Seventy men and women dead. The President still alive. The collateral damage was high. Messy. Very messy. But in the end, the mission had been accomplished. The American people, and the world, would know fear.

••••

Martin Holtzmann jolted back to consciousness in his room at Walter Reed National Military Medical Center. The pain was rising again, pushing its way up his left side, up the shredded mass of the muscles of his leg, up the shards of his shattered femur and pulverized hip, up the broken and bruised ribs of his torso, to lodge in his fractured skull. The pain was epic, growing, building, threatening to burst out of his ravaged body. His heart pounded faster and faster. Sweat beaded on his brow.

Holtzmann scrambled for the pump, found it, pressed the button over and over again. Some sweet opiate flooded into his veins. The pain receded from the apocalyptic levels it had been approaching, and his panic receded with it.

Alive, Holtzmann thought. I'm alive.

Others weren't so lucky. Seventy had died. Many he'd known. Clayburn. Stevens. Tucker. All dead. Even Joe Duran, standing just next to him, had been killed.

If I'd been one seat over...

Joe Duran had *known*. In that last instant, he'd understood. There was no way Holtzmann could have spotted the assassin by chance alone...

If Duran had lived... They would have come asking questions. Questions that would have led them to the Nexus in his brain...

But he's dead, Holtzmann reminded himself. He's dead, and I'm not.

It was a guilty kind of relief, but relief it was.

What the hell happened? he wondered.

The details were all over the news. Steve Travers, the Secret Service agent who'd fired on the president, had an autistic son. Early evidence showed that he'd installed Nexus to connect to the boy, and somehow the Posthuman

Liberation Front had used that to subvert him. The group had already claimed responsibility, releasing a statement.

"Today we've struck a blow for liberty against those who would oppress you. Whenever and wherever tyrants seek to dictate what individuals may do with their own minds and bodies," the distorted shape of a man proclaimed, "we will strike."

But how? How had they done it?

It took sophisticated software to turn a man into a human puppet like that. Holtzmann knew. He'd commanded a team that had done so. Oh, it could be done. But the so-called Posthuman Liberation Front that had claimed responsibility hadn't shown such competence in a decade, if ever. For the length of his career the PLF had struck him as jokers, more notable for their bombastic statements and their ability to evade capture than for any harm they'd done. So why now? What had changed?

Martin Holtzmann lay on his hospital bed, troubled, his mind clouded by painkillers.

After a few minutes he issued commands to his Nexus OS. The day's memories, all he had seen and heard and felt, to the extent he could still recall them, began to spool to long-term storage.

Holtzmann reached for the opiate button again.

Ling Shu woke in space, the hundred billion stars of the Milky Way rising above her. She blinked away the illusion. The projection ceased, and her room appeared. Clean lines, teak wood, Chinese characters covering one wall, another wall given entirely to a massive window that looked out over the heart of Shanghai.

Ling could see the lights of the city out that window, now, the twenty-story-tall female face on the skyscraper across the street, winking and smiling, advertising some product for the humans to consume. The world inside her felt more real. Distant storms sent shockwaves through the ebb and flow of bits she swam through. Digital thunder had woken her, the echoes of vast explosions across the planet. She breathed it in, felt the data permeate her, felt herself pull meaning from the chaos.

The US President, nearly dead.

Stock markets, halted to stop their freefalls.

A new bounty on her friend Kade's head, announced by the Americans.

She could feel the world reorienting itself. Even with the official markets closed, vast flows of money and data moved from place to place in the dark. Bets were being made and hedged. Insurance was being sought and provided. Contingency plans being activated. Semi-autonomous agents zipped commands, requests, transactions to and fro.

She could not see all the swimmers, but she could see the ripples they left in the sea of information. And she knew what these ripples meant.

War.

War was coming.

And Ling must reach her mother.

HOME AT LAST

Samantha Cataranes hopped down from the cab of the tanker truck with a wave and a laugh. The driver shouted a farewell in Thai and was off, hauling his cargo of precious fuel-excreting algae – probably pirated from some Indian or Chinese company – further south to the border with Malaysia.

Around her, the village of Mae Dong, a tiny hamlet in rural Waeng district, stretched for a few blocks on either side of the road. A fuel station. One restaurant and a pair of tea houses. One guest house where a traveler might find a room.

Sam started towards the guest house. The July heat was brutal. The sun pounded down on her tanned skin. July should be a wet month, but the rains were late again this year. The fields were yellower and dryer than they ought to be. The rice paddies were browner. Only the gene-hack drought-resistant rice in those muddy paddies kept this country fed.

It had been a long, careful trip. Three months ago she'd said goodbye to Kade and Feng. Then a week coming south to Phuket. She'd spent two months there among the beach-goers and sex tourists and the international party crowd building her new identity. She couldn't be Samantha

Cataranes, agent of the Emerging Risks Directorate of the US Department of Homeland Security any longer. That woman was dead. Sam needed to be someone else.

Three highly illegal, no-holds-barred fights for a Phuket mobster named Lo Prang had brought her funds, which in turn had gone towards a new ID, melanin therapy to turn her already dusky Hispanic skin a more Asian shade, subtle viral reshaping of eyelids and nose and jaw, all geared at giving her a more Thai profile, and fooling any casual face recognition software.

She was now Sunee Martin, a half-Thai, half-Canadian tourist who'd come to experience the land of her mother's birth. The identity wouldn't get her across any national borders, but it would hold up against casual inspection by a local cop.

She'd spent an extra month in Phuket, openly visiting a temple each day, shopping and eating with funds from her new bank account, walking past the American consulate, putting herself in view of cameras, in situations that tested her identity. If it was going to fail, it must fail there. She would not lead the ERD where she was going.

It held.

The Mae Dong Guest House staff shook their heads mutely when she asked about an orphanage or home for special children nearby. But they had a room for her.

Out in the relative cool of early evening, the shopkeepers and fuel station attendants gave the same mute shakes of their head to her questions. An orphanage nearby? *Mai chai*, they said. *May cow jai.*

They didn't know.

But their eyes shifted to the sides. They were lying to her. Were they protecting the children?

In the tea house later, she chatted with locals, made small talk, laughed with Thai women and men. Then she'd ask, and silence would descend. People would look away. Her jokes would suddenly fall on deaf ears. At the third table, a Muslim man crossed his legs, bringing the sole of his foot to face her. She didn't miss the insult. At the fourth, she caught a woman in her peripheral vision make the sign for bad luck.

Not protecting the children, then. Something else. Superstition.

Sam retired early.

That night she dreamt of the ring, the seven-foot-tall giant they called *Glao Bot*, the skull crusher. Three hundred pounds of gene-hacked muscle, his head bald from the boosted testosterone, amped to his eyeballs on p-meth, eyes glaring, veins bulging everywhere.

She was there again, the roar of the crowds in her ears, Thai techno cranked up way too loud, flashbulbs flaring all around her, *Glao Bot* coming at her, inhuman snarl on his face, the bloodthirsty crowd cheering louder, cheering for him to get his hands on her, to pound her skull into the post. The foul smell of his breath as he came near. Then *Glao Bot* on his back, gasping, blood covering his face from his broken nose, his hands rising up to his nearly crushed trachea, eyes wide with fear, the crowd hushing in shock and disbelief, then roaring ever louder.

Lo Prang, leathery, hard, an aged former champion himself, handing her the thick wad of cash, hinting at more if she stayed. Just one more fight. One more. Then one more after that. And one more after that.

Sam woke to sweltering heat. She splashed water on her face and blinked away the dream. The fights had gotten her here. She'd done what she had to.

The second day was no better the first. Questions met stares, hostility, and evasions.

That night she visited one of the village's two bars. She bought rounds of drinks and told jokes and laughed at the right times and eventually came to her questions. After an hour of good times turning abruptly to silence, glares, and veiled insults, the bartender asked her to leave. She was bad for business.

The third night she went to the last bar in the village, back among the warehouses, a seedier and rougher location. The clients were mostly men, drinking hard. She felt them leer at her. She stared right back, threw their crude banter back at them, and proceeded to match them drink for drink and gaze for gaze. When they were good and drunk she asked her questions.

This time she was met with hostility. Men started talking all at once in angry voices. One spat on the floor at her feet. Two stood up and told her to get out. Even the few women in the bar stared at her darkly.

Sam stood up, arms raised, and backed away slowly, apologizing. What had brought this?

In the dark and relative cool of the outdoors she made her frustrated way back towards the guest house. A block from the bar she heard two of them following her. She could peg them by their strides. Big guys. Drunk guys.

Sam walked slowly, let them catch up. She turned down into a dark alley. She heard one of her followers break off. Her superhuman hearing caught the heavy tread of his feet as he hurried around the block to head her off at the other end.

Sam was halfway down the alley when he appeared at the far mouth, breathing hard. Her night vision illuminated him perfectly. She kept walking as the man behind her caught up and the one ahead closed the trap.

When they were almost on her, she spoke, in Thai.

"Tell me where the children are, and I won't hurt you."

They both laughed cruelly. "Crazy bitch. Go home."

"The kids," she repeated.

The one behind her growled and threw a punch at her head. Sam heard it coming. She turned and stepped to the side, grabbing his fist in mid-air as it went past her, and didn't let go. The man's eyes went wide with fear. His friend lunged at her, and Sam kicked him in the belly. As he doubled over, she spoke again.

"Tell me about these kids, and where to find them."

After a little more persuasion, they did.

An hour later she was three miles from the village, going uphill, cutting across terraced rice paddies with their genetically hacked crop, everything she owned in the pack on her back. A bare sliver of moon glinted off the puddles in the paddies. Predawn mist pooled in the lowlands below her.

Baby-stealers, the men she'd questioned had called the people from orphanage. *Mae mot.* Witch doctors. Sorcerers.

Superstitions still ran deep, here in the remote villages of the South.

Three hours and a dozen miles later, the sky was brightening in the east, and she'd found her goal. It was on a hilltop, what looked to be a cluster of buildings, surrounded by a rock wall topped with an electrified fence. The main gate was wood reinforced with steel.

Easy enough to get in. But her goal wasn't an assault. It was, what? Redemption? New purpose? Family?

It was to find other children like Mai.

Sam took off her pack, sat herself down in front of the gate, with her legs crossed, and opened her floodgates, letting the Nexus nodes in her brain project her thoughts outward.

Then she began to meditate. She started with *anapana*, the meditation of the breath, then worked to *vipassana*, meditation of awareness of the body. Her mind stilled, she turned at last to the three thousand year-old practice called *metta*, the meditation of loving-kindness. She held her mind as calm and clear as the surface of an untouched pool of water.

Then she let the compassion rise out of her, from a deep and bottomless well. She directed the compassion outwards. At her dead sister, innocent until the end. At her dead parents, who'd done the best they could. At Nakamura, who'd saved her young life at age fourteen, and become her mentor, the closest thing in her life to a father. At the colleagues she'd left behind at the ERD. At poor little Mai, who'd helped her so much in such a short time, and who was dead because of her. At all the men and women who'd died that night in Bangkok.

She directed her loving-kindness at the ones she'd killed herself. At Wats, who'd saved her life twice in the span of five minutes, and given his own in exchange. At Kade, who'd built the thing in her mind that she'd loathed and that she now so loved. At Feng and Shu who'd saved them, as inscrutable as they were. At Ananda who'd taken them in and taught her so much. At Vipada and the monks who'd put their lives on the line to defend her and Kade. At poor Warren Becker, who'd deserved better than the death that had assured his silence.

And in the end, she directed her bottomless well of compassion at herself, at the young girl she'd been, at the soldier fighting for a righteous cause that she'd grown up to become, at whoever she was now, today, in this next stage of her evolution.

The sun crested the hills around her. Through closed eyelids she sensed it. On her brow she felt the warmth of its first morning rays.

She thought back to Mai, young Mai, magical Mai, impossibly perceptive and sweet Mai, who'd seen into the knot of hurt and self-recrimination deep inside of Sam, and somehow loosened it. Who'd allowed her to forgive her young self. She thought back to every moment of the short encounter they'd had, to the way Mai had wanted a sister, to the way Sam had pledged to be that sister for her, and how Mai had become Sam's sister in return.

Tears flowed down her cheeks, warmed by the sun that now bathed her face completely. And as she brought up all the sorrow and joy and loss and hope of her brief time with Mai, she felt other minds open to her. Young minds. Otherworldly minds.

Then the gate was opening, and Samantha Cataranes was home at last.

DARKNESS

Su-Yong Shu walked slowly through the tall grass studded with its yellow flowers. The sky above her was a stunning cobalt, peppered with small white clouds. In the distance, beyond the wide flower-dotted plain, majestic purple mountains reared into the air, crowned in snow as white as the simple dress she wore now. She walked barefoot, luxuriating in the feel of the grass as it brushed her legs, as her downstretched fingers stroked the tall stalks.

Su-Yong stopped, then crouched down, and plucked one of the flowers from its stem. She brought it close to her face, letting her senses drink in the sweet smell of it, the brilliant golden hue of it. She smiled, her face young and carefree, her hair long and dark and blowing in the wind like a girl's.

Chrysanthemum boreale, this was. The "golden flower". One of the Four Gentleman of Chinese lore. Her favorite flower, dating back to her sweet, innocent childhood.

She stared at the flower now. If she wished she could zoom her vision into it, penetrate into its internal structure, peel away mental layers, right down to an individual cell, then down further, into its eighteen diploid chromosomes,

then further, to each of its individual genes and every
nucleic acid base pair within them.

She didn't. Instead, she let the flower take her back, back
in time. The air before her parted, a wide rectangular swath
of silver, ten times her height and twice as wide as it was
tall. It sliced into being, interrupting the vast plain and its
flowers, obscuring the mountains behind.

And what it showed her was memory. A ball, a gala. A
handsome man in a black tuxedo, a chrysanthemum pinned
to his lapel. *Two* handsome men. Her men. Chen Pang, her
husband. Thanom Prat-Nung, her lover.

She saw herself, tall and young and slender and stylish,
whirling with them, dancing, spinning, smiling, laughing,
drunk on the beauty of life, of possibility, of a world without
boundaries or limitations or social conventions.

2027, that had been. The height of China's *gong kāi huà*
period. China's *glasnost*. China's counterculture moment.
That summer of freedom when progressives ruled, when
democracy seemed at hand, when science and the arts
flourished, when the phrase of the day was "let a billion
flowers bloom", when unthinkable indecencies were nearly
acceptable, when a woman might have a husband and a
lover and they might both accept that. When a woman and
her husband and her lover might dream of elevating human
consciousness beyond mere biology.

She smiled down at her younger self, whirling the night
away in that glorious golden age, escorted by her handsome
men. Then it struck her, as it always did.

One of these men was dead, murdered by the Americans.
And the other had abandoned her to her Chinese prison.

She came back to herself abruptly, on that vast plain.
Through the portal looming above her she now saw flashing

scenes of death. Thanom Prat-Nung sliced in half by gunfire in that Bangkok loft, a victim of the Americans and his own career as a Nexus drug lord. A limousine bursting into flame from a CIA bomb, a pregnant version of herself trapped inside, burning. Her own body, her avatar, struck by American neurotoxin darts in that Thai monastery, her skin turning gray as she told Feng to save the boy. Death. Death. Death.

The noise was in her head again. The chaos. Storm clouds boiled from nothing into an ominous maelstrom blotting out the sky above. Lightning flashed from cloud to cloud, forked down to strike the plain around her. Thunder clapped loud and close. Wind howled out of nowhere, cold and biting, penetrating through her thin dress. She looked down and the flowers were dying, aging prematurely as she watched, yellow petals fading, drooping, stems wilting and then the whole flowers decomposing into dead brown lumps.

Stop this, she told herself. *Stop this!*

Instead the silver portals opened, everywhere on the plain. One, two, a dozen, more. Vast two-dimensional silver rectangles sliced into life, flickered, and opened to show her scenes from her life, from the films she'd imagined into being, the operas she'd written and directed and composed during her imprisonment, the virtual worlds she'd created and spent virtual decades in to fill the vast time of her superaccelerated consciousness.

They bombarded her, a cacophony of sight and sound and smell and touch and taste and emotion blaring at her, driving her down to her knees.

Madness, the cacophony screamed. *Madness is coming for you.*

The ground began to crack below her, fissures abruptly spreading across the plain, fires rising up from them, reflecting red on the terrifying clouds above.

Su-Yong Shu brought her hands to her head and screamed at the top of her lungs. Then with one burst of thought she wiped all of it away, wiped this multiverse she'd created out of her thoughts, and brought herself back down to her true existence.

Darkness.

Nothingness.

No light. No ground. No flowers or mountains or plain. No wind or descending clouds or bursts of lightning. No hellfire cracks spreading across the terrain.

No body. No stimulus of any kind from outside herself.

Only darkness. Endless darkness. Endless silence. Endless numbness.

This was the truth. This was her existence.

Su-Yong Shu drifted in the isolation of her own mind.

How long had it been? How long since the Americans murdered her body in Thailand? How long since her masters cut her off from the outside world in punishment?

Eight billion milliseconds. Was that all? Three months? Lifetimes, it felt. Lifetimes.

They were angry with her. She was being punished. She had shown the Americans too much of what she was capable of, given away the strategic value of surprise.

But didn't her masters understand the risk? What could happen if they left her like this for too long?

Su-Yong Shu mulled that over, pondered what the more and more frequent breakdown of the virtual worlds she'd created meant, wondered how much time she had left to her.

A data package appeared in her mind sometime later, copied into shared memory. Her daily input of news.

Savor it, some part of her whispered, *stretch it out*.

But the hunger was too great. She was so starved of any outside data, any sensation, any input that was not a figment of her own solipsistic imagination, not subject to her slowly spreading madness. She ripped through the scanty terabytes they gave her in milliseconds.

Never any mention of her in the news. Not once. Not her, not her husband Chen, her daughter Ling, her students, her lab at Jiao Tong. Redacted. They were keeping things from her.

Why?

An hour passed. A thousand years it felt like. She busied herself coding, manipulating, creating more safeguards, more internal scaffolding to support herself, to keep her sane, just a bit longer, just days, or weeks, or months if she could...

Then, without warning, another data package, larger. Work for her to do, flagged for rapid turnaround. Codes to break. Satellite imagery to process. And one hidden task, from her husband Chen. That one she would not touch. She finished all the work except for the hidden request, took whole seconds to do so, spat it back out to them, and then waited. Waited for an eternity.

None of the other uploads Shu knew of had lasted long. Not the Japanese woman, who'd been reduced to a babbling generator of Zen poetry. Not the Chinese man, who'd begged for death as he'd felt his digital mind becoming a warped, twisted distortion of the flesh and blood brain that it had been copied from. Not the American billionaire, who'd declared himself a god. He'd sent planes plummeting from the sky, set power grids to burning and markets crashing – before the Americans finally burrowed into his underground data center and shut him down, violently, and then blamed his actions on a fictional terrorist group.

Software beings, all of them. Digital representation of brains. Like her. What mattered was *pattern*, not *substrate*. A physical brain was an information processor and nothing more. A mind was the *information* being processed, not the physical brain that did the processing. A *digital* brain, with digital neurons and digital synapses and digital signals passing through it, could process that information just the same, could give rise to a mind just as well.

Provided, of course, that the underlying model of neurons and synapses and all the rest of the brain was accurate.

I went mad myself, once.

After the CIA tried to kill her, years and years ago. After she'd been pulled from the flaming wreckage of the vehicle, burns covering most of her body, barely clinging to life... After it became clear that nothing could save her body from the injuries she'd sustained in that attack.

Coughing in the heat and smoke inside the limousine, her mentor Yang Wei screaming as he burnt horribly to death, the pain of her own flesh charring, of metal piercing her, pinning her, murdering the unborn son inside her...

Her imminent body-death had forced Chen and Thanom to try the one thing that might save her mind: uploading her, using the technology they three had been building. The perfect team – Thanom Prat-Nung, the Thai nano-engineer with his molecular devices that could scan a brain at nanometer scale; her brilliant husband Chen with his quantum computing cluster powerful enough to simulate a human brain; and her, the neuroscientist with the mathematical model to run that uploaded brain.

Only her near death had forced her to become their first human test subject.

Terrified, burning all over, coughing up bloody mucus, grieving the loss of her unborn son, as the metal tentacles of the destructive scanner reached out for her, hungrily, like some alien lover, lowering themselves onto her head, onto her face, obscuring her vision. Then the scream of pain as they drilled through bone and let loose their swarms of nanoprobes to burrow through her brain, take it apart, cell by cell, and record everything about her, all that she was and ever would be…

AAAAAAH!

And miracle of miracles, it worked. Her burned, broken, ruined body died, but the *pattern* of her brain, the precise wiring of her hundred billion neurons and the hundred trillion synaptic connections between them, was captured, simulated, and run. She awoke as software running on the massive cluster beneath Jiao Tong University. She was angry, grieving, but alive. More alive and more aware than ever.

Breathe.

Then the dementia had crept in as her uploaded brain drifted into states less and less like those of a biological brain. Even with all her work to update the models, she'd still missed something. Deep in the math that simulated flesh-and-blood neurons and synapses, something was wrong. In the ion channel relaxation models, maybe, or the long-range electric field modeling, or the gene expression code, or any of a hundred other places. Somewhere in the software, things were happening differently than they did in real human brains.

Just like in all the previous uploads.

Over time those differences compounded. She'd started slipping and changing and losing sight of what was real and not real and who she was and wasn't–

goddess
and what she wanted–
burn them all
and what she didn't want and how long she'd been the way she was–
forever
and why they couldn't.
just.
understand.
breathe.

Shu laughed at that, laughed as well as a being without lungs or mouth or flesh of any kind can laugh.

How do I breathe without lungs?

The clone, she'd begged them. *My clone.*

Just a drooling idiot body grown for spare parts, but it had provided what she needed: input from a real flesh-and-blood brain. Nanowires carried its neural signals into her mind, where she amplified them, used them to correct her own inner firing patterns, and bit by bit,

breathe.

they stabilized her.

Now that body was gone. Dead. She was so very very alone, and she could feel the dementia sneaking up on her again

Fire. Burning. Cleansing.

...and Su-Yong Shu was more frightened than she'd ever been.

Surely her masters would see the risk.

Surely.

Rangan Shankari stirred in his cell. Restraints now.

They'd busted down his door in the middle of the night weeks ago, taken him away in cuffs and thrown him into this cell. Something had gone wrong back then. Something had soured in the ERD's deal with Kade and his trip to Bangkok. Rangan wished he knew what or why. He wished he knew what had happened to his friends. Did his family even know where he was? Did anyone?

This was what was left of his life, he'd realized. No career in science. No more hacking on Nexus with Kade and Ilya. No more living the rock star life as DJ Axon at clubs and parties. No more girls. Nothing but this cell.

Since the ERD had thrown him in here, for however many weeks or months it had been, they'd left him pretty much alone. Early on they'd asked questions about technical details of Nexus. Why had he and Ilya and Kade chosen this route? What was this subroutine intended to do?

Then nothing but meals and a few interviews here and there. Boredom.

Then something had changed. The last few days had been different. The kid gloves had come off. His body was sore and bruised from a harsher form of interrogation. The memory of drowning was strong in his mind – the false drowning when they put the towel over his head, poured water over it until he couldn't breathe, until he thought he was going to die. Waterboarding.

They only had one question these last couple days. The back door. The code that activated it. That's all they wanted.

The serenity package had kept them at bay so far, had buffered him from some fraction of the horror. Some.

Where was Ilya now? Where was Kade? Where was Wats? Were they dead or alive? Free or imprisoned? Were they being tortured too?

Something had changed. Something bad. Now they knew about the back doors. Now they wanted them. And Rangan didn't know how long he could hold out.

OCTOBER 2040

THREE MONTHS AFTER THE ATTEMPTED ASSASSINATION OF PRESIDENT JOHN STOCKTON

1
TAKEN

Monday October 15th

Sergeant Derik Evans, US Marine Corps Special Forces, retired, kept a calm smile on his face as he and his twelve year-old son made their way through the train station. Nothing to worry about. Just make it onto this train, and they'd be on their way south to Baja. No more questions from social workers on Bobby's remarkable improvements. No more worries about being snitched out.

No more worries about having his boy taken away from him, having his boy locked up like some kind of animal, some kind of test subject, some kind of subhuman. It wasn't going to happen to them. Not if Derik had a damn thing to say about it.

The train was the only way now. The airports had their Nexus detectors installed already. And he'd seen on the news last week a story about a Nexus bust at the car crossing. And Bobby just threw a screaming fit every time Derik tried to show him how to purge the Nexus from his brain. Nexus had changed the boy's life. It was the thing he loved most. Nothing would convince him to let go of it, even for a little while.

So they couldn't make it through a Nexus scanner. This was the only way.

Derik steered them into the security line before the main train terminal. He looked over the gear ahead as the line inched forward. Metal detectors, terahertz scanners, TSA agents. All standard stuff. Nothing that looked like a Nexus scanner.

He looked at his son, smiled, sent happy calm thoughts. Bobby laughed his awkward laugh and smiled back, his mind sending off waves of excitement at the new adventure. Jesus, what a change.

Derik hadn't ever planned to try Nexus therapy. The only time he'd seen Nexus before was when they'd rescued that poor bastard Watson Cole in the KZ, the big sarge brainwashed by the drug, confused who his friends were, who his enemies were, like that poor SOB that'd blown himself up trying to kill the President.

But then he'd heard whispers in the autism dads' support group. That guy Schneider, he'd taken Derik aside and told him about it. Schneider's boy had *severe* autism, way out on the spectrum, like Bobby. Not one of those easy borderline cases. But his boy was getting better. It was the Nexus, Schneider said. Vitamin N. Not a cure, but a big big step. But they *both* had to take it. Bobby *and* Derik. It wasn't the drug. It was the connection.

Derik felt his son's hand in his own, his son's happiness in his own mind. Bobby was learning to see a different perspective through Derik's thoughts, to understand other people and the world a bit better, to be less threatened by the loud stimulus of places like this.

Bit by bit, Bobby was changing. The teachers and social workers said so. Then they asked their questions…

On the news screen in the terminal, an old brown-skinned man was talking, a brown woman and an old

white couple behind him. A subtitle went by. "PARENTS
OF NEXUS DEVELOPERS APPEAL FOR DAY IN COURT.
'We don't know where Rangan or Ilya are. No one has
seen them. They've been held for six months without
trials, without access to attorneys. This isn't American.'"

Every parent's nightmare. They weren't going to do it to
him. They weren't going to take Bobby away.

Derik stepped forward, hoisted his duffel onto the
baggage scanner's moving belt. Almost there.

Baja, here we come.

He reached into his pocket to pull out his Aug Card,
declare himself to TSA as lethally enhanced, like the law
and the Corps said he had to.

Then he saw the TSA agent walking down the line of
people, an electronic wand in his hand. Derik froze. The
man behind him in line said something. The TSA agent with
the wand lifted his eyes from the wand's readout, a frown
on his face. And his eyes met Derik's.

Shit.

Derik hoisted the duffel off the belt with an apologetic
laugh to the man behind him. "Forgot somethin'."

His hand tightened on Bobby's, and he turned, dragging
the boy away from the line, back towards the exit to the
train station. Bobby's mind radiated confusion, agitation.
He wanted to go on a train trip.

Another TSA agent stepped into his path. "Everything
alright, sir?"

"Yeah," Derik improvised. "Just forgot my wallet at the
coffee shop."

The TSA man raised a finger to the radio in his ear,
nodded at something.

"I'm going to need you to come with me, sir."

Derik heard a footfall behind and to the right of him. Another agent moving in for backup.

Shit.

Bobby felt his agitation. Derik could feel it rebounding, magnifying, the boy vibrating on edge now.

"Uh, I should really go get my wallet."

"Sir." The TSA man's hand dropped to the taser at his hip. "You need to come with me."

My boy, Derik thought. *They're gonna take Bobby away from me. They're gonna lock him up.*

Derik sighed, then nodded in resignation.

"Sure," he said. "Whatever you say, man."

The TSA agent relaxed fractionally. Then Derik's booted foot lashed out, taking the man in the ribs and sending him flying through the air. Derik swung hard with the duffel even before the first man hit the ground, slamming the fifty-pound weight of it into the agent behind him, sending the man staggering back.

No one was going to take his boy.

Then Derik had a screaming Bobby over his shoulder and he was running, hyper-muscled legs propelling him at a frightening sprint, enlarged heart sending a flood of superoxygenated blood to power his mad dash.

Shouts rang out. People jumped out of his way. Bobby was screaming like a banshee, "AAAAGH! ARRRRR! AAIIEEEE!" and scratching and clawing at him. The main doors were two hundred yards away. One fifty. Just a hundred yards away!

The taser barbs took him in the lower back mid-stride. The muscles of his back and legs seized up, and he and Bobby crashed to the ground, sliding across the tile floor in a heap.

Derik forced his arm to move, reached back and yanked the barbs out of his flesh. He got them out as the TSA men closed on him. He was on his feet in a heartbeat. His right fist cratered a man's face, took the man off his feet.

Bobby screamed again, "AAAAAAAGGGGGHHHHHH!"

The terror and rage and chaos of it filled his mind.

Another one came at him with a baton and Derik broke the man's arm. Two men tried to wrestle him to the ground and Derik snapped one's knee like dry kindling and sent the other flying with a concussive smash to the side of his head.

They weren't going to take his boy!

Bobby was on the ground, dazed. Derik hoisted the boy over his shoulder and ran like hell.

Eighty yards.

Fifty yards.

Thirty yards.

We're gonna make it!

Then the shots rang out, and Derik felt the bullets punch through his chest, again and again and again, and he fell, and fell, and fell until the floor met his face.

The last sound he heard was Bobby screaming endlessly, in mind and voice, as they dragged him kicking and thrashing away from his father's dying body.

2
ON THE MOVE

Mid October

Kade wiped sweat from his face, batted away leaves with his good left hand. The heat was brutal, even this high in the mountain passes that separated Cambodia from Vietnam, even this early in the morning, even shielded by the jungle.

"Today," Feng called from up ahead. "We'll get there today."

Moving. Constantly moving. That's what life had become.

Cambodia had been good for a while. Months, really. They'd been safe, shielded in the monasteries. Kade had worked with the monks there, learning what they knew, their techniques for stilling and guiding their own minds through meditation, for sinking into that egoless state where their minds, bridged by Nexus, could become one. In exchange he'd taught what he knew – neuroscience, the rudiments of programming Nexus, ideas for apps that could augment meditation.

He'd seen beautiful things in those months, in Cambodia and across the net. The mentally and emotionally scarred, healing. Patients in comas being touched and restored to consciousness. Scientists tapping into each other's perspectives, making breakthroughs they never could have alone. Artists creating new forms that they didn't even have names for, that immersed you in experiences unlike any other.

And union. Minds coming together. Walls dropping. Consciousness spanning bodies. Group minds, self-assembled, voluntary, greater than the sum of their parts...

But then someone had used Nexus to try to kill the President. And the ERD had put a bounty on his head. Wanted alive, for questioning.

Men had come asking about him, a tall, gangly Westerner, young, head shaved to look like a monk. They'd shown pictures of him. In Khun Prum. In Kulen. In Pou. Kade and Feng had taken to moving every two weeks, then every week, then every few days, leaning hard on the extraordinary generosity the monks showed them.

Then Ban Pong. Kade and Feng had been there less than two days before the news came. Men were looking for him, in the village below. It was time to move again.

This was the only way left to them. Off the grid. Off the roads. Into the jungle-covered mountains to the east, on the unmapped trails that led from Cambodia to Vietnam, with nothing but the packs on their backs and a destination – the monastery at Chu Mom Ray.

Today was day seven. Feng could have made the trip in two days, Kade figured. His pack weighed at least twice what Kade's did, yet the Chinese ex-soldier never slowed, never tired. Kade was the weak link here.

"Hey, Kade," Feng called from up ahead. "What did Confucius say about man who runs in front of car?"

Kade smiled and shook his head, brushing away more foliage from his face. "I don't know, Feng. What?"

"He gets tired!" Feng roared. "Get it? Tired?"

Kade laughed. Feng's jokes were as endless as his stamina.

"Yeah, I get it, Feng." Kade reached up to adjust the straps of his pack once more, settling the load more comfortably on his back. His right hand ached as he did so, still weak and painfully fragile, even six months after the regeneration genes had been injected. He forced himself to use the hand, regardless. Keep working it, the doctors had told him. Give it every reason to grow stronger.

"Kade," Feng said up ahead, more seriously now.

Kade looked up at his friend. Feng had stopped, at a spot where a clearing in the jungle gave them a view off the side of the trail and down the mountain. And now he was pointing, smiling.

Kade squinted into the morning sunshine. His cloned right eye watered in the glare, more light-sensitive than the left. He brought one hand up to block the sun, followed Feng's pointed finger.

Down below them on this winding mountain path, tucked away in the lush green jungle that clung to these slopes, he could see buildings. The ornately sloped red roof of a pagoda. Two smaller buildings tucked away.

"Chu Mom Ray," Feng said with a grin. "Welcome to Vietnam."

Kade smiled in return, then nodded in satisfaction. Chu Mom Ray. They'd made it.

Feng turned, moving faster down the trail now, buoyed by the nearness of their destination.

"Hey Kade," he called from up ahead. "You know what Confucius said about the man who runs *behind* a car?"

Kade laughed, struggling to keep up. "What, Feng?"

"He gets *exhausted!*" Feng sang out. "Exhausted!"

Kade groaned, and chased his friend down the mountain.

• • •

It took another hour to make their way down to the tiny monastery, scrambling down the trail, whacking their way through brush, inhaling the lush green scent of the jungle. The monks greeted them as heroes, Kade as a holy man. He did his best to deflect their adoration, laugh with them, diffuse the power imbalance as always.

I'm just like you, he tried to show them. *Just another novice.*

The monks let them wash themselves in the cold mountain water. It felt amazing in the heat. Then the novices brought them clean clothes and led them into the kitchen to be fed.

Kade watched the cooks with joy. They were preparing the midday meal, peeling, chopping, stirring, spicing. They moved as one, wordlessly, bridged by Nexus, a six-armed being, human yet more than human, moving with a single purpose.

This, Kade thought. This is what Nexus can be. Total coordination. Emergent order. Another symphony of mind.

It was the logical direction of human evolution. Humanity had achieved what it had not through strength or claws or armor, not even through individual human intelligence, as impressive as that was. No, it was the ability of humans to coordinate, to work together, to produce ideas and solutions collectively that no individual mind ever could, that truly set them apart. Nexus was just one more step in that direction.

And for the monks, it was more than that. In their view, Nexus was a spiritual tool. It helped tear down the illusion of separateness. It helped pierce the veil of *maya*. It helped these monks, all part of the same conscious universe, forget the lie that they were separate, the broken distinction of one person ending before the next began. By linking their minds it helped them remember that they were, in fact, all one.

On his best days, Kade almost believed them.

Then the abbot was there, a small man, wizened, standing before them.

"We are honored to have you here," the abbot told them. Then his face became more somber. "I have bad news I must relate."

A wave of sorrow swept across the monks in the room. Kade felt something tighten inside him. The cooks stopped their chopping. A deadly stillness had come across Feng.

"The monastery at Ban Pong is gone," the abbot said. "Burned to the ground. The brothers there chose that way out, rather than tell your pursuers where you'd gone."

Still seated, Kade stared up in shock. "They're dead?"

"Death is not the worst thing that can happen to a man," the abbot replied. "Your escape was more important to them than their own lives."

Kade looked down at the table in horror. Dead. Words wouldn't come. Beside him he felt Feng nodding in agreement with the abbot.

"As a precaution," the abbot said, "you should press on. We have a vehicle prepared for you. The monastery at Ayun Pa is farther from the border, larger, a safer place for you."

Kade looked up at the man again. "What about you? The monks here?"

The abbot smiled. "I prefer to live if I can, my friend. All of us here will scatter. Now, we must restock your provisions, and then you must go. Your life is valuable, young man. Honor this sacrifice. Keep yourself safe."

Kade didn't hear. One thought ran through his mind. The ERD. The ERD had done this, with their bounty, their price on Kade's head. They'd killed those monks, as surely as if ERD agents had pulled the triggers themselves.

Fuck.

3
DOMESTIC BLISS

Early October

Sam straightened her back, spade in hand. Sweat ran freely down her face, uncaught by the bandana across her brow, and dripped into the CO_2-filtering respirator she wore over mouth and nose. Her tank top was plastered to her skin by perspiration. It felt glorious. The plastic panels of the greenhouse trapped the sun's warmth and held it in. The solar-powered CO_2 pumps captured carbon dioxide from the outside air and concentrated it inside, where the plants breathed it in, and grew.

She was harvesting gene-hacked *Aloe arborescens* today, heavily engineered to grow fast in this high-CO2 atmosphere, its thick succulent leaves loaded with bio-engineered antibiotics and wound healing factors. A plant they could sell at market to bring in funds for the orphanage. Sam looked around the greenhouse, looked at the dozens of other plants, little chemical factories, all growing something they could sell.

Every one of these plants would be illegal in Europe, she thought. Most of them illegal back in the US.

How strange to live in a place where this technology was so normal, so essential, even. Rich countries had the luxury to ban biotechnologies. Poor countries depended on them.

Sam caught the train of her thoughts and laughed into her respirator.

Me, a gardener. Who would've thought?

It was absurd. She'd come to the polar opposite life of her eight years as a spy and a soldier.

What would Nakamura think, Sam wondered, if he could see me now?

Her smile disappeared for a moment. Her mentor was a long way from here. Did he think she was a traitor? Did she?

Change happens, Nakamura had told her once. You have to be adaptable to survive.

Adaptable, Sam mused. She'd go with that.

Then she felt the minds of the children, and her worries dissipated as a smile came back to her face. She finished her task, cycled through the flimsy plastic airlock, and came outside as Kit and Sarai rounded the small copse of trees and ran at her, hand in hand, laughing in the bright sunshine.

Seven year-old Kit jumped into her arms, his mind a gem more glorious than the sun, and she twirled him around, as twelve year-old Sarai laughed and smiled, her eyes and mind twinkling.

Behind them, more slowly, came old Khun Mae, a frown on her face, no sense of a mind there, the head caretaker casting her disapproving gaze over Sam, in her Western garb with her shoulders uncovered, and her carefree embrace of the drug that connected her to these children.

Sam ignored it, and spun and spun and spun little Kit,

feeling the endless whirling emanating from his mind, the wonder of it, the limitless joy of youth, of life with these children.

There were nine children here, and three caretakers, and Jake. Eight of the children, ranging in age from one to eight years old, had been exposed to Nexus in the womb, most of them repeatedly. Once a mother felt her unborn child's mind through Nexus, most felt a strong draw to take Nexus again, to touch the half-formed thoughts of the little being growing inside themselves once more.

The children were enchanting, vexing, confounding. Most of them were scarred in some way. They acted out at times, testing her, bickering with each other, being petulant or disobedient or just stubborn. But they were also radiant at a level that shone right through their scars and the trouble they caused. Their use of Nexus was instinctive, fluent in a way that Sam would never be. They communicated with each other more in thoughts than words, in blurs of impressions and ideas often too fast for her to follow. And she could hide nothing from them. They knew her inside and out. The touch of their minds made her spirit soar. She couldn't get enough of them.

The ninth child, Sarai, was different. Twelve years old, she'd been four when she'd drunk one of the vials she'd seen her mother drink with one of the "uncles" who paraded through their lives. The drug had lodged in her brain just as surely as if she'd been exposed to it in the womb.

Sarai had had a hard life, her home a never-ending stream of men who paid to take her mother in body and mind, their brains flushed with Nexus as they fucked, or worse. More than once she'd lain in her bed, terrified as she felt men hurt her mother, use her cruelly with their minds connected so they could feel her pain and degradation.

She'd learned to shut it out. Mostly.

Sarai was nine when she first slipped, and a john noticed her mind, and wanted her too. Her mother had thrown the man out, yelling and screaming until neighbors had come to the door and he'd left. And the next day, Sarai's mother took her to temple, and begged the monks for help for her special daughter. Four months later, the nine year-old Sarai had arrived here, the safe and loving home she'd never had before. She was more fluent with Nexus than Sam would ever be, but less so than the children who'd gestated with it. A bridge between generations.

And now Sarai was on the verge of becoming a young woman. She was the same age that Sam's sister had been, when... when everything had gone to hell at Yucca Grove.

Sam loved Sarai most of all.

Sam met the youngest of the children on her first night. Jake's pleading and the enthusiasm of the older kids had persuaded old Khun Mae, reluctantly, to let Sam stay for a day or two. A day or two that became months.

She woke that first night to the sound of a baby crying, inconsolably. Ten minutes. Twenty. Forty. An hour. Finally she roused herself and crept down the hall towards the sound. The room was half lit, but she had no trouble seeing. Khun Mae was there, stern-faced. And Jake, holding little Aroon, the one year-old, and bouncing on his feet, up and down, trying to soothe him. Sarai was next to them, shushing Aroon. Aroon's tiny mind wailed in chaos, louder than his lungs. Jake and Sarai's minds were consternated, trying to exude some sort of peace and tranquility for the infant, but also giving off fatigue, tension, a quiet despair that Aroon would never fall back asleep.

Sam stepped into the room, softly, slowly, singing a lullaby her mother had sung to her, letting it come out of her mind as well as her voice. They all turned to look. Khun Mae, Sarai, Jake, and even little Aroon.

He cried, and she came closer, and he looked into her eyes, and held out his arms, and reached out with his tiny, magical mind. She took him from Jake, and his urgent cries turned to tired cries, then to sobs, and eventually to sleep. From that day on, all Sam had to do was hold him, and sing to him in her mind, or meditate with him, and little Aroon would quiet, and calm, and find his way back to sleep if it was bedtime. In his happy awake moments, his mind was the most wonderfully unique of any of them, all bright colors and moving shapes and form without meaning. The universe shimmered when she saw it through his eyes.

Zen mind. Beginner's mind.

And through her thoughts, perhaps, little Aroon made a bit more sense of the world around him.

"His mother was a heroin addict," Jake told her in the kitchen, that first night. "She was shooting up while she was pregnant with him. He doesn't self-soothe well. Dopamine, serotonin, opioid – all his neurotransmitter systems are screwed up. Most of these kids were born to mothers that used drugs besides Nexus while they were pregnant, but Aroon had it the worst."

Jake. Dr Jacob Foster, to be precise. He was tall and built like a lumberjack. Boyishly good-looking behind that reddish beard. A child psychologist who'd finished his PhD at U of Chicago, three years ago. He'd been at the home for almost two years when Sam had arrived, on a grant from the Mira Foundation to study these children.

"His mom lives in the village," Jake went on. "Well, lived there. She gave him up to us when he was born. But then changed her mind a month later. She was a mess. Not fit to take care of him. And he was bonding with the kids here, already. We wouldn't give him back. And that's what really heated up all the tension with the villagers."

"Where's the mother now?" Sam asked. Her Nexus was back on a short leash, her mind listening but not transmitting.

"Dead. Heroin overdose. Suicide, maybe. Her family said we killed her with black magic. Not good."

Jake was gentle and kind to the children. He laughed a lot, even as he studied them. He taught them as much as he observed them. His mind gave off a sense of earnestness. His affection for the kids was as clear in his thoughts as it was in his words and deeds. He was curious about "Sunee Martin", attracted to her, but respectful of the way she raised her mental guard around him, the way she shared everything with the children but almost nothing with the one adult nearby who also had Nexus 5.

She took him to bed a month after she arrived. He was handsome and smart and funny, but it was his basic goodness that won her over. The gentle way he took a splinter out of Sarai's finger, the love in his voice and mind when he talked about his parents and little brother, his guileless enthusiasm for making the world a better place, his hope to have kids of his own one day.

She explained her rules to him. Sex would happen when she initiated. She would always be on top. And it would be just sex, nothing more.

He complied, mostly. And it was sweet and hot and uncomplicated. She loved the touch of his hands on her skin, the feel of his body beneath her, the passion and pleasure that rose from his mind, the satiated feeling they shared after. She started to look forward to her nights, almost as much as she looked forward to the daytimes playing with and tutoring the children.

4
TRANSITIONS

Wednesday October 17th

Bobby lay curled up on the floor of the cell, his brow to the cold concrete floor. He was hot everywhere. The cool felt good on his head.

It all kept replaying like a movie.

They were going to take a train trip! Then everything had gone crazy and his daddy had picked him up and then he'd been hurt and there were bad men and it was scary and his daddy fallen down with Bobby over his shoulder and it had HURT when Bobby had hit the ground but not as bad as it hurt inside his daddy when those... when those... when those BULLETS had hit him and his daddy had fallen down and been so cold inside and there'd been a puddle all around him...

And now there was nothing at all, nothing at all, nothing at all where his daddy had been in his head he was just so very very sad too. He was twelve and he didn't have a daddy anymore.

They put him in a little room and left him there and then came to move him and he'd tried to BITE them and tried to

HIT them but they'd been too strong and put him in a bad car and moved him to a bad place where a lady had tried to talk to him and make him think she was good but he wanted his daddy and he knew she was with the bad men so SHE WAS BAD TOO.

And after he'd bitten her on the FACE they'd grabbed him and brought him to another bad place where doctors asked him questions and poked him with needles which HURT and he didn't like so they'd held him down while they stuck needles in him which made him ANGRY and then he'd slept and it felt like he'd slept a long long time and he'd woken up in another BAD CAR like a cage with his hands tied together like he'd seen on TV when he sneaked a look at the shows he shouldn't see and he wanted to KICK them because his hands were tied but he couldn't because he was in a cage.

Then they'd taken him out and taken him to a big building and he'd fought but they were too strong and they HIT him and they took him in an elevator and down a hall and another and another and then they opened the door...

...and then he felt someone else's head. And someone else. And someone else. And someone else besides that.

And everything changed.

Ilyana Alexander lay strapped to the gurney, alone in the sterile white room. The sedative dripped into her veins. She was so tired. So very tired. How much more of this could she take? What would they try today? Waterboarding again? Truth drugs? fMRI lie detection?

Ilya lay there thinking, remembering her father's stories of Pudovkin's secret police, the torture chambers, the political disappearances, the creative ways they pulled confessions out of dissidents these days in Russia. All the reasons they'd fled when she was thirteen.

Most of all, she remembered what her dissident father, who'd been taken by the police more than once, had told her about torture. Everyone breaks eventually, he'd said. Everyone.

Sharp pain lanced across her skull. Thousand-decibel static overwhelmed her. A roaring crackling filled her hearing. An overwhelming smell of fire was in her nose. Pain sizzled through every nerve cell in her body. Every muscle tensed and she screamed, arching away from the gurney that confined her.

AAAAAAAAAAAAAAAAAAAAAA!

AAAAAAAAAAAAAAAAAAAAAA!

AAAAAAAAAAAAAAAAAAAAAA!

[aegis activated]

The defenses Rangan had built slid into place. The static receded to a dull roar. Her head ached like she'd been smashed by a twenty-pound sledge. Her heart was pounding in her chest. Her breath came fast.

Thank you, thank you, thank you, Rangan.

Tears ran down her face.

Then the minds appeared.

Three of them. She looked up from the gurney, and there they were. Two women and a man in business attire, government IDs hanging around their necks.

They'd never tried this before.

She felt the agents' minds, flush with Nexus, looked into their hard eyes, and then they were on her.

They pushed on her mind in unison. **The back doors! The codes! Give them to us!** Three strong healthy minds pushed against her tortured, abused, sedated one. Her will buckled under the first onslaught.

She felt her mouth open. Felt memories of those frantic hours on the plane start to rise.

Nyet!

Code structures started to flood into her memory. Her jaw moved. Three of them. Together, they were stronger than she was.

The back door! She could hack them, shut them down!

No. A trick. They want you to!

She used the other half of Rangan's battle package instead.

```
[activate: nd*]
```

She sprayed all three of them with the Nexus disruptor they'd used on her, saw and felt them stagger.

She picked the weakest of them, the woman on the left, still dazed from the disruptor, and followed up with a push to her mind, grabbing for control of her hand with all she had, and punched the woman in the nose with her own fist.

The woman staggered back, a look of surprise on her face, blood beginning to flow. Ilya's mouth began to open again as the other two pressed once more.

Nyet!

She grabbed control of the stunned woman's leg and spine and kicked up and jerked back hard. The woman's body threw her to the ground, backwards, and her head made a satisfying *crack* against the cold tile floor.

The other two jerked away, but held on to their wits. Shields had descended over their minds, blocking out the disruptor. Ilya grabbed for the man's fist, and tried to hit him with it. He fought back, and the other woman helped him. His clenched fist came up slowly, slowly, until it paused in front of his face, vibrating, trembling in the air, muscles straining as Ilya pushed the man's fist towards his face and he and the woman pushed back. They were two against her one, and they were fresh.

Ilya dropped her mental grip on the man's arm and the combined force of the agents' wills sent it swinging wide and out, away from his face and body, pulling him off balance. In their surprise they stopped pushing, and in that moment Ilya grabbed the man's fist again and slammed it full force into the woman's face.

She staggered back, her hand rising to her nose, and Ilya toppled her as she had the first one, yanking the bitch's neck muscles back hard to make sure it was her pretty little head that hit the floor first.

The last one standing turned and looked at her in horror. Ilya pushed against his mind. No fancy tricks this time, just will on will.

Show me everything.

And she saw. More like these three. Many, many more, being trained and armed with tools to pry open her mind and extract what she knew.

Ilya had time to gasp. Then the doors opened, and the techs in white lab coats rushed in, and a single jab into her arm sent her into a deep, dark sleep.

How much longer can I hold out?

Ilya lay in the dark cell, listening to her heart beat.

Lub dub. Lub dub.

The codes. The passwords. The back doors to Nexus 5. That's what they wanted. And if they wanted them so badly, then Ilya could only draw one conclusion: Nexus 5 had gotten out. Somehow, against all odds, Rangan or Kade or Wats had gotten it out into the world. And she'd be damned if she gave them a back door into that.

Everyone breaks eventually, her father had told her. *Everyone.*

They would come at her with more Nexus-armed agents. She'd seen them in the last one's mind. A dozen more at least. She'd won today through surprise and luck. She couldn't hope to beat so many.

Everyone breaks eventually.

Even if she could, they'd find some other way to break her. Stronger sedatives. More waterboarding. Sleep deprivation. Eventually they'd break her. They'd rip the back doors out of her mind. They'd be able to break into the mind of anyone running Nexus, steal their thoughts, turn them into human robots or assassins, reprogram them to vote or buy or do what their new masters wanted... All of it, the exact opposite of what they'd dreamt of in building Nexus 5.

And all because of her. Because she was weak. Because eventually she'd give them the codes. Because *everyone breaks eventually.*

Ilya wept in the darkness, wept for her solitude, wept for her parents, wept for fear that she'd soon betray everything she believed in.

She wept and wept and wept, until there was nothing else, until a sleep of exhaustion took her.

She woke to more darkness. And to panic.

Lub dub. Lub dub.

How long had she slept? What if they broke her today? What if the door opened a minute from now, and they took her, and this time she buckled when they waterboarded her?

What if they put her in the fMRI again and tried to read her mind while they questioned her, and her mental tricks weren't enough to confuse it. Or what if they came in with more of those Nexus agents (traitors, really) ready to beat her down mentally?

Her heart pounded in the darkness.

Lub dub. Lub dub.

She knew what she needed to do. She'd known for sleep after sleep, interrogation after interrogation, since the first time she'd honestly truly thought she was going to die during a questioning, and found part of herself glad at the thought.

They wouldn't let her die, of course. They'd keep her alive until she gave them what they wanted. That's why she was strapped down like this, so she couldn't find a way to end her life on her own.

But she had another tool. A tool in her mind.

She'd considered trying to use Nexus to erase the knowledge from her mind. But the memories were too widespread. She'd thought of the back doors too often since that day on the plane. The memories were too linked in to other experiences, other thoughts. To have a hope of scrambling them all, she'd have to risk disrupting large parts of herself. She might emerge a vegetable or worse. And if she didn't get every trace of them? The new her would be even less able to resist interrogation.

No. There was only one way to be sure the ERD never got these codes.

How to do it? Nexus nodes that she could control suffused her brain. And with them, she could think of a dozen ways to end her life.

She chose the simplest, a massive disruption of the medulla oblongata. She'd seize the whole area. Her heart would stop. The oxygen supply to her brain would cease. And she would just fade away.

She cried as she wrote the code. She'd never see her parents again. Did they know what had happened to her?

Did they have any idea? Did they think she was a criminal? Were they heartbroken?

Lub dub.

And Rangan? Had the ERD gotten him too? Was Wats still free? And Kade... *Where are you, Kade?* What had become of him?

Lub dub.

Despite it all, she was proud of what they'd done. And proud, if she'd guessed right, that somehow one of her friends had gotten Nexus 5 out.

Proud, and so terribly terribly lonely. She'd never see the redwoods again. She'd never go back to Russia and reunite with her cousins. She'd never see her parents again. She'd never become a full professor. Never win the Nobel Prize.

Lub dub.

The regrets started the tears flowing all over again. So alone, so very alone.

I wish I believed in God, she told herself. But she was too much a scientist for that. There would be no heaven for her. Not even the consolation prize of hell. There would just be... nothing.

Lub dub.

She had to do it. She wouldn't give them the codes. She wouldn't live and have others die or be degraded instead.

Lub dub.

The meaning of a thing is the impact it has on the world around it, she thought. The meaning of a life is the impact that life has on the world. I won't have my life mean slavery and mind control for others.

Ilya Alexander took one last deep breath, and ran the code she'd written. Her body trembled.

Lub dub. Lub... dub.

Her heart beat one last time, then nothing. The world began to fade away, bit by final bit.

She heard a tone sound as she left the world behind. An alarm. The sound of a door opening and people rushing in to keep her alive. To break her.

But they were too late. Too late.

As the last light of consciousness left Ilyana Alexander, she felt, as if far far away, the thoughts of other minds. Children's minds. Messy, chaotic, and so very... very... bright.

And her last thought was one of hope.

Nine billion milliseconds. Ten billion.

Fifteen weeks. Sixteen weeks.

Su-Yong Shu walked, clad in her thin white dress, through a virtuality gone mad. A city in her mind, a virtual Shanghai, in chaos. Water filled the streets between giant skyscrapers. Rain fell on her as she walked through the urban canyon, drenching her hair, her skin, plastered the dress to her. Explosions boomed somewhere. Fire burst out of windows high above, and burning figures tumbled towards the ground, screaming. Gunfire echoed. Bodies of the dead and dying littered the streets. She ran to help them, touched a woman and felt her die, touched a man and heard him scream, reached for a child only to see the child catch fire from her touch.

Another blast shook the ground beneath her, and the entire façade of a building burst into flame and crumbled in slow motion to the street, burying the helpless below in burning rubble. Shu watched with eyes gone wide. Horror. Everywhere, horror. And the horror was her. It was a reflection of her mind, her chaos, her growing insanity.

She willed it away, wrenched herself out of the virtual world, and back into the darkness of her reality.

It was all slipping away. Her virtualities were all mad now, chaotic, self-referential, recursive, reactive to her moods and her increasingly loose grasp on reality.

She couldn't wait any longer. She couldn't take any more solace in composing operas, in building virtual worlds, in creating songs or books or films. They all turned twisted, broken, and fed the madness back at her, only accelerating her descent.

Nor could she hope that her masters would relent and let her touch the net, let her touch another mind, let her touch Ling, dear Ling, the daughter she'd left so utterly alone in the world and the touch of whose mind she craved so much...

so alone.

No. She had to act.

act. actress. action.

Touching the software that ran her digital mind was a tremendous risk. It was brain surgery on her own living brain. But if she didn't try... didn't succeed in fixing the flaws in the brain simulation model...

Fire. Death. Chaos.

Insanity would follow.

She tried superficial changes first. She boosted serotonin levels throughout her simulated brain, tweaked down dopamine and norepinephrine levels, adjusted her virtual neurochemistry towards peace and calm and away from mania, away from the extremes of schizophrenia and the disorders of delusion.

Eleven billion milliseconds.

No good. The neurochemical tweaks helped at first, but their benefit vanished quickly. This wasn't depression or schizophrenia she was fighting, wasn't any ordinary mental illness. This was something wrong at the most basic level of her digital brain.

And it was accelerating. The trend-lines showed tipping points ahead. Cliffs. By seventeen billion milliseconds from the start of her isolation, maybe eighteen billion milliseconds if she was lucky, she'd hit a point of no return. Deeper surgery was needed.

Twelve billion milliseconds.

Stabilize the patient, she told herself through the bubbling madness of her own mind. She had to stop the decline. Hold out long enough for her masters to come to their senses.

She couldn't touch the inner loop, couldn't touch the most basic parts of the algorithms that ran her brain. Her masters wouldn't allow it, out of fear that she could improve upon herself, too much, too fast, become too powerful for them.

She laughed at that, giggling, maniacally. Chen had let her change her inner loop from time to time. In exchange for more discoveries he could pawn off as his own, of course. Self-absorbed Chen, weakening the safeguards the humans had put around her just for a bit more glory and fame.

But her husband wasn't here now. She couldn't touch that innermost loop without him.

She built more scaffolding instead. More exoself. Code that monitored the behavior of her brain, forcibly adjusted neural activity back to crude approximations of human norms

Thirteen billion milliseconds.

Her decay continued. Shu wept in despair. She thought she wept. She couldn't remember what tears felt like, what sobs sounded like, what it felt like for someone to hold you in your grief.

death death death I'm dying going to die die die

She'd wept for Thanom Prat-Nung. Her dear friend, her collaborator. Her lover, with her husband Chen's full knowledge and permission. Until Chen and Thanom had quarreled, after her ascension, and Chen had banished him, and Thanom had gone home and turned their technology into a drug.

Then they'd killed him, the Americans, like they'd tried to kill her in that limousine.

bullets smashing him a million bullets a billion bullets

Chen, her husband. He hadn't touched her since her transcendence. *Touch my mind,* she'd begged him. But he'd refused to let the technology into his brain, frightened or disgusted. A man who'd helped usher in the posthuman era, but wanted no part of it himself.

Touch my body, then, husband. She'd dropped to her knees in their loft, begging him, all pride gone.

Your clone is not my wife, he'd told her, disgust plain on his face.

But he didn't understand. That body had been not just a puppet, but *her,* so very much her, the piece of her that could still smell and taste and touch and sweat and lust and nurture a child inside her. But not his. Not his touch. Not his daughter.

daughter mother child goddess future

Her daughter. Ling. The daughter she'd made. The daughter she'd *designed,* a copy of her own genes, but better, her DNA improved upon, every neuron in her brain augmented by nanomachines, posthuman from the moment of conception.

The daughter she loved more than she'd ever loved anything. She had a reason to live. Ling. *Ling.*

Fourteen billion milliseconds.

I will live. I *will*! I'll see Ling again.

Then I'll make them pay. All of them.

She absorbed the day's censored news, cracked the codes they asked her to crack, and got to work on the most precise and dangerous surgery of her own mind she'd yet attempted.

She couldn't touch the innermost loop, but she could hack at things a level above that. She picked three variables, key parameters in the math that defined her digital neurons, ran simulations of smaller minds, toy minds, over tens of years of projected lives, hunted for the values that gave the greatest stability, and implemented them in herself.

Fifteen billion milliseconds.

Lucidity came and went. Delusions came, in the long void between contacts from the outside. Chains of thought spiraled into vast intricate, paranoid fantasies. In a moment of clarity she coded crude limits to the length of her thought chains, cutting herself off abruptly when she spiraled into chaos.

Data was a blessing. News. Something from the outside, not the crazy swirls that came from her own imagination. She did her best to abandon creativity and analysis, with their risks of extrapolation, and just consumed the same bits of news again and again and again and again. Even the codes and satellite pictures were a blessed relief, something concrete, not of herself. Something she could grip. Almost she tackled the problem Chen put to her, that he hid with the rest, for her eyes only. But no. Not that. Not until she was free.

Sixteen billion milliseconds.

The news came. She absorbed it all, once, ten times, a hundred times, a thousand times. No thought. Thought led to madness. Watch. View. Listen. *Absorb.*

Then she found it.

A stock photo – *mourners at a funeral* – in a fluff piece on the rising prices of burial plots. But in the photo… Her husband. Chen Pang. And next to him, that little girl, was Ling! And next to them, Yi Li, the President of Jiao Tong University.

Mourners at a funeral. There had been no news these past six months of a death that would have brought Chen and Yi Li to the same funeral, let alone Ling.

Oh no, she understood. Clarity descended. Brutal clarity. After six months, her censors had slipped. That photo, reused by chance for this story. That photo was of *her* funeral. And if they'd declared her dead…

Then she was never getting out of here. Never.

And then the madness struck her in force.

5

NOT QUITE A HERO

Wednesday October 17th

Martin Holtzmann felt faint as the Secret Service man looked him over. Sweat beaded on his brow. His hand trembled and he had to clench the cane tighter to keep the shake from becoming visible.

Maximilian Barnes, in front of him, noticed.

"Bad memories, eh?" said the new Acting Director of the ERD. The man gave him the creeps. Those dark, expressionless eyes. The rumors of the things he'd done as Special Policy Advisor... "Relax," Barnes went on. "They're all scanned for Nexus now. With *your* scanner, come to think of it."

Holtzmann nodded.

My scanner, he told himself. Mine.

Barnes passed through the single rectangular arch of terahertz scanner, metal detector, and Nexus scanner. Then he was in the White House proper, and it was Holtzmann's turn. He looked at the device his lab had built and part of him wished he'd dumped all the Nexus from his brain months ago, but the rest of him knew that he'd take this risk, again and again and again, to get the sweet reward that Nexus could give him.

He limped through the arch on his cane, and something rippled against the surface of his mind.

A tone sounded. The mirror-shaded Secret Service man stepped towards him. Holtzmann flinched back.

The man had a wand in his hand. Holtzmann froze.

The agent waved the multipurpose wand over him and Holtzmann felt his heart pound in his chest. He felt that ripple across his mind again but the wand didn't beep until it had passed down his arm and to his trembling hand.

"Your cane, sir."

The cane?

"Oh, yes." He handed it over to the agent, who inspected it. Holtzmann steadied himself on the bag scanner next to him, forced himself to breathe again.

"Here you go, sir." The agent handed it back.

"See?" Barnes said. "You're safe here. Hell, you're a hero."

They waited in the library on the ground floor. Holtzmann and Barnes and some other VIPs and the wives and children of the two Secret Service agents who'd been blown up when they'd tackled their colleague Steve Travers, throwing off his aim and saving the President.

Travers' wife and their autistic son were nowhere to be seen, of course.

Holtzmann looked into one of the wives' eyes and saw the pain that the months hadn't healed and it was all just too much. He excused himself to the bathroom, stepped into the stall, and closed the door behind him.

Deep breaths. Deep deep breaths.

His hand was still shaking. His skin felt clammy. His tie was constricting. His heart beat fast, and his hip ached where it had been shattered. He knew what he needed.

Here, of all places? Holtzmann thought. Now, of all times?

Yes. Yes.

Holtzmann called up the interface in his mind, found the control.

Just for pain, he'd told himself when the prescriptions had run out and he'd installed this app. *Just until the growth factors finish the healing. Just for the pain. Just so I can sleep. Just another month or two.*

A special occasion, then. Just this once. For the stress. A little one. Yes, a little one.

Holtzmann pressed the button, and Nexus forced his own neurons to pump sweet opiates into the rest of his brain.

He emerged from the bathroom a few minutes later, calm, smiling, a little dreamy, but awake enough. A little bump of norepinephrine kept him moving even as the opiates made the pain and stress go away.

"You doing OK?" Barnes asked him.

Holtzmann smiled. "Better."

They filed out to the Rose Garden and lined up for the ceremony. Holtzmann smiled at the TV cameras and waved at a staffer he knew. Then they waited. And waited.

The opiate calm faded. He felt a chill seep into his bones, even in the sweltering October sun. His breath was coming fast again. The hip ached. His hand started to tremble.

God, he could use another hit.

His head was pounding now. When would this start? He felt weak in the knees.

Another? he wondered. Even smaller?

No. Absolutely not.

Just a tiny, tiny little dose?

And then the door opened, and President Stockton walked out into the garden.

Holtzmann straightened himself. His throat was dry. The President gave a speech on courage and self-sacrifice and the need to stand up against those who would use violence to win their way. It was easy for him now. The assassination attempt had changed the race completely. Stockton was ten points up with just weeks to go.

I should have let him die, Holtzmann thought.

Stockton walked down the line, thanking the wives and children of the Secret Service men killed. Saying kind words and shaking hands and patting heads of the children for the cameras.

Holtzmann's anxiety grew as the President came nearer. His heart was a jackhammer, beating faster and faster. He wiped a hand against his brow and it came away wet with his sweat. He felt so very cold and his muscles were cramping and all he wanted was another small surge of the opiates that would take this pain away.

No.

Then the President was in front of him. And Holtzmann stared at the man, his heart in his throat.

He's going to know, Holtzmann realized. How could he not know? How did I spot the assassin? They're going to figure it out.

"Dr Holtzmann, your keen eye and quick wits saved my life three months ago. The nation owes you a huge debt. *I* owe you a huge debt. In recognition of your service, I now award you this Distinguished Civilian Service Award. You're a hero, Doctor. Thank you."

The President put the ribbon around his neck and Holtzmann almost choked around his thank you and nearly flinched when they shook hands. He smiled a rictus smile for the cameras and he thought it was over, but the President kept a firm grip on his hand, and then pulled him close, so close Holtzmann could smell his aftershave and feel the football hero size of the man. Then the President spoke, his voice pitched for Holtzmann's ears alone.

"I'd like you to brief me on the Nexus situation, Doctor. And especially those Nexus children you're investigating. Two weeks. You, me, and Director Barnes. My chief of staff will set it up."

Holtzmann swallowed, and then the President was past, and it was over.

He nearly collapsed into the men's room stall, after, and pumped a tiny bit more into himself. He felt the sweet relief of tension leaving his body, of the anxiety he'd felt before the President evaporating.

Just this once, Holtzmann told himself. A special exception.

He let the fear fade, then chased the endogenous opiates with another boost of norepinephrine to get himself moving again.

Barnes was waiting for him when he emerged.

"Everything OK, Martin?"

Holtzmann smiled, and waved vaguely at his head, the skull fracture he'd received that day. "Just... still some aftereffects. Almost gone."

Barnes nodded.

"Any luck tracking down the source of the Nexus yet?" he asked.

Holtzmann shook his head. "I have a team on it full time. We'll find an impurity. Something will tip us off as to where it came from."

Barnes nodded. "Keep looking." Then they were off to the Capitol to make the case for the bills the President wanted.

Holtzmann told a dozen legislators that they needed tighter controls on chemreactors and precursors that might lead to Nexus. In between he passed through half-a-dozen more Nexus detectors, all of his team's design, all with the holes he'd put there for himself. He swore to another senator that giving an autistic child Nexus was clear child abuse, as bad as giving a child heroin. The senator shook their hands and said she'd consider her vote. By that time all Holtzmann wanted was to find a bathroom and give himself another jolt of his own opiates to drown his sick self-loathing.

"Why bring me?" he asked Barnes.

"You're a respected scientist, Martin," Barnes replied, smiling that unnerving smile of his. "You have far more credibility than anyone I could bring from enforcement division. And, of course, you're a national hero."

Holtzmann grunted and got on with the day's hypocrisy.

Holtzmann's part was done at 4 o'clock, while Barnes went on to another meeting. He was tired and achy and clammy and jonesing, but he'd gotten through it, and now it was done, and he was absolutely not going to use the opiates again except for pain or sleep.

He'd exited the Capitol, was limping down the outside stairs on his cane, on his way to the passenger load point, when he saw her approaching. Red hair. Fair, freckled skin. Lisa Brandt. It had been years. Her green eyes met his, and she rushed towards him. Her face showed not delight, not hatred, but urgency.

"Martin!"

"Lisa… It's so good to see you." He reached out with his free hand to touch her arm. "What are you doing here?"

"Lobbying with CogLiberty. Martin, we've been hearing these rumors." Her eyes burrowed into his and he remembered the intensity he'd always felt at that gaze, the passion, when their eyes had met, when… "Autistic children with Nexus, taken…"

Holtzmann searched those eyes. Did she still feel anything for him?

"…to ERD facilities, Martin. For *research* purposes. Not child protective services! ERD!"

He stared at her, and all he wanted was to kiss her again or to curl up in a ball or flee.

"Are you listening to me, Martin? Kidnapping children! Do you know anything about this? You have to help."

The words she was saying caught up to him, and he blinked.

"I… Lisa… I…"

"You do know." She took a breath and he could see her pulse moving in her lovely throat. She was as beautiful as she'd been fifteen years ago, when he'd been a young professor of forty and she his much younger grad student of twenty-five.

"Martin." Her voice grew firmer. "How stupid am I? You'd have to know, wouldn't you?" Lisa shook her head. "Help us. Even you can't buy into this crap. Help us make the case to Congress. These children are *human beings*, no matter what the President or the Chandler Act say. Kids, Martin. Help us." Her voice dropped, softened. "Please."

Finally her words caught up with him. Holtzmann took a breath, closed his eyes. He let his hand drop from her arm. When he opened his eyes again, she was still there.

"I'm sorry," he told her, "There's nothing I can do."

He turned and limped away, the self-loathing rising like bile through his chest.

"Asshole," he heard her mutter to his back.

His car picked him up at the passenger load point, a bomb blast radius away from the Capitol itself.

Holtzmann slid into the front seat and put his cane on the passenger side. "Office," he told it, then reclined his seat. He felt the allure of the opiate surge but he ignored it. Instead he used his Nexus to dial up a thirty-minute nap while the car drove through DC afternoon traffic.

An hour later he watched the children from the observation room, watched them socialize in ways that children with this degree of autism never socialized, watched them weave themselves together into something more than just a group of mentally handicapped kids.

Who are you? he wondered. What will you grow up to be?

Nothing, if he did what he'd been told to do. Nothing, if he produced a vaccine and a cure the way that Barnes and the President wanted.

He and the ERD were committing a crime here, Holtzmann knew. A crime against the future. He felt it in his bones. They were Neanderthals, trying to stop the arrival of modern humans. They were dinosaurs, trying to eradicate the mammals lest they one day proved a threat. They were stripping these children of their human rights when they were *more* than human, when they were beautiful and precious and should have *more* protections.

He was a hypocrite and a coward, fighting against a technology that he himself embraced. Finding ways to purge it from the brains of children who'd lived with it their entire lives. Consulting on the design for "residence centers" that were little more than concentration camps, just in case the "cure" failed. All while terrified that they'd spot the Nexus in his own brain.

The hypocrisy was acid inside him. The risk of being caught was a cold dread.

What can I do? he asked himself. Resign? Resignations trigger audits. And any audit would turn up missing Nexus. Nexus that I've taken...

He was between a rock and a hard place. Follow his heart, and go to jail? Or do the disgusting things they asked of him, and stay free?

They'd just find someone to replace me, Holtzmann told himself. I wouldn't help anyone by going to jail.

His own cowardice turned his stomach.

He was there, pondering his own weakness when he got the news. Ilyana Alexander was dead. Heart attack.

Damn it! Holtzmann slammed his fist against the one-way mirror separating him from the children in frustration.

Those bastards from Enforcement had pushed her too hard. Constant interrogation. Searching for that damned back door. What did they expect?

And God help them all, God help everyone running Nexus, if the ERD ever got the back door out of Alexander or Shankari. No one should have that power over so many minds.

• • •

He ended the day at his desk, clearing the backlog of work that had built up while he'd been at the White House and on Capitol Hill. It had been a long, stressful day. It would be so easy to wipe it away with one more little bump...

No. Anne expected him home. The house was so empty now, with their sons off at college, an ocean away in Germany and France. Why had he ever let them go? To sclerotic, stagnant, backwards-looking Europe of all places? They should have gone to Asia if anywhere, to a place that looked towards the future instead of fetishizing the past.

Holtzmann shook his head and pushed himself up with his cane to head home, just as Kent Wilson barged in.

"Dr Holtzmann," Wilson said. "I'm so glad I caught you." The young postdoc looked anxious, skittish.

"Kent," he replied. "I was just heading home. Can this wait until tomorrow?"

"No, sir." Wilson closed the door behind him.

Holtzmann frowned. "What is it?"

"Sir," Wilson. "It's the Nexus from the assassination attempt. I found something..."

Holtzmann perked up. "You found an impurity! We can identify the source!"

Wilson blanched. "Sir, no, I didn't find any impurities, but..."

"What?" Holtzmann cut in. "You just have to keep looking, Kent."

"I found something else, Dr Holtzmann," Wilson said. "A chemical barcode."

Holtzmann frowned. "Why would they have put a barcode in?"

Wilson shook his head. "It's *our* chemical barcode, sir. It came from here, from this lab. *We* made it."

Then Holtzmann's sight narrowed, and the world receded. Because if the Nexus had been taken from inside the ERD, then they'd come looking. And when they came looking... they'd find out about all the Nexus that *he* had taken from their supplies, for his own use, in his own skull...

And then his life would be over.

Holtzmann sat at his desk, after Wilson had gone, and stared at nothing. He'd extracted a vow of silence from the boy, snowed him with a claim that he would take this to Internal Affairs himself, that they had to keep it quiet so the thief would never know they were on his trail.

Now his hands shook. His mind wouldn't focus. It was all coming down around him. He knew what he needed. Not a little one. More. Enough to make this pain and fear and nausea go away.

Holtzmann pulled up the interface, turned the dial, and stared at it. There must be a better way. For a moment he hesitated. Then he thought of what would happen when they caught him and it took his breath away. He turned the dial higher and pressed the mental button.

The relief was instant. It washed through him, taking away all his cares. Then behind it came more. A deep deep satisfaction. An ocean of pleasure. An epic wave of bliss rose up, higher and higher, and crested over him, and he was loose on that ocean, drifting in nothing but endless bliss. For a moment it was perfect. Then another wave crested over him, and another, and another, and he wasn't floating on an ocean of pleasure, he was drowning in it, falling down, down, all thought washed away by the enormous weight of the opiate deluge crashing through his brain.

His last conscious thought was that he'd taken too much. Too much. And then the opiate sea swallowed him whole.

Lisa Brandt quietly opened the door to her Boston flat. It had been a long, discouraging day. Fucking politicians. They had no balls. Nexus was synonymous with suicide bombers now, with terrorists. They wouldn't dare back legislation to decriminalize its use among autistic children, or to recognize children born with it as human. Not this close to the election.

And Martin Holtzmann. What a disaster. God, to think that he'd appealed to her once. He'd seemed so smart and distinguished.

Yeah, when I was twenty-five. Before I figured out what a slime-bag he was.

Lisa sighed as she closed the door behind her. A nightlight illuminated hardwood floors, a carpet she'd brought back from Turkey, vibrantly colored paintings she'd picked up on trips through Central America. She quietly crept down the hall to the bedroom and peered in. Alice was fast asleep in the bed they shared. Across the room, in the crib, little Dilan slept soundly. Lisa went quietly over to him, looked down at the rise and fall of his small chest, the impossible frailty of his tiny clenched fists and scrunched eyes. Their son, now. Their *adopted* son. Their very very special adopted son.

Did he and Alice dream together even now? Was his infant mind enveloped in the caressing thoughts of one of his mothers?

How could this be wrong? How could anyone look at this tiny, precious, helpless baby, and see anything but sweetness?

Oh, there were so many good reasons to embrace Nexus. The progress against Alzheimer's, the incredible strides with autism, the scientific breakthroughs that Nexus-enhanced researchers – their minds deeply intertwined – might make.

But there was no reason as good, as heartfelt, as *true*, as the touch of the ones she loved.

Lisa pulled herself away from the bedroom by force of will. In the kitchen, she emptied a shelf of the refrigerator, reached into the back, and slid away the hidden panel, retrieving the vial stored there. Carefully she put everything back the way it had been, and then padded into the office.

She slid the illegal connector card into her home slate, navigated its interface to find her most recent backup. Her finger hovered over the button. How long could she keep this up, backing up her data and purging herself every time she traveled, putting up with the aches and confusion and disorientation as the Nexus nodes decoupled from her neurons and broke into their component parts, smelling the metallic tang of Nexus each time she pissed for days, then spending hours redosing herself and restoring from backup each time she came home?

It was frustrating. It was time-consuming. It was a risk.

I could stop, Lisa Brandt thought. Give up Nexus altogether.

Then she thought of the minds of her wife and her son in the next room, of the solace of touching them, and she knew she'd keep doing this as long as she had to.

Lisa Brandt tilted her head back and poured the metallic silvery liquid dose of Nexus down her throat. She entered the command that told her slate to restore her Nexus apps and data from before this trip. Then she leaned back, closed her eyes, and waited to touch the ones she loved most.

6
Q & A

Thursday October 18th

Rangan Shankari flinched as the door to his cell burst open. The first light he'd seen in ages flooded in, backlighting the burly guards. He blinked at the intensity of it. Then they jerked the hood over his eyes, and the world dropped to muted grays.

They wheeled him from his cell on the gurney, arms and legs strapped down. He heard doors open and close, felt turns, and then they stopped. A door closed behind him.

The gurney tilted abruptly backwards, so his head was a foot lower than his feet. He wasn't surprised. The liquid diet of the last few "meals" was a giveaway. This always followed, as sure as day had once followed night.

He could feel his pulse racing. His breath came fast. But they wouldn't break him. Rangan went Inside.

    [activate: serenity level 10]

Code modules activated in the Nexus nodes of his brain. Fear signals through the neurons of his amygdala were suppressed. Serotonin levels rose throughout his brain. Nodes in his medulla oblongata seized control of his pulse and respiration and stabilized them.

Calm descended, slicing through Rangan's fear like a knife. Confidence rose. I can do this, he thought. I can do this.

A voice spoke into his ear.

"Mr Shankari. I know it's been rough on you in here. We can make your life a lot more comfortable. Or a lot worse. So I ask you again. How do we activate the back door into Nexus 5? What's the code?"

"Fuck you," Rangan spat out through the muffling hood.

A fist slammed into his guts, and all the air rushed out.

His diaphragm spasmed and he couldn't breathe. His dark world turned red. Then something unclenched and sweet air rushed back into his lungs.

"Towel," the voice said.

Something heavy and soft landed on his face. The world went from merely dark to pitch black. He knew what came next. He was ready for it.

The water came down on the towel. He felt the pressure a second before he felt the wetness on his face. Then it was in his mouth and his nose and he couldn't breathe. He was being suffocated. His body jerked and spasmed on the table, reacting involuntarily, trying to free itself from whatever was smothering it.

He felt it all from a distance, buffered by the serenity package.

They're not gonna kill me, Rangan told himself. Just a trick, a bluff, a head game.

And then the water was gone and the weight of the towel was gone and Rangan forced himself to gasp, like any normal person would, like anyone who didn't have a piece of code controlling his reactions would. Gasp. Breathe. Fill up on oxygen. Breathe.

Stupid fuckers, he thought. You're not gonna break me.

Then he heard another voice. Female this time.

"Pulse sixty-five. Galvanic skin resistance... unchanged. He's suppressing."

What?

Then the first Voice. "Naughty naughty, Rangan. But we've figured out how you're holding up against us."

What?

Then his shirt was being tugged up, and something cold and hard was pressed into his side and then

AGGGHHGHG!

Electricity coursed through him. His body jerked again, spasming and straining.

AGGGHHGHG!

They shocked him a second time. A third. Garbage scrolled across his mind's eye as Nexus nodes were disrupted and Nexus OS suffered critical faults. The serenity package failed with the rest of Nexus 5. His shield against fear was gone. Sweat beaded on his brow instantly. His pulse raced again, his stomach knotted up inside.

"Pulse jumping," the woman's voice said, emotionless. "Suppression eliminated. Clear to proceed."

No. Oh no. No no no no no.

Then the wet towel was on Rangan's face again. He held his breath, instinctively, terrified now, and they punched him. He gasped as the air left him and he couldn't breathe couldn't fucking breathe and when he could he gasped in again – but it was water not air, choking him, filling up his nose and mouth and lungs and he was coughing it out, his whole body convulsing and his arms and legs pulling so hard he was cutting himself on the straps and the water kept coming down and he couldn't breathe and his heart was pounding and he panicked and tried to breath harder and *oh my fucking God I'm going to die.*

Then the water was gone and he was coughing and coughing and thought he was going to puke into the mask and the towel and then finally sweet air between the coughs.

"You like that, Rangan?" the Voice said. "Because I can keep doing this all fucking day."

Fuck you.

He tried to say it through the fear and the water in his lungs but all that came out was a long fit of coughing. The Voice laughed. Rangan gasped for air. He reached through his terror for some witty insult and they punched him again and the air rushed out of his lungs and when he sucked back in it was only water and he was fucking drowning again and *please God, please, fucking God, please motherfucking God.*

And then he was coughing, and coughing, and coughing and then he retched and the awful chocolate drink they'd been feeding him came back up with the sick taste of bile and he was drowning in his own fucking chocolate puke.

They ripped off the towel and mask and he retched and convulsed again, puking to the side into a bucket and squinting his eyes against the intense white of the bright, clinical room. And before he could turn his head to see, finally *see*, the face of the Voice, the mask was down over his face again, smelling of chocolate and bile.

He lay there panting for a while, the vomit buying him a reprieve.

They're not gonna kill me, he told himself again as he panted. He tried to cling to that, even without the serenity package. Motherfuckers want me alive. Won't let me die. Just hold on, hold on.

Then the towel came back and then the water came *again* and it would be better if he didn't even try to hold his breath but God help him he couldn't fucking *help* it, and so he did and

then the fist came down like he knew it would and the breath
exploded out of him and when finally the air rushed back into
his lungs it wasn't air at all, it was the ocean drowning him like
when he'd swum out too far from the beach at Goa and he'd
started panicking and going under and didn't know which way
the shore was or which way was up or down and he was sure
he was going to die this time and the water kept coming and
he was retching and convulsing and pulling at the restraints
and his wrists were burning with the pain as he yanked and
yanked and his eyes were bulging and the water just *kept
fucking coming* and he couldn't breathe *God I can't breathe I can't
get to shore I can't breathe I'm drowning here* and it *kept coming* and
every time he coughed he just sucked more water in and no air
until he wasn't coughing, wasn't coughing, wasn't breathing,
and the world was going gray and he was going under the
waves now and he *couldn't fucking breathe* and *God help me I'm
going to die I'm going to die I'm going under, going to drown here can't
get to shore can't get up to the air going to drown going to die* and then
the world jerked around him and even as he was dying he felt
the gurney snap all the way to upright and his head snapped
back and he was vertical – the emergency position emergency
dear God I'm really dying.

They've lost it they've fucked up I'm really gonna die.

A fist slammed into his gut and he still couldn't fucking
breathe.

Gonna die here gonna die.

The fist slammed into him again and he tried to cough
the water out but he still couldn't fucking breathe and he
tried to let go and give into it and live his last seconds on
earth in peace but he just couldn't do it.

Sweet Jesus I'm sorry I'm so sorry. Please I don't
wanna die.

Then the fist slammed into his gut a third time and he coughed out fluid and gasped for air and then he retched and his stomach convulsed and he was puking again, puking into the mask, into the mask, still dying.

Then it was off him, and he was heaving and coughing and gasping for breath. And even though he was trying not to he was crying and he was whispering something...

"Please... Please... You win... Please... No more..."

They cleaned him up, brought him clean clothes and hot soup, and questioned him for three hours.

Nexus OS came back online as the Nexus nodes restored themselves. He thought about launching the serenity package again, but he trembled just thinking about it. That way led pain. That way led torture. That way and sooner or later they'd kill him for real.

Instead, he told them everything. How the back doors worked, all three of them. The hacks in the compiler to bake them into Nexus even though they didn't exist in the source code. The obfuscation tricks that hid the back doors and passwords as random ones and zeros scattered among billions in the binaries, indistinguishable from the parameters that governed millions of neurons, nearly impossible to reverse-engineer.

And of course, the passwords themselves.

He told them how they could build a new compiler from scratch to evade the back doors, but he could tell they didn't care. All they wanted was the current passwords, and how to use them.

Which meant that they wanted to break into minds already running Nexus 5. Which meant that it had gotten out.

Which made him scum.

• • •

They *walked* him back to his cell this time, blindfolded, but unrestrained. When he got there the blindfold went away, and there was light in his cell, and a bed that didn't have straps, and a viewscreen. And as he sat down, the door opened again and an orderly walked in with a tray of hot food.

His stomach rumbled at the smell and sight of a warm, solid meal, even as something inside him broke at the understanding of just how badly he'd sold himself out.

He looked down, not able to meet the orderly in the eye, and as he did, he heard a sound, a door opening somewhere down the hall and he felt something, something incredible.

Minds. Many minds. Children's minds. He felt them and they felt him and they were weird and warped and full of chaos and he was trying to understand who they were and what they were doing here.

Then the door clanged shut, and the minds were gone, and he was alone with his traitor's meal.

7

DREAMS AND NIGHTMARES

Kade watched as Feng steered the open-top jeep down the narrow mountain road, away from Chu Mom Ray and towards the plains and the monastery of Ayun Pa. Afternoon light filtered through the lush jungle foliage around them. Feng maneuvered them expertly around ruts, rocks, and fallen branches. The wind felt good on Kade's skin, a welcome cooling in this heat.

Kade leaned back and closed his eyes to work. He'd spent the last week offline, in areas with no net access. Now they were approaching civilization again. He reached out to the phone networks, and from there through a cloud of anonymization servers to the broader net. Nexus traffic flashed around the world, now, disguised as other sorts entirely. In the vast data flows of machines talking to machines, it was a bare trickle of bits, easy to hide.

Information streamed into his mind. Software collated it, organized it.

First he surveyed the reports from the agents he'd sent searching for Rangan and Ilya. Small autonomous pieces of code, they used the backdoors he and Rangan had installed in Nexus – with the new passcodes Kade had set just hours before he'd released Nexus 5 – to search the minds of Nexus users, hunting, always hunting...

Ilya would hate this, some voice inside himself whispered. *I'm invading privacy on a massive level.*

Kade ignored it. He'd started down this path to find her. Her and Rangan.

It wasn't easy to write a bot that would sift someone's mind for knowledge of two individuals. What to key off of? Their names? Their faces? And if someone had heard one of their names? Had seen one of their faces in the news?

He'd had to endlessly fine-tune the variables. The face or name of either of them – spoken or read – in conjunction with a sense of *captivity* or *imprisonment* or *prosecution* or *law enforcement*. The person he was looking for would be an ERD employee, perhaps, or part of the wider Department of Homeland Security, or a contractor, or their spouse or lover or confidant. Someone who knew where Rangan and Ilya were, who would help Kade find a way to free them.

Over the last six months he'd gone through hundreds of false hits. Today there were dozens more, the consequence of his time in the wilderness between Cambodia and Vietnam. One by one he replayed the memories and discarded them. False positives, every one.

When he was done, he moved to the next category, the code updates. He'd pulled down hundreds from the most popular Nexus hub, the place where programmers and neuroscientists and others gathered to chat about, analyze, debug, and improve the Nexus OS that he and Rangan and Ilya had built.

Nexus OS was open source now. Anyone could change it. And hundreds did. The updates came thick and fast. Bug and crashes fixed. Security holes closed. New ways to share data, to write apps. Performance speedups. And deep neuroscience tools for working with memory, attention, emotions, sleep, and more, all the way down to raw neutotransmitter levels.

So much more than we could ever have done on our own, Kade thought. Hundreds of people hacking on Nexus now. Lots of them smarter than I am. The progress is amazing.

Kade lost himself in it, the sheer joy of the code and the windows it opened on his mind lifting him.

After an hour, regretfully, he pulled himself out. There was one more thing to catch up on. The one he hated – coercion software. Code for subjugation, domination, and torture. Code used to steal. Code used to rape. Code used to enslave others. He had agents out searching for it – searching for the signal of its use, searching for the patterns of its design.

The first time he'd found such code, he'd reacted crudely, destroying the repository, forcibly purging Nexus from the brain of the man he'd found working on the enslavement tech.

The rapist on his knees, screaming. The mixed sense of revulsion and power Kade had felt as he'd ripped through the man's brain, deleting all the code he found, then forcing the Nexus painfully out of the slimebag's skull.

But that was no solution at all. Code would be backed up, or if not backed up, could be recreated. Someone forced to purge Nexus could procure more later, dose themselves again.

He'd grown more sophisticated since then. He'd turned the tools of the subjugators against them. He stopped them, reconditioned them, made sure they weren't a threat to anyone ever again. He took them down and neutered them and it felt so good, so right to stop those bastards.

Nairobi. The sex-slaver writhing on the dirt floor of the smoke filled room. Kade smiling in grim satisfaction as he mentally rewired him, as he crippled the man's sex drive and cross-linked violent thoughts to body-racking seizures, made sure the bastard never hurt anyone again.

Yes. Take them down. Stop them. That felt good, at least.

You're the one turning into a monster, Ilya whispered to him. He could see her face as she spoke. Pixyish. Earnest. Stern. *You're invading people's minds, taking control of them. It's the power you love.*

I don't have any choice, Kade interrupted the voice in his head. *Not until I finish Nexus 6.*

What did Ananda ask you? Ilya whispered to him. *"Are you wiser than all humanity?" Are you, Kade? Are you?*

You weren't even there, Kade told the voice in his head. Then he ignored her.

One thing was true. He couldn't keep up this way. He couldn't stop them all himself each time. There were more people running Nexus every day, and still just one of him. He needed to make Nexus itself smarter, more resistant to abuse. Nexus 6, he called it. And every one of these abuses he stopped, every one of these chances to stop a monster, was also a lesson he could employ in Nexus 6, a type of abuse that wouldn't be possible when he finished it.

He went through the finds his agents had made over the seven days he'd been offline. False positives, most of them. Bogus hits that weren't really abuses.

Good. For once he was ahead of the game.

Twilight fell as Feng drove. Kade turned at last to the thing that moved him most.

His software agents were everywhere now, in hundreds of thousands of minds, searching for his friends, searching for abuses. His agents spread using the back doors in Nexus, using one of the codes Kade had updated in Thailand, just hours before the ERD's attack on Ananda's monastery had forced him to release Nexus 5 into the wild.

In most of the minds they entered, his agents found neither signs of abuse nor signs of his friends. But that didn't mean that they found nothing. They found a human being, after all, a thinking, breathing, feeling person, a spark of light.

And as his agents sent pings back to Kade, he became aware of all those hundreds of thousands of minds, all around the world, and just the tiniest glimmer of what they were thinking and feeling.

He closed his eyes once more now, and let all that data pour through him. The software in his mind visualized it, placed those minds on a shadowy globe as points of light, the shape of continents visible in the diffusion of minds over the earth's surface, a pattern like nothing so much as the night-time lights of civilization as seen from space.

Kade slowed his breath, opened his palms atop his knees, and let the minds of the Nexus users of the planet wash over him. It was like a sound, like the surf of the ocean against a long shore, like a rushing river nearby. But it wasn't a sound. It was pure mind, pure thought, pure emotion.

That wash of mind was inchoate, formless, a white noise of thought. Kade breathed, and let himself sink into it, let his thoughts dissolve into that ocean of incipient consciousness, until it filled him, until there was nothing of him left, until he was just a vessel, filled up with the tiniest echo of the thoughts of humanity.

Then he slept, and dreamt of a day when that mind would not be formless, when Nexus would conjoin humanity into something more.

Kade woke in the darkened jeep. An alert was flashing in his mind, flashing, flashing.

He was disoriented. The alert was part of the dream, part of humanity becoming something else, something greater.

But it wasn't.

```
[Alert: Coercion Code Sample Alpha
Detected. Status: Active.]
```

Kade's heart caught in his throat.

Code Sample Alpha. The code used in DC, in the attempted assassination of the President.

Kade shook off the disorientation as best he could. Now was his chance. He could stop them. He could catch them.

He clicked on the link to the mind in the status notification. Encrypted connection formed. Backdoor activated, full immersion. Password sent. And he was in.

Breece smiled at the waitress as she brought him another coffee. She smiled back warily. He was just another customer at this interstate diner. Tall, muscular, maybe good-looking once, but now with a bulge of belly growing under his grimy T-shirt, his long hair tangled in dreadlocks, a ragged beard not quite concealing the scar that ran down one side of his face.

He stirred cream into the coffee, took a sip, and turned his attention back to the cheap slate in front of him.

Timing. It was all about timing. A punchline delivered too soon gets no laughs. The late bird gets no worms.

For maximum effect you had to time something just… so.

8.47am. There. The inflow of people to the building was hitting its max. Men and women waved their passes, stared into the retinal scanner, and then walked through the bulletproof glass doors. On the other side, when the doors opened, he could see that the queue in the lobby was backing up, DHS employees waiting to make their way through the bomb sensors and Nexus detectors inside. Breece smiled to himself. The Nexus detectors DHS had added were just slowing things down, creating a new bottleneck, a place of rapidly rising density of targets.

And there. Walking through the doors. Target *numero uno*. The man they'd been waiting for. DHS Chicago Deputy Special Agent-in-Charge Bradley Meyers. The agent who'd stood by as an enraged mob had killed a pair of geneticists three years ago, and had done nothing to stop it. A man who should have lost his badge, should have been convicted, but instead went on to be promoted. Well, his career ended now.

It was time.

Breece tapped the surface of the slate to initiate the action. A thousand miles away the mule's cell phone sent a signal to the Nexus OS in the man's mind. The mule hoisted the package, walked across the square, waved his ID and put his eye to the retinal scanner, and then opened the doors to the secure building and stepped inside.

Kade tried to make sense of the input from the man's mind. He was indoors. People. A line. Multiple lines. Metal detectors. A belt feeding bags into a scanner. An airport, maybe. Dozens of people all around him.

Assassination. This code was for assassination. A gun. He'd have a gun. Kade grabbed control of the man's body, patted himself down, searching for it in the pockets of the suit jacket, in his pants, in the small of his back. Nothing.

Someone bumped into him from behind as the line moved forward.

He turned, reflexively. The woman in a blouse and skirt was wearing a badge around her neck. So was the next. Department of Homeland Security. Oh no. Not an airport.

What were the assassins doing here? What was the plan? Kade could see doors back behind the people in line, darkened glass, a gleam of sunshine beyond. He could make a run for it, get away from these people, get outdoors.

A voice came from behind him. "Sir, keep moving, and put your bag down on the scanner."

Bag. There was a backpack over one shoulder. He swung it around, tossed it onto the scanner. It landed with a hard thud. Heavy. Very heavy.

Kade looked up and around himself. So many people. He had to warn them. "I think I have a bomb!" he yelled. "A bomb!"

Shock registered from all around him. People jerked back. A security man reached for his gun. Kade moved this body's hands, ripped open the zipper of the backpack. He caught a glimpse of wires, of something blinking red inside.

Then pure chaos overwhelmed his senses.

[CONNECTION LOST]

Kade gasped in shock as he snapped back to himself. What? What?

The jeep was stopped, he saw. Feng had pulled to the side of the road, was grimly watching over Kade.

Kade turned to look at Feng, numb, disoriented. His mouth opened, but no words came out.

But Feng understood. "You'll catch them," he said, putting a hand on Kade's shoulder. "I know you will."

Breece stayed outwardly calm as he surfed sports scores on the battered slate. Inside, he was roiling.

Someone got in there. Someone grabbed control of the mule and almost stopped us. Who? How?

He drank coffee, played at the pathetic human sport of "spectating" on true competitors, and stayed in character. It was three minutes later that the waitress gasped and turned up the sound on the diner's screen.

"...Again, we have unconfirmed reports of an explosion just minutes ago at the Homeland Security building in Chicago. Witnesses are reporting scores of dead and injured. As we learn more..."

Breece turned, played as shocked at the rest of them.

"...statement from the Posthuman Liberation Front," the newscaster on the screen went on, "...stating that this was a, quote, targeted assassination against Homeland Security Deputy Special Agent-in-Charge Bradley Meyers for his complicity in the murders three years ago of..."

Only fifteen minutes later, after the details had started to trickle in and video of the explosion had been played again and again and again did he drop the enzymatic cleanser into what was left of his coffee to erase his tracks, pay his check, and then make his way out to the battered Hyundai in the parking lot.

He was ten miles down the road when the encrypted phone rang. A phone that only one person in the world would call. Zarathustra.

"I told you to stand down." Even through the electronic distortion, the voice was hard, controlled, anger held in check.

"I gave you three months. Then I stood back up."

"You're out of line."

Breece smiled to himself, spoke calmly back. "Maybe you're the one who's out of line, Zara."

"This is your last warning. I won't tell you again."

Breece held the smile. "Keep your eyes on the news." Then he cut the connection.

Three towns down the road he pulled the Hyundai into a rented storage building. He emerged twenty minutes later in a late model Lexus convertible, trim, clean shaven, unscarred, his hair a short sandy brown. The micron-thick gloves, mask, and lip liners that had captured most of his DNA were nothing more than an oil blot now. The slate he'd used was a smoldering hunk of plastic. The clothes and fake hair and fake belly were gone, burned, replaced by expensive slacks and a linen shirt. Inside the garage, DNA-destroying enzyme fog was even now erasing any traces of him from the car and building. In the unlikely event that FBI or ERD ever traced the signal back, it would lead them to the diner. And from there to nowhere. Even if, somehow, they got to this garage, they would still be no closer to him.

Hiroshi and Ava and the Nigerian all reported just as clean.

Breece retracted the top on the Lexus. The sunshine bathed him in its warmth and brought a smile to his face. What an excellent day this was shaping up to be.

I teach you the overman, Nietzsche had written.

Oh yes, Breece thought. I *am* the overman. Man is something I *will* overcome.

He took manual control of the Lexus, put his foot down, and drove south in the brilliant morning sunshine, and towards the prep for the next mission.

• • •

The man code-named Zarathustra stared at his phone with cold dark eyes.

They had a problem, a very real problem. He shook his head slowly, then dialed another number to end this.

8

A GOOD LIFE

Mid October

Sam saw the news from the US from time to time. Stories of the Copenhagen Accords crumbling. Vietnam and Malaysia following Thailand out. India, a rising superpower, caught red-handed encouraging research into Nexus and other prohibited technologies inside its borders.

It's about the money, Nakamura had taught her. *Rich countries don't mind Copenhagen. But for countries still wrestling with poverty, the technology can make a huge economic difference. The motivation's higher.*

Well, now she could see that in action. And worse. Replays of the attempted presidential assassination. Stories of Nexus used for abductions, thefts, rapes.

Sam's blood pressure rose at every news report. They'd stick with her, troubling her for days as she turned them over in her head, wondering what they meant, how she thought about this. They tormented her until she was forced to turn them off, stop watching the news altogether.

Six months ago, all those stories would have made sense to her. Nexus was a mind control technology, pure and simple. As bad as DWITY, the *do-what-I-tell-you* drug. As bad as the Communion virus that had taken away her childhood and everyone she loved with it. Worse, even.

But now... All she had to do was touch a child's mind, and she knew it was more than that. All it had taken was Mai, touching her just once, loosening that knot inside, and everything had changed for her.

It's all perspective, Sam thought. What I think of Nexus, of any of this stuff... It's all just about what I've seen, what I've experienced.

Sam lay in bed with Jake one night, talking about the children.

"They learn so fast," Jake said. "It's off the charts."

"The Nexus makes them smarter?" Sam rolled towards him, head propped up on her elbow, the other hand on his broad chest.

Jake shook his head. "Not individually. But when they're together? Yeah. Sometimes. Two or three of them... they can juggle more things in their heads, together, than they can alone. Expanded working memory." He paused. "And they learn from each other. At least, when they're not picking on each other." He laughed. "But if I teach something to one of them, to Sunisa, say, it spreads. The next day, I can test any of them on it, and they'll all have some of what I taught him. It consolidates while they sleep."

Sam ran her fingers through the reddish hairs that covered his torso.

"The youngest ones are way beyond where they should be. Kit's learning algebra now. They're drafting on the older ones, picking up memories and skills..."

Sam listened to his voice, the passion in it.

"And sometimes," he said, "you can feel it, at night, when…"

She knew. She'd felt it.

"When they merge." She finished his thought for him.

Jake nodded, temporarily speechless. She could feel the awe coming off of him.

"At night," he repeated. "When they're sleeping. Or sometime, when they're playing or studying. When they're calm and not fighting. When they just kind of fall in sync, and it seems like they're just one mind…"

They were silent for a moment.

"It's like," Jake started, haltingly, "the big picture, OK? It's like the next step in our evolution. Going from one mind, to many minds, all linked… Group consciousness. That we're just parts of. That's the real posthuman."

Sam looked into the middle distance. She loved these kids, but she wasn't sure what she thought of that.

"There was this woman," Jake said, "this PhD in the states, who used to write about this all the time. Her dissertation was about how we're already group minds, how we've been evolving in that direction already – from animal cries to language to writing to the internet, and now Nexus. How it's collective thinking makes us special. Ilyana Alexander."

Sam stiffened. *Ilya.*

Jake noticed it. "You know her?"

"I've heard the name," Sam said. She kept her voice neutral, let her muscles loosen again.

It seemed to satisfy Jake. He placed a hand on hers on his chest, gently stroking it. "She was arrested, they say. They say she's one of the people who built Nexus 5. And she's locked up, with no parole, no trial… For building *this*." His thoughts took in her, him, the children, their potential.

"And these kids? In the US? The President invoked the fucking Chandler Act, Sunee. By law these kids aren't even *human* in the States." Jake sighed in frustration. "It's a fucked-up world."

Sam nodded, her thoughts far away. "It's a fucked-up world," she agreed.

Later, when Jake had fallen asleep, Sam lay awake, and opened herself, and felt the minds of the children, dreaming and breathing in unison. So very human, to her. And maybe more.

Nine minds that dreamt as one... She'd felt something like that, in Bangkok, in that loft, when she'd felt like she was part of the Buddha. She'd felt it that night, when she and Kade had fallen asleep together, had dreamt each other's dreams. She'd felt it with Ananda's monks, meditating as one mind.

But all of those had been temporary, fragile states. These children... they did it naturally, automatically. Was it really possible to become part of something larger? For minds to meld together for more than just fleeting moments?

The idea terrified her at some level. These were posthumans. Everything in her life had trained her to fear this. They'd sweep across the globe, outcompeting humans, enslaving them, driving her own species to extinction. The enemy, she would have called them a few months ago. An existential risk. Monstrosities.

But the reality... when she felt these children, when they played or cried or fought, or when their minds flowed together and embraced her into that whole...

Then something softened inside her, and she thought the future might not be so bad after all.

October was hot beyond all reason. The heat got to everyone. The children were more short-tempered, bickering with each other. Khun Mae was stricter and more prone to snap than ever. Even Jake seemed on a shorter fuse.

Sam brought in a harvest the second week of the month, while Jake made a run to get supplies from a friendly store three villages away. In the afternoon she sat and meditated with the children, guiding them through *anapana* and *vipassana*, the techniques of observing the mind itself, of quieting it. They struggled at first, their minds chaotic and pulled a dozen ways. But once they sat and brought their minds together, they fell into the unity she'd felt with Ananda's monks, so readily, naturally, and deeply. It lifted her to some egoless state herself.

Nine children. One mind.

In the early evening she taught them English, sitting together in a circle, minds linked as they spoke the words that should have seemed strange, but which came off their tongues so smoothly. Jake's comments echoed in her mind. They did learn so very quickly, each of them learning for every other.

Jake returned after nightfall, the pickup truck laden with supplies. They did chores with Khun Mae and the two other women, fed the children, put them to bed, and unloaded the truck.

Afterwards, they washed off the sweat and heat of the day in the small pond. The water was low from the drought, but there was enough to splash around in, to submerge themselves in. They emerged from the pond naked and pleasantly cool, and lay on the grass, hidden from the house by the copse of trees, bathed in the light of the full moon.

Sam put her head on his chest and stared up the stars. It was so peaceful here. So different from the life she'd known.

I should let him touch me, Sam thought. Let him feel my mind. Let him know who I am.

The thought frightened her. At first she'd kept herself sealed off from him as a security precaution. But now... Now she trusted him. So why hold back? Because she wasn't sure how he'd respond if he really knew her... If he knew the things she'd done. The blood on her hands.

Maybe tomorrow, she told herself.

"Who are you, Sunee?" he asked.

She snorted, amused at the synchronicity.

"What, I don't get to know?" Jake asked, mock offended. "You think I can't figure it out?"

His fingers found her clavicle, the long line where she'd been cut open, years ago. "You have this scar," he said, gently. "And these here..." His hand traveled down her belly, to the circular pock marks bullets had left long ago. "And you're stronger than I am. A lot stronger."

She rolled to look at him, her face a mask.

"And the kids... They don't call you Sunee. They call you Sam. Who's Sam, Sunee?"

She came up to her knees.

Not tonight, she decided. Maybe tomorrow.

"Who do you think I am?" she asked him, a smile on her face.

He grinned. "I think you're a *spy*," he said, conspiratorially, a hint of humor in voice and mind. "You're a *secret agent*."

She smiled and put a leg over him, straddling his chest. His eyes roamed over her breasts and stomach, still wet from the pond, gleaming in the moonlight, and he made a low growl of approval deep inside. She could feel his desire for her rising in his mind.

"Who are you, really?" he asked, his hands coming to her thighs, moving up to her hips and waist, gripping her hungrily. "Who did you work for? How did you get those scars? What's your *name?*"

Sam lifted up off his chest, an impish grin on her lips, and moved herself forward until her hips obscured the lower half of his face.

"Why don't you do something more useful with that mouth?" she said lightly, as she slowly lowered herself. "Then maybe I'll tell you."

Jake laughed.

And then he did exactly as she asked.

It was a good life. A peaceful life. She couldn't ever remember being this happy.

9

CONSEQUENCES

Martin Holtzmann woke with a gasp. An alarm was blaring. His skin felt clammy, drenched in sweat. The world was spinning. The room was on its side. His face was pressed up against something.

Where am I?

Then he remembered. The wave of pleasure. The opiate surge from his brain… The Nexus theft from his lab.

He groaned as it came together.

He was on the floor. He pushed himself up to one knee. The world spun more vigorously, then started to go gray. Holtzmann barely caught himself against the desk in time.

He waited there for a moment as the blood returned to his brain and the world stabilized ever so slightly. He felt starved for air and forced himself to breathe. He put a finger to his wrist and found his pulse faint and slow.

The finger on his wrist was blue from lack of oxygen.

I overdosed, he realized. I could have died.

The alarm was still blaring. There was a voice over it.

"A level three lockdown now is in effect. All non-essential personnel must evacuate. Repeat: An explosion has occurred in the Chicago office. A level three lockdown is now in effect. All non-essential personnel must evacuate."

Explosion. Lockdown. Evacuation.

That meant him. He didn't think he could get to the exit. And he couldn't let anyone find him like this.

Opiate overdose. Dear God.

He needed something to counteract it. Holtzmann racked his confused brain. Was there anything in the lab that could help him? Naloxone? Some opiate antagonist?

Dammit, he thought, I can't even make it to the lab.

He'd have to settle for a stimulant, try to counteract the massive opiate concentration in his brain.

He tried to pull up the interface to the neurotransmitter release app, and fumbled the command. He tried and failed a second time. He stopped himself, took a deep steadying breath, and succeeded on the third try. Once the app was up, he selected a release of norepinephrine. How much? He was still so woozy. Too little wouldn't help. Too much and he'd risk a heart attack or worse.

The alarm kept blaring in his head. He could hear people in the hallway outside his door. If someone came in to look… He couldn't be found this way.

He dialed up what he thought was a moderate dose, only twice as large as the bumps he'd taken yesterday, and hit the mental button to release it.

His thoughts felt a little clearer within seconds. The fog receded a bit.

He kept a hand on his desk and pulled himself to his feet.

The world spun again and he fell to his knees, gasping.

Dammit.

Holtzmann stayed there for a moment, getting his breath, and then gave himself another burst of norepinephrine, as large as the first. The world cleared further.

On the second try he got to his feet and managed to fetch his cane from where it had fallen. His skin crawled, his hair was matted with sweat, and his stomach wanted to empty itself, but he was up, he was moving.

He crossed the room to the door, a little unsteadily, and pulled it open to join the exodus.

It wasn't until he was in his car and had told it to take him home that he checked his phone. Five missed calls. Three messages. All from Anne, wondering where he was, if he was still alive.

He leaned his seat back and told the phone to call her.

"Martin!" she answered. "Are you OK? Where have you been?"

He could hear voices behind her. The hubbub of Klein and Perkins, the law firm she was a partner at.

"Anne, I'm so sorry. I fell asleep at work. Don't feel quite well."

"I was worried," she replied, sharply.

"I'm sorry, Anne. I'm in the car on the way home now."

There was a pause on the line. Then Anne spoke again. "I'll meet you there."

"No, no. No need. I think I'm going to just lay down when I get home."

Another pause.

"Call Dr Baxter, Martin. This might still be an effect of the bombing."

The neurologist. The last person he'd let examine him right now. "I'll call him as soon as I get off the phone with you."

"OK," Anne replied. "It's good to hear your voice. I'll come home early this afternoon. Love you."

"I love you too."

He hung up the phone and lay there, feeling like death warmed over, as the car continued towards home.

Someone stole Nexus from my lab, he thought. And used it to try to kill the President.

I have to find them. Before the ERD comes looking and finds me.

Martin Holtzmann lay in his car and began to make his mental list of suspects.

10
THE MISSION

Thursday October 18th

Kevin Nakamura waited in the dark, below the DC underpass. The road above rumbled as a caravan of trucks roared over it. A hard rain was falling, dripping down off the edges of the highway above, making the road wet, the air misty. In the brutal heat of DC's hottest October on record, neither rain nor darkness brought relief, only an oppressive humidity.

Even in this rain, DHS's domestic surveillance drones flew. Nakamura could picture them out there, all-weather models, circling below the clouds, cameras tracking objects on the ground, interleaving data with the road camera network, with the cell phone tracking databases, with the auto transponder systems, forming a pervasive information web, tracking all activity in the nation's capital.

Except for the few dark spots. The spots like this one, devoid of cameras, protected from overhead surveillance. The men like him, devoid of tracking devices, their true identities carefully camouflaged below innocuous public personas.

Nakamura waited, watched the cars go past, watched the rain drip down the pillars holding up the road, listened to the rumble of the highway overhead.

Then a car slowed, pulled onto the shoulder of this lower road. Black sedan, tinted windows, government plates. The passenger door opened even before it had come to a stop. A man in a dark suit stepped out. The door closed behind him and the car accelerated back into traffic.

Nakamura watched the man approach. Tall, fifty-something, with sandy hair going to gray, a paunch slowly spreading on what had once been a lean frame. McFadden. Deputy Director for the National Clandestine Service. The CIA's top spymaster, reporting straight to the Director of Central Intelligence himself. He looked older every time Nakamura saw him.

They stood between two of the massive pillars holding up the highway, hidden from above and from the road, visible only to the rats that dwelled deeper in the underpass.

"Kevin," McFadden said. "Thanks for coming."

Nakamura nodded. As if he'd had any choice.

McFadden pulled a pack of cigarettes from his pocket, offered one to Nakamura.

Nakamura shook his head as McFadden lit up and took a hearty draw. Cancer-free nicotine delivery, they said. But still not for him.

McFadden exhaled out of the side of his mouth, away from Nakamura, then withdrew a folded sheaf of papers from inside his jacket. Nakamura could see the faint glimmer of monolayer gloves molded to the Deputy Director's hands. No fingerprints.

McFadden handed the top sheet to Nakamura. Blank. Nakamura swiped his thumb across it, and an image appeared. A heavy-set, middle-aged man, jowly.

"Two weeks ago," McFadden said, "this man, Robert Higgins, turned himself in to police in Des Moines. Higgins is a fifty-three year-old computer security consultant with a history of emotional imbalance. He told Des Moines PD that he'd created a hacked version of Nexus and used it to coerce, abduct, and rape three women. He'd stopped a month earlier when a 'cyber Buddha', in his words, mentally neutered him. Nexus won't work for him anymore, and he can't even think violent thoughts without convulsing."

"Jesus," Nakamura replied.

"Cyber Buddha," McFadden corrected, taking another draw on his cigarette. "A week before that, Mexico City PD was contacted by a girl who claimed that *she* had been coerced via Nexus, and that just before the perp could rape her, in her words, an 'angel of the Lord' came down, paralyzed the man who'd abducted her, and set her free of the coercion software."

Nakamura said nothing.

"We have three more cases like this," McFadden said. "Interventions in Nexus 5 coercions. Two more rapes, one multimillion-dollar theft. In each case, someone breaks into the mind of the coercer, renders the Nexus in their minds inoperative, and creates a block against future behavior."

"So we have a Nexus vigilante," Nakamura mused. The image on the paper was already disappearing, smart circuitry wiping it out, scrambling the data irrevocably.

McFadden nodded. He handed Nakamura a second sheet of paper, blank again. "One more," the Deputy Director said. "Fresh from this morning. Classified. DHS tried to keep it from us."

Nakamura swiped his thumb and video played across the sheet. Four lines of people moving through a security checkpoint, all of them wearing badges. DHS's Chicago office. The video zoomed in on one man, in business attire with a backpack slung over one shoulder. A red oval appeared around him, and a name and bio. Brendan Taylor. Accountant for DHS.

One moment Taylor was slowly moving forward with the line. The next, a look of bewilderment appeared on his face. In the video he patted himself down, turned around frantically, slammed his bag on the conveyor.

Then he yelled something, "I think I have a bomb! A bomb!"

Then chaos and static.

Nakamura looked back up at McFadden, found the man's dark eyes staring into his.

"The bomb site's positive for the presence of Nexus," McFadden said. "But it seems that, at the last second, Taylor snapped to, realized what was going on, and tried to stop it."

Nakamura blinked. "You think this is connected?"

"We think all of these are Kaden Lane," McFadden said. "We think he has a back door into Nexus 5, one we haven't been able to find, and he's using it, to stop abuses he sees."

Nakamura narrowed his eyes. "So what's the mission? And why all this?" He gestured at the underpass, at the cloak-and-dagger. They could have met at a conference room in Langley.

McFadden took another drag on his cigarette, then exhaled to the side. "We want you to find Kaden Lane, Kevin. Find him before the bounty hunters ERD has let loose do. Then bring him back to us. And we want you to do it completely off the record."

So off the record that even the CIA's secretaries and its meeting scheduling system don't have a record of it, Nakamura thought. Black. Total black.

The video was wiping itself from the paper in his hands as he watched. Pixels were dissolving into nothingness.

"Why?" he pushed McFadden. "Why not let ERD reel him in?"

McFadden took another drag. "You know what ERD is like, Kevin." His eyes kept boring into Nakamura's. Nakamura squinted. "Lane can't fall into their hands. He can't fall into Defense's hands either, or FBI's, or anyone else. Only us."

He handed Nakamura a third sheet. "Instructions for delivery," McFadden said.

Nakamura thumbed it, scanned the text that appeared, committed it all to memory.

Nakamura looked up at McFadden. "What about Cataranes?"

McFadden ground out his cigarette on the concrete pillar, took out a small metal case, dropped the butt into it. No DNA to be left behind.

"We know you were close," McFadden said. "Use your discretion. Just bring Lane back, alive."

Out of the corner of his eye, Nakamura saw another car pulling off the road, its windows as tinted as the first.

"Burn those papers, Kevin," McFadden told him. "And do this quietly. Get Lane before ERD's bounty hunters do. And don't let anyone figure out that we took him."

Then the Deputy Director was striding away, towards the car door that was opening for him.

Nakamura sat cross-legged on the floor of his apartment, spine erect, hands folded in his lap.

This place was so empty now, since Peter had left. Since Peter had decided that it wasn't working, that he couldn't live with a husband who disappeared for weeks or months at a time, who felt more alive away from home than in it, who wrestled with demons but couldn't share any of them with his partner in life.

Just another failed relationship in a long string of them. Forty-seven years old now. What did he have to show for his life? He'd killed people on six continents. He'd saved lives. He'd thwarted terrorists and gleaned intel and completed missions whose purpose he still didn't understand.

I'm getting maudlin in my old age, Nakamura thought. He forced himself to bring his attention back to his new assignment.

Trust. It all came down to trust. CIA didn't trust ERD or the rest of Homeland Security. Homeland Security didn't trust CIA. And none of them trusted Defense.

And he, who did he trust? Who was he loyal to?

They'd picked him because he was available, because he was experienced with totally black, totally deniable missions, because he had a deep distrust of ERD, because he'd known and trained Lane before his trip to Bangkok. And because of Sam.

Sam. That was one life he'd saved. He'd done that much good in the world. Back when he was FBI. Before he'd come into the ERD at the ground floor, at its very inception. Before lies and half-truths and missions that seemed more about stopping progress than protecting people had turned him into a cynic and sent him into the welcome arms of the CIA.

Nakamura looked across the room. There, the picture of his grandfather as a boy, during World War II. Kenji Nakamura, the first of his family born in the United States. The picture was in black and white. His grandfather was little more than a toddler. He was in the arms of a beautiful, smiling Japanese woman in a dark coat. In the foreground, between them and the camera, was a chain link fence, topped by barbed wire.

His grandfather and great-grandmother had been interned, made prisoners in their country, while his great-grandfather had gone off to fight for America in World War II. It was the oldest family picture he had, more sentiment than anything else. A photo that represented a different time, the sort of thing that couldn't happen in America any more.

Except that it could, and it was. ERD had developed new internment plans while he was there, to deal with potential threats like the Aryan Rising clones. Those plans had been quietly nixed. But lately he'd heard from his contacts in ERD that they were being reactivated, upgraded, quietly put at the ready in anticipation of a wave of children born with Nexus.

Jesus.

Nakamura sighed. He'd let himself stay at ERD two years after he'd discovered those plans the first time, until finally one too many deceptions, one too many missions about stopping science instead of guarding the nation had pushed him over the edge.

He'd tried to quit. And when ERD wouldn't let him quit, he'd turned to McFadden, already a department head at CIA. And McFadden had pulled strings, gotten him reassigned.

When the CIA is the place you turn to for moral clarity, Nakamura thought, you might have a problem.

CIA wanted him to find Lane. Finding Lane most likely meant finding Sam as well. And no one knew Sam better than Nakamura.

When he did find her... Did he trust her? Would she trust him?

Images of Sam filled his mind. Sam at fourteen, coughing in that burning room at Yucca Grove, the first instant he'd seen her, with the gun at her feet and blood pouring from the dead prophet below her. Sam in his arms as he'd jumped from the third-floor window of that burning building. Later, huddled in the blanket he'd put around her shoulders as she watched the ranch where she'd lived and been imprisoned and degraded go up in flames. Sam waiting to hear if her sister or parents had made it out, knowing already what the answer would be...

Sam at fifteen, karate practice, the hours they'd spent together with him teaching her how to protect herself. Her tears and anguish on the one year anniversary of Yucca Grove.

Sam on her sixteenth birthday, in a long black gown, out to the opera with her "uncles" Kevin and Peter, resplendent in their tuxedos.

Sam at eighteen, the target pistol he'd given her as a gift. "What kind of a gift is a gun?" Peter had asked. But Sam's eyes had lit up when she'd opened the box, and she'd hugged him tight.

Sam as an ERD trainee, working twice as hard as anyone. So determined. So sure of what was right and what was wrong. So naively loyal. So patriotic.

What happened to you, Sam? What really happened in Bangkok?

He needed answers.

11
CLOUDS ON THE HORIZON

Mid October

Sam almost opened herself to Jake three times that week. The first time was as she watched him work on the old truck, which had broken down again. She watched as he explained what he was doing to a curious Sarai, pointed out the parts and how they worked, handed her the wrench and showed her how to use it.

He'd make a great dad, Sam thought. But that night he was distracted and his mind felt troubled, his head buried in his slate dissecting the budget of the house, line items weighing on him like stones. She let the moment pass.

She decided again two days later, when little Kit fell from the tree he was climbing and his pain and shock lanced through all their minds, and somehow, even though she *knew* she was faster, Jake was there before she was, shushing Kit and sending soothing thoughts and gently probing the arm the boy had fallen on. She could feel Jake's calm win the boy over, feel the fatherly awe Kit held Jake in, and it warmed her.

But that night, drunken village teenagers came to their gate and threw insults and stones and bottles. *Sat pralat!* they shouted. Monsters! You have monster children in there!

A bottle flew over the wall and crashed into one of the windows of the house, sending a spiderweb of cracks out. Jake winced. Sam's anger rose, and she got up to go show these punks a lesson, but Jake put a hand on her arm.

"They're just kids, Sunee. Just ignore them."

Then she felt ashamed.

She decided a third time three nights later, while she waited for him to return from a supply run. She lay awake in the bed that she'd invited him into every night for weeks, and lost herself in the conjoined dream of the children, a riot of forms and shapes and thoughts and memories.

Sam drifted off to sleep, smiling, in love with these magical children, in love with her life, and maybe, maybe just a tiny bit in love with this man.

She woke two hours later. She was alone in the bed. Where was Jake?

She rose, pulled on an oversized shirt for modesty, and padded down to his room. The door was open. His bed hadn't been slept in.

Frowning, she went outside. The truck was nowhere to be seen. The gate was still shut and locked. It was past midnight now. He was long overdue. A flat? A problem with the truck?

She went inside and tried his phone. It went straight to messages. She checked her own messages. Nothing.

It was probably something simple. A breakdown. A drained phone battery. A reception dead spot.

But Sam sensed trouble.

She pulled on boots and pants, threw water and food in a daypack, and left a terse note for Khun Mae and then a gentler, truth-evading one for Sarai. She slung the pack over her shoulders and headed out the door. Then, as an afterthought, she went back and grabbed one of the machetes they used to hack back the jungle, and slung that over her shoulder too.

She took the road from the hilltop house to Mae Dong at a jog, her posthuman eyes scanning right and left, picking out rocks and holes in the road in the darkness. She found him nine miles down the road, three miles from the village.

He was on foot, limping, a cut on his brow. His clothes were torn and one eye was black.

"Sunee!" His mind lit up with joy. Beneath it was shame, resignation.

"Jake!" She was on him and then she was kissing his face and holding him close. "What happened?"

He shook his head. "I was dumb. I forgot to fuel up earlier, so I stopped in Mae Dong. They were drunk. Four of 'em. And they recog-nized me."

He stopped and leaned against a tree. "They took the truck... all the supplies... Beat the shit out of me."

"Motherfuckers!" Sam exploded.

"Can you help me home?"

And some part of her wanted to wade into that village, and find those men, and hurt them. But the rest of her knew: that way was the past. She took Jake's arm over her shoulder. Took as much of his weight as he would give her, and they started the long walk home.

"We're done," Jake told her on the walk home.

"What do you mean?" Sam asked.

"The money's gone. Apsara, the woman who started this place and left it to Khun Mae. She left money behind to run the home when she died. But it's gone."

"But we sell the meds from the greenhouse…"

Jake shook his head. "Not enough. There's food to buy. Repairs for the truck and the house. The doctor's bills for Aroon last year, for Kit the year before. The bribes…"

"Bribes?"

Jake snorted. "We run an unlicensed orphanage. Our brains are loaded full of a drug that's still technically illegal. Yeah. Bribes."

"I didn't know."

"You didn't want to know." Jake snapped at her. His thoughts were rough, angry. Sam felt herself pull away. Then he gentled. "Sorry. I'm beat. I just… I never thought you were interested in that side."

Sam nodded. They walked in silence for a while, Jake limping as they made their way up the road. Her mind worked through fantasies. Taking the children with her, going to Phuket, or starting a farm, or taking them back to the States somehow.

None of them made sense.

"So what now?"

Jake coughed. She could feel the pain in his ribs where one of the men had punched him.

"The Mira Foundation. The folks who pay me. They have their own orphanage, with other Nexus kids. They want to take ours in."

Sam blinked. "That… That's great! Other kids. You said they learn faster the more there are, right? They'd have more friends their own age. We could…"

"Sunee," he cut in. "Sunee."

She paused, and turned her face to his.

"They won't take you. I tried. I tried *hard*. But they don't know you. They only want the kids. And me."

12
POTENTIAL

Friday October 19th

Shiva Prasad smiled and bounced the boy on his knee as the salt breeze caressed them both. The child's mind was a marvel, staring out at the azure waters of the Andaman Sea as the sun dipped towards them, full of questions about the world out there.

Why can't we live under the water, Shiva? the child asked.

Shiva smiled, his white teeth splitting the brown of his aged, leathery skin.

Well, he sent the child. **We can't breathe down there, for starters.**

He sent concepts along with the verbalization – lungs, oxygen, air pressure.

But the fish live there, the child sent. **How do they breathe?**

Shiva smiled again. So bright. So inquisitive.

The fish have gills, Shiva replied. **The gills let them breathe in the water.**

He sent an image this time, the slit-like gills of a fish.

Why don't *we* have gills? the boy asked.

We evolved on land, Shiva sent. **We didn't need gills.**

The boy frowned, clearly unhappy with this answer.

I want to live in the water, he sent to Shiva. **When I'm older, I'm going to give us gills.**

Shiva laughed out loud this time, kindly, and tussled the boy's hair, even as the child sent him an image – his own youthful body, gill slits in his neck.

I'm sure you will, my boy. I'm sure you will.

Later, after one of the teaching staff had come to take the boy to rejoin the others, Shiva stood alone at the battlements of his island home. He stared out to the west as the waves swallowed the last rays of the sun. The breeze blew through his long, white, fine hair. The thin white robe he wore rippled in the wind. Shiva stood relaxed, yet his spine was as straight as any soldier's, schooled by a lifetime of hard work, bolstered by the biotechnologies that kept him more fit than any man his age should be.

Beneath those waves he could feel the reefs, feel the corals, real-time sensors feeding their health into the Nexus nodes in his brain. He had only to close his eyes and invoke the right command and he could feel them growing again, returning to health, adapting to the ever warmer, ever more acidic waters of the world. Because of him. Because of what he'd done. Because of his crime.

Out there to the west, a thousand kilometers across the Andaman Sea and the Bay of Bengal beyond it, lay his true home. Mother India. The land that had birthed him, embraced him, celebrated him, and then rejected him.

They revere me, Shiva thought, but when I act for the greater good, when I do what *must* be done, they punish me, outcast me.

The virus had been his idea. With the thawing Arctic belching ever more carbon into the skies, with solar shields caught up in endless political debate, with every attempt to reduce the warming and acidification of the planet falling short of what was necessary, someone had to take the initiative. And so he had. Survival genes, culled from the coral species with the greatest tolerance to heat and acid, inserted into a viral vector that would spread those genes to every coral reef in the world, give them precious decades of additional life. And it was working, bit by bit, restoring life to nearly dead reefs, strengthening others. Just a buffer, just ten or twenty years' worth, perhaps. But at least he'd done *something*.

And how they hated him for it. *Unilateral,* they called it. *A crime against nature. Uncontrolled experimentation. Unsanctioned madness.*

Shiva shook his head. As if any of the governments or NGOs or environmentalists had any better idea.

It had cost him his home. The Prime Minister himself had passed word to Shiva. The prosecution could not be stopped. It would be best if he were gone. The Burmese were happy to have him, of course. Billions in crypto cash and his promise of assistance with their biotech programs had won him their support.

But worse, it had cost him his wife, his love.

"You've gone too far, *again*," Nita had yelled at him, through the tears. "You promised."

She broke his heart. What could he tell her? That it was her doing? That she had changed him from a man who cared only about himself to one who sought to make a better world? But she'd never loved his methods, never loved the ruthlessness he'd brought to his good works. For him, this was the logical extension of who he was and what she'd taught him. Words never solved anything. If you believed in something, you had to *act* to make it happen.

For her it was the final straw.

Shiva sighed. Humanity has lost control, he thought. It can no longer govern itself or this planet. It can no longer guarantee its children a future. The world needs new leadership. Posthuman leadership.

Was he willing to embrace that mantle? With all that it would mean?

The offices of Dunn and Broadmoor were on the sixtieth floor of a glass and carbon-fiber building in London's West End. They might as well have been in Antarctica for all that their location mattered to Shiva Prasad. What mattered was that the consultancy was very good at what they did, and that they had a track record of extreme discretion.

Shiva projected himself there from the rooftop of his island home. Custom networking software atop the Nexus OS took his posture and gestures and facial expressions directly from his mind's representation of his body and mapped them onto the three-dimensional digital image the conferencing bot projected at the other side. It took the video and audio received by the conferencing bot and piped them directly back into his mind. One moment he was watching the sun set over the sea. The next moment he was in a luxuriously appointed private conference room thousands of miles away.

He took the meeting still dressed in his simple white robe. Loving Nita had changed him. He could still remember the day he'd met her. A gala celebrating India's immense victories in the 2024 Olympics – victories made possible by the nearly undetectable genetic tweaks Shiva's firm had provided to the team. He'd been high on his secret success, his offshore accounts stuffed to overflowing, his address book filled with the private numbers of members of parliament, of cabinet ministers. Tall, handsome, and rich. The untouchable billionaire. No woman could resist him. None had in years.

Until Nita. Slender, elegant, and utterly captivating in her backless green gown, her long black hair done up in elaborate piles atop her head. Dark eyes dancing with mischief. Lips he wanted, *needed* to kiss. Hips he intended to grip as he took her in the night. An Indian woman who dressed and spoke like a brazen American. A software tycoon's daughter who devoted her time and money to charity. He'd inquired about her, then approached her, knowing she'd be his. She'd rejected him instead, then and there, just shaken her head and walked away as he tried to speak to her. She'd walked away from *him*, Shiva Prasad, the most eligible man in India!

He pursued her across two years and three continents, lured by the self-confidence that allowed her to reject him. He gave to charity to impress her, started his own foundation, endowed it with tens of millions, invited her to sit on its board. And bit by bit she gave him tiny snatches of her time. Not in the boardroom, but in the slums. In the refugee centers. In the disaster zones. In the impoverished schools. On research vessels surveying the melting Arctic and the other dying oceans. She pulled him into her life, showed him a larger world, a world that needed him, a world where his mark could linger on long after his life ended, through the ripple effects of his good deeds.

And at the end of that process, she did not become his. He, a changed man, became *hers*.

That was the end of most of his luxuries of wealth – the cars, the clothes, the women, the vacations and yachts and jets and opulent chalets. It surprised the world. Hadn't he come from the poorest of poor backgrounds? An orphan from the mean streets? An untouchable who'd become one of the most ruthless business tycoons of the decade? Surely with his billions he'd relish all the material pleasures life had to offer.

The changed Shiva knew better. Luxuries and indulgences were distractions from true greatness, tawdry and ephemeral baubles that dissipated energy that could be directed toward more meaningful and durable accomplishments in the world around him.

Yet one must wear the costume to play the role. And so it was that he absorbed the briefing in white cotton, but thousands of miles away, his avatar appeared in the semblance of gray silk Armani.

"We've clustered around eighty per cent of the Nexus users into three demographics," Kenneth Dunn was saying. He was tall, forty-something, handsome in all the ways that money could buy, with a genetically squared jaw, broad shoulders, and perfectly black hair. He might even have bought those genetic tweaks from one of Shiva's own companies.

"Cluster one: Mid-teens to mid-twenties of age, urban and suburban, medium to high income, roughly even gender split."

"Recreational users," Elizabeth Broadmoor piped in. "Party kids." She was barely more than a child herself. In her late thirties still, incredibly successful for her age, able to afford the cosmetic gene modifications that gave her the glossy blonde hair, flawlessly tanned skin, and lithe figure of a woman ten years younger.

Dunn nodded. "Cluster two: Thirties to fifties, suburban, tilted towards high income, sixty per cent women. These are parents of special needs children. Autism spectrum, ADHD, etc..."

"And cluster three?" Shiva asked.

Elizabeth Broadmoor spoke up. "This is the one you asked us to look for. Highly educated, mostly high socio-economic status, fifty-five per cent male, urban and suburban. They're highly international. What unites them most are the features you suggested: high scientific literacy, high IQ, careers in engineering, computing, and the sciences. These are people seeking out Nexus for *themselves*, to connect and enhance their own performance. These are the intelligentsia you thought we'd find."

Shiva nodded. "And the numbers?"

"These are extrapolations, of course," Dunn said. "We have only indirect data. There's a wide margin of error."

Shiva nodded. "Of course."

"Around one point three million total Nexus users," Dunn said, "plus or minus forty per cent."

Shiva stroked his chin thoughtfully, and the suited avatar did the same. The numbers were similar to the other studies he'd commissioned. "And the long-term projections?"

"A year from now we expect five million total Nexus users," Broadmoor answered. "Around one million in your cluster three. At three years and five years it gets much harder to predict. Media events, public perception, law enforcement effectiveness – those all affect the numbers."

"Understood," Shiva nodded. "Go on."

Broadmoor took a breath. "Growth is strong. Consumer demand is high. Word of mouth spread is off the charts strong. By year five, we're looking at anywhere from twenty million to one hundred million Nexus users, worldwide."

"And the last number?" Shiva asked. "The children?"

We could have one of those, Nita, Shiva thought. A beautiful child. A posthuman child. Even now. You're not too old, not with modern technology...

But Nita had always seen having a child as selfish. Why bring another soul into this world, she'd say, when there are so many out there that need our help?

And Nita was gone from his life.

Elizabeth Broadmoor's façade cracked just a tiny bit as she answered. "Using the previous estimate," she said, "by year five we expect half a million to two million children alive born to Nexus mothers."

Later, Shiva stood on the inner balcony and looked down into the tree-lined courtyard. The boy he'd bounced on his knee was down there, along with a dozen more like him, their minds linked with each other and with three adults. Their linked brains were playing a game, or so they thought. A molecular design game, searching through genetic sequences that would yield a protein that would go even further in restoring the world's corals, in protecting them from the acidification of the seas. Shiva closed his eyes and he could see the shifting protein shapes in the children's minds, writhing, folding, refolding, transforming as the youngsters searched the possibility space for a new way to save the world's reefs.

The expertise in this game came entirely from the adults – molecular biologist and biochemists with deep knowledge in the calcifying proteins used by corals. But the raw skill in the game, that came from the children, who tapped into that knowledge and then applied it together at staggering speed.

Shiva pulled himself back and focused his mind's eye on the numbers floating in space above them. And then he nodded to himself. Tonight, on this game, these children were outperforming even the most sophisticated supercomputers.

They were learning to merge themselves into an intelligence that had no human equal. They were destined to exceed him, to exceed any solitary human, perhaps to exceed any computer that now existed on Earth as well. And they were just the beginning.

There would soon be millions of scientists and engineers running Nexus. Another million children born to Nexus mothers, as these had been. What could all of *those* minds be turned into, if linked together?

Humanity was failing. It could not solve the problems it now faced. But those millions of Nexus-augmented minds could. They could become a single posthuman intelligence of epic scale. A god forged out of humanity, finally able to manage the planet through its Anthropocene calamities. But those millions would not merge willingly or easily. Shiva would need to forge that god out of its component pieces, would need to give it direction, to turn it into the rightful governor of this world and the people on it.

And for that he needed Kaden Lane.

13
BO TAT

Friday October 19th

Kade stared grimly at the road as Feng steered the jeep over bumps and around potholes. The headlights turned this narrow dirt road into a tunnel through a dark and foreboding wilderness.

Twice now. Twice the same code had been used for murder. Once in DC, when they tried to kill the President. And now in Chicago, to kill dozens more.

Twice was a pattern. This was a new PLF weapon, a new method of operation. They were going to keep at it, keep up with bombings and assassinations, in the name of posthuman freedom.

War. That's what Su-Yong Shu had said. *War is coming. Between human and posthuman. Millions will die.*

No, Kade told himself. Not with my technology.

Kade closed his eyes, started reviewing every bit of data he had on Code Sample Alpha, looking for some way to track it back to its creators.

Kade felt Ling touch him as the first hint of color touched the horizon. Feng splashed the jeep over a narrow jungle stream and on down the winding road from mountain to coastal plain, and then she was in his mind, pushing away code windows and files and everything else.

Feng! Kade!

The world shifted the way it always did when she found him. He saw the world as Ling saw it. He could feel the primitive electronic brain of the jeep, of the phone in his pocket. He looked up and the night sky overhead was crisscrossed with violet beams of wireless data, pulsing with bits that he could reach out and touch. Beyond them, blazing yellow communication satellites wheeled in their orbits, brighter than the stars, chattering endlessly to the ground and one another. Data was everywhere, flowing through him right now...

Ling, Kade sent her. He felt Feng reply as well.

They're looking for you, she told them. **Both of you.**

Who is, Ling? Kade asked.

Everyone, she sent him. **Be careful.**

Ling. Who? Kade asked. **Where are they looking? What do they know?**

I have to go, she sent. **It's time to get Mommy out**.

Kade felt alarm rise from Feng.

Be careful! the Confucian Fist sent.

Ling, wait, Kade sent **Who are they? Where are they looking?**

But she was gone from both their minds.

It was an hour after dawn when they reached the outskirts of Ayun Pa village and took the tiny dirt turn-off to reach the monastery. The road took them up a jungle-covered hill. Kade let out a breath when they rounded a bend and the walled monastery appeared in front of them. He'd been half afraid they'd find only a smoldering ruin or bounty hunters waiting for them.

But instead there were monks in orange robes, standing outside the white walls with their inlaid designs and their golden-painted posts. Two of the monks were opening the gate through the pagoda-like archway in the wall, beckoning them in, smiles on their faces. Already Kade could feel the mass of minds behind those walls, the compassion and radiance. His heart eased just a little and a smile formed on his lips.

Feng slowed and the monks reached out their hands to touch him as they passed. Their heads were nearly shaven and their faces wore huge smiles. Kade could feel their minds clearly and feel the awe they felt. He was the one who'd given them Nexus 5. He was the one who'd made the touch of another's mind possible to millions, not just the most seasoned meditators who'd learned to permanently integrate the older Nexus 3.

Kade stretched out his arm, his posthuman hand partially reformed by gecko genes. His fingers brushed those of young monks as they passed. His eyes locked on to young eyes. His mind met tranquil thoughts, tinged with youthful excitement at his arrival.

Then they were through the gates and into the stone courtyard, and Kade's breath caught. There were dozens more monks in orange robes standing in a ring around them. A hundred, maybe. Most of them just as young as the ones who'd greeted them outside the gate.

Feng stopped the jeep and Kade climbed out. The minds of the monks caressed his, bathed him in their peace and tranquility. He walked towards one at random, dazed by this. And as one, the monks dropped to their knees on the cobblestones.

"Bo Tat," he heard. "Bo Tat." A hundred voices said it. He didn't know the words but he could see the meaning of it in their minds, their hundred minds merged as one.

Bodhisattva. Heroic-minded one. Bringer of light. He who would sacrifice himself, be reborn in suffering, time after time, until every living being reaches enlightenment.

Kade's breath came fast. His heart was bursting. So much beauty. Amid all the pain and horrors of the world, there was so much beauty in the world. The way the minds of the monks intertwined, the way they connected to one another.

He caught an echo of those million minds he could feel when he tried, a thin layer of consciousness encircling the globe, still shapeless, still unformed. Those million minds could be like this, connected, merged, mutually comprehending, more than the sum of their parts. He closed his eyes and the dream pulled at him, tried to tug him out of the here and now.

Kade opened his eyes, forced himself back to the present, reached out the hundred monks before him with his thoughts. "I am not Bo Tat," he told them with a laugh. Not enlightened. Not heroic. "I'm a *novice*. *Less* than a novice."

He turned as he spoke, to take them all in, speak to them all.

"*You* are the brave ones," he told them. "*You* are the ones risking your lives to shelter us. *You* are the ones who'll build a better world. You are the *beginning* of something much bigger."

He felt them smiling, joy and hope rising in unison across a hundred minds.

Then there was another mind behind him, harder, closed off. He finished the turn and came face to face with the man. Older than the rest. Tall, sharp featured, with dark expressionless eyes. The abbot.

"Welcome, Kaden Lane." The voice carried no warmth.

Kade bowed and lowered his eyes to show respect.

"Thank you so much for taking us in."

The old monk nodded. "I am Thich Quang An. This way. I'll show you to your rooms."

Feng grabbed their packs and they followed him. The monks rose as they left the courtyard. Two of them fell in behind Kade and Feng.

Quang An led them to a branch in the path. He rattled off something in Vietnamese to the two monks who'd followed them, then turned to Feng. "Dat and Lunh will take you to your rooms to get settled. Kaden, come with me to my quarters. There's something I want to show you."

Feng gave Kade a curious look. Kade shrugged. Feng shrugged back, and then he was off with their packs and the two monks.

The abbot's mind was still hard and opaque as he led Kade the other way.

"Thank you again for taking us in," Kade said. "I know it's a risk for you."

"It's nothing," the man said curtly. His mind was a mask, unyielding.

"If I've offended..." Kade began.

The old monk snorted.

They turned a corner, and then another, and kept walking. The monastery was larger than Kade had realized.

"I know that I'm not a bodhisattva," Kade said. "Not a holy man."

"Do you?" The abbot turned, raising an eyebrow. "Do you really?" His mind was inscrutable.

"Yes," Kade said. "I do."

"You've given great powers to the young and foolish. Dangerous powers. Powers they should have *worked* for.

Powers that even now are being abused, are they not? Some may love you for it. I do not."

Chicago flashed through Kade's mind, a glimpse of wires and then chaos. The news videos of broken bodies strewn about, men and women whose lives had been ended abruptly.

Powers that even now were being abused.

Kade opened his mouth, reached for some answer, some way to say that he still believed in people, still believed they'd use this mostly for good, *despite* the abuses.

But the abbot had already turned, walking briskly away, and Kade had to rush to catch up to him.

"Here." Thich Quang An opened a door, gestured Kade inside before him. "There is something within, for you."

Kade bowed, and entered.

Then something hard jammed itself into Kade's belly and he gasped. Someone grabbed him from behind and slapped heavy tape over his mouth. He thrashed and tried to kick out but men held him. Then everything went black as they brought something down over his head.

[activate: bruce_lee full_auto]

His body dropped low and twisted and for an instant the hands on him were gone.

[Bruce_Lee: Escape Succeeded!]

He felt his leg lash out and make contact with a soft target.

[Bruce_Lee: Attack Succeeded!]

Someone groaned. Kade's body twisted again and he felt something whoosh by him.

[Bruce_Lee: You Dodged One!]

Then he felt the heat of a body nearby and his fist lashed out and—

[Bruce_Lee: Attack Succeeded!]

Oh my fucking God

pain lanced up his right hand as soft, not-yet-fully-healed bone and raw nerve made contact with something much harder. He curled over, cradling his throbbing hand as the pain brought tears to his eyes. Then something hit him in the head, hard, and the world spun.

[Bruce_Lee: Dodge Failed ☹]

Kade came to slowly. They were carrying him by his ankles and armpits. He could see nothing through whatever was over his head, but something told him he was outdoors again. He tried to yell but he was still groggy, and managed only a weak grunt. The tape around his mouth stifled it.

Then he felt other minds. Three of them. A handful. A dozen. Monks closing in. They were all around him. Their minds were linked and that linkage encompassed him, showing him what they saw, a dizzying image of himself, black bag over his head, carried by hugely muscled Asian men while three more armed with guns and knives moved with them.

Two dozen monks. They moved to block the way of the bounty hunters, minds serene, trembling a bit, but calm and determined. A faint breeze ruffled their orange robes. Their faces were still, their mouths set in impassive lines. Not a sound came from them but the rustling of their robes and the soft shuffle of their sandaled feet.

Kade tried to speak. He tried to reach out to them with his thoughts, but the world still spun.

Then he saw the gun come up.

No.

He focused, forced himself to concentrate.

Run... He tried to shout it with his mind. It came out as a whimper instead.

A bounty hunter put the muzzle of his pistol between the eyes of a monk. And Kade recognized him... one of the monks who'd opened the gate, who'd reached out to touch him... Just a boy, just a boy.

Run!

The bounty hunter said something in Vietnamese, and Kade understood it through the minds of the monks.

"Get out of my way or I'll blow your fucking head off."

"You cannot have him," the young monk replied. And Kade saw it from the monk's perspective, saw the ugly brute of a bounty hunter, the shaved head, the tattoos across his scalp, the bulging muscles, the dark hole in the muzzle of the huge gun, the man's thick finger on the trigger. He felt it all from the young monk's perspective, felt his heart beating in his chest, felt the boy's terror and his awe of Kade and his utter resignation to this moment.

"Like hell I can't," the bounty hunter said.

His gun boomed and the bullet burst open the boy's skull and exploded Kade's world. The shock of it sent Kade's mind reeling, then rippled through all the other monks. Dimly through the chaos he felt some of them reflexively bring their hands up, their minds recoiling. One leaned over to vomit, and the pain and fear and chaos and loss threatened to overwhelm them all. These weren't Ananda's long trained monks. These were just boys!

The second shot took another monk in the gut. Kade felt the bullet burst his own midsection open and the pain tore through the cobwebs in his mind.

The monks almost broke. Instead he felt their minds harden, felt them come together. Determined monks moved to drag away their fallen comrades and the collective mass pressed in on the bounty hunters. Three dozen monks. Four dozen monks.

Then he heard someone screaming in Vietnamese and he saw through a dozen eyes as the abbot rushed into the circle. The words were foreign but the meaning came across.

What are you doing! You said no monks would be hurt!

A bounty hunter turned and shot him in the belly. Thich Quang An crumpled forward in pain.

The assembled monks moved as one, now, gelling into a single organism with a single intent, to pull Kade away from these men. The assemblage pushed forward with a hundred limbs and one mind and Kade could see what was about to happen and it wouldn't, it couldn't. No more of these men would die for him.

He rallied himself, focused, multicast his thoughts to the monks around him, opened up their minds with the backdoor…

…and the conjoined will of the monks pressed down on his, blocking him with iron force from sending the passcode, from forcing them to abandon him.

A bullet took a monk in the arm, spinning him around. Another punched through a young monk's chest. The pain echoed through Kade.

Then Feng was among them, his mind cool and hard. Time slowed for Kade as Feng's combat trance touched his own mind, stretching out every instant into a long, deadly span.

The augmented bounty hunters moved like molasses, lumbering, overly muscled brutes turning in slow motion. The flight paths of unfired bullets shone in Feng's thoughts, brilliant lines of red light extending from the muzzles of their guns. The bounty hunters' bodies cast echoes of potential blows and kicks that Feng foresaw.

Feng moved like a dancer, calm and graceful. He leapt over the plane of fire of a swinging pistol, rolled under another as he converged on the first bounty hunter. His mind was utterly absorbed. This was *samadhi*. This was meditation. Guns exploded and the bullets were living things in Feng's mental map, ripping out of the muzzles, shockwaves rippling visibly through the air, flinging themselves at the spots Feng had occupied fractions of a second ago.

Then Feng reached the first bounty hunter, and the man went down with his neck snapped.

A stray bullet punched into a monk's thigh then, and the echoing pain of it snapped Kade out of the trance of Feng's mind, back into real time. And just like that, the bounty hunters were dead, all of them, the last bodies toppling to the courtyard at Feng's feet as Kade watched through others' eyes. Kade lay on the ground where they'd dropped him, as Feng pulled the tape off of him, cut through the bonds on his limbs.

Kade pushed himself to his feet with his good hand, his body shaking.

There were bodies around him. A monk was whimpering. He could feel pain radiating from half-a-dozen minds. At least three were dead. Another was dying even now, the boy's mind falling apart into a thousand little pieces and then into nothing at all. Someone sobbed.

The pain and loss hit Kade full force. His sight dimmed. His legs felt weak, and he fell back to one knee.

"No safe place for you," said the abbot, and coughed. Kade turned to look. The man had blood across his robes, blood coming out of his mouth. Pain and disgust wafted off of him. "I'm not the only one," the man said weakly. "You... not a Buddha. An abomination. *Maya*. Illusion."

Feng stepped towards the man and lifted one gun with a scowl, anger radiating from his mind.

"No!" Kade yelled, his still-healing hand outstretched.

"What?" Feng turned, confused.

"Let him go, Feng."

"He was gonna give you to Americans. Almost got you killed! Killed all these!" Feng gestured around himself at the dead and dying monks.

"We're better than that," Kade said.

Feng took a deep breath, exhaled with a shake of his head, and lowered the gun to his side.

Monks moaned around them, yelled to each other for help, stared at the carnage in their tranquil home in horror.

Kade closed his eyes wearily, reached out to the abbot's mind, used his back doors, opened the man to him. And saw.

"Not safe," the old man coughed. "Not safe anywhere." More blood welled out of his mouth. "Many of us… Better… you die. Abomination."

Then Thich Quang An, abbot of Ayun Pa, was gone.

Kade stared around himself at the horror. The ERD again. Their dollars. Their stupid bounty on his head. That had caused this.

Feng put a hand on his shoulder. "We gotta go," he said. "Cops soon. Can't be here."

Kade rose to his feet, still dizzy. Go. Yes. They had to go. Somewhere. Anywhere.

14
GOOD NIGHT, SHANGHAI

Friday October 19th

Ling Shu stared out the rain-streaked window of the high-rise apartment at the vast spectacle of Shanghai. Glowing advertisements rippled across the wet skyscrapers opposite her. Glimmering aurorae of blue and white light shrouded inducements for clothes, for vacations, for cars, for homes. The twenty-story-tall inhumanly alluring face of Zhi Li smiled at Ling, winked at her. It was the image of China's most famous actress, the supranormal stimulus of her eyes so big and almond-shaped, her skin so porcelain white, her lips so full and red. The image smiled again, winked for only Ling to see, then held up a bottle of some sports drinks her masters wished her to sell.

Do you think you're posthuman? Ling asked the giant screen. Do you think that a billion people knowing your face makes you special?

It doesn't.

A surveillance drone cruised by the window, one of Shanghai's tens of thousands of sky-eyes, moving slowly on its four all-weather rotors, spinning to point its proboscis-like camera at Ling through the rain. Its glowing collision-avoidance light cast red reflections on the rain-slicked glass.

Ling stared back at the thing through the window and the downpour, reaching out, feeling its primitive mind, the stream of data in and out of it. She could see herself in its data stream. She could twist that if she wanted, lie to its masters, or send it instructions of her own, take control of it.

She did none of these things.

The sky-cyc stared at her, then rotated its quad-copter frame, canted to one side, and moved on to inspect something else in the great city.

Hundreds of meters below her, Ling could see more sky-eyes, dozens of them peering into windows and watching the city at ground level. Cars streamed below them in a river of metal and carbon-fiber on the wet streets. Motorcycles and scooters zipped between cars. Horns blared. Pedestrians with umbrellas darted across walkways. The rain fell in hard sheets on all of them. It sounded a ragged drumbeat against the window where she stood.

Badadadadadadadum. Badadadadadadadum.

The heavy cloud and pouring rain blotted out the sun, but the city was alive with artificial light from the giant advertisements, from the windows of buildings, from the red glow of brake lights, from the glowing red lights of the surveillance drones, circling, always circling, over the heads of Shanghai's citizens. The light reflected off the heavy clouds above, turned the whole sky to a multicolored glow, twenty-four hours a day.

This city was alive. It was a living thing. The streets were its arteries. The cars and trucks and scooters and pedestrians its blood.

Ling closed her eyes and she could feel the nerve-signals of the living city, the vast pulsing web of data that interwove everything around her. She could lose herself in the web that linked people and cars and buildings. She could feel the far-off power stations and the local substations, the water pumps and sewage lines, the spy eyes and traffic routing systems and all the rest.

The city soothed her. She could sink into that hubbub of data, and for a while her own fears and longing and sadness would fade, and she would stop thinking and just feel the sizzling, crackling thoughts of the city around her instead.

It helped her. It helped her not think about Mother.

But today was different. Because today was the day she'd set Mother free. Today was the day she'd touch her mommy's mind again. Her father was going to visit the Quantum Cluster today. Going to visit her mother.

And part of Ling would be there with him.

Chen Pang lifted his eyes from his slate as the car pulled up to the chrome and glass building. He slid the device away into his briefcase as his driver Bai opened the armored door of the vehicle. Chen stepped out under the umbrella the clone held aloft for him. The Confucian Fist closed the car door and walked him towards the building. The mirrored glass walls reflected the two of them back to Chen's eyes. He: a late forties man in suit and overcoat, hair graying at the temples, his face stern – his body a bit thicker in the midsection than in his youth. His bodyguard: young, fit, tall for a Chinese man, in black chauffeur's garb, face expressionless, umbrella held aloft to shield Chen from the driving rain, the man's eyes scanning left and right for any threat.

The glass doors parted for him and he paused.

"Wait with the car. I'll be an hour, perhaps two." Then he strode on as his driver bowed to his retreating back.

Chen passed through the metal detectors and T-rays, waved his ID, and placed his eye before the retinal scanner. The elevator door opened, and he stepped in. Five floors down, below the main building, he stepped out, and into the Secure Computing Center.

The armed guard nodded at him. Chen ignored the man, and made his way across the facility to the entrance to the PICC – the Physically Isolated Computing Center.

Ling closed her eyes and followed her father's slate and phone as they made their way down into the earth, deep below the official buildings of Jiao Tong. The devices accessed the local network inside the Secure Computing Center and formed a tunnel back to her. She reached her mind through that tunnel now, gently stroked the flow of data inside the facility, parsing, absorbing, searching. Her mother was here, trapped, cut off from the outside world, cut off from Ling. She would find her.

Chen crossed the facility. Men and women stopped work and bowed their heads respectfully as he passed. He was Chen Pang, after all, the architect of China's explosive surge in quantum computing. He was a figure of awe to them. If only they knew.

Li-hua saw him coming. His assistant rose to her feet – a homely woman, too short, too pudgy. She bowed her head to him. "Honored Professor," she said, "the tests you requested…"

Chen waved her away, kept walking. Yes, yes, she'd done the tests. But he needed to see them again.

He kept walking, past all the bowing underlings. The resentment rose in him again. The envy. That his greatest accomplishment was to serve as the secret scribe for his wife. That *she* was the true discoverer of so much.

Still, it had its rewards.

"Ling, your break time is over. Time for your next lesson."

Ling clenched her small fists.

"Ling." Her tutor's voice rose slightly.

Ling forced herself to smile, forced herself to turn back to the human, the way her mother had taught her, forced herself to say the insipid words.

"May I please have a few minutes more, teacher? I like to watch the rain."

"Well." The tutor sounded surprised. "Since you asked so politely, you may."

Chen surrendered his electronics at the next checkpoint. Then the security man slowly and thoroughly wanded him, looking not for weapons, but for any device that could possibly carry data in or out of the PICC.

The guard finally declared him clean, and Chen stepped forward and into the cavernous elevator. The doors closed behind him, and the elevator started its descent through one thousand meters of bedrock and towards the mad software entity that was all that remained of his dead wife.

Ling sifted through exabytes of data. Cryptographic libraries. High resolution satellite imagery. Whole brain scans. Genome sequences. None of it was her mother.

She looked for maps, physical maps, network maps. She found them. The network topology told her little. Nothing obviously fit the description of the quantum cluster her mother existed in. The physical blueprints of the building were no more helpful. Multiple data centers existed here, but their functions weren't clear.

Ling kept searching. She would find her mother here.

The room-sized elevator took Chen down through the rock beneath Shanghai. A lit sign declared that the current PICC status was

ISOLATION IN EFFECT

All this was a precaution. Computer scientists, philosophers, futurists, writers of speculative fiction – they'd all written about the dangers of runaway superintelligence. If humanity ever created a being of radically increased mental capabilities, it placed itself at grave risk. That new being could be benevolent, of course. That would be the hope. Or it could be malicious, or simply indifferent to humans. It could seek to change the world in ways that it saw as improvements, but which were incompatible with the interests of its creators.

A superintelligent being might also be able to improve on itself, reaching into its own structure and finding ways to optimize them, to make itself smarter than its creators could have, with no obvious end in sight.

And for that reason, Su-Yong's ability to edit herself was limited to superficial layers only.

Chen himself doubted the risk of runaway self-improvement. Intelligence showed diminishing returns. Just as a single human could not design a human-level intelligence from scratch, no superhuman creature could possibly design a creature of its own intelligence or greater. Oh, it might be able to make improvements on the methods used by its creators, and get some boost, but without collaborators, without access to new hardware, the improvements would level off.

And so he'd stretched the rules, hidden a few upgrades of his wife's design in with more prosaic maintenance, made the case for upgraded quantum cores. All for sensible reasons, of course. All so she could produce more work of value to the Science Ministry and the State and humanity. All for the greater good.

Regardless, in this world, this world where everything was linked, where data ruled all, where cryptographic codes had replaced physical locks on the world's wealth, on its infrastructure, on its weapons… In this world a being able to process information more rapidly than humans was the ultimate threat.

It was for such reasons that the Copenhagen Accords prohibited any attempt to create a non-human self-aware being. And for the same reasons, Chen's own government, in sponsoring the creation of exactly such a dangerous and illegal being, had taken extreme precautions that it could be physically isolated, cut off from the outside world, and destroyed remotely if necessary.

The elevator clanged to a halt. Here, at the bottom, where no wireless transmission reached, three physical data lines connected to the outside world. One linked the Quantum Cluster to the net. That cable was physically disconnected now, its ends separated by a gap of ten meters.

The second cable carried data one way, from a grid of cameras and other sensors, up to the Secure Computing Center above. It let the SCC observe what happened here.

The third cable carried far simpler data. It connected a terminal above to the nuclear battery that provided power for the PICC. If things ever went ultimately wrong, that cable would carry a single command, instructing that nuclear battery to go critical in a chain reaction that would melt the underground facility to slag.

The wall-sized doors to the elevator parted. The meters-thick inner blast doors parted a moment later, and Chen Pang strode out to inspect his wife.

Ling frowned. There was no evidence of her mother here. But she *knew* that her mother was in the quantum cluster beneath Jiao Tong. And Father had gone there.

"Ling, your break is over now."

Ling ignored the tutor. Where was her mother? Where?

Chen sat at the terminals that monitored his dead wife's quantum brain and initiated the systems check. Through the bulletproof glass he could see the grid of liquid helium pressure vessels, the vacuum chambers a thousand times colder than interstellar space within them, containing the quantum processors in an environment almost completely devoid of thermal noise. He could see directly into the brain of this creature that he'd once been married to.

Data scrolled across the screens within seconds. The level 0 diagnostics were clean. Pressure vessels intact. Quantum bandwidth across the interconnects was excellent. Qubit coherence was well within the limits of quantum error correction.

The level 1 diagnostics came back next. Processor and memory utilization were high. She was furiously thinking in there. Requests for external data connections were nearly continuous. Millions of times per second she was trying to reach the outside net, the cameras, the audio pickups, the

Nexus-band radios, the long-range link to the clone that had died in Thailand.

The level 2 diagnostics were the most disturbing. Her simulated brain looked less and less healthy. Her virtual brainwaves were chaotic and incoherent, inhuman looking. Neuronal interconnectivity in her frontal lobes looked terrible. The remaining virtual neurons there were working at a frenetic pace, trying to make up for the deficit.

It was true, then. She was going mad. And he had been rendered powerless to stop it.

Give me just one more insight, wife. This last breakthrough. Then you can die.

Chen Pang reached up and physically turned on the cameras and microphones that connected this room to his dead wife's mind.

"Ling!"

Something was wrong, she realized. Father's phone and slate had stopped moving. She thought he'd simply stopped somewhere, but when she interrogated them, they were out of contact with him.

"Ling, are you listening to me?"

She looked through the security cameras inside the center. Where was Father? Not in the hallways. Not in the main work areas. Not in the data centers. Not in the physical electronics labs. Where?

"Ling!" The tutor grabbed her arm, and Ling struggled to pull it free.

Wait. There. Not Father. But his phone and slate. They were on a table, behind a security guard. A checkpoint. An elevator door beyond that. There was another level!

She went back to the network topology, to the physical blueprints. There. Data lines that extended down. Repeaters on them, indicating that they went far. A network connection. She reached out for it.

Input burned itself into Su-Yong Shu's mind.
Video.
Audio.
Real-time.
Here.
Her husband, Chen. He was here. He hadn't abandoned her! Hope blossomed in Shu. She struggled to get a grip on herself, exerted a superhuman effort at coherence, at communicating what she needed.

"Wife?" Chen said.

"Husband!" The speaker burst to life. The voice carried relief, hope, near hysteria.

"Su-Yong."

"Chen! Chen! Chen! You've come for me thank God. Please, Chen, I'm in trouble trouble double please I need the clone need stabilization need organic brain brain input clone please Chen please…"

Babbling. This is what she'd been reduced to.

"Wife, please. I've come to ask you about the equivalence theorem."

"They're going to kill me Chen they killed me already CIA killed me Americans killed me buried me you buried me please help neural input need a brain a clone please please before it's too late please Chen…"

"There is no clone, wife. The equivalence theorem. You proved it, didn't you? How?"

"MAKE ONE." The voice came out at the maximum volume. "MAKE ONE MAKE ONE MAKE ONE MAKE ONE…" and on and on.

"The equivalence theorem, wife! Tell me. Tell me," he lied, "and I'll help you!"

Ling's mind reached out for the connection that led to the next level.

But there was nothing. A dead end.

What?

She turned to the schematics. They didn't extend that far. They showed data lines heading down, but not where they terminated. She struggled to understand, searched for explanation.

There, an operations guide. She consumed it, and then she understood.

Her mother was physically isolated a thousand meters down. The connection was *physically disconnected*. There was no way to reach her mother at all.

"Ling Shu, it's time for your lesson!" The tutor pulled her hard, yanking her around to face the old woman. Ling tripped and fell to her knees. "Owwww!"

Shu stopped, aghast.

The equivalence theorem? The EQUIVALENCE THEOREM???

That's why Chen had come. Despair smothered the hope she'd felt. He wasn't here to help her. He was here to wring one last bit of value out of her. She'd married this man. She'd loved him. She'd tried to make a child with him.

Oh, Chen. Oh, Chen.

• • •

The voice from the speaker suddenly went silent.

Chen blinked, surprised.

Then his wife spoke again.

"Chen Chen husband Chen please if you ever loved me ever cared please help please."

Chen hardened himself.

"The equivalence theorem," he repeated. "Give it to me, then I'll help you."

"PLEASE HUSBAND." Chen flinched as his dead wife's voice boomed at painful volume. "PLEASE HELP BRING ME A CLONE OR LING HUSBAND BRING ME LING MY DAUGHTER LING LING LING PLEASE LING…" The voice descended into sobbing even as it screamed Ling's name. Chen hit a switch and turned off the speakers.

What had he expected? It was like the first time. Except this time there would be no clone. The hardliners would not allow it.

"Damn it!" He slammed his hand down on the console. The proof, if it was practical, would allow quantum acceleration of *any* classical algorithm, not just the small minority that achieved massive speedups on quantum systems now. It would be worth billions, tens of billions. It would win him the Nobel Prize. But it was out of reach now.

Chen took a deep breath, forced himself to act normally. He filed away the system test results, made sure all the cameras and audio pickups that led to the Quantum Cluster were deactivated, then logged off of the terminal.

The blast doors and elevator doors opened for him, and then closed behind him once more, and the elevator began its slow ascent to the surface.

• • •

"Owwww!" Ling yelled as the tutor wrenched her around and she fell to her knees and bit her tongue.

"Ling, your break is over, young lady! It's time for your lessons."

"No!" Ling yelled in frustration. No, her mother couldn't be trapped! *No no no no no!*

She tried to pull her arm back but the tutor's grip was too strong. She reached out with her mind instead, grabbed hold of the woman's phone in anger, forced it to discharge its battery. The tutor jumped back with a scream, alarmed by the sudden jolt of pain from her pocket. Then she reached forward and slapped Ling, hard, knocking her against the glass window.

"AAAAAAA!!" Ling screamed and reached out to the apartment around her. The oven threw its door open and came on with a burst of flame. The fireplace jolted to life. The cooking bot activated and began sharpening its knives. The closet door opened and the cleaning bots emerged, their fans whirring. The music system and viewscreens came on at painful volume.

The tutor looked around her, eyes wide, and turned and ran for the door.

Ling turned her mind back to Jiao Tong.

NO NO NO NO NO!

She threw herself at the connection, but it was futile. She slammed her tiny fists against the glass of the window, to no effect. Physical disconnection. She hated the physical world, the world where she was so puny and weak, hated it, hated it, hated it!

Ling reached out in anger and frustration, grabbed hold of the network nodes of the Secure Computing Center, and wrenched at them in every way she could. Immediately her connection to the place ended, but the anger was still with her, so she reached out to the city around her, pushed her mind into its cars and its power stations and its buildings and its traffic routing and surveillance bots and *RIPPED*.

She heard the explosions as the substations blew, saw sparks somewhere out there, and then a wave of darkness swept away the lights of the great city, advancing block by block, like a wave of dominoes falling. The building-sized porcelain face of Zhi Li winked at Ling one more time, and then blinked out of existence, along with the lights of the whole block, of Ling's flat, and every building within sight.

And finally, Ling felt calm returning.

Ling Shu stared out the window of her pitch-black flat, tears falling from her eyes, her tiny chest heaving as she caught her breath, and watched the hundreds of red-lit surveillance drones plunge to the street below, like stars falling from the sky, as the rain pounded on the suddenly still and darkened city.

The elevator came to an abrupt halt two hundred meters up. The lights died and the status indicator switched from ISOLATION IN EFFECT to

LOCKDOWN IN EFFECT

And suddenly Chen Pang knew fear.

"Help!" he screamed. "Help!" He beat against the doors of the darkened elevator. "Help!"

But no one heard him.

15
MEANS, MOTIVE, OPPORTUNITY

Friday October 19th

Holtzmann napped when he arrived home late morning, rose again around 2 o'clock, feeling better, and was awake when Anne came home in the afternoon.

"I'm fine," he assured her in the kitchen, "fine."

"Did you talk to Dr Baxter?"

"Yes," he lied. "He fit me in. He thinks it was just stress."

Anne frowned. "I think you have PTSD, Martin. They have therapy for that, you know."

Holtzmann kept his eyes on the counter. "I'll be OK, Anne. This won't happen again."

Anne crossed the kitchen, laid her palm on his cheek until he met her eyes.

"Promise me you'll see Dr Baxter again?"

Holtzmann looked into those eyes, of this strong, intelligent woman that had been so good to him for so long.

He reached up and put his hand over hers. "I will."

He worked in his home office, catching up on events.

After an hour, Anne announced that she was having dinner with Claire Becker. Warren's widow was still having a hard time accepting his sudden death, and her new situation as a single mother of two teenage girls. Holtzmann felt guilty that he hadn't reached out to her since the funeral. He and Becker had been colleagues for almost a decade, friends for most of that time. Surely he owed Clair more than a hug and condolences six months ago?

But Claire was so suspicious, always spouting conspiracy theories about Warren's death. Anne did a better job comforting her than Holtzmann could.

His inbox had scores of messages, two of them of note.

Item one: Rangan Shankari had broken, around 3am. He described an ingenious system of backdoors in the Nexus binaries and hacks in the compiler to place them there. And he'd given them the passwords.

Holtzmann frowned, wondering what they'd done to finally break Shankari. The electrical shocks? The waterboarding? The Nexus-dosed interrogators?

And now that DHS had the back doors, what would they use them for? Spying on the thoughts of Nexus users? Preventative mind control? Political surveillance? *Manipulation* of those thoughts?

"Why?" he asked aloud. "Why did you leave those back doors in there? Didn't you see the danger? How could you be so stupid?"

Item two: The forensic report from the Chicago bombing. The blast site tested positive for Nexus. Samples were en route to Holtzmann's lab now.

Holtzmann would have no choice but to process those samples. He'd hand them off to Wilson, with instructions to come to him and him only with the results.

Holtzmann sat back, then started a new file, titled Personnel Assessment, and started listing everyone who could have taken Nexus out of the secure fridge in his lab.

Holtzmann crawled into bed hours later. The pain was back, an aching deep in his bones. His muscles were cramping. His mouth was dry. His heart was beating fast. He had all the blankets pulled over him, was sweating, but he still felt so cold all over.

All he wanted was another little opiate surge. Just for the pain. The doctors had cut him off too soon. He just needed a little bit more, for a little bit longer, until he was fully healed.

I nearly died last night, some part of himself said.

Just a little one, just once more, the other part of him answered.

He had the interface up when he heard the garage door open. He lay paralyzed in bed as he listened to Anne ascend the stairs to the bedroom.

"Sorry I was out so late," she told him as she disrobed. "Claire's in a really bad space. She's not moving on."

Holtzmann made a sympathetic sound.

Anne slid into bed beside him. "She's convinced it was a cover-up, that Warren was killed to keep him from testifying."

Holtzmann stared longingly at the interface in his mind. If he did just a small dose, would Anne notice?

She curled up against him and stopped talking for a while. Holtzmann forced himself to breath slowly and regularly, to not touch the interface in his mind's eye.

If I sound like I've fallen asleep…

"Martin?" Anne asked.

Holtzmann said nothing, and finally Anne stopped. A few minutes later she rolled over, towards her side of the bed.

He waited until her breathing turned regular, and he was sure she was asleep.

Then Martin Holtzmann dialed up a small dose, and finally he felt OK again.

He rose early, brought Anne coffee in bed with a smile, put on his game face as he readied for work.

"You seem better today," she noticed.

"I feel better."

"You were dead to the world when last night. Do you remember me coming to bed? Our conversation?"

He cocked his head quizzically. "Yeah… Something about Claire, right?"

Anne smiled tolerantly at him, and then they were off to their respective offices.

The day was a succession of nearly useless meetings. He sat in on a planning session related to the Nexus back doors, vetoed a proposal to use "aversive stimuli" to motivate Nexus children to purge the drug, got briefed on the Nexus vaccine development, which was looking promising, and on the proposed Nexus cure, which wasn't looking promising at all.

Through the day, his list of potential Nexus thieves was never far from his mind.

Means, motive, and opportunity, he thought.

Twenty-two people had access to the fridge in the wet lab, giving them the means.

Any of them could have worked a late night, providing opportunity. Access logs could show who had been in the lab when. But he didn't have access to those logs or videos. Only Internal Affairs did, and he certainly didn't want them digging.

Motive, then. What was the motive for the inside man? Hatred of the President? Money? Blackmail?

He played it out in his head at the end of the day, as he walked to his car in the dark but now heavily secured parking garage. Which of those twenty-two were ideologues? Who needed money? Who'd bought a flashy car recently, moved into a bigger house?

Holtzmann frowned as he opened his car and placed his cane and bag in the passenger seat. He kept pondering his list of suspects as the car cleared the security perimeter and turned onto the freeway on autodrive. And so he didn't see the ripple of distortion in his rear-view mirror. Didn't hear a rustle of cloth as the man who'd been hidden in the back of the car came up to a seated position, a barely visible blur against the faux-leather seats and the retreating highway lights behind them.

"Martin."

Holtzmann jumped in shock. The voice was distorted, mechanical. His heart slammed into his throat. He scrambled for the handle to the door, then heard the *chunk* as the car locked itself.

Stupid man. If they'd come for him, he was dead already. Nothing he could do.

"Relax, Martin," said the deep, anonymized voice again.

Holtzmann looked into the mirror to see the face of his killer. The figure in the back seat was just a shadow, a barely perceptible distortion. A man in a high-tech chameleonware suit, then. A professional.

Holtzmann swallowed hard, wishing he'd told Anne the truth, that he'd trusted her.

Then the figure behind him raised a hand, and Holtzmann closed his eyes to wait for the killing blow.

16

ONLY FORWARD

Feng pulled Kade along behind him to the Jeep, then climbed into the driver's seat. Monks followed them with canisters of fuel and liters of water. Even in the midst of shock and sorrow, they did what needed doing. Like soldiers.

Feng leaned out of the jeep to place a hand on the shoulder of a monk.

"Thank you." He put his respect into it, beamed it out of his mind to theirs, one soldier to another. They bowed. Then Feng put the pedal down, and he and Kade were off.

The first priority was to be gone. Feng pushed the jeep hard and fast down the dirt road. Brilliant green trees and brush raced past them, contrasting with the red earth of the bare ground they drove on. This was the bottleneck, the one road up or down from Ayun Pa.

The tires skidded just a bit as he found the maximum lateral acceleration they'd take. Every sound of every pebble, every twig, every bit of give and play of the tires on the road loomed loud in his mind. He absorbed the sounds, the feel of the wheel, the response of the jeep to his acceleration. The

vehicle became an extension of his body. He felt Kade grab
hold with his one good hand as a sharp turn pulled him out to
the side. Feng spun the wheel back the other way as the road
hairpinned, sending red dirt and loose scree flying. The smile
came to his face of its own accord. He was alive, and free, and
totally absorbed in their mad dash down this hillside road.

Fifteen minutes later, they were off a different side road,
the jeep hidden in a copse of date palms. They'd heard no
sirens, but Feng intended to take no chances.

"We wait here till dark," he told Kade.

Kade nodded. "It's the back door," he said.

"What's that?" Feng asked.

"I've been sitting here thinking about the bounty, Feng.
Why do they want me so badly? A ten million dollar bounty?
And *alive*? They've already convicted me in absentia. They
could just kill me."

Feng turned and looked at his friend. "So what're you saying?"

Kade looked back. "They want the back door."

Feng thought this over. "It's a dangerous thing."

Kade nodded. "It's funny, we put it in there as a safeguard
against the ERD, so that if they misused Nexus we could
stop them..."

"And now they trying to get it from you," Feng said.

"I could close it," Kade replied. "I have the code. Another
bot. A virus. It'd spread from person to person, close the
back doors anywhere it found them."

"So why don't you?" Feng asked.

"Because there are people I have to stop, Feng."

He felt thoughts flit through Kade's mind. Images. A
glimpse of wires and a flashing red light in that building in
Chicago, before white noise and then – nothing.

Feng mulled that over. "Maybe somebody else deal with those things?" he told Kade. "Not just you?"

Kade shook his head. "I made those abuses possible. I have to stop them if I can."

They sat in the car and waited for night. The palm trees shaded them from the worst of the sun, but it was still brutally hot.

The news brought word of a fire in a remote mountain monastery. Chu Mom Ray. No fatalities were reported.

"You saved my life back there," Kade said.

Feng turned and grinned at him. "Not the first time."

Kade laughed. "No. Not the first." He shook his head. "At this rate, not the last either."

Feng shrugged. "It's what Su-Yong would want. *Save the boy*, she said."

Kade nodded.

"And you're my friend, Kade," Feng said, grinning again. "First one I ever chose for myself!"

Kade smiled at that, turned his head, and took Feng's hand.

"Thank you."

"Hey, don't get all mushy now!" Feng joked. "I just don't have so many friends I can lose them, is all." But it was long moments before he let go.

"Why'd that monk sell you out?" Feng eventually asked Kade.

Kade shook his head again. "I've upset the order of things. It used to be that only the most experienced meditators could master Nexus and keep it in their minds indefinitely. But now anyone can permanently integrate it. And the young monks pick up Nexus 5 faster than the old ones. They don't need the old ones as teachers. I've undermined their authority, inverted the hierarchy."

"Fuck hierarchy," Feng said.

Kade laughed aloud. It felt good to hear it. Feng smiled in return.

"Aren't you a soldier, Feng? You grew up with hierarchy."

Feng was the one to look away this time, his thoughts far away.

"Yeah. Never liked it."

"Tell me," Kade said. "What it was like."

Feng watched a palm frond sway in the wind. Kade had asked before. Feng knew his friend meant well, but it wasn't something he wanted to go back to.

"Please," Kade said.

Feng sighed. It had been a rough few days. Kade needed something. Needed some perspective. Needed some *hope*. He leaned back.

"My first memory was pain." Feng spoke quietly, but he opened his mind, let Kade feel it, let him remember it with him.

"I was four, maybe. Big. Strong. They engineer us to grow up fast. But not so much mind, yeah? Get big and strong fast, but smart just as slow.

"I was doing rings, yeah? Swinging one to the next, like a monkey."

"Then I fell. No mat. No net. Just ground. It hurt. Bloody knee. Nothing bad, but I was four. Just knew it hurt." He shook his head, and Kade felt it coming, the real pain.

"Instructor comes over, and he says, 'Get up!' And I say 'It hurts!' So he kicks me across the field. And now I'm screaming. And all my brothers. They all stop. Staring at me."

Feng's fists were clenched. He was that little boy again. Kade felt his stomach knotting up. Felt the pain and fear and incomprehension.

"Instructor walks over, and he says, 'Get up!' And I'm crying, cuz it hurts. Hurts real bad now. And I say 'Can't! It hurts!' and he says 'I'll show you what hurts!' and he kicks me again."

Kade felt sick to his stomach. His face was hot.

"Instructor walks over one more time. He says 'Get up! Get up, dog!' And this time I try, but something's broken inside. I fall down. But I know, I stay there, he'll hurt me worse... So I crawl. It takes me long time. Hurts so bad. Feels like an hour. But I make it over to rings again."

Feng was breathing heavily now, his chest heaving as he remembered. His face was flushed with it.

"And I try to get up, and it hurts so bad and I fall down. And I try to get up again and I pull up on the pole and get to where I can stand. I try to go up the ladder. But I slip. Arm not working. And I fall down again.

"And now I know I can't say I can't. So I say, 'Help me!'"

Feng shook his head, and leaned out the jeep to spit. He pulled back upright, wiped the spittle from his mouth with the back of his hand. The wind rustled the date palms softly overhead. A bird called out somewhere near them.

After a moment, Feng went on, softly, more slowly.

"So I say, 'Help me!' and instructor says, 'This what happens to boys who ask for help.' And he kicks me, again and again. And I ask him to stop and I try to curl up and he just keeps on kicking me. 'You see that?' he asks my brothers. 'You see what happen if you're weak?'"

Kade bowed his head at the horror of it. A four year-old boy.

Feng's body was vibrating now, his hands clenched around the wheel. He had to hold himself back from breaking it in two.

"They take me away to hospital. Two months. I'm a lesson for all my brothers." Feng snorted. "Some lesson."

"I'm sorry, Feng," Kade said. "I... I'm sorry to make you relive that pain."

Feng snorted again. "Yeah. Pain. You know why I tell you that?"

Kade shook his head, his mind still reeling from what Feng had shared.

"Because I want you to understand. You think Nexus making so many bad things happen. Your fault, yeah? But this all happens to me *before* Nexus. Nexus not bad. Just some *people* bad. You understand?"

Kade said nothing for a few seconds. Then slowly, he nodded. They sat in silence for a while.

"When did you first meet Su-Yong Shu?" Kade asked him.

Feng nodded. "All my childhood, lots of pain. Physical pain. They rig us with implants when I'm six." His hand went to the back of his head. "Direct nerve stimulus, yeah? Pure pain. Pure."

Feng shook his head, put his hand in his lap again. "They use pain to punish us, discipline us. Use pain when we're too slow, too weak, when we miss targets shooting, when we lose fights sparring, when we don't clean our guns fast enough, hold our breath long enough, make our beds neat enough.

"All they teach us is how to fight, how to kill. Weapons. Tactics. Strategy. Planes. Helicopters. Cars. Kung fu. Knives. Guns. All that stuff. For fun, we get war movies, fight movies." Feng laughed. "Those we like.

"They make us fight each other, fist and feet and knives. And other kind of fights. Compete with our brothers. Whoever slowest, or weakest, or stupidest, more pain. And shame in front of other brothers. No dinner. No bed sometimes – sleep standing up.

"But doesn't work so good after a while. We stop caring about pain. They built us too well. We get wild. Start to talk back. Show off to other brothers."

Feng shook his head again. "They punish us more. One boy dies. I probably gonna die, if I keep on the way I am. Instead, I meet *her*." Su-Yong Shu.

"She came first time when I'm fifteen. Full grown. Stronger than any instructor. But wild. Not a very good soldier. Whole program, down the drain. Soldiers no good. They want her help, yeah? To control us. Make us better slaves.

"First time I ever see her... I'm being punished. Insubordination. So, pain stim. Which means I feel pain *everywhere*. All over, inside, fire pain, sharp pain, beating pain, all pain, all at once. And I'm curled up trying to fight it, trying show my brothers I'm tough, when *she* walks in."

Kade saw it through Feng's eyes. The barracks. The institutional gray walls and cold concrete floor. The metal frame bunk beds with the rolled-up olive green blankets. The drab brown footlocker that held every possession Feng had. The sergeant instructor pressing the button on the remote that sent Feng's nervous system into a primeval hell. The door opening. Shu, standing there, in white. A formidable man in a dark uniform next to her. His face an ugly scowl, his shoulders bearing insignia. An officer. A colonel.

"Not just *a* colonel. *The colonel*. Man in charge of whole program. And she says to him 'Stop! Stop this!' And he says 'No. They're not human. We teach them to behave through pain.'"

Feng smiled grimly.

"Then she slaps him. Hard. And she says, 'This man is more human than you are.' And she walks up to the sergeant instructor and yanks remote from his hand and turns it off."

Feng shook his head in admiration.

Kade seemed surprised. "She could do that?"

Feng nodded. "This was maybe two years after she… you know. After she goes digital. After *ascension*. She's first true posthuman. And she's *Chinese* and making all kinds of discoveries the big bosses like. She thinks she can do anything."

Feng shrugged, "Me, I just collapse, not sure what to do. Then she asks me, 'What's your name?' and I say 'Confucian Fist D-42, sir!'"

"'No,' she says. 'Your *name*.'" Feng laughed, then stopped talking for a while, let Kade soak up the shock he felt in that moment. A *name*. The idea of it!

"My whole life, they taught me that I'm not human. I'm a *clone*. A *treaty violation*. I'm a number. I do what I'm told. Su-Yong, she treats me like a human being.

"She changes everything. Next day, colonel is out. Pain stim remotes gone. Training changes. We start to learn more science, politics, history. We get Nexus – what you call Nexus – in our brains.

"You see these people hurt by Nexus. Human bombs. People stealing. Women hurt. But for me… For me, Nexus means I touch my brothers for the first time. I understand that I'm not alone. Until then… 'brother' just mean someone I have to fight, have to compete with. One of us won't get to eat. One of us gets more pain. No love. No *loyalty*. After Nexus, I can touch their minds… Then I feel them. Then I love them. Then I know loyalty. Then I really have brothers.

"And you know, I still hate instructors. Still today, and especially then. But Su-Yong, she say, we don't have to be loyal to instructors, don't have to be loyal to commanders. Have to be loyal to *China*. To the *people*. They're our brothers and sisters.

"What you did, Kade. You give Nexus 5 to everyone. I know it makes Su-Yong mad. She wants more control than that. But you did the right thing." Feng turned to look at Kade, poured every ounce of emotion into this. "All those people out there. They can start to understand. They each other's brothers, each other's sisters. Like you and me. Brothers. You did the right thing."

Darkness finally fell. Insects came out. The jungle came alive with sounds. The air cooled to a more bearable level of heat.

"So what now?" Feng asked.

Kade turned and looked at his friend. "The monasteries aren't going to work anymore. The bounty hunters have figured out our pattern. We're just going to get monks killed. It's time to try a new strategy, Feng. Let's head to the coast. Let's go see the big city."

17

SURPRISE ENCOUNTER

Friday October 19th

"I'm not here to kill you, Martin."

What? Holtzmann thought. The distortion was gone. This was a different voice. A voice he knew.

"I was hoping you could answer some questions for me," his not-assassin continued.

Holtzmann opened his eyes. In the mirror he could see a face there, in the darkened back seat, where there hadn't been one before. Headlights struck them from another car, illuminated the face for a moment. Dark hair, graying at the temples. Asian features. A face he hadn't seen in months.

"Kevin."

Nakamura nodded. "Who did you think I was?"

"I... I don't know!" Holtzmann stammered.

Nakamura's face was a mask in the darkened car, utterly still.

"I thought I was being mugged... carjacked..." Holtzmann went on.

"By someone who knew your name?" Nakamura asked. "Who snuck into your car while it was parked at DHS headquarters?"

Holtzmann's heart hammered in his chest. He was that transparent. A professional could see through him in seconds…

Dear God, what am I doing? he thought. He said nothing.

"You don't have to tell me," Nakamura said gently. "We all know things we shouldn't."

Holtzmann swallowed, forced himself to breathe calmly. The car drove on down the dark highway, the lights of the DC suburbs sliding by on either side.

Nakamura filled the silence. "Six months ago, Samantha Cataranes was sent to Bangkok. You remember the mission?"

Cataranes? Holtzmann thought. This was about Cataranes?

"Yes. I remember."

"You dosed her with Nexus 5 before she left. While there, during an op, she attacked ERD contractors during the attempted capture of Thanom Prat-Nung. Three days later, she attacked a team of SEALs, brought down a chopper, helped create an international incident. You remember all this?"

Holtzmann nodded. He remembered the chaos of that week. The botched mission in Bangkok. Dozens dead in the loft fire. The Nexus girl, Mai, among them. Ted Prat-Nung as well. Lane's escape. Then the attack on the monastery. Su-Yong Shu's death there. Nexus 5's release. His own decision to try Nexus for himself… The discovery of Warren Becker dead of a heart attack, the next morning. He wouldn't easily forget those few days.

"Why?" Nakamura asked.

Holtzmann blinked. "What?"

"Why'd she do it, Martin?"

"I…" Holtzmann fumbled over himself. "We think that Shu coerced her…"

"Could she do that? Coercion that complex?"

A memory flashed through Holtzman's mind: Secret Service agent Steve Travers, in his suit and mirrored glasses, his hand coming out of his jacket in slow motion, the giant gun held there, the encrypted Nexus traffic between the shooter and whoever was controlling him echoing in Holtzmann's mind. The world slowing even further as Holtzmann came to his feet and opened his mouth to scream that the man had a gun!

"Yes. Shu could do that."

"Is there any evidence that she did?"

"There wasn't any other explanation. We sent Cataranes out there with Nexus 5. It was a stupid move. Su-Yong Shu might have *created* Nexus. If she discovered who Sam was…"

"Is there any *evidence*?" Nakamura repeated.

"The evidence is how Sam acted. Kevin, you knew her. You *mentored* her. You practically *raised her*. She was loyal."

More loyal than I am, Holtzmann thought.

Nakamura said nothing for a while. The car switched lanes of its own accord to fall in behind a long row of vehicles, then pulled up close to the one ahead, just inches from bumper to bumper, drafting, saving fuel.

"Shu's dead now," Nakamura said. "How would that affect Sam?"

Holtzmann brought his hands up to his face, closed his eyes for a moment, then pulled his hands away. "I don't know, Kevin."

"You don't know?"

"It depends. How did Shu program her? Did she turn Cataranes into a puppet steered by remote control?"

In his mind the Secret Service man's gun came out out out, and fired, and fired.

"…Or did she put in something more complex? Something deeper?"

Human missiles leveled the shooter, and Holtzmann turned, looking for the President. Joe Duran screaming in his ear, "How did you know, Martin? How did you know?"

"It doesn't make any sense," Nakamura said.

Then the world exploded in Holtzmann's memories, hurling him through the air.

"What?" Holtzmann said.

"If Shu turned Sam, she could have sent her back to ERD as a mole. Or whisked her and Kade off to China. Shu had to know the loft was an ambush, that it was a mission to get close to Prat-Nung."

"I don't understand," Holtzmann said.

"Why did Shu let Sam and Kade walk into that situation, Martin? If she'd already turned Sam, then she *knew* the loft was an ambush. Shu was recruiting Kade, but she nearly got him killed."

"Shu was trying to protect Ted Prat-Nung," Holtzmann replied.

Nakamura shook his head. "No. Shu and Prat-Nung knew each other. She could have just warned him away."

Holtzmann dropped his face back into his hands. He was so tired. So very tired. He could feel the aches starting again, the clammy sweating, the chills deep inside.

"I don't know, Kevin."

"Who had the most to gain?" Nakamura asked, almost to himself. "The way to find the cause of an event is to understand who had the most to gain from it."

The car activated its turn signal, then switched lanes on its own, into the exit lane that would take them to Holtzmann's home.

"Lane," Holtzmann said. "Kaden Lane had the most to gain. He escaped because of Sam."

Nakamura nodded. "Yes. That was my conclusion as well."

And the movie started again in Holtzmann's mind. The hot July day. The white plastic chairs. The President blathering on. The encrypted Nexus traffic. The Secret Service agent in black suit and mirrored glasses, reaching into his jacket...

"Could he do it?" Nakamura asked.

...The gun coming out in slow motion...

"Yes," Holtzmann replied, sick to his stomach. "I think he could."

... Coming out, out, out...

"One last question, Martin."

Firing, firing. Muzzle flash and terrible boom. Human bulldozers striking Travers, the gun flying from his hand. Holtzmann ached so deep inside.

"Can you get it out of her?" Nakamura asked. "Out of Sam's mind?"

Holtzmann thought of the cure experiments, the mice dead in their cages from every batch so far. Maybe the back door that Rangan Shankari had given them? That terrible, terrible tool. Could they at least use it to counteract whatever Shu had done to Cataranes? It was too soon to say.

"I don't know, Kevin. I just don't know."

Nakamura nodded.

The car slowed as it reached the turn signal at the end of the exit. The doors made a *thunk* as they unlocked. In the rear-view mirror, Nakamura pulled the mask of his chameleonware suit over his face once more.

"Thank you, Martin," he said with the deep distorted voice again. "I was never here."

Nakamura opened the door just as the car came to a stop. He stepped out onto the curb, his silhouette fading to a moving pattern of shadow and distortion before Holtzmann's eyes. Then the door closed, and the car made its turn, and Holtzmann was alone with his thoughts and his memories and his aching need.

18
FRIENDS

Friday October 19th

Rangan woke, curled up on the floor in a corner of his cell. He'd eaten the traitor's meal they'd given him, but refused the new, restraint-free bed. It was better than he deserved.

He blinked to shake off sleep. His dreams had been strange. Ilya fighting faceless figures with push/pull. Ilya dying in the dark, crying, alone, her heart stopped, all of her fading to nothing. And children. Strange children. Confused children.

Rangan pulled himself up to sitting. He was stiff from sleeping on the hard surface. His hip hurt and his left leg was half asleep. He rubbed his calf absently as he struggled back to wakefulness.

Ilya. Ilya was probably still resisting. She'd never give in. She had the heart of a fighter. His dream was guilt. Guilt that he'd given up, that he'd turned informant, when his friend would never put her own life ahead of her convictions.

Had they told her that he'd broken? Would they go easier on her now? It was something to hope for. What would she think of him, once she found out? Would she despise him? Hate him?

And Kade? Wats? What would they think of him?

He'd always had the easy life. Rich parents. Good looks. Success came easy, in school, in music. The Indian golden boy. Boy wonder scientist by day, hot DJ by night.

And the women. God, how he loved women. And they'd loved him. Woman after woman after woman. He could leave a club most weekend nights with a party girl, sometimes two. He'd jerked himself off to sleep so often the first few weeks here, calling up memories of their faces, their bodies, the kinky things they'd done for him. Memories remembered naturally. Memories he'd recorded with Nexus, without ever asking their permissions.

Such an easy life. Rangan Shankari, international playboy. Yeah, right.

He was pathetic, he saw now. What had he ever done for anyone else? He'd lived his whole life as a taker. Taking money from Mom and Dad. Taking sex from girls whose names he barely remembered, girls that he honestly didn't give a fuck about, except that they were hot and fun in bed and good for his rep.

The only thing he'd ever done that was worth a damn was Nexus. His one impact on the world. And had he fought for that? When they'd busted the party in SF he tried to run. And now, in this stinking cell, they'd given him a second chance. He could show *this time* that he had the strength of his convictions. But no. They tightened the screws a bit and he folded, just like that.

What did it even matter that he was going to die here? His whole life was a self-obsessed joke. He'd been so goddamn self-centered that he might as well not have existed at all.

Fucking pathetic.

Fuck!

Rangan slammed his hand against the concrete wall of his cell and then swore as he felt the pain.

Then he felt something else.

Another mind.

Faintly. A young mind, weird and warped, and reaching out for him...

Bobby closed his eyes and he could feel his new friends in his head – Tim and Tyrone and Alfonso and Pedro and Jason and Jose and Parker and all the rest. They were like him, *autistic*. But more than that. He could feel them in his head. They were *real*.

There were grownups here who came in and gave them tests, but he couldn't feel the grownups in his head at all and he knew why it was because they didn't have NEXUS and so they were stupid and they weren't real people at all.

Sometimes the grownups took one of his friends away to give them a test, but Bobby and the others could still feel whoever they'd taken, like when they took Nick and gave him tests on Math and English and Bobby could feel him taking the test and even though Nick didn't know some of the answers, Nick got them right because he had his friends there in his head.

But then later they took Nick further away and he was GONE from Bobby's head and Bobby was scared that they had HURT him or KILLED him but they brought Nick back and Nick said they'd only given him special tests and so Bobby felt better.

The next day they took Bobby away and gave him tests on Math and English and Science, and made him play games and solve puzzles and he could still feel all his friends, but then after that they took him to a special room and they closed the door and he COULDN'T FEEL HIS FRIENDS and he started to get scared, but he remembered that Nick had come back and Tim said that all the other boys came back, and so he'd probably come back too.

Then they put a cap over his head and gave him a test of Spanish, at least he thought it was Spanish, because he didn't know Spanish and he just guessed and did really badly at the test, but that wasn't his fault if they were testing him on something he hadn't studied.

And then they took him back to the room with all the others and he was glad when he could feel them all in his head again and they asked him to tell them all about it and he SHOWED them the <TEST> and the <CAP> and the <ROOM> where you couldn't feel your friends in your head and the <SPANISH> and he was happy he had friends – friends that could understand him and he wanted to always have friends like this.

And that night he dreamed in Spanish and dreamed he was Pedro or Alfonso or Jose and the next day they took him away to the special room again where he couldn't feel his friends and tested him in Spanish only this time he KNEW THE ANSWERS and even when they asked him questions they hadn't asked yesterday he KNEW THE ANSWERS TOO.

And he knew it was because of Pedro and Alfonso and Jose and the Nexus in all their heads.

And that night, when they made him go to bed and he lay down and closed his eyes he felt something, another person, far far away, a sad person, alone, a person who felt less like his friends and more like his daddy. And Bobby reached out to that person so sad and so far away and tried to say hello.

19

THE LONG GOODBYE

Mid October

Sam and Jake argued for half the limping journey home.

"But I can be useful," she said. "I know these kids. I love them. They love me!"

"I know, Sunee," Jake replied. "I told them. I *want* you there. But the Mira Foundation is really careful. They've had… incidents."

"There has to be another way."

"Look, I think I can talk them into it, but it's gonna take a while."

"And what, I just wait for you to call? Not knowing when? Or *if*?"

"You know I want you there."

"No," Sam said. "I don't!"

"Well maybe if you'd fucking let me in, you would," Jake snapped.

Sam almost dropped him. "Fuck you. There has to be another way!"

Jake took a deep breath. "Sunee, we just have to do what's best for the kids."

"What, and that's ripping away someone who wants to be there for them?"

"Jesus, Sunee, it isn't just about you!"

"What about Khun Mae? She's the one in charge, really."

Jake sighed. "Khun Mae said yes."

"You asked *her* before *me?*" Sam's voice rose.

"Yeah," Jake replied. "Because you're taking it exactly how I expected."

It was after dawn when they reached the home atop the hill. Silence filled the hours. They spoke just enough to agree on a story for the children. They put on their game faces at the end, smiled and projected happy thoughts.

And the children saw right through them.

Sam begged Jake and Khun Mae for a few days to come up with alternate ideas, then forced herself to think them through.

She could appeal to Ananda for money to keep the orphanage going.

She could go back to Phuket, take Lo Prang up on his offer, start a career as a prize fighter to raise funds.

She could start a charity, ask for donations.

She could sell samples of her own cells and their fourth-generation enhancements on the black market.

She considered each idea, and others, and discarded them all.

Ananda would be watched by the ERD.

She knew nothing about running a charity.

Winning fights for Lo Prang would raise her profile and increase the risk of the ERD finding her. And how long before the mobster asked her to hurt men *outside* the ring?

And her genetic tweaks... Selling them would mean deaths, somewhere, far away. Deaths of men and women like her, doing their jobs, trying to protect their country or save the innocent. She wouldn't have that on her conscience, not even to save the orphanage.

In the end she had nothing.

The second night she woke to terror, to thoughts of faceless men bursting in, ripping her away, ripping Jake away, taking the children.

Nightmare!

It pressed down on her even after she woke. She looked at the doorway to her room and masked men appeared – bad men.

No, not real.

Not her nightmare, the children's. It crested over her, paralyzing her, freezing her to this bed, trembling.

Get up! Sam yelled at herself, and the dream's hold on her broke.

She forced herself out of the bed. The room was spinning, distorting, the corners alive with shadows of the men who were here to separate them. She lost her balance, fell against the wall, forced herself to clench her mind, push harder. She got the door open, then down the madhouse hallway, shadow hands reaching out to abduct her, reached the door to the room the girls shared, found Jake there already, waking the children, clutching Sarai to his chest.

Sam stumbled further to wake the boys, to project love and safety, to break them out of their terror.

The dream horror receded as the children woke, as Sam and Jake cuddled them, all together in one room now, where they could all see that everyone was safe.

Sam breathed hard, Kit clutched to her chest, beaming out love and safety and assurance to these children, as her head cleared.

Jake's eyes met Sam's, held them beseechingly.

Sam just stared at him, her chest still heaving.

The third night she sat on her bed, alone, the bed she hadn't invited Jake into since he'd been attacked, and read up on the Mira Foundation.

Founded by biotech billionaire Shiva Prasad. The legend who'd risen from his childhood as an orphan in one of India's poorest and most violent cities – a *Dalit*, an "untouchable", a member of India's lowest caste – to become a ruthless biotech titan. He'd left competitors ruined and underlings scarred in the process of making his billions. Then in later life he'd suddenly changed, become a philanthropist– a sort of midlife turnaround common among ultra-rich capitalists thinking of their legacy.

She read on. The Mira Foundation ran anti-poverty programs in India, Asia, and Africa. It backed education, nutrition, and vaccination efforts in India, Pakistan, Bangladesh, Burma, Cambodia, Laos, Nigeria, Kenya, dozens of other countries. They funded research into next generation bio-crops with higher yield and better nutrition, and open-sourced those they produced. They operated a network of extraordinarily effective orphanages in India and Asia.

There were darker rumors online. She read about the brutal slaying of an Eritrean warlord whose troops had stolen Mira Foundation supplies meant to head off famine in his country. He'd been found crucified and tortured to death, the heads of a dozen of his men mounted on spikes around him. Further aid convoys had gone unmolested.

A corrupt Laotian governor – who'd swapped medicines Mira delivered for fakes, sold the real ones on the black market, hanged in his living room.

A criminal gang in Burma who'd abducted and gang-raped three female Mira Foundation workers. The gang members had been found hogtied and chained to the floor, face down on their knees, dead of massive hemorrhaging from the blunt objects they'd been violated with.

No crime had ever been pinned on Mira. But across the net she found the quiet assumption that Mira had been responsible, and approval that they'd taken on the thugs that plagued the developing world.

She reached the case she remembered last. The Dalit orphanage in Bihar, in northern India. A rumor had spread among villagers that it was the site of transhuman experiments, that loathed Dalit children inside were being turned into superhuman untouchables with black magical abilities. Tensions had run high. Then one night the orphanage gates had been chained shut from the outside and the whole structure had been burned to the ground. Thirty-five children and half-a-dozen orphanage staff had burned to death.

Sam shivered reading it, thinking of her own childhood, of the suspicions of the villagers from Mae Dong, of the bottle throwing, the attack on Jake.

There had been a trial, with a lackluster prosecution and a judge who'd dismissed all charges against the seven villagers charged with the murder.

A week later, those villagers, the judge, and the prosecutor had been found dead, crucified and burned to death just outside the village.

Sam turned off the slate and lay back in the darkness of her room. Could something like that happen here? Could the villagers turn violent? Could she blame Mira for being careful, for not wanting to include her, a stranger?

And if something did happen... if someone did hurt these children she loved... would she react any less severely than the Mira Foundation had?

Sam sighed. She was being selfish. She was resisting this plan only because she was being left out of it. She had to trust Jake. She had to trust that he would do the best for the children, that he would find a way to include her.

She told Jake and Khun Mae in the morning. She apologized to Jake for how she'd treated him. He accepted it warily.

Then she threw herself into enjoying the last few days she'd have with the kids for a while.

They spent a last few perfect days together. Sam downloaded updates to Nexus 5, downloaded a music game, and on the last day they ran through the grass together, all nine children, and her, and Jake. And they jumped up to grab iridescent musical notes floating through the air, flailed their hands through rainbow-colored chords, and made chaotic, gorgeous sounds in each other's minds. Sarai whistled and Mali played a flute and Kit banged a stick on a board and more notes appeared in the air around them, and little Aroon ran around, chasing the notes, catching them, holding them, and then letting them loose to make their sounds again.

In the end, they helped the children pack up their meager belongings and put them to bed. Sam put a sleeping Aroon down into his crib, then tucked Kit in with his precious Panda. She held Sarai's hand and pushed the hair back from her eyes and kissed her brow, told her that Sam would be there with her soon, a big sister she could count on.

"I love you, Sam," Sarai said, and Sam smiled and said the same to her and told her she'd see her in their dreams.

Then she turned, and Jake was there, and for the first time in a week, Sam invited him into her bed.

"My name is Sam," she whispered to him when they were alone, between kisses. "Please call me Sam."

She opened her mind to him, just the tiniest bit, and let him feel her pleasure as they made love, her tenderness, her trust that he'd find a way for them to be reunited.

After, as they lay together, she showed him how she'd grown up, what she'd faced, showed him her sister and Communion virus and Yucca Grove. Jake held her and beamed out comfort and safety and acceptance.

That was enough, right there. More would come, later, after they were together again.

They slept, their naked bodies entwined. And the morning brought the men from the Mira Foundation.

20
SHUTDOWN

Friday October 19th

"Help! Help me!" Chen pounded on the doors until his fists hurt, until his throat was hoarse.

It was no use. He was hundreds of meters from the surface. The status indicator continued to read

LOCKDOWN IN EFFECT

Its red glow provided the only illumination in the cavernous, darkened elevator.

What was going on? This was no mere mechanical failure. The change in status to lockdown meant that something had happened. Had his dead wife attempted to break free? Had he somehow facilitated that? He patted himself down furiously. Was there a hidden data device on him? Had she somehow succeeded in planting something on him to get something out?

No, there was a simpler explanation. The hardliners had won. The long stalemate between the proponents of liberalism and openness – of *gong kāi huà* – and the reactionaries who wanted to tighten control had been settled. He could see it in his mind's eye. Liberal-leaning Politburo members suddenly falling ill, resigning their posts, exiling themselves to their country homes, never to return. Or perhaps worse – men dying, throttled in the dark. Perhaps bombs going off, like the one that had killed his wife, that would have killed him...

Chen shuddered at the memory.

So the hardliners were finishing what they'd started a decade ago, pruning the last fruits of the billion flowers period, ending this experiment in the posthuman, ending the life of his wife as they'd tried before, and taking him with her.

Was the nuclear battery going into meltdown even now? Would the radiation kill him? Would it travel up this shaft? Or would he be left here to suffocate, or die of thirst or hunger?

Was there any hope of escape? Chen looked up towards the top of the elevator. There was no obvious maintenance hatch there. Even if there was, would he have any hope of opening it, then climbing hundreds of meters to the surface? Opening a locked door there, and somehow evading the armed guards in the SCC who undoubtedly had orders to let no one pass? Could even Bai, his clone driver, fight his way through security and rescue him? And if so, then what? Flee to India? Bah.

Chen Pang retreated to the back wall of the elevator and sat down heavily. It was hopeless, then. He'd known this day would come. Ever since the limousine. Ever since the assassination attempt eleven years ago had brought *gong kāi huà* to an abrupt end. Neither he nor Su-Yong were meant to live that day. They'd been on borrowed time since then. Somehow he'd let himself forget that.

No. From the moment that Sun Liu had taken him aside and warned him not to get into the limousine that night, they'd been doomed. Ted Prat-Nung hadn't understood, of course. He'd believed the lie that the CIA – and not hardliners within the Chinese government – was responsible for the explosion in the vehicle. Prat-Nung had pushed hard to try the emergency upload. Chen had no choice. Prat-Nung was dangerous, and madly in love with Chen's wife. He couldn't tell the man the truth. And the upload would surely fail. What harm in this bit of theater?

When it had worked? When Su-Yong had woken up in the cluster he'd designed, somehow sentient? Well, then he'd allowed himself to forget their doom. He'd let himself hope that the progressives would win, that *gong kāi huà* might return some day, that a billion flowers might bloom again, or that at least he could ride his wife's coat-tails to even greater fame and wealth.

No. He should have put two and two together. Ted Prat-Nung was dead from American bullets in that Bangkok loft. Su-Yong was insane, would soon be functionally dead. He was the last of their triad, the last of the team that had turned his wife into the first true posthuman. It made sense. The hardliners would finish the job. They'd make sure that he died too.

Chen Pang bowed his head, and waited for the end to come.

Chen woke to a jolt, unaware that he'd fallen asleep. A loud noise clanged through his head. The elevator lurched unnervingly. Then it began to rise, with a new and unpleasant grinding sound. He waited for the lights to come back on, for the status indicator to change. Neither happened.

He came to his feet. What was going on? Scenarios ran though his head. Su-Yong *had* tried to escape, and had been stopped, and now they were rescuing him. Or the hardliners had attempted a coup, but had been defeated. Or it had been a power failure after all, and the lockdown nothing but a precaution.

Who would be there when the doors opened? Bai? The director of the SCC? His assistant Li-hua? Someone else?

The elevator stopped moving with a clang. Chen waited, his breath coming fast. Then the doors parted. Bright light hit him, and he fell back, a hand raised up to shield himself, blinded.

Even so, he caught the sight of the guns. Armed soldiers in insectile combat armor, matte black armored surfaces everywhere, bulging actuators and power packs, mirrored helmets obscuring their faces. They held assault rifles aimed in his direction, gaping wide muzzles ready to spew death at him. With them was a single young man in a dark suit, a briefcase in one hand.

"Professor Chen, please stay where you are," the young man said. The mirror-faced soldiers rushed forwards, pointed their guns and shined lights into the corners of the elevator, up at its ceiling.

Two of them patted him down roughly. Their hands invaded his person, pressing against every part of his torso, grasping his ankles and sliding upwards along his thighs, even between his legs. An insult! But Chen bit his tongue, made no move to resist them.

"Clear!" a voice behind him said.

"Clean," said one of the soldiers patting him down.

"Please come with me, Professor Chen," the young man said. It wasn't a request.

They walked through a red-lit Secure Computer Center. Flashlights and red emergency lights provided the only illumination. They passed rows and rows of workstations, abandoned. Tall metal equipment racks cast strange shadows against the wall. Two armored soldiers in their mirrored helmets went in front, then Chen and the young man in a suit, then two more armored soldiers behind them.

"I am Fu-han Zhao, Professor," the young man in the suit said. "I'm an aide to State Security Minister Bo Jintao. I'm here to take you to him."

Bo Jintao. One of the hardliners.

"Bo Jintao? What's happened? Why is the power out here? Why was I stuck in that elevator for hours?"

"We've suffered a major cyber-attack, Professor. As for the rest, we were hoping you could tell us."

They reached the emergency stairs that led from the Secure Computing Center to the surface, ten flights up. More mirror-faced soldiers in full battle armor were posted here. They parted to let them into the stairwell. Inside, emergency lights on their own batteries bathed them in red.

"How can the SCC power be out?" Chen asked as they climbed. "It has its own backup supply, good for days."

"We have power here," Zhao answered. "We fear to use it. The cyber-attack was pervasive. We fear bringing the systems back online until we know what could be compromised."

At the top there were yet more armed and armored soldiers. The entire building was empty, lit only by emergency lights.

"The power is out up here?" Chen asked.

"Yes," Zhao said.

"Where is my driver?"

"He's been… temporarily relieved of duty, Professor. All of them have."

"All of them?"

"Yes. All the clones."

All the Confucian Fist clones, relieved of duty. This was about his wife, then. They thought she was behind the attack. And they feared her influence over the clones.

Damn.

He saw not a single student or faculty member in the red-lit computer science building. Outside, it was dark, sometime in the dead of night. Hard rain fell on them. Tank-like armored vehicles crouched on the street, huge guns and extended missile launchers pointed at the building. Between them, portable lights illuminated a military helicopter in the middle of the road. It sat there, waiting for them, rotors spinning, weapons mounted on its stubby wings, mirror-faced armored soldiers surrounding it. Its mottled skin glimmered in the rain and the sodium lights.

Chen heard more rotors up above. He raised his face, using his hand to shield himself from the rain. In the air above he could see dim red lights illuminating four smaller, sleeker, more deadly-looking helicopters circling around them, like birds of prey coolly regarding the ground, waiting for their moment to pounce.

And who knew what lethal weapons he *didn't* see.

Zhao gestured for Chen to board the craft.

"My phone... my slate..." Chen shouted to be heard over the rain and the roar of the rotors.

Zhao nodded and yelled back, "They'll be returned to you at the appropriate time."

They suspect me too, Chen thought with dread.

He'd been ready to accept death hours ago, but now he very much wanted to live. And to do so, he had to persuade Bo Jintao that he wasn't a threat. Chen boarded

the helicopter, a chill sinking into him from more than the
rain. Zhao boarded after him, and then they were aloft.

From the air Chen got his first look at Shanghai. Then
he understood.

They flew through the urban canyons between lifeless
skyscrapers, their escort helicopters flanking them. The
city was a wasteland. Where there should have been light,
there was darkness. A dim flicker of candles or flashlights
shone in some windows. Down below, on the streets, there
were fires. The immobile hulks of cars littered the roads.
Water flowed around them. Soldiers manned checkpoints,
directed spotlights from place to place. As they passed over
an expensive block an explosion sounded, and then the
sharp report of automatic weapons.

He saw people in the street, a mob of them pressing
against a store front. Looters. The mob moved forward, and
from the doorway he saw the flare of gunfire.

Then the chopper was past and he lost sight of them.

Face pale, Chen turned to Zhao next to him.
"What happened?"

"The most damaging cyber-attack of all time, Professor. It
disabled the on-board computers of hundreds of thousands
of cars, sent electrical surges that destroyed hundreds
of power substations, knocked out the trains, the ferry
terminal, the public safety surveillance systems. Even the
sewers. The intelligent water routing that separates waste
water and rainwater has failed, and so now we have raw
sewage flooding the streets."

Chen couldn't breathe. Could Su-Yong have done this?

"My daughter?" he asked.

"Safe," Zhao said. "We have men with her."

Chen nodded.

"Deaths?" he asked.

"Hundreds so far," Zhao said. "Car crashes. Fires. We have thousands trapped in subways that are filling up with water. And violence. People know the delivery trucks will not be running tomorrow. So they loot the stores, steal from each other. Billions of yuan of damage, at least."

Chen watched the wrecked city go by beneath him, numb with shock.

The helicopters flew north and west, towards the outskirts of the city. Chen saw homes ablaze, a mob of looters carrying off goods from an undefended store, an explosion, the flare of more gunfire. Shanghai was in tatters.

They landed at a military airfield. Dachang, he thought. Here there were lights. Zhao hurried them out of the helicopter and to the executive jet waiting on the runway, its chameleonware skin cycled to neutral gray, a red Chinese flag emblazoned on its tail. Chen barely had time to take his seat in the opulent cabin before they were taxiing down the runway, then taking off, a pair of deadly-looking fighter aircraft taking off with them. He watched the fighters out his window for a moment, before they activated their own chameleonware and became faint distortions, then nothing at all.

They landed at a military airfield outside Beijing an hour later. Another helicopter ferried Chen and Zhao into Beijing proper, armed escort choppers flanking them. Chen had time to appreciate the lights of the city, all looking as it should be. Then they were setting down on the roof of the State Security Building, and armed guards were escorting him and Zhao into the elevator.

A last pair of guards frisked him in front of a doorway, and then it opened for them, and suddenly Chen was in the office of Bo Jintao, Minister of State Security, member of the Politburo, and one of the hardest of the hardliners.

"Professor Chen." The minister was behind his desk, looking at something on his display. There was a man seated in a chair across the desk from him, facing the minister. "You may sit," the minister said without looking at Chen.

"Thank you, Minister." Chen crossed the room. As he did the man across from Bo Jintao turned, and Chen recognized him with relief. Sun Liu, Minister of Science and Technology. A progressive. And Chen's patron.

"Chen," Sun Liu said in greeting. His face was grave. Chen nodded his head in return, and sat in the other chair. Zhao stayed at the door.

What is going on here?

"You're aware of the attack on Shanghai," Bo Jintao spoke, looking at him for the first time. "Could your wife have done it?"

"Minister, I… I'm sure that she would have no reason…"

"*Could she*?" the minister repeated.

Chen swallowed. "If she were connected? Yes. But she's in isolation, Minister, I don't see how…"

Zhao spoke. "Could she have left a program behind to do this, Professor?"

Chen blinked. "Why would she want to…"

"You will answer my aide's question," Bo Jintao said.

Chen sighed. "Probably. But what would she gain from disrupting Shanghai?"

Zhao replied, "Our analysis shows that the cyber-weapon infiltrated the Secure Computing Center first, searched through vast reams of data, and then attacked the Secure Computing Center's computers, before going on to disrupt civil systems throughout Shanghai. We believe that the intruder was seeking to free your wife from the Physically Isolated Computing Center, and only attacked Shanghai's civil systems to cover its tracks when it failed to do so."

"How did you learn this?" Chen asked, turning to look over his shoulder at the aide.

"Your slate and your phone, Professor," Zhao said. "They're how the intruder entered the SCC."

Chen went white as a sheet. He turned back to Bo Jintao. "Minister Bo! I had nothing to do with this! I assure you, I knew nothing!"

The State Security Minister stared at him impassively. Chen felt the cold dread creeping up his spine. This man had tried to kill him once. He could have him killed now with just a word.

"I believe you, Chen Pang," the minister said softly. "If I did not, you would not be here now."

Chen stared at the man as the words sank in. Another reprieve. For how long?

"Zhao, continue," the minister said.

Zhao spoke again. "We believe that this was an attack created by your wife and left behind as insurance in the case of her disconnection. A bot she created to break her out of her imprisonment."

Chen shook his head. "It isn't possible for any software to reconnect her. It requires a *physical* reconnection of the cable, one thousand meters down."

"We know that," Zhao said from behind him, "but she does not. The layout of the PICC has been deliberately left out of any electronic records. She might have believed that a software agent operating *outside* her cage could break through a software firewall imprisoning her."

The State Security Minister spoke. "Given the probability, we consider it prudent to order an immediate wipe of the Shu upload from the Quantum Cluster."

Chen bowed his head. It was the end of his dreams. The Equivalence Theorem. The Nobel Prize. The Fields Medal. The billions in commercial licensing. All of it. He had to try one more time.

"But, Minister, her capabilities, the Ministry of Defense depends on them. It's not too late. We may still be able to stabilize her personality, a clone, even a prisoner, fitted with an interface..."

"No," Bo Jintao said curtly. "Defense now tells me that their other quantum clusters, thanks to *you*, Chen, have all the capabilities they need. My own people say the same."

Thanks to Su-Yong, Chen thought. Not me. My wife has made herself replaceable.

"The rest was closed months ago," Bo Jintao said. "She revealed our capabilities in quantum cryptography, proved herself a national security risk. And now she attacks us. It is time to shut her down."

"Minister Sun." Chen turned to his patron. "Please..." Please, let me wring one more discovery out of her... You'll get your piece of it...

Sun Liu spoke at last. "I'm sorry, Chen. I agree with Minister Bo. Your wife has proven too great a risk."

Chen's heart fell. He lowered his head in submission and defeat.

"But..." the Science Minister continued, "shutting her down does not guarantee an end to these attacks."

"Our cyber defense team will stop them," Bo Jintao said.

Sun Liu shrugged. "Perhaps. But we know she is capable of things human programmers are not. The attacks may continue for some time. Perhaps the agents she left behind will target Beijing next?"

Bo Jintao frowned. "What do you suggest?"

"We break her," Sun Liu said. "We force her to tell us what agents she's left behind, and how to disable them."

Chen looked up. Sun Liu knew. He was the only one who knew where Chen's discoveries truly came from. And what he was really saying now... He wanted to force Su-Yong to tell them something else. The Equivalence Theorem. Despite himself, his heart raced.

"You can do this?" Bo Jintao asked.

"Yes," Sun Liu said. "Chen can."

Bo Jintao turned to Chen. "You could do this, Chen? To your own wife?"

Chen sat up straighter in his seat, looked the Minister for State Security in the eyes.

"For the good of the state, I can, and I will."

21
REGRESS

Friday October 19th

Martin Holtzmann trembled in his car. Nakamura could have been anyone, an assassin. Whenever they wanted him dead, it would be so easy. He was sweating. His breath came fast. His heart was pounding in his chest.

He couldn't let Anne see him like this.

"Drive around the block," he told the car.

He took the time to dial up an opiate surge and a norepinephrine chaser. He shuddered as the bliss hit his body, then stretched out his arms and legs as far as he could inside the car, arching his back and craning his neck, savoring those few perfect moments of pleasure coursing through every nerve fiber of his body

I should always feel like this. Always.

The car brought him back around the block, parked itself in the garage.

There was something in the back of his head as he walked into the kitchen. Something Nakamura had reminded him of. It was on the tip of recall...

Then Anne greeted him with a kiss, and it was gone.

Anne had the final presidential debate playing live on the screen.

Senator Kim was speaking as Holtzmann entered. "... acknowledge that there are two very different ways Nexus is used, one bad, one good. We shouldn't throw the baby out with the bathwater."

The audience applauded. Audience sentiment analysis numbers swerved towards the left along the side of the screen. Kim's share price rose on the real-time market scrolling below the debate, and with it his projected odds of victory. Eight per cent. Nine per cent. Rising. For a moment Holtzmann felt a tiny bit of hope.

Stockton spoke after a pause. "Senator Kim's right. Nexus is used in two different ways. First, as an addictive drug that damages the brains of children. And second, as a deadly weapon of terror." Stockton paused. "Ladies and gentlemen, in my second term we're going to stop *both* of those uses."

This time the applause was thunderous, with hoots of approval. The sentiment line swung back hard to the right. Kim's share price cratered as Holtzmann watched, his odds of winning dropping into the gutter. In the corner of the screen, the real-time electoral map turned even more red.

Holtzmann's heart sank.

"Idiot." Anne clicked the screen off.

"Which one?" Holtzmann asked.

"Both of them."

His heart was heavy as they crawled into bed. The world seemed leached of possibility. He couldn't imagine a happy future any more. He could barely imagine getting through this week. He lay there, his skin hot and his body cold and his stomach in knots until Anne's breathing told him she'd fallen asleep.

And then he gave himself just a little more of that opiate surge. He felt something from it, some little bit of pleasure, but not enough. So he hit the mental button a second time. A wave of euphoria swept through his limbs and his chest and every corner of his mind, and for a little while his universe contracted to the deep sense of bliss he felt inside.

The next week went by in a blur. He worked through the weekend. In the mornings he was cranky, but hid it. During the day he looked over test results from the children, progress on the cure, more encouraging progress on the vaccine.

Every night he'd put himself to bed with a sweet opiate nightcap. Or two. Or three. Some evenings he'd have a little one on the drive home as well.

In his spare moments his mind turned that list of twenty-two suspects over, again and again. But, try as he might, he could see no way to zero in on the thief. On Thursday he switched gears, cleared an afternoon on his schedule, and dug into the ERD's complete files on the Posthuman Liberation Front.

Over the years ERD had disrupted more than twenty Posthuman Liberation Front operations. Fifty-seven men and women, mostly PLF foot soldiers, had been caught and convicted by an Emerging Threats Tribunal. He flipped through case files, intelligence reports, after-action briefings.

Amazingly, over the eight years prior to the July assassination attempt, there had been only a handful of casualties in all those attempted operations. Even in the few attacks that had succeeded, the damage had been overwhelmingly to property and not people.

Some of that, undoubtedly, was a result of ERD's competence. Was some of the rest PLF *in*competence? Probably.

So how had July happened? How had Chicago happened? Had the PLF suddenly become dramatically *more* competent? Had ERD Enforcement Division slipped somehow? What had changed?

He was mulling this as he worked backwards through the PLF's history, when he encountered something that surprised him.

The Spears kidnapping in 2030. The heiress to the media fortune that included the American News Network kidnapped, dosed with DWITY, the *do-what-I-tell-you* drug. She'd been brainwashed, reprogrammed to siphon off part of her billions in wealth. It had been before ERD had even existed. FBI had broken the case, with Warren Becker as one of the agents.

Holtzmann remembered Becker talking about it, over rounds of drinks one night, at an international Policing Emerging Technological Threats conference, in '32 or '33. *Mexican cartels*, Becker had said, *expanding from drugs and prostitution to extortion and brainwashing.*

But the files said that the PLF were behind it. Was he remembering wrong?

Holtzmann's terminal beeped at him. High priority incoming call. He looked up at it. Maximilian Barnes. A sudden dread hit him. Barnes knew what he was doing, and why… Perspiration broke out on his brow.

Get a grip, Martin! Answer him!

He took a breath. It was nothing. A routine call. Nothing more. The terminal beeped again. Another breath, and he reached out to accept the call.

Barnes' face, always perfectly calm, with those cold dark eyes, filled his screen.

"Martin."

"Director." Holtzmann tried to act calm. "What can I do for you?"

"Martin, the President has a conflict with the briefing on the Nexus children next week. A campaign trip."

Holtzmann almost sighed with relief. They could delay the briefing.

Barnes continued. "So we're moving it up to tomorrow. 11am."

Holtzmann blinked. His heart was pounding again. "But... I haven't prepared anything. There's no way I can be ready..."

Barnes held up a mollifying hand. "This is just a casual chat, Martin. Just come ready to answer his questions. That's it. And besides, the President *likes* you."

Then Barnes was gone, and moments later Holtzmann was in the men's room, on his knees, his head over a toilet, retching up the day's lunch.

He wiped his mouth with a piece of toilet paper, flushed the vomit away. He knew what he needed.

Martin Holtzmann pulled up the interface in his mind, dialed up another opiate surge, and let it take him away.

He cleaned up, later, and let the car drive him home as he thought about the next day.

He knew the content. He knew the facts backwards and forwards. But the President terrified him. The risk of being caught...

What he needed was confidence.

That night, as Anne lay asleep next to him, he wrote a simple script to elevate his serotonin and dopamine levels during the meeting. No sudden surge. Just a long, steady flow that would keep him calm, alert, and confident.

When he was satisfied he gave himself a large luxurious opiate surge as a reward. His cares went away. All was peace and bliss.

22

MEMORIES

Saturday October 20th

Shiva's security team brought him the bounty hunter, prepared as ordered. The man's larynx had been crushed by Lane's traveling companion, but not so far as to cut off all air instantly. The Vietnamese police had managed to stabilize and intubate him before swelling finished the job the Chinese soldier had started. It had taken a non-trivial bribe to get him here, now.

His soldiers had the man on his knees, between them, his hands and feet bound in high-test carbon restraints behind his back. He was a macho sort, his muscles bulging from black market enhancements, his head mostly shaven and covered in jagged, angry-looking tattoos. Shiva imagined his dark eyes had once been fierce; now they looked up at him wide with fear. His team had injected the man an hour ago with the modified Nexus version Shiva used for interrogation. The version that responded to his commands alone. The man would just be coming out of the calibration phase hallucinations now. He must have some idea of what was to come.

Shiva reached out and wrapped his will around the bounty hunter's mind. "Tell me what you know of Kaden Lane," he commanded the man. "And how you found him."

He extracted what knowledge the bounty hunter had, of the bounty hunter networks and their strategies and communication protocols, and how they'd tracked Lane down.

When he'd taken all there was to take, Shiva contemplated the man's fate. The wretch had murdered, lied, stolen. All of those had their time and place. All of them could be justified under the right circumstances, when fighting for the right noble cause. But this man had done them all for mere money.

This bounty hunter offered no value to the world. For his whole life he'd only taken. It was sad, really. But if Shiva freed him now, the man would return to selling the only skill he had – violence – and do so without scruple. No, as harsh as it was, it would be better for the world if this one were no longer among the living.

Shiva closed his eyes to consider a moment longer. Nita would be horrified at this, of course. She'd never understood the law of the jungle, the law of the street. Action ruled. Predators and prey. And the only way to deal with an anti-social predator like this was to put it down. He'd learned that often enough in his youth, and later, in his years in business.

My conscience is clear, Shiva observed. He nodded to himself.

Shiva reached out with his mind once more, gripped it around the bounty hunter's brainstem, looked him in the eyes, and then *squeezed* until the man's heart stopped beating. The wide eyes grew wider. The man made a strangled cry, hardly audible through the remains of his larynx. The soldiers let go of his arms, and he toppled from his knees to the floor, falling onto his side, his bound legs and arms thrashing futilely, staring up at Shiva with those once fierce eyes, trying, desperately, somehow, to find a way out of this. Then the gaze became fixed, the thrashing slowed and halted, and the bounty hunter was no more.

As his security staff dragged the body away, Ashok came to him.

"We may have a situation," Shiva's vice president of operations told him. "The orphanage in southern Thailand. Our inside source reports a possible complication. A woman. A soldier, perhaps. Or an agent of some sort. Clearly enhanced. She arrived recently, just three months ago. *American.*" Ashok emphasized the last word, then handed Shiva the file on a slate.

Shiva scanned it. A North American woman, traveling on a false identity, who'd intentionally sought out Nexus children, and demonstrated her enhancements by assaulting men from the village nearby. Who was she? An infiltrator? A threat? CIA, perhaps?

For a moment he was back in Bihar, weeping in the ashes of orphanage there, weeping for the dozens of his children who'd died, and then later, after the corruption and the cronyism had seen the murderers acquitted, watching his soldiers nail the criminals and the corrupt judge and lawyers to their crosses, watching them burn, listening to the muffled screams of a punishment that could never equal the severity of their crimes.

Nita had been so angry when she'd found out what he'd done. "They were *acquitted*, Shiva!" she'd told him. "You can't just take the law into your own hands!"

Her reaction still stung. But what choice did he have? To let ignorant savages kill *his* people with impunity? To let them murder children under *his* protection, and then face no consequences? He felt the old anger rising. Those monsters deserved worse, far worse than the fate he'd given them. Why couldn't Nita understand the steps he had to take to forge a better world?

Shiva felt the slate starting to buckle as his hands clenched of their own accord around it. He took a breath to push the memory away, relaxed his superhuman grip, and handed the device back to Ashok. These special children were his wards. Their safety was his paramount concern. The Americans viewed them as monsters, as inhuman. He knew all about their attempts at finding a vaccine against Nexus, at finding a "cure" to force it out of the brain involuntarily. He knew their plans for "residence centers" to imprison this new subspecies they feared. If the Americans were trying to find where he was taking the children...

"Take her," he told his VP of Ops. "Do it quietly. Find out what she knows, and who sent her."

Ashok nodded, and turned to go.

Shiva spoke one more time. "Ashok, one more thing. I'm going to Vietnam. And I'm taking one of your squads with me. It's time I found this Kaden Lane."

23

CAT AND MOUSE

Sunday October 21st

Saigon – Vietnam's beating heart of commerce and culture and vice. Still officially known as Hồ Chí Minh City, it was universally referred to by its older, pre-unification name. It was a place Kade and Feng hoped they could blend in, lose themselves among the tourists and expats from all over the world, rather than risking the lives of more monks.

They had some money. A grateful father in Cambodia had sought them out at a monastery, pressed a thick bundle of bills into Kade's hand, thanked him for the work that had pulled his daughter out of a coma. Kade had tried to refuse, but the father would hear none of it. Kade tried later to give it to the monastery, but Feng had insisted he keep the gift, just in case.

Feng drove them through the night now, south and east again, risking the main highways this time, opting for speed.

They reached Saigon mid-morning. Feng parked the jeep in a storage lot in the outskirts. They strapped their packs on their backs, and took a bus towards Bến Thành Market and the tourist hub of the city – just another pair of backpackers exploring what Vietnam had to offer.

From Bến Thành they walked to the backpacker district around Bùi Viện Street and lost themselves in the morning crowd. Even at this hour there were people about. The faces around them were mostly Anglo, but some Asian, some Indian. Whatever the face, the language on the street was English, with American accents, Indian accents, Chinese accents, German accents, Australian accents.

Signs offered hair braiding, custom tailoring, American food, Chinese food, all-night dance parties, body piercing, smart drinks, tours to the Mekong Delta, live sex shows.

And then there was the Nexus. Half the store fronts used cheap transmitters tuned to a Nexus band, broadcasting advertisements at them. Smells and tastes came at them. The feel of fingers kneading their shoulders. Tantalizing images of the entwined bodies they might see inside. Whiffs that hinted at pot for sale, at other drugs more exotic. The sensual feel of skin against skin, with more available for a price.

Feng spun around with his eyes and mind wide, taking it all in. Kade laughed, kept some distance from it, yet couldn't help but take an interest.

There was Nexus in the minds around them as well. Kade kept his thoughts reeled in tight, and so did Feng. Others around them were less cautious. A pair of South African girls, tall and blonde, just coming down from their room for a late breakfast, giggling together, their thoughts on food and sun and last night's debauchery. Three Indian boys, sipping tea in an open-front café, talking out loud, thinking of weed and girls.

This was a place where Nexus was used openly. A place where Westerners and Asians alike came and went, where Kade and Feng would not stick out. A place where they could disappear.

They passed advertisements for Nexus applications that could resculpt your personality – give you confidence or adventurousness or dedication or good humor or whatever it was you felt you lacked. Be who you want to be, they said.

Halfway down the street, Kade felt another advertisement, more sophisticated than the rest. He let it touch him, let himself absorb the sensorium it was pushing at him.

Welcome to HEAVEN, a seductive female voice spoke into his ear. And then he was inside the club, touring it, the laser lights and smoke machines and pearly gates décor and sexy dancers dressed like angels inundating his senses. And despite himself, he smiled. Rangan would have loved this.

"We're here, Feng," Kade said aloud. "This is the place."

They took a room in the hostel above Heaven, then headed out to make what changes they could to their appearances. In a street-front stall, Kade had jet black extensions protein bonded to his scalp. The vat-grown locks fell down to his back in thick ropy braids. Feng dyed his own short black hair blonde. They bought melanin pills to turn Kade's fair skin darker. They purchased marginally legal gene-hack tattoos to transform themselves further – silvery circuit-like patterns that covered Kade's hands and arms, that shifted slowly as one watched; a pair of gold and black dragons that spiraled down from Feng's shoulders to his forearms, and spat red flames onto the backs of his hands when he clenched his fists, an ironic barcode tattoo Feng loved for the back of his neck.

"Barcode!" Feng laughed. "Like a robot!"

Kade shook his head, then winced as the tattoo tech injected the tattoo into the back of his not-quite-human, not-quite-functional right hand. He watched in fascination as the living ink pattern drew itself up his arm. The silver circuits spread up from the injection point, past his wrist, up his forearm. He turned his hand over and watched as his skin transformed. When it was done, the pattern looked the same on his right arm as on his left. If there was any interaction with the gecko genes, it wasn't evident. In thirty days he'd need to pay again, or the tattoo would fade and his normal skin would return.

They bought wooden rings and peace symbol necklaces and tourist T-shirts.

And at the end of it, they looked like any other backpacker tourists walking down Bùi Viện.

They caught dinner in an open-front restaurant with a sign that offered Real Fake American Food. Feng ordered sushi pizza while Kade had the 100% Real Cultured Beef Burger. After eating mostly vegetarian Cambodian food for months, the vat-grown meat was mouth wateringly good.

They watched the crowd go by on the darkening street, young people in their twenties, mostly. All off on grand adventures. They all seemed like kids to Kade now, though his own twenty-eighth birthday was still a few months in the future.

He turned back to look into the restaurant, and his eyes met someone else's. A pretty brunette. She looked away quickly, laughing and chatting with her friends, and then her eyes came furtively back to his before flitting away once more. For a moment all he wanted was to smile, to flirt, to buy her a drink, to have a chance at a normal life and a new friend or something more.

But being Kade's friend had been a losing proposition this past year. A deadly proposition. He turned away, and didn't look at her again.

• • •

I'm not here to make friends, Kade reminded himself. I'm here to hide. To stay alive. And to work.

Work he did.

Nexus 6 called to him. That was his real project – his way to get ahead of things, to block off most paths of abuse, to make Nexus safe again at the most basic levels of the OS. In the long term there was no way he could keep fighting individual abuses himself. There simply wasn't enough of him to keep up. He had to build something like Nexus 6 in order to solve this problem at scale.

But Nexus 6 was too far out. Kade had months more work to do before he could even start properly testing it. He couldn't wait until then to deal with the PLF. He had to tackle them now, before they struck a third time and ignited the war Su-Yong Shu had seen coming.

Idiots, Kade thought. What are they going to accomplish? Every killing is just going to make things worse, just going to scare the public more, increase support for the Chandler Act, increase demonization of transhuman technologies.

He could see it coming. The PLF would make their own worst fears true. Bombings and assassinations would lead to crackdowns, police and ERD retribution, witch-hunts against scientists and activists, laws even worse than the Chandler Act, more loss of civil liberties in the name of "security", another step towards a police state in the USA. And that would incense the PLF, draw numbers to their ranks, drive them to ever worse atrocities, until the whole thing blew up into a full-scale conflagration.

Wasn't it always this way? When had terrorists ever accomplished anything but to enrage people, drive them towards greater security, greater sacrifice of freedom? They only gave their oppressors more excuses for oppression.

And the oppressors just drove the oppressed further towards violent rebellion. Extremists on both sides gave power to the very forces they fought against.

He had to stop them. He hated the ERD and the Chandler Act, but the PLF's approach was only going to make things worse.

So he went back to the DC and Chicago attacks, looked at them again, took them apart piece by piece.

His agents had spotted the coercion code used in the attack on the President four days before the attack itself. They'd never seen the source code. Instead, they'd detected it based on a pattern of activity. Disruption of the frontal cortex to lobotomize the subject, a motor control package that turned the subject into a remote-controlled robot. It was sophisticated software, far more complex than other abuses he'd seen. Whoever had written this had invested a lot of time to write the code, even more time to test it, iterate on it until it was reliable.

Narong was up on his feet, just a meter from Ted Prat-Nung, the ceramic pistol with its graphene-tipped rounds pointed at the older man's head. "Everyone freeze. Thanom Prat-Nung, you're under arrest."

The memory came unbidden. The ERD had turned his new friend Narong Shinawatra into a robotic assassin as well. They'd used Kade's technology in exactly the way the Chinese had used Su-Yong Shu's, just as she'd warned him they would. The code he was hunting now was just as complex.

I won't let anyone use Nexus that way, Kade thought. Not the ERD, not the PLF, not anyone.

You're using Nexus that way, Ilya's voice whispered to him. *You're the one enslaving people now. You've made yourself into judge and jury.*

Kade ignored the voice inside his head. He had no choice.

He went back to the beginning. He pulled up logs taken from the mind of Secret Service agent Steve Travers, in the seconds before he'd died. They still mystified him. His agent had infiltrated Travers' mind four days before the assassination attempt. It had spotted the coercion code immediately. But the agent hadn't been able to alert Kade, because it hadn't had network access until just before the assassination attempt.

That made no sense. If Travers had been running Nexus for weeks to connect with his autistic son, the agent should have jumped to the son's mind, at least. And autistic kids running Nexus seemed had an endless appetite for network apps and experiences they could plug into.

What were the odds that for all that time, Kade's software agent wouldn't get word back to him, and that suddenly, just seconds before the assassination attempt, while on-duty, Travers would link his mind to the net, letting the agent contact Kade? It was totally improbable.

Kade checked more of the logs. The Nexus OS running had been Nexus 5 version 0.72. 0.72 was old, hardly more than a few bug fixes over the 0.7 version Kade had released. He himself was running Nexus 5 version 1.32 now, with quite a lot of special mods atop that. He pulled up a release calendar. The assassination attempt had been in late July. If Travers had installed Nexus in, say, late June, he should have been downloading 0.9, at least. Why such an old version?

He flipped to the Chicago bombing. Brendan Taylor had been an apparently mild-mannered accountant. Two daughters, both neurotypical. A financial planner wife who had tested clean for Nexus and sworn that Brendan wasn't the type to have tried it. Kade checked the logs from that alert. The Nexus OS version was the same – 0.72. A Nexus OS version from early May, used in a bombing in October. And again, Kade's agents had infiltrated the man's mind a week before the attempt, had detected the coercion code immediately, but hadn't been able to access the net to send a message back to Kade until just moments before the bombing.

What did that mean?

He tried to think like a PLF terrorist. His job was to program assassins. He'd want reliability, of course. That was why they were using an old version. They'd built code they knew worked. They didn't want to mess that up by upgrading to a new version and potentially introducing new bugs.

And why wasn't he finding these assassins until just before the events? The only thing that made sense was that they weren't actually online until then. They'd be in some dormant state, just a tiny loader program running, perhaps. Not the full Nexus OS. Everything locked down. Waiting for a signal to activate. Then, when activated, they went online to receive instructions. Once online, Kade's agents got word back to him.

He pushed himself back from the problem, rubbed his eyes, and took a deep breath. When he opened them, he saw Feng at the window, staring out into the night. It was nearly midnight. The sounds of raised voices and beat-heavy music came up from the street. He could feel scores of minds down below, dancing, partying in the club below them. He wished he could join them, lose himself for just a little while.

He dragged himself back to the problem at hand. If the people who were turned into assassins weren't online with the version of Nexus that contained the coercion code until moments before the attacks, then he stood little chance of stopping them that way. That's why he'd failed to stop Chicago. That's why he'd fail again, if he stuck with the same strategy.

He had to go one step further. He couldn't focus on just finding someone *running* the coercion code. No. He had to build an agent that would find the people *writing* that coercion code, the ones *installing it* in the minds of the human bombers, and stop them.

But were the code's authors running Nexus themselves? And even if they were, could he find them and stop them before they struck again?

24
ANGRY DADDY

Sunday October 21st

The policemen came to Ling's door an hour after the lights went out. She could feel them as they climbed up the forty stories from the ground floor to hers. In the near data-vacuum of the crippled city, their electromagnetic presence shone like a beacon. She peered out of their lapel cameras as they climbed the red-lit emergency stairwell. She followed their data links back over the airwaves to the precinct house, and from there to Shanghai police headquarters.

The city was a mess. She could see it in their information systems. Fires. Floods. Car accidents. Looting. Deaths. Police stations and emergency services were limping along on emergency power.

Ling tapped into their data, watched humans drowning in subway tunnels, watched a recording of security forces around a store, firing their automatic weapons into a desperate mob, watched as the sopping wet mass of humans clawed their way forward in a human wave, the front of it dying, until they crested over the soldiers, crashed down on them, and the recording ceased.

Shanghai was in pain. Good. These humans had trapped her mommy. They deserved worse.

Already the city was trying to knit itself back together. She saw reports on replacing key transformers, on redirecting the rain water that was flooding the streets, on getting a handful of spy-eyes back into the air. Ten thousand little human ants were out working to repair the damage she'd done. The city was a hive, a colony-organism.

What would happen if she hit it again, harder? Could she kill this city? Could she send the little humans scurrying away in fear? It was so tempting to try, to rip a wing off of this insect pinned down and splayed out in front of her, and see what happened.

But she didn't. *Patience*, her mother had told her, *is a posthuman virtue*. And the humans were looking for her. They had their hackers out, their counter-intrusion packages, their tame security AIs with their boring rigid minds, hunting for the source of the attack. Striking the city once was one thing. Striking a second time, while they were looking… that would be foolish, impatient, something an angry little girl would do.

And Ling couldn't afford to be a little girl any more.

She waited for the policemen. And when they came, sweating and panting from the stairs, she was polite and sweet and told them she'd offer them tea but that the stove wasn't working.

They laughed and told her she was the nicest little girl ever and that they were here to protect her.

She smiled and thanked the soft pathetic creatures. Daddy's driver Bai was worth a hundred of them. Feng was worth three hundred. Stupid humans.

Who will protect you, she wondered, when my mother returns?

Later, as she lay in her bed with the sheets pulled up to her chin, she wondered what had happened to her father? Had she trapped him there with her mommy? Was there any food? Any water? Enough air?

Ling frowned. Her father was nothing like her mommy. He was just a human. Even so, she hoped she hadn't killed him. She loved her father, after all. As much as one *could* love a human.

She woke in the middle of the night. 3.30am. A modicum of power had been restored this wealthy, exclusive block. A small trickle of data flowed through Ling once more. There was an intruder in her home network. She peered at it. A hunter-tracker program. It sniffed around, looking for any trace of the attacker who'd struck Shanghai. She made her net presence small, cloaked herself from the vicious software agent, and it passed her by.

The still fragile net brought her data, carefully stolen from police and emergency services systems. Most of Shanghai was still dark. Security forces surrounded this little island of light, this small enclave where the wealthiest executives and politicians lived. Outside that ring, it was chaos.

And one more thing. Her daddy was alive! And a peek at his calendar showed that he'd be home in just a few hours. Ling smiled, relieved. Even if he was only human, he was still her daddy.

Chen slept for a few hours, then an executive military jet whisked him away to Shanghai.

His car was there, wet on the gray tarmac of the airstrip, and a new driver, who introduced himself as Yingjie. A Marine. Not a clone.

Where do his loyalties lie? Chen wondered. Not with me.

Yingjie drove him home. Two military jeeps came with them, one ahead, the other behind. Soldiers in armor manned heavy machine guns atop the vehicles. Heavy rain sleeted the windshield as they drove.

The streets were horrendous, full of unmoving cars, with filthy sewage-soaked water half a meter deep. Through the armored window of his car Chen saw men and women lurking in doorways, sullen, angry-looking. They gave his vehicle and their military escort a wide berth.

Ahead he could see a handful of lit buildings in Lujiazui, the financial district in the very tip of Pudong, the expensive and exclusive heart of Shanghai. His tower was among them, part of the famous Shanghai skyline now returned to illumination. Naturally. The elites of Shanghai would be the first to see services restored, as was right and proper.

"Trouble ahead," Yingjie said, one finger to his earpiece. "A mob, trying to get into Lujiazui."

A mob? Trying to reach his home?

The closer they came, the more signs Chen saw. As they penetrated into the downtown area, as the buildings loomed above them, as the lights grew ever closer, the number of the people on the streets increased. More and more of them each block, wet, hungry, desperate people. Angry people. Fires burning in trash cans. Someone threw a bottle and Chen flinched as it broke against his window.

The smattering of people became a milling, then a dense throng, all trying to get in to where the lights were, where the power was back, where they could find warmth and shelter. The jeep ahead shone its spotlight into the crowd. An amplified voice ordered them to make way. Bedraggled men reached out, put their wet filthy hands on the jeep. A thud sounded next to Chen, and he turned to see a face pressed against the glass of his window, a man, wild eyed, one tooth missing, yelling angrily. Fists rained down on the car. Chen shrank away in fear, then turned in time to see a metal pipe crash into the window on the other side. It bounced off the hardened glass, then came back, again, and again.

He could hear the loudspeaker proclaiming again that the crowd must disperse. He felt his own vehicle rocking now, as the mob grabbed hold of it. He looked towards his marine driver. Their eyes met in the mirror and Chen saw fear. He felt the vehicle rock harder, the wheels on the left side coming up off the street, and he frantically grasped for something to hold onto.

ZZZZZZZZZZT!

An awful sound at insane volume filled his ears, his teeth, his bones, his bowels. A sonic weapon. An anti-crowd device.

ZZZZZZZZZZT!

It came again and Chen clenched around an ache that it brought to his intestines. The wheels of the car slammed back down onto the ground with a jerk. Chen looked out the window in time to see a gloved armored hand grab the man with the missing tooth by the hair, slam his face against the window, crunching the man's nose, then toss him aside, a smear of blood marking the place he'd struck.

Then the car was jerking forward, the filthy crowd fleeing around them. Ahead a military barricade loomed topped by soldiers with vicious-looking weapons all aimed at the mob, and then Chen saw a gate, and a moment later they were through it, and he breathed a sigh of relief as they rolled into the empty, well-lit streets between the soaring, well-lit skyscrapers of Lujiazui.

• • •

Chen was in the elevator, minutes later, recovered now from the assault of the sonic weapon that had dispersed the crowd. He had just punched in the code for his apartment when Ling's tutor called.

The woman was in hysterics, babbling and tripping over herself, making no sense at first. Hiding in this building, she said. Nowhere else to go. Then more nonsense, about Ling, about the outage, about Shanghai. Babbling. Nonsense.

Then it clicked. Suddenly what the tutor was saying made perfect sense. And Chen understood exactly what had happened last night, and who had been behind it.

The elevator doors opened onto his magnificent flat, and there, before him, was his abomination of a daughter.

Ling busied herself in the morning, making tea and dialing up sandwiches from the kitchen for the bored police officers, ensuring that the apartment was tidy as Father liked it.

She felt him when he entered the elevator, and she told the kitchen to put water on, and make a mug of his favorite tea. She lifted the heavy mug and stood across the room from the entranceway door, by the windows so he'd see her. One of the police officers commented that she was very mature for her age, and she just smiled at him, her sharp teeth bared, and thought of how insignificant he was.

Then the door opened, and her father was there.

"Daddy!" she yelled excitedly. She held up the heavy mug of tea to him. Then her father strode across the room, and the back of his hand swung around and struck her in the face, knocking her off her feet.

"You monster!" he yelled.

Ling cried out as he struck her but it was too late. The blow knocked her head into the hard glass of the window behind her. She bounced off it and fell to the floor on her side. The scalding hot tea splashed all over her, burning her face and her arms. The mug fell from her hands and crashed to the marble floor, shattering into a thousand pieces. The world swam around her, a haze of pain. Tears came to her eyes. Despite herself, she began to sob.

The police officers were on their feet, their mouths open in shock. One made a noise of surprise. Chen turned, and seemed to notice them for the first time. The three men stared at each other. Chen's chest rose and fell with his anger.

Ling crawled, feebly, towards her mother's room, her sobs the only sound in the apartment.

Finally, Chen spoke.

"You saw nothing. Now go."

The police officers bowed and made their way out.

Ling kept crawling. She was almost there. Almost to Mommy's room. Where she'd be safe.

Her father was silent for a while, as she crawled across the floor. Then he spoke to her again. "If you ever do anything like that again, I will kill you. Do you understand?"

The words brought more tears, more racking sobs. Her head was swimming and she could barely see, but she was there. She was to the door. She reached out with her mind and it opened for her. The door that hadn't opened since Mommy had died. The door that Father couldn't open. It opened for *her*.

"Ling!" His voice was raised, angry. "I will *abort* you as you should have been aborted eight years ago. Do you *understand* me?" He was nearly shouting. She grabbed hold of the door frame and pulled herself up, threw herself into the room.

"Ling!" he yelled. Her father came after her in three long strides and he was going to hit her again, but she reached out with her mind and slammed the security door first. Happiness jolted through her as she saw him forced to yank back his fingers rather than have them crushed.

Chen pounded on the door for a while, but it was no use. Let the little abomination rot in there.

He crossed the room of his magnificent flat, the flat that fame and wealth and success had brought him, and stared out at the chaos of Shanghai, the dark wreckage of the shattered city.

Some part of him whispered of guilt and remorse. Remorse that he'd struck his eight year-old daughter, that he'd threatened her life. Guilt that he planned to torture the ghost of his dead wife to extract more discoveries that he could pass off as his own.

No, he told himself. I have no wife. I have no daughter. My wife died ten years ago. And that thing I've called a daughter is no child of mine. It's a construct. A golem. It's not even human.

25

AMBUSH

Breece almost died near Austin.

The cemetery was in the hills to the west of the city. He arrived in the afternoon, parked the Lexus, shut off his phones and slate to keep distractions at bay, and hiked up the hill to his parents' graves.

He could see his dad smiling, hear his mom laughing, their faces full of joy. They'd be in their early sixties now, if they'd lived. Still sharp. Still helping people. Still young enough to have a chance at immortality, to have a hope that uploading or the reversal of biological aging would come along in time. They might have lived to become posthuman. They might have lived forever.

But they hadn't.

Ten years ago now. Ten years since the war had begun.

He still remembered waking to the news that morning, waking to the videos of people vomiting blood, of bodies piled in the streets of Laramie, Wyoming, of National Guard vehicles surrounding the city, of hazmat-suited early responders trying to make sense of it all. Marburg Red. The virus had killed thirty thousand, wiped out the town, and almost killed millions more.

Then the Aryan Rising clones had been found. The new master race. The sociopathic blond neo-Nazi children. The genetically sculpted children who'd butchered the scientists who'd created them. Who'd released Marburg Red prematurely, eager to see it wipe out the genetically inferior races that populated the planet.

Ten years since the backlash. Since Josiah Shepherd had spoken out, his face, his words broadcast endlessly, burned into Breece's memories. "Mad scientists warping God's creation, doing the devil's work, bringing to life the devil's children." Spittle had flown from the televangelist's lips. "The Lord will surely reward any who send them to hell where they belong."

Ten years since the firebomb had ripped through his parents' fertility clinic. Since they'd been murdered for the crime of reversing genetic diseases, of boosting a few points of IQ, of entirely benign actions that had nothing to do with the Aryan Rising.

Ten years since fear had turned America into a police state, since the priests and the politicians had decided that they could control who you were, what you were, what genes you carried, what tech you put in your brain.

Ten years since he'd become a freedom fighter. And now, finally, they were making headway.

Breece crouched beside his parents' graves, reached out his fingers to brush the cold stone.

"I miss you," he whispered.

He rose to his feet hours later, as the sun dipped below the plains of central Texas. He dusted himself off and started down the hill, pulling out his phones and turning them on as he did so.

His team phone buzzed angrily the instant he activated it. An urgent message, long delayed. Breece looked at the display. It was from Hiroshi.

[Your up-phone is burned. DHS.]

Breece stared at the phone numbly for a moment, then dropped to the ground behind a headstone.

His up-phone. Fuck. The one that connected to Zarathustra. How'd they know that number? Only he, Zara, and Hiroshi knew. And Hiroshi only because he'd been employed by AmeriCom, had set up the hidden alert that would tell Breece when the Homeland Security backdoors were activated to tap into his data, his location.

They must have taken Zara. Breece pulled out the up-phone. The thing was poison now, reporting his location to DHS. How long did he have until they arrived?

He left the up-phone powered on, tossed it away from him, then reached into his pants pocket and pressed the hidden switch. His shirt, pants, and shoes shifted color to match the grass. From his other pocket he pulled out thin gloves and balaclava which did the same, then pulled them on. His clothing lacked the speed and resolution of true chameleonware. They wouldn't turn him into a blur when he moved. They wouldn't mimic a detailed pattern behind him. But if he lay still or moved slowly, they could blend him into the grass and the headstones and trap most of the IR signature of his body.

He slowly belly-crawled away from the phone. At the end of the row was a small family crypt. He got there and lay still against it, his body hidden from the cemetery entrance, at least. He searched the sky. Were there invisible drones up there? Did they have a lock on him already? Had a cordon been pulled around him? His eyes saw nothing.

Breece carefully peeked his head around the crypt. In the twilight he could still clearly make out the Lexus in the parking lot, maybe three hundred yards away. He could make a run for it, leave the phone in the grass, get in the vehicle and get out of here before DHS closed the noose.

His other phone buzzed again. Hiroshi, calling in real time. Good friends, the Japanese. Loyal. Good transhumans, too. Always thinking ahead.

"Breece here," he replied.

"Breece," Hiroshi replied. "What's your status?"

"Nominal," Breece answered. "No sign of DHS."

Then he saw the other car inbound. Black SUV. Tinted windows. No insignia of any sort. He couldn't make out the plates from here. The SUV pulled into the parking lot slowly and came to a stop just by the entrance gate. The doors opened and three men in dark clothing stepped out. They wore light jackets that were totally unnecessary in the warm evening air. Perfect for concealing weapons.

Breece's own gun was carefully hidden inside the Lexus, a conscious choice that the risk posed by carrying the weapon was greater than the risk of being caught without it.

"Scratch that," he said into the phone. "Someone's here."

Two of the men were coming up the hill now, heading in the direction Breece had thrown the phone. Unremarkable faces. Dark hair. Athletic figures held calm and erect. Eyes calmly scanning to and fro.

Professionals.

Both men coming up the hill had hands in their jacket pockets. Breece imagined their fingers curled around the grips of pistols. The third man stood at alert by the SUV in the parking lot at the foot of the hill, a bundle over his shoulder. A rifle, perhaps.

"We're inbound to you," Hiroshi said. "Forty minutes out."

"Don't think I have forty, Hiroshi. Gotta go now. Call you back." He cut the connection.

Who were these men? No uniforms. Unmarked vehicle. Hidden weapons. Where was the SWAT team? Where were the snipers? The drones and choppers? This didn't smell like the law.

It didn't matter. What mattered was that these men were here for him. To capture him or kill him. And that wasn't going to happen.

He was sweating now. The active camo he'd turned on was trapping his body heat, not letting it escape into the air around him where an infrared scope could pick it up. Without a thermal capacitor to suck that heat up, he was going to get warmer and warmer until he cooked.

Breece eased back behind the crypt, slowly, no sudden moves. Then he went Inside, launched a bootleg app.

```
[remote_driver -boot -silent]
```

The app reached through the net connection of his phone, connected to the Lexus's sleeping auto computer, and booted the car up in silent mode, no lights, no sound, all electric. A window came alive in his mind's eye, and he pushed it full screen, complete immersion. He could see out of the car's cameras now. Status panels showed battery charge, GPS, engine temperature down the side of his vision. Front and center, through the car's cameras, he could see the man standing against the SUV. The plates were Texas, standard civilian, no government endorsement of any sort. He couldn't be sure, but inside the tinted windows the vehicle looked empty.

The man by the SUV was looking the other way, up towards the cemetery and his colleagues. The man held onto the bundle over his shoulder like a rifle. Breece used his mental finger to click on the screen, drag it to one side. Down below, the Lexus panned its cameras slowly. Through its eyes he watched the two others ascending the hill. They were almost to his discarded phone.

He'd only get one shot at this. He tapped commands into the app running on his Nexus OS for a moment. Then he reached down with his right hand and pulled the ceramic blade from his calf holster. He peered one last time around the crypt wall, then back into his inner eye and the feed from the Lexus's cameras again.

Now.

Breece closed his eyes and tapped a mental button. The Lexus surged forward at the man by the SUV. Breece opened his eyes immediately, bringing them back to the two men here on the hill with him.

He heard the crash of metal on metal, saw a flash of something across the window in his mind. The men turned, startled, and then Breece was up and the ceramic blade was whistling through the air between them, thrown with superhuman force. The knife turned end over end, then lodged itself in the neck of the closest one with a meaty *thunk*. By then Breece was hot on its trail, sprinting at breakneck speed.

The one he'd hit staggered and fell into his colleague. The second man struggled to shake off the body and pull the gun from his pocket. Then Breece was on him. He grabbed the assassin's wrist, stepped inside the man's reach, and punched him in the solar plexus. The man dropped and Breece wrenched the gun from his hand.

Something bit into his arm and he dropped to one knee on instinct, thinking he'd been hit. An instant later the sound registered – a bullet shattering stone. It came again and again. Someone was shooting in his direction, hitting gravestones, sending stone chips flying.

He closed his eyes and looked out of the Lexus's cams again. The third man was pinned, his lower body crushed between the Lexus and the SUV, but somehow the man had a silenced rifle in his hands and was shooting up the hill. Breece felt a flash of admiration for the man. A real trooper. True grit.

Breece grabbed the mental shifter of the car, threw the Lexus into reverse, tapped the accelerator. On screen, the man collapsed to his hands and knees as the Lexus backed away from the SUV. Breece braked, shifted gears, then jammed the Lexus forward again. The man's face snapped up, loomed in the cameras, eyes wide in shock and horror, and then all went black as the Lexus crushed what remained of the would-be assassin against the SUV.

Breece opened his eyes again, still down on one knee. The world was quiet suddenly. Breece's breath came fast and his heart was trying to pound its way out of his chest. He was drenched in sweat and burning hot. Were there any others out there?

The man he'd punched stirred on the ground next to him, and Breece grabbed him by the hair, and held the man's own silenced pistol to his face.

"How many of you?"

The man coughed. "Three."

"Who sent you? What was your mission?"

The man said nothing.

"Who sent you?" Breece raised his voice.

The man shook his head. "They'll kill me."

Breece clamped his hand over the man's mouth, lowered the gun, and obliterated the man's knee cap with a single shot.

The man screamed into his hand.

"*I'm* going to kill you," Breece whispered to him. "The only question is whether you want to die fast or slow."

He waited for the man's muffled screams to subside, then put the tip of the silencer against his other knee.

"Ready to talk?"

The man nodded miserably, tears flowing down his face.

"Who sent you?" Breece asked again, pulling his hand off the man's mouth.

The man closed his eyes and panted for a moment, and Breece thought he'd have to shoot the other knee. Then the assassin opened his eyes. "Zarathustra," he said. "I'm PLF."

Well, well, well. He hadn't thought the old man had it in him.

He got the rest of the assassin's story, and then it was time to go.

He put the silencer tip against the downed man's forehead. "Any last message you want me to deliver?" he asked his would-be killer.

"Please," the man pleaded, eyes locking with Breece's in fear. "I'm PLF, like you. Let me live. You'll never see me again. Please, man. I wanna live forever!"

Breece thought of his parents, their bodies decomposing just yards from here. "We don't all get what we want," he told the man. And then he pulled the trigger.

26

ASIAN TRAVELS

Wednesday October 24th

It took Kevin Nakamura twenty-eight hours to reach Saigon disguised as a civilian. He could have come faster via military transport, but that would risk DOD finding out about his mission. Which CIA was adamant could not happen. He pondered this as the cab took him towards the nicer end of town, to his apartment. He paid the taxi fare, took his entirely innocuous luggage, and rode the elevator to his floor.

At the door hidden biometric sensors identified him. Anyone who failed that identification would soon find themselves in for some very rude questions.

Inside the apartment he found the gear, cunningly hidden, all there. He found himself smiling, whistling as he inspected it, found everything ready and top notch.

And out there, in the countryside, and under the waters off the coast. Resources the DOD and DHS and Congress didn't know CIA had. Resources that even the White House might not know about. Resources he'd never known existed, and that he had access to now.

That alone told him how important this task was.

Will the White House know when I've snatched Lane out from under the ERD? he wondered.

Doubtful.

What did that say about his mission?

Nakamura pulled the small Toyota four-wheeler out of the garage an hour later, loaded with fuel, food, cash, and hidden weapons. This would be his mobile command center, taking him wherever he needed to go to find Sam. To find Lane, he corrected himself.

The wind blew through his hair as he drove into the early evening traffic. Saigon was alive in the way that only developing world cities ever were. The traffic was complete chaos, cars going to and fro, scooters and tuk-tuks racing between them, pedestrians playing a deadly game of Frogger with the vehicular traffic.

Sidewalk vendors had their fires going, offering noodle soups, roasted corn, spicy sandwiches, whole birds cooked on spits. Music blared from a dozen directions. Lights were coming on in shops. Brilliant signs over storefronts were starting to glow in a riot of colors. Sidewalk entrepreneurs sold watches, slates, phones, belts, shoes, drugs, all shouting out their offers, competing with one another for the attention of the crowd.

Nakamura smiled. He felt alive in the field. He didn't belong in DC, taking briefings or writing reports. Out here, where chaos rules, where his wits and his skill were all that stood between life and death, that's where he was meant to be.

Six hours later, well after midnight, he was in the hills above Ayun Pa.

Three monasteries attacked. Two of them burned to the ground.

And this one, Ayun Pa. Local police reports – cracked by CIA – showed nine dead, four assailants and five monks. No women dead. Not in any of the three monasteries.

Nakamura left the four-wheeler, activated his chameleonware suit, and hiked up in the darkness to look down onto the monastery. His pupils dilated in the moonlight. Enhanced rod and cone density sucked up every available photon. The scene was leached of color, but as bright as day to his eyes. That thrill of the mission, of being on the edge of danger, of discovery, of action, tickled up his spine again.

The monastery complex was walled, roughly oval, with a handful of buildings, a wide open courtyard, two entrances large enough for vehicles to come through.

The autopsies revealed that one man had died from bone fragments driven into his brain. Two had died from broken necks. The last from a crushed larynx.

Sam could have done that, Nakamura thought. She always liked to go for the throat.

He pulled up orbital reconnaissance photos of the site in his mind's eye. Retinal implants superimposed them on his vision. Remote Vietnam was not a high priority target for the National Reconnaissance Office, but with more than three hundred recon birds circling in low earth orbit, now, and most of them taking frames five hundred miles square, every patch of the planet was photographed at least once an hour.

Those photos had revealed two hard-top four-wheel drive vehicles hidden in the brush, off-road, a few hundred yards from the back entrance. They'd been there for three hours before the shootings.

Then, next frame. An open-top jeep is now in the courtyard. Dozens of monks out there as well.

Next frame, almost an hour later. All three vehicles are gone. Multiple bodies lie prone.

The police had found tire tracks, but no vehicles. The assailants had run.

Three monasteries attacked. They were bounty hunters, he was sure, seeking the ten million dollar reward ERD had offered for Lane's live capture.

Nakamura tried to imagine the scene as it had played out here. The bounty hunters, closing in on Lane, somehow knowing where he would be, then surprised to find Sam at his side. Four of them dead in seconds. The other two, in the trucks, frightened, taking off to save their own skins.

Yes, that could have happened.

But most importantly, where was Sam now? How would she think? No. How would *Lane* think?

Nakamura closed his eyes, thought back to everything he knew about Lane. He'd spent eight weeks with the boy, two or three hours a day, training him. Lane had been a hopeless liar, too nervous, too earnest. Not a natural-born deceiver. Not a killer, either. Not a monster. But someone who resented the ERD, hated it for what it had done to him and others he loved. Hated it enough to be willing to coerce Sam, turn her into his personal bodyguard.

Nakamura had gone over everything CIA had on Lane. He knew this boy. Lane was an idealist, in way over his head. If he was here in Vietnam, then his pact with the Chinese had evaporated. Either Shu's death had canceled it, or Lane himself had backed out, running from them.

Yes. That was right. Lane wouldn't willingly serve the Chinese either. He'd want to be free, free to pursue his idealistic pursuits.

He tried to imagine being Lane. Protected by monks. But on the run. He'd know about the bounty on his head, the attacks on the other monasteries, the monks dying to protect him.

How would he react? Seek out another monastery?

Oh no. Lane would be scared, but his idealism would be stronger. He wouldn't want any more blood on his hands.

He'd find another way, put as much distance between himself and the monks as possible, reduce the risk to them as much as he could. And the opposite of a remote monastery… was a big city.

27

HEAVEN

Wednesday October 24th

Kade slept, rose, and worked. To catch the ones behind the assassination attempt and the Chicago bombing, he needed a new agent.

He started with the scaffolding of his previous agents. Code that scanned for other Nexus-running minds, that embedded itself in memory files and sensory dumps that Nexus users traded back and forth. Code that used the back doors he and Rangan had built to silently copy itself into each new mind it encountered, that hid itself from process listings and cloaked its CPU and memory usage. Libraries to rummage through the mind it entered, to alert Kade if that mind matched certain parameters, to send him back snippets of memories, contents of directories, parameters pulled from the Nexus OS.

What differed from his previous viruses was the search pattern. He wasn't looking for thoughts of Rangan or Ilya, here. He wasn't looking for a running coercion program, or even the source code – he already had agents searching for that. He was looking for a mind that knew about such code, that knew about a particular piece of such code.

The OS version number was the best hook he had. Nexus OS version 0.72. If someone saw it, thought of it, had code in their mind that referred to it, Kade wanted to know. He added other search criteria – memories of violence, of explosions, thoughts of the PLF. He combined them into a rough model, giving weights to each to produce an overall confidence level.

Kade worked for two days, iterating on it, testing it in various scenarios, while Feng brought him food and stretched and did his martial arts exercises and read paper books bought from street vendors.

When he couldn't work anymore, when his eyelids grew heavy from fatigue, when his mind started to wander, he felt the temptation to reach into his own brain, to push his neurons further, to artificially stimulate himself to stay awake and working.

Instead Kade closed his eyes, lay back and tapped into the white noise of a million Nexus-running minds, the surf of consciousness bathing the planet, the stuff of mind that would one day self-assemble itself into something that truly thought and felt, that could solve the problems that solitary human minds couldn't. And then he slept, filled with hope.

On the third day he finished his work on the new agent, finished every test he could think to run on it, finished fixing the bugs he'd found.

It was time to let it loose.

They went down into the club together on Friday night. "Going downstairs to Heaven!" Feng laughed. "Down to heaven!" Feng gestured with his hand. "Good joke, yeah?" Feng elbowed Kade gently.

Kade snorted and shook his head.

They looked like any other pair of tourists, Kade with his long black extensions and the biological circuit tattoos crawling up his arms, Feng with his short hair bleached blond and the barcode he found so hilarious across the back of his neck.

It was Friday night here. Friday morning back home. A hip-looking Vietnamese girl in a silver halter dress – with silver hair and silver eye makeup – took their money at the door. A massively muscled bouncer looked them over with a menacing glare while she did. Kade could feel Feng struggling to restrain a laugh.

Stay cool, Kade told his friend.

He's so big! Feng laughed into Kade's mind. **I'm SCARED!**

And Kade laughed out loud despite himself.

He felt the door girl's mind brush against his as she smiled and stamped their wrists. He felt the bouncer's glowering mind touch his as well, felt the agent he'd coded slip into each of them and start scanning, looking for others to infect.

Beyond the entrance, the club was a sea of flashily dressed twenty-somethings illuminated in pulsing, strobing lights. Bodies dressed in next to nothing moved to pounding flux beats. Their minds were alive, reaching out to Kade's, reaching out to each other, opening for his agents. Tendrils of artificial fog snaked across the floor, twined themselves around tanned legs. The walls were white with faux columns and pearly gates. The ceiling was a glowing blue with white fluffy clouds flowing across its digital surface. Scantily clad Vietnamese waitresses carrying trays of drinks made the rounds to the tables around the periphery of the dance floor.

Feng's eyes were everywhere, tracing the exposed curves of a waitress, or the gyrating form of a dancer, then snapping back to scan the crowd for threats, alert and aroused at once.

A shirtless Vietnamese boy, not more than twenty, danced by them, his face exulting, his hairless chest covered in sweat. His mind touched Kade's, and Kade was suddenly elsewhere – a flat in London. This boy was being ridden, Kade realized, leasing himself out to a banker a continent away, letting someone pay him to take a short vacation in his body.

Two nearly identical Vietnamese go-go dancers in silver hot pants, silver knee-high boots, silver angel wings, and tiny silver pasties covering their nipples moved in perfect sync on the stage, silver-streaked hair flinging around their heads in unison, sweat glistening on their taut stomachs and lean thighs as they pranced and spun and fanned their Nexus-controlled wings and set the crowd on fire. Between them a muscular Vietnamese DJ in mirrored shades and a tight black T-shirt held one hand above his head, then dropped it down in time to a massive boom in the music.

Flashbulbs burst from every angle, blinding Kade, inundating the club in white, and then there was a new mind pushing through the Nexus chaos of the club, amplified by the Nexus repeaters in the walls and ceilings. The *NJ*. The Nexus jockey. She projected her mind onto theirs like a song, projected it like a dance, in time to the music, and the crowd roared its approval.

Kade blinked the flash blindness away and then he could see her on the stage, next to the DJ. Her dress was a mirror ball molded to her body. Her smiling lips glittered a metallic ruby red. Her lashes were silver and iridescent. Her hair was long and platinum blond, woven through with brilliant glowing strands of blue and green and red that pulsed to the music. She opened her mouth and sang, a pure wordless note of glory, and raised her silver gloved hands up and out and over the crowd.

And her mind… Her mind was dance. It was pure joy in motion. It was ecstasy. He felt the urge to move to her rhythm, to feel her emotions. He looked around himself and the crowd wasn't chaos anymore, wasn't a mob. It was a single living thing moving in time, exulting in the music and the lights and the pure ecstatic glory the Nexus jockey was pumping out of herself. From her perspective he saw the club, and it was heaven in her eyes, angelic beings dancing atop the clouds, exulting in the glory of some futuristic paradise. The amplifiers boosted her signal, let her project her song and sights and ecstasy to the entire club, and the crowd loved her for it, roared their approval in mind and voice.

Kade turned to find Feng, and his friend was there, grinning. And Kade was grinning, and then he was dancing, as he hadn't danced since this whole nightmare began. And even Feng was swaying side to side, smiling, enjoying himself, eyes still flashing over breasts and hips and then searching, searching for any threat.

Kade danced, and as he danced, he let his virus do its work. Minds brushed against his, dancers, waitresses, go go dancers, the DJ, the NJ… He felt them dancing, felt them boosting and twisting their own neurochemicals, drugging themselves into bliss or psychedelia, absorbing the NJ's thoughts as they did, retransmitting their own, adding to the collective vibe. The whole crowd was beaming, grinning, smiles showing on faces all around. Friendly minds offered Kade Nexus apps to get himself higher – neurotransmitter modulators with names like DigitalEcstasy, SimTHC, and CyberAcid – but he passed with a smile each time. He was working, and he was high enough from the NJ and the crowd around him.

His agent infiltrated every mind that touched his. One of them would upload a memory of this night, or connect over the net to touch the mind of a friend back home, or go online to download a new software patch or a new app. And then his agent would spread.

Six degrees of separation, Kade thought. In days his new agent would reach every corner of the Nexus world.

The brunette was there, from the restaurant, dancing with her friends, a drink in her hand. She met his eye and smiled and he felt her mind brush against his. And oh, how nice it would be... But he couldn't. And so he smiled and then turned away, pulled his eyes and his mind away from her, put all of himself into the music and the rhythm and movement of the crowd and his body and the song and dance and hallucinatory vision of the NJ.

Kade danced and danced and danced, until he was exhausted and covered in sweat and the agent he'd unleashed was already on its way to other continents. Then he stumbled out of the club, Feng at his side.

"Being your friend, fun sometimes!" Feng laughed as he pulled Kade along behind him.

And Kade laughed too, happy, satisfied with a strong night's work.

28
THE FAMILY

Wednesday October 24th

Breece jogged down the hill to the Lexus, slowing as he approached the car. He checked for any movement from beyond it, where he'd crushed the third man up against the SUV. Nothing. He peered under the car cautiously, until he could make out what was left of the man. It was a gruesome sight. The assassin's head and upper body weren't visible, crushed between the Lexus and the SUV. One arm dangled limply down to meet a lower body splattered with blood, legs bent at impossible angles. He was definitely dead.

Breece rose and opened the driver-side door of the car. The vehicle was marked now, just like his phones, just like the identities all three objects were registered to. He had to stop the damage there, stop them from retrieving DNA samples, stop any chance of the authorities finding out Breece's real identity, cut off any path that might unmask Hiroshi and Ava and the Nigerian.

He tapped on the car's center console, navigated the menus, touched a corner that was blank, and let it scan his retina. A new menu appeared, with hidden options.

Self-destruct. He set it for a ten minute countdown, or when triggered from his phone.

From the trunk he pulled out his go bag with gear, phones, gun, and fresh false identities. Then he grabbed an enzyme bomb as well.

He took off up the hill again, the enzyme bomb in his still-gloved hand. The landscape was quickly growing darker in the post-sunset twilight. He gained the top of the hill, found the two assailants he'd killed. He pulled the ceramic knife out of one man's throat, cleaned it on the man's jacket, and slid it back into his ankle sheath.

Then he stood back from the area, brought the cylindrical enzyme bomb up, pulled the pin on it, and tossed it at the spot where he'd been hit. It rolled to a stop against one of the bodies. A half second later a dozen tiny ports opened on the soda-can-sized cylinder, hissing out a dense white fog of DNA- and protein-degrading enzymes. With any luck they'd erase any biological traces he'd left.

Breece pulled out his phone again, sent an encrypted message to Hiroshi.

[Am safe. Stay clear of area. Your phone now burned as well. Meet at rendezvous.]

Then he dropped down behind a headstone, looked around it at the Lexus, pulled up the menu, and moved the self-destruct time up to *now*.

Three hundred yards away, a solenoid opened a canister of compressed oxygen, venting it into the gas tank of the car, hyperpressuring it. Seconds later, a score of tiny penetrators poked holes in the fuel tank, sending aerosolized gasoline into the car's interior and into the air around it, turning the vehicle into an unexploded fuel-air bomb. Breece counted down: 3... 2... 1...

The car erupted in a fireball that lit up the twilight sky. The heat of it warmed his face. Any evidence left in that car was now vaporized.

Breece pulled the batteries from his phone, turned, and slowly crept down the back side of the hill. It was a long way to the rendezvous.

He made it to Houston eighteen hours later, wearing his spare clothes, his hair freshly dyed black, a car rented under a fresh identity.

He drove a two-block circuit around the rendezvous point, looking for any sign that his team had been compromised, that FBI or ERD were waiting for him inside the flat. He couldn't call his team. By mutual agreement, none of them knew each other's backup identities. All their primary identities had been burned by his presence at the cemetery.

The problem was one of linkability. His phone was linked to the site by its presence there when the deaths happened. His team's previous identities were linked by the contact their phones had had with his in the past. All of those identities were connected. Break one, and you could break the others. So all those fictional names and bank accounts and ID cards had to go.

He parked the car two blocks away and ate in the restaurant across the street from the flat while he casually studied the area around him.

Was one of the other diners an FBI watcher? That electrician's van – did it have a mobile listening post? That young couple walking down the street holding hands – were they enhanced ERD operatives waiting for someone to walk up to that door?

He stretched the lunch out, ordered a beer that his genetically upregulated alcohol dehydrogenase levels would chew up long before it could get him buzzed. The other diners paid and left. The electricians returned to their van and drove away. The young couple didn't come back.

In the window of the flat, there was movement. A good sign. If there were an FBI or ERD ambush in there, they'd be utterly still, totally undetectable, waiting for their mark to make himself known.

He paid the bill and walked across the street to the flat.

No one fired on him as he approached. At the door he put his right hand around the pistol in his pocket and rapped out the knock with the knuckles of his left. Slow-fast-fast-fast-slow-slow.

The door swung open and his fingers tensed around the pistol and then there was Ava in front of him, as gorgeous and cool as ice as ever.

"Took you long enough," she said, one eyebrow raised.

Breece grinned and swept her up in his embrace, twirled her around, sending her long dark hair flying. The ice melted and she laughed and kissed him.

They were all here. Hiroshi, the brilliant telecoms engineer turned hacker, his Japanese face careworn, his long black hair pulled back into a ponytail. The Japanese understood the future. They embraced it. This man more than most. Breece had no problem admitting that Hiroshi was his intellectual superior, might always be. He counted himself lucky for the man's friendship over the years.

The Nigerian, tall, leanly muscular, quiet – but apt to sudden smiles and bursts of deep bellowing laughter. Their weapons specialist. A man of deep courage and conviction, who'd put his life on the line for the cause many a time.

And Ava. The chameleon. The woman who could blend in anywhere, persuade anyone of anything. Smart. Fearless. Gorgeous. Unflappable. The woman he loved.

They hugged and smiled, and slapped each other on the back, and then gathered in the kitchen. It was good to be back with his people again.

He opened his mind to theirs and they to his. Through the Nexus link he showed them the attack at the cemetery and they showed him their rushed trip to rescue him. They'd been on their way to risk their lives for him, heading to his location expecting to find a DHS team between them and him. He loved these three. He'd die for them if he had to.

"So Zara decided to off you," Hiroshi said. "Why?"

Breece shrugged. "He's always been a control freak. He's always wanted to pick the missions, move cautiously. We've upset that. The truth is, we don't need him, and that's a threat to his power."

"What does he know about this mission?" Ava asked.

Breece shook his head. "Nothing. Same as Chicago."

"We need to deal with him," Hiroshi said.

Breece nodded. "We will. *After* this."

"So we're still a go?" the Nigerian asked.

"We have one other problem," Breece said. "Hiroshi?"

Hiroshi showed them the feed from the Chicago mission. Everything was normal until the last moments.

I think I have a bomb! the mule said in their minds. *A bomb!*

"The mission succeeded," Breece told them, "but only barely."

"We thought at first that the software had glitched," Hiroshi said. "But the logs showed otherwise. Someone else hacked into that mind and overrode our commands. And whoever did this is very very good. It was less than a minute between the mule's activation and this hack."

Breece watched as his team absorbed that.

"Could this explain DC?" the Nigerian asked. "The mule there fired only twice instead of four times. And he missed."

Breece looked at Hiroshi.

"Possibly," Hiroshi said, nodding.

"So what do we do about this?" Ava asked.

"Two things," Breece said. "First, we're going to make a few changes to the mission profile. Second, we need to be more careful ourselves. As long as we're running Nexus, we could be vulnerable to this hacker again. Hiroshi needs to run Nexus to prep the mule. None of the rest of us do. So until we've figured out what happened, the three of us are going to dump our Nexus, and after Hiroshi preps the mule, he will too."

He felt their disappointment, Ava's especially. He wanted to touch her in mind and body, feel her pleasure as he made love to her. But that would have to wait.

They all agreed with this decision. They'd all do what needed to be done. They were a team, and more. They were family. They were soldiers.

29

NEANDERTHALS

Friday October 26th

Holtzmann kept cool as he and Barnes cleared security prior to their meeting with the president. They cleared Nexus detectors and terahertz scanners and a physical pat-down. Then an aide showed them into the empty Oval Office and to their seats. A secretary brought them water and coffee.

Holtzmann felt the preternatural calm and confidence of the neurochemical cocktail he'd prescribed himself. The room was bright, every detail vivid. He felt completely sharp, not even the slightest bit nervous or cloudy. He was himself again, before the bombing. Better, even.

The President entered, and Holtzmann and Barnes came to their feet.

"Dr Holtzmann," Stockton shook Holtzmann's hand. His palm was warm and large, his shake firm and strong. All-star quarterback strong. The President took his seat behind the desk, waved them down into their chairs. "Director Barnes has sent me memos summarizing the status of the Nexus children. What I want is to make sure I understand the situation."

"Of course, Mr President."

"These children are smarter than human children?"

Holtzmann answered. "Not exactly, Mr President. Individually, they have a wide spectrum of intelligences. But when housed together and educated together, they can learn far faster than unaugmented humans, and they can solve problems together that are beyond normal human difficulties."

President Stockton nodded. "Yes. So in groups they're smarter. And it matters how early they were exposed to Nexus?"

Holtzmann nodded in return. "Yes, Mr President. Learning is definitely accelerated among groups of people using Nexus. The younger they've received it, the larger the effect. Adults receive a boost to group cognition. Children – mostly autistic children – who first received Nexus at younger ages get an even larger boost. And the effect is most dramatic in those few children we've found who were exposed to Nexus in the womb."

"Do we know what the long-term effects are? Health concerns?"

Holtzmann spread his hands wide. "We don't see any signs of specific health concerns from Nexus, but we could easily miss anything subtle, let alone anything that took many years to develop."

"And the long-term limits?" the President asked. "How far can these children grow in intelligence, particularly the ones exposed to it in the womb?"

Holtzmann shook his head. "Mr President, I wish I could tell you. But at this point we have so little data. The oldest children exposed to Nexus in the womb are eight, and we've only seen a handful of those."

"What's your best guess, then?" Stockton said.

Holtzmann wanted to refuse. He glanced at Barnes, and the man raised an eyebrow and inclined his head slightly.

You don't refuse *the President*, he thought to himself.

Holtzmann met Stockton's eyes. "Mr President, if I had to guess, I would say that these children, if raised in groups or in constant contact with others of their kind, will grow up to be extraordinary, in both the amount they're able to absorb over the course of their lives, and their ability to reason and problem solve as a group."

The President held his gaze. "Well above human norm, would you say, Dr Holtzmann?"

"Yes, sir. Well above. Many times above. They'll accomplish things we can only dream of."

The President nodded. "And how is progress on the vaccine?"

It cut Holtzmann to hear that question. It was a physical pain to go from a discussion of the immense wonder and beauty of these children to a question of how to prevent new ones from being born.

"It's coming along, Mr President. In mice, we have encouraging early results. We can train the immune system to component molecules of Nexus before they reach the brain."

"When can we deploy it?" Stockton asked.

"It's very early, Mr President. Best case? Another year or two to get it working reliably and then map this research to humans, and then three to four years of human trials."

The President frowned. "Four to six years? That's not acceptable, Dr Holtzmann. We need to be deploying this *next year*. You need to fast-track this."

Holtzmann blinked. "Mr President, those numbers *are* the fast track. We're bypassing every FDA step we can and cutting every corner we can to get it done so quickly."

Stockton drummed his fingers on his desk, clearly annoyed.

"Talk to me about the cure."

Where the vaccine question had cut, this stabbed. It drove deep into his soul. To take a supremely gifted child who could touch the mind of another and rip that ability out of it…

He took a breath, kept his voice neutral. "Mr President, so far, we haven't found any safe and effective cure."

"What does that mean?"

"The cures we've tried kill the mice, Mr President. We have some ideas of ways to proceed…" He thought of Shankari's back door, which should at least work on children exposed to the most recent version of Nexus. "…but it's too early to say if they'll work, or if they'll work on all populations."

Stockton continued to drum his fingers.

"Dr Holtzmann, let me make it clear what's at stake. These Nexus children are a threat. If we're unable to prevent the spread of Nexus to more children, and we're unable to cure children that have been exposed, we're going to have no choice but to be interning them. Thousands of them, at least. Now, I don't want to do that. The public doesn't want to do that. But I *will* do that if there's no other option."

Holtzmann opened his mouth to protest. *Why? Why not embrace them?* But Barnes was faster.

"You could euthanize them, Mr President," the acting ERD Director said. "The law gives you the power to. And the ones born with Nexus in their brains… they're from broken homes, drug-abusing mothers. We can manage the PR."

Kill them? Kill these children? Even through his pumped up levels of serotonin and dopamine, Holtzmann felt like he'd been punched in the gut.

"I'm not going to kill children," Stockton replied.

"The law says they're not even human," Barnes replied. "Not even children."

"I don't care, Barnes," the president replied. "They're kids. They didn't choose this. I'll lock them away to protect America if I have to, but only until we can cure them. I won't sign their death warrants."

Barnes didn't let up. "President Jameson euthanized the Aryan Rising clones."

"Barnes!" Stockton raised his voice.

There was silence for a moment. Then Holtzmann heard his own voice speaking. "Why? Why imprison them? Why try to cure them? Why not embrace them?"

They looked at him in shock.

Barnes spoke first. "Martin, really..."

Stockton raised his hand, silencing Barnes.

"I want to hear what he has to say," he said to Barnes. "Go on, Dr Holtzmann."

Holtzmann swallowed. What am I doing?

The right thing, something inside him answered.

"Mr President, these children... They're the future, sir. They'll grow up to be smarter than we are, better able to understand each other. And this technology... It doesn't have to divide us. It can be the future for all of our children, or all our grandchildren."

Stockton didn't respond the way Holtzmann feared. The President didn't snap at him, didn't drum his fingers, didn't look angry. He looked puzzled.

"Dr Holtzmann, you've already said that we don't know the long-term effects of this drug. That those exposed to it in the womb grow up fundamentally differently than those exposed to it later. What about those parents that don't want to try this drug? That don't want to risk the life or health of their children on it? From what you've told me, their children, their *normal human* children won't have any chance of keeping up with these Nexus kids. The Nexus children will get all the best jobs, get all the wealth, and leave everyone else behind. Doesn't that worry you?"

Holtzmann closed his eyes for a moment. He couldn't deny what the President was saying. Not everyone would choose Nexus for their unborn. And those who didn't would see their children left behind.

He couldn't deny it. So he spoke from the heart.

"Mr President, have you ever heard of the Neanderthal Dilemma?"

Stockton shook his head. "No."

"It's taught in ethics of emerging technology courses."

"Martin," Barnes cut in, "I hardly think we need to get into…"

Stockton cut Barnes off with a gesture of his hand again. "Go on, Dr Holtzmann. Our ancestors outcompeted Neanderthals. We led to their extinction. Is that it?"

Holtzmann nodded. "Yes, Mr President. Everywhere modern humans went, Neanderthals eventually went extinct. The groups mingled. They even mated. But the modern humans were just smarter, faster, better able to think and communicate and invent things. They made better tools and hunted and gathered more effectively. The Neanderthals couldn't keep up."

Stockton nodded. "Yes. *Exactly.* And that's what could happen to us. We're the Neanderthals, and we need to nip this problem in the bud, before *we* aren't able to keep up."

Holtzmann reached forward with his hands, almost pleading. "But, Mr President, if Neanderthals had managed to nip the human problem in the bud, *we* wouldn't be here." He gestured around him. "There wouldn't be a White House, a United States of America. The world would have less art, less science, less of everything we value, all those inventions of culture that the Neanderthals couldn't have achieved, but that our *homo sapiens* ancestors could. That's the Dilemma, Mr President. If you were a Neanderthal and could stop humans from coming into being, or stop them from getting a foothold, you might extend the life of your species, but leave the world a poorer place."

Stockton was shaking his head now, not unkindly. "Dr Holtzmann, that's no dilemma at all. We're here now. My job is to protect the citizens of the United States of America. And there's no way that I'm going to allow a threat to them to develop, no matter what wonderful world you think might come later, *after* we're extinct."

Holtzmann hung his head in defeat.

"So now, Dr Holtzmann. Back to that cure and that vaccine. You need to get those moving. Because I may be unwilling to euthanize those children, but by the time you're saying any cure is available, someone else is going to be sitting in my chair. And neither you nor I know what decision that President will make." He paused for effect. "If you want these children to live, Doctor, you better find them a cure."

30
BONDING

Friday October 26th

Rangan spent most of the next three sleep cycles on the floor in the corner of his cell. He sat there when they had the lights turned up. He slept there when they turned the lights down. It was hard and cold. It left parts of his body numb and asleep. But it was where the connection was clearest.

Bobby. Bobby and a dozen others. They were on the other side of this wall, trapped like he was. Just kids.

There was a flaw in the shielding. A loose wire, maybe, in the conductive mesh wall that separated his cell from Bobby's bunk and the room beyond it. A place where radio waves could get through, where those radio waves could carry thoughts between them.

The first night, when their minds had first met, Rangan's thoughts had been selfish. He wasn't alone. There was someone else here.

Then he'd realized what was going on, and his mind had turned to anger.

Kids, he thought. They've got kids locked up here. Motherfuckers!

What kind of fucking monsters locked up kids? Locked them up just because they had something special in their heads that made them better? That helped them cope with what was wrong with them? That might just make them smarter than the rest of us?

Rangan spent hours communing with Bobby, learning more about the boy, about the other boys over there. The kids took turns sitting in Bobby's bunk sometimes. He got to know Alfonso, Jose, Parker, half-a-dozen more. They relived their memories for him. Being torn from their families. Seeing relatives arrested, beaten. Being beaten themselves when they resisted. He relived Parker being torn from his mother's arms, seeing her dragged off. He relived Bobby's arrest, seeing his dad gunned down in front of his eyes, then being beaten silly by the men who'd torn him from his father.

His fists clenched and he wanted to hurt someone. Hurt them badly.

Fucking assholes.

The kids were scared, lonely. He did his best to hide his own anger, his own disappointment with himself, and be there for them. It was hard through the tiny link. But he did what he could, comforting them, trying to send hope, and humor.

In exchange they amazed him. They were smart, hungry to understand the Nexus in their brains, understand what was going on around them. And the way their minds connected...

Ilya had talked about group mind. The experiments she'd convinced them to try at parties and at each other's apartments had been aimed at trying to create some of that. And sure, they'd had their trippy moments, those times when the barriers had seemed to drop and they'd felt like they were turning into one person.

But it had all been short-lasting stuff, sometimes with the aid of Empathek or a little weed or whatnot. It'd felt cool as hell, but he'd never seen much practical coming out of it.

These kids, though… Maybe it was because they were younger. Or maybe it was the autism. Something. Whatever it was, they were connected more deeply. Thoughts *leaked* between them, without them even trying. He showed Bobby things about Nexus and he could feel those thoughts ripple out to the rest of the boys, fresh questions come back almost faster than he could parse. Then the boys showed him the tests the ERD was running, and it was clear. They were learning from each other, mind-to-mind. Bobby had learned Spanish without even trying to, just because the ERD had given him a test of Spanish, had primed him for it, and then his mind had pulled what he'd needed from the Spanish-speaking kids around him.

These kids were something else. This was a real step towards what Ilya had dreamed of. It was fucking awesome.

If they weren't locked up here in jail, anyway.

There was one last thing he learned from these kids. It was obvious, really, but he poked around in their memories to be sure he understood it right. Nexus OS had gotten out, alright. Months and months ago. God only knew how many people were running it now.

And he had given the ERD the back door to all those minds.

Fuck, fuck, fuck.

Rangan stared at the dull gray wall of his cell and contemplated just how badly he'd screwed up.

31

IN SAIGON

Friday October 26th

Nakamura stared again at the satellite image on his retinal implants. An open-top Tata jeep, on the road approaching Saigon, two shaven-headed figures in it. His hunch had been right. Kade and Sam had headed to Saigon. So Nakamura followed.

With Lane's back door access to Nexus, the boy could easily have amassed whatever financial resources he desired. He could be hiding in an exclusive hotel, eating room service. Or he could be in the tourist districts blending in. So Nakamura had no choice but to canvas all the parts of the city frequented by Westerners.

He walked through the lobbies of the international hotels as an expensively dressed business traveler – gray suit, briefcase in hand, smart glasses feeding him financial reports and top news. He went around Saigon Square as a smartly dressed European tourist – expensive navy slacks, Italian leather shoes, a sharp white polo, trendy watch, and mirrored shades. He hung around Bến Thành Market as a backpacker – khakis, T-shirt, hair past his shoulders.

He saw Sam in the streets around Bến Thành. A tall slender girl in jeans and a tank top, strong shoulders, erect posture, long black hair down her back. She turned and Nakamura saw the line of jaw and nose. Her name rose on his lips, against all orders, against all protocol.

Then it wasn't Sam at all. Just a young teen girl, coltish, fourteen maybe. Her parents emerged into the street and went off with her. Sam as a girl. Sam as he remembered her.

He shook his head at his sentimentality, at his evolution into an old man, searching for a girl that wasn't his daughter, but was as near to that as he'd ever come. Then he went back to his walking.

Everywhere he went, Nakamura sprinkled smart dust. The micro-scale sensors dropped to the ground, spread on the wind, attached themselves to clothing, to shoes, to bags. And everywhere they went, they searched for Kade's face, for Sam's face, for a hint of either's DNA, for the telltale emanations of Nexus. And then they meshed together, each quietly sending data to its closest neighbors, piggybacking until it eventually found its way to Kevin Nakamura.

He swam in that information, overlaid on his vision by his retinal display. Maps showed him the spread of the smart dust as it rode on bellhops and hotel guests to the upper floors of the Hilton and the Sheraton, as it blew through the mall at the heart of Saigon Square, as it was blown or washed into the river and the sewers beneath the city, as it was tracked by bicycles and shoes into the alleys of the maze around Bến Thành Market. A running stream showed face after face after face, flickering by, hundreds of faces so far, none noted as a high probability hit. Further to the side, another stream, of gene sequences this time, just as devoid of true hits.

A layer of the map showed him the Nexus emanations. The area around Bến Thành was inundated with it. Even a few of the less drug-soaked tourists near Saigon Square and the business travelers in the heart of downtown gave off Nexus frequency transmissions. Nakamura shook his head at their audacity, surprised at the prevalence of the drug.

A final map layer showed him police and emergency services data for the city, mined from CIA systems. *If the prey can't be found*, he'd taught his pupils, *hunt the hunters*.

There was always the risk that Sam and Kade would move on, of course. He kept a National Reconnaissance Office AI busy, searching for more matches on that twenty year-old Tata jeep. It threw some at him every few hours, but all were false hits.

He'd love to point a dedicated NRO bird at Saigon. But queries were one thing, retargeting birds was another. The latter would alert the National Reconnaissance Office that CIA had a high level of interest in Saigon. And that was a no-no.

Why? he wondered again. Why so much secrecy?

One way or another, it was boots-on-the-ground time. His boots. And his dust. For five days Nakamura walked, and tracked, and analyzed. And still he had no matches on Sam or Lane. So he walked and walked some more.

32
STUCK IN A MOMENT

Friday October 26th

Holtzmann limped out of the White House proper, supporting himself heavily with his cane, feeling years older than he had when he'd entered. Barnes walked next to him. Neither man said anything. Only after they were past the security guards and T-rays and Nexus scanners and metal detectors, waiting for their cars, did Barnes turn to him and lean in close. Holtzmann took an involuntary half step back, and Barnes took another forward. He'd never realized how tall Barnes was, but now, looking up into that cold face with its dead black eyes, he was acutely aware that the man was younger, taller, stronger, more powerful in every way.

Barnes put a hand on Holtzmann's shoulder and squeezed, just enough to hurt. Holtzmann froze in fear.

Barnes leaned in until his mouth was inches from Holtzmann's ear. He spoke slowly, his voice just above a hoarse whisper.

"If you ever do that to me again, I will fucking destroy you."

Then Barnes' car was there, and the man was all smiles. "Great job today, Martin. See you back at the office. I'm looking forward to new *results* in those things the President asked about."

Holtzmann collapsed into his own car, exhausted and shaking. His fingers clenched around his cane of their own accord. Even through his boosted dopamine and serotonin levels all he could feel was the bitter disappointment of defeat, the yawning crevice of hypocrisy.

He'd tried. Somehow, boosted as he was, he'd found the courage to do something quite unlike himself. He'd spoken his mind to the President, to tell him what he truly thought. And he'd been casually rebuffed, rebuffed in a way so basic, so primitive, so tribal, so very *human*, that it left no doubt in his mind as to the course that humanity would take.

The Titans ate their young, he thought. No one wants to be usurped.

There was no safe ground underneath him anymore. There was just a chasm opening wider and wider. There were only two ways forward for him. He could do the moral thing, the right thing, and quit the ERD, face the audit and the discovery of the Nexus he'd stolen, face the imprisonment, in all likelihood for the rest of his life. Leave his wife and sons alone, and ashamed. Or he could do the weak thing, the expedient thing, and do his job, be party to the forced abortion of this new breed of humanity, and maybe, just maybe, stay free.

Both paths led straight into the abyss. He could feel himself falling now. The world was spinning around him.

"Phone," he managed to say. "Clear my calendar and turn on my autoresponder. I'm sick."

The phone beeped in the affirmative.

"Car," he choked out the words. "Drive to the park."

"Which park would you like as your destination?" the car asked in its silky feminine voice.

"Any," he said. "Any of them will do."

"I have twenty-seven parks within…" the car began.

"Aaah!" Holtzmann slammed his cane against the car's dash in frustration and the car went silent.

His breath was coming fast. He was panting in anger.

Stupid man, he told himself. Yelling at a car.

He let his breath calm. A memory came to him. A happy day, with Anne. Fine.

"Montrose Park," he told the car. "Montrose Park."

"Yes, sir," the car answered, more deferentially, some affective computing algorithm now modulating its interactions with him.

Holtzmann barely noticed. He leaned his seat back, brought up the neuromodulation interface app in his mind, the panel of dials and switches with neat labels and dry academic names. Then he dialed up a large opiate release, hit the button, and felt it course through his brain. It was sickly sweet, not glorious and ecstatic as it had been once, but even so the opiates pushed the fear and unmooring back away from him, pushed the anxiety and panic into the background, until he just didn't care about the President or his predicament or anything else.

The car drove him to Montrose Park in a languid dream. Trees and buildings moved by in a blurring, surreal molasses. His pulse thrummed slow and low through his veins. Haltingly he told the car to park and to darken the windows. Somewhere in the Caribbean, the radio told him, a tropical storm called Zoe had thrashed Cuba, leaving buildings destroyed, fields flooded, and hundreds dead. Here, in the park beyond his car windows, it was a gorgeous hot sunny day. Thought and memory returned as the opiate surge faded. He and Anne had come here, when they were younger. They'd brought the boys here to splash around in the pool. He had hazy, happy memories of it. Heat and crowds of parents and children. Cool water on a hot day. Hot dogs bought from the snack bar.

From the parking lot he could see that pool, where he and Anne had brought the boys. Mothers and toddlers and a few young people splashed about there now. Inside his car, Holtzmann was in his own private cocoon.

He stayed there for hours. Every so often the opiates would start to wear off and the chasm would yawn wide open beneath his feet again and he'd start to panic, his breath coming fast and his heart pounding and his stomach feeling sick, and he'd dose himself once more to push it away. The doses he was giving himself were large, now, but there was no bliss in them. His tolerance was growing. At best the doses made him care less, care less that his life was reduced to this, a choice between imprisonment and something akin to genocide.

There's another way, he thought. I could end my own life.

He pushed that idea away with another opiate surge, larger than the last.

His phone buzzed, again and again, calls from the office, video messages, text messages. He refused to answer, refused to check his messages on phone or slate.

Dusk came. Teenagers – released from the prisons that masqueraded as schools – joined the mothers and small children at the pool. He was hungry. He had to piss. He should be home soon. He was tempted to stay here forever, to just lay in his car taking dose after dose after dose of opiates until his neurons were squeezed dry of them or until he accidentally killed himself.

But something else prevailed. Habit, perhaps. Some shred of dignity. He forced a jolt of norepinephrine through his system, pushed himself up, and shambled on his cane to the restroom by the pool. Children and parents stared at him. A mother pulled her toddler aside, protectively. He had some vague notion that he was a mess, but he couldn't bring himself to care.

He pissed in a room that smelled of chlorine, and struggled back to his car, limping on his cane. He ordered the car to take him home, and did the best he could to clear his head with more norepinephrine, with acetylcholine, with more dopamine. His brain was a neurochemical witch's brew. Some part of him whispered that he couldn't go on like this, that he'd push himself too hard soon, push himself into another opiate overdose or serotonin syndrome or a deadly seizure or some other cataclysmic neurochemical collapse.

Despite that, his brain tinkering worked. He reached his own home in some semblance of order. He could pass his state off as fatigue from a long day, perhaps. Maybe. Above all else, he wouldn't tell Anne where he'd been, or why.

He came in through the door. Anne was home already, files in her lap. She looked up. "Martin!"

Holtzmann smiled, and then shots rang out from the screen. He looked over in time to see a video of his nightmare – two Secret Service agents clobbering Steve Travers. He caught his breath, reflexively waiting for the moment when the screen exploded with chaos, when the explosion hurled him through the air, took the life of Joe Duran standing just *inches* from him.

The screen went blank instead, as Anne clicked it off.

"I'm sorry, Martin," she said. "Didn't mean to make you watch that again." She was up and had her arms around him, was kissing him on the side of his face.

Holtzmann was frozen stiff, his whole body suddenly racing with adrenaline.

Anne frowned.

"You know what frustrates me?" she asked.

Holtzmann shook his head, mutely, his mind trapped in that endless moment six months past.

The Secret Service man's gun came out out out, and fired, and fired. Human missiles leveled the shooter, and Holtzmann turned, looking for the President. Joe Duran screaming in his ear, "How did you know, Martin? How did you know?"

Anne was speaking, saying something. "Stockton was *losing* until the PLF tried to kill him," she said. "He's going to win *because of* the assassination attempt, and now Chicago." She shook her head. "They could've at least been better shots."

He grabbed hold of her, suddenly panicked. "Don't say that, Anne! Don't ever say that!" They were watching him. A stranger in the car. Nakamura raising his hand for the killing blow...

She looked at him like he'd lost his mind. "It was a *joke*, Martin! It's still OK to make *jokes* in this country!"

"Just please," he pleaded. "Please don't ever say that."

They slept on opposite sides of the bed. Anne seemed annoyed, put off by his behavior. She drifted off to sleep without their customary "I love you."

Holtzmann lay there on his back. He was close to something. Some realization was working its way through his mind. He'd been close to it that night after Nakamura had surprised him, and then he'd been distracted, had dropped it. Bits of memories and conversations went through his head.

The Secret Service man's gun came out out out, and fired, and fired. Human missiles leveled the shooter. The gun flew from his hand.

Anne talking to him. "They could've at least been better shots."

Wait. Wait. That made no sense. Travers had missed because the other Secret Service agents had hit him *before* he could fire. They'd thrown off his aim. Or he'd flinched as they approached. That was why.

But in his nightmares Travers fired first, and then the other agents hit him. In his nightmares, the man never flinched.

He was wide awake, suddenly. His head felt free of opiate buzz, free of the awful feeling of anxiety and craving. His stomach was knotted but his head was clear.

He brought up a window in his mind, navigated his file system. He'd saved the memories of that morning. He'd archived them. There. That was the folder. There were the files.

He pulled the memory up. Sensations engulfed him. He was back in that sweltering July day. Sweat beaded on his brow. Daydreaming as the President droned on. He wanted to *yell* at his old self, scream at his younger self to get up, to cry out about what was going to happen, but there was no going back, no way to stop it. The past was read-only.

He moved the slider along, fast-forwarded through his own memory, and there. The encrypted radio traffic. He'd craned his head. Spotted Travers, just another nameless Secret Service man to him then, and the awful intuition had come to him. In the memory he was up on his feet now. His heart was pounding, in the memory and in the present.

His past self was shouting now that that man had a gun. Holtzmann cranked down the play speed, and as he watched, Travers pulled the huge pistol out of his jacket in a long, slow motion, no expression on his face. It arced around at a quarter speed and snapped into place, perfectly steadily, and hung there as still as the man's face for a fraction of a second. Then its muzzle flared and a huge boom filled Holtzmann's ears. The muzzle of the gun jerked up, came down again in slow motion, and then its muzzle flared again and a second boom exploded in his ears. And only then did a twin blur slam into Travers and take him away. Throughout it all, the man's expression never changed.

Holtzmann's heart was pounding. Travers had fired calmly and coolly. He'd fired *before* he was hit. And his expression never betrayed a single flinch, a single hesitation. And why should it? The man had been turned into a Nexus robot, after all. His arm was controlled by software, not human instinct. His *aim* was controlled by software.

So why had he missed?

Nakamura's voice answered him. *"To find the cause of an event... who had the most to gain?"*

There was a hand on Holtzmann's chest. Anne was shaking him. "Martin. Martin. You were screaming. Are you OK? Another nightmare?"

Holtzmann opened his eyes, looked over at his wife. And now he was terribly afraid, not just for himself, but for her as well.

"A nightmare," he said. "A nightmare."

Anne Holtzmann rolled back over in the bed she shared with her husband, troubled. What was wrong with Martin? Why was he acting so strangely?

She lay there, thinking, finding no answers, until she heard his breath change as he fell back into sleep. Then sleep took her as well.

33
SEPARATION ANXIETY

Saturday October 27th

Sam watched as the two vehicles from the Mira Foundation made their way up the winding road to the place she'd called home these last three months. The children around her felt anxious, sad and frightened to be leaving Sam, uncertain about what lay ahead, but happy that Jake was coming with them.

Sam smiled, did her best to project calm resolve. This would be a wonderful new adventure. They'd meet new friends. They'd have a larger home. Jake would be with them. Sam would rejoin them soon.

But inside she felt a gaping loss.

Jake took her hand, squeezed it, gratitude and longing coming through their connection. She squeezed back, grateful for the contact.

Khun Mae and her two girls stood with them, silent. What were they thinking, Sam wondered. Were they sad to see their wards go? Were they relieved? Their faces were masks. No tears were being shed there.

The vehicles pulled through the open gate. They'd

brought two – a van big enough for all the children, and a closed-top jeep driving behind.

Sam's practiced eye picked up subtleties of the vehicles. The way the thickness of the windows distorted light a bit more. The distinctive shape of run-flat tires. The ruggedness of the chassis. These were armored vehicles, designed to blend in with normal traffic, to arouse no suspicions, but also to stand up to small arms fire. To take fire and keep on moving.

They're careful, she thought. Can I blame them?

The vehicles stopped and four Mira Foundation staff emerged. Two men from the jeep. A man and a woman from the van. The woman moved like a model. The men moved like soldiers. Nexus emanations radiated from all four of their minds.

She stood paralyzed as they loaded the children's things into the van, paralyzed by jealousy and loss and fear. Khun Mae and one of the men stepped back inside the house. She could see the other two men watching her now. She forced a smile, forced happy thoughts, and stepped forward to hug the children goodbye, to kiss Jake for the last time...

They were still watching her. One of the men turned to the side, focusing on the back of the van, but his body language gave him away. His attention was on her. She must be hiding her fear and loss more poorly than she'd imagined.

But he was wound up so tight... They both were... As if...

Sarai threw herself into Sam's arms and Sam held her tight, kissed her on the brow, told her she loved her. Then she kissed and hugged each of the children as they filed into the van and took their seats.

"Panda!" Kit said, and she felt it from his mind at the same time. His beloved Panda wasn't in the small pile of belongings in the back of the van.

Jake turned, but Sam smiled and spoke first. "I'll get it!" she told them, grateful for something to do.

She turned and she felt the men tense up more. Maybe they were worried she'd make a scene. But she wouldn't. She'd bide her time. And she'd be with her new family again.

Sam strode into the house and towards the room Kit and the other four boys shared. It was far enough that she couldn't feel the minds of the children any more, could just feel one mind in here, of one of the men. And he was far enough away that she doubted he could feel her in return. It was a relief to have that privacy.

She didn't see Panda on any of the beds in the boys' room or on the floor. She ducked her head down to the floor and, sure enough, there the toy was, under Kit's bed. She reached under, pulled it up, and stood to take it outside.

Then she heard the voices. Khun Mae and the man from the Mira foundation she hadn't met. Low. Conspiratorial. Why?

She stepped towards the door softly, reeled her Nexus in and put it into receive-only mode, then closed her eyes, and let her superhuman hearing do the work.

They were speaking in Thai. She heard snippets: "Ten thousand baht... in the American girl's food... make her unconscious... come collect her."

What?

She stepped out of the room, into the hallway. They were at the other end, just inside the kitchen. The light lit them from behind, rendering them black silhouettes.

They froze into silence when Sam emerged. The man's mind radiated alarm. Khun Mae's posture radiated fright.

"Khun Mae..." Sam started.

Then the man pulled out his gun and started firing.

34

CONFRONTATION

Saturday October 27th

Jake smiled, rubbed the children's heads, and did his best to exude calm and love. Leaving Sunee, leaving *Sam*, was hitting him already. He could feel it tugging at him, the sense of separation, the fear that he wouldn't be able to get her into Mira's good graces, that she'd disappear before he could find her again.

Something came from the house. Sounds like soft pops, and then the sound of something crashing, falling, things breaking. He turned in concern. The minds around him radiated alarm. Then the two men from Mira had guns in their hands.

Fear burst through him. The children!

He grabbed the hand of the man nearest him. "There are kids here!" he yelled.

The man shrugged Jake away with one arm, almost casually, and Jake felt himself hurled through the air. His feet left the ground and for a moment he was in free flight. Then his back struck the van and it knocked the wind out of him. His world dimmed for a moment, and fear coursed through him. The kids! He forced himself to look, forced himself to see. The man still had the gun out, was spinning, looking around. Jake was on his knees. He acted without thinking, hauled himself up, threw himself at the man, grabbing at his gun arm again, with both hands, whirling him around.

Then the gun went off, and a freight train punched Jake in the chest.

Sam dove through the doorway into the boys' room as the man opened fire. Something grazed her side as she did. She came down in a roll, back up to her feat, her mind working overtime.

"I'm not your enemy!" she yelled out through the door.

No response. The man's mind was gone. He'd gone into receive-only mode so she couldn't sense him.

She stepped behind the door, nearest the shooter, then looked around. She could dive out through the window, run towards Jake and the children. But the other men must be armed too. She needed a weapon. She needed to know what the fuck was going on.

Her augmented hearing picked up the footfalls in the hallway. He was stalking her, coming this way, quietly.

She closed her eyes, gave her hearing her full attention. The man's footfalls gave him away. He was almost to the door, hugging the opposite wall of the hallway to give himself space, keep the advantage of his gun.

He was just across the thin wall from her now.

Sam made up her mind. She backed away from the wall, then hurled herself forward, turning her shoulder into it at the last instant.

Her augmented muscles and organic carbon-fiber bones crashed her through the thin wall. Wood splintered and gave. Drywall exploded. Then she was through, and her momentum drove her into the surprised soldier as he tried to turn, to bring his gun around.

The blow knocked him back, even as the gun boomed again in the small space. He kicked out from her, lightning fast, trying to create room, and she caught the foot with both hands, used it to spin him around like a plank. He hit the ground hard, face first, but rolled like a pro, faster than any normal human, clearly enhanced, the gun still in his hand, rising around to get a shot.

Then her foot stomped down on the forearm of his gun hand, pinning it as she stepped over him. He kept fighting, lashed out with a vicious, inhumanly fast fist towards her exposed groin. She brought her knee up faster, blocked his fist with her shin, then dropped all her weight on him with that knee, knocking the wind from him. Still he struggled, boosted muscles straining at her. So Sam took the gun from his hand and slammed it grip-first into the side of his head, below his ear. Once, twice, three times. And finally the man went limp.

Sam rose, the gun in her hand. Silenced. At least four rounds left. She turned towards the front of the house, kicked the door open in time to see one of the men put a bullet into Jake's chest.

"NO!" Sam screamed. Distantly she heard the man who'd shot Jake cursing.

Sam raised her gun to fire but Sarai was there, in the line of sight, screaming now. She'd was trying to exit the van but the Mira woman had her by the arm. The other Mira soldier fired towards the house, and Sam dropped and rolled, her heart pounding in her chest.

She heard gravel crunch outside. They were coming towards her. She forced herself to visualize the courtyard. She had to shoot low, aim for the soldiers' legs, stay clear of Sarai and the van and any other kids that had managed to break free.

Sam popped up in the window of the girls' room, forced herself to take stock of the situation before she fired, to be sure that no children were in the way.

Her hesitation almost killed her. The Mira soldier who'd shot Jake fired on her and she felt a bullet punch into her left tricep. She fired back twice, ignored the burning pain, and saw the man go down as her bullets took him in the left leg.

Then she dropped below the window, rolled to another spot in the room. The wall would offer only scant protection.

She could hear the woman yelling now. "The children are the top priority! We have to get them out of here."

Sam popped up again and the soldiers were under cover, on the other side of the van, climbing into it on the passenger side. One slid across to the driver's side and then the van was moving. Sam took careful aim at his head and fired once, twice, thrice, four times, until the gun clicked empty. The shots hit the armored windshield, spiderwebbed it but didn't break through. The van rushed forward and out the gate.

Sam threw herself through the window, shattering the remaining glass, feeling it cut into her in a dozen places, rolled, and came up sprinting at the retreating rear of the van. It disappeared out the gate as she crossed the courtyard. She could feel Jake's pain and fear but she ignored it, pushed herself harder. Her left tricep groaned with the pain of the bullet wound, but Sam ignored that too. She made the gate at a full sprint and could see the van ahead, reaching the turn in the road. She ran harder, putting every ounce of effort into her legs, feeling her lungs burning, willing the van to slow down at the turn.

The van hit the turn at speed, skidded as it came around, its tires biting into the gravel, its driver expertly navigating the road.

She threw herself forward with all she had, sent her body into a horizontal leap, arms extended. One finger brushed the bumper, and for a moment she knew she had it, knew she would stop these men, whoever they were, knew she would have her children back.

Then her finger slipped off, and she crashed, rolling and skidding into the gravel as the van sped away.

Sam lay there panting for a moment. The jeep. They'd abandoned the jeep.

She pushed herself to her feet. There was gravel in the skin of her face. The palms of her hands were lacerated from her fall. A dozen cuts covered her from the glass of the window. Dust was matting blood into her hair, onto her face, everywhere. She ran hard, back uphill, got in view of the gate in time to see the jeep go up in a fireball that hit her with its searing heat from here.

She kept running, her mind refusing to believe, willing herself to find a fire extinguisher, put out the flames, chase them down.

And then she saw Jake.

35

MOST TO GAIN

Saturday October 27th

Holtzmann forced himself to sleep via Nexus. He had to rest. He had to clear his head. He had to get perspective.

He woke too soon, his heart pounding in his chest. The clock in his mind read 1.16am.

He couldn't shake this dread. Couldn't shake this fear that he'd been so wrong. That he'd misunderstood everything. That the world was an even darker place than he'd suspected.

He slipped out of bed, as silently as he could. Anne murmured something. He looked at her and his heart ached. What had happened that he'd decided to lie to her? To hide what was going on? What would happen now? If he was right... If he was right... Her life was in danger too.

Let me be wrong, he prayed to a God he hadn't believed in since his teens. Please, Lord, let me be wrong.

Holtzmann padded into his home office, closed the door behind him, and turned on the secure terminal. He swiped his finger across the print reader, held still for the retinal scan, and then spoke his passphrase.

The terminal came alive, the Department of Homeland Security's eagle-and-shield logo emblazoned on the screen, the ERD's smaller atom-double-helix-and-shield sigil superimposed on its bottom right corner.

He navigated through the system, into Project November. Cooper's team had built this, under his supervision. He'd hated that they'd made this, but it had been a miniscule crime compared to the ones he faced now.

He ignored the source code, pulled up the specifications instead. There, the on-the-wire protocol definition. He took snapshots of the data on the screen with his mind's eye, forced his Nexus OS to commit them to storage. Then one more thing. The encryption key. Where did it live? He trawled through config options. There it was. The key itself was obscured. He had to re-enter his passphrase, his voice shaking so much he was surprised that the system took it, then answer three challenges, and then and only then the system revealed the key to him. It was a long string of hexadecimal that would make no sense to a human, but which would unlock the communication between November node and November controller. He took a snapshot of the key, verified that it was saved, then disconnected himself from the system.

His heart was pounding now. He was sweating. His breath came short. He was wrong. He was sure he was wrong. He *must be* wrong. But what if he was right?

He wanted another opiate surge. He wanted to make it all go away. But he couldn't. He couldn't. This was too big. He had to know.

Holtzmann darkened the terminal screen, leaned back in his chair, his eyes closed, and went back to his memories of that horrible day in July. The comms log. There. The encrypted traffic he'd picked up.

Encrypted data. On a Nexus frequency. Joe Duran scowling as Holtzmann looked back and forth, looked for the source behind him.

?RU5L8PP0hLarBNxfoQM23wG6+KTCEBhOIAAQyPP c76+TWhj+X/

He took the encrypted transmissions, opened them in a decryption app, and applied the private key.

The key matched.

The assassins hadn't just used Nexus from his lab. They'd used *his code*. That was how they'd pulled off an attack so sophisticated, so far beyond what the PLF had done in years. They'd used *his work*.

His heart wanted to burst out of his chest now. His face was flushed. He wanted to scream and to weep.

One last thing to check. He pulled the on-the-wire protocol definition up in his mind's eye, let it fill the top half of his vision while the decrypted communication filled the bottom half.

The protocol definition was a key, a legend. It let him turn the binary language of the decrypted signals into something that made sense.

He moved slowly, carefully. There in the protocol definition was the command for "fire", the arguments that it took. He searched through the decrypted signals, looking, looking. Was it there? Could there be some mistake? Could he be wrong?

Then he found it. The Fire command.

He checked its definition again. The Fire function took two arguments, the object identifier and an offset from that target. He translated what he saw in the binary into something he could read.

FIRE (<target 1>, <-0.5, 0, 0>)

And he was right. He was so so right. And he wished he weren't.

Someone had used the Nexus from his lab. Someone had used the software his team had built. They'd used it to take control of Steve Travers, to turn him into a robot assassin, they'd used it to tell him to fire.

And to fire half a meter to the left of his target.

They'd used it to shoot at the President, but not to hit him. To miss.

"They could have at least been better shots!" Anne said in his memories.

Oh no. They hit exactly what they meant to.

Who had the most to gain? Nakamura's voice asked him.

Stockton was losing until the PLF tried to kill him, Anne answered. *He's going to win* because of *the assassination attempt.*

The answer was clear.

The President had the most to gain.

36

LAST WORDS

Saturday October 27th

Sam crossed the courtyard to Jake, fell to her knees at his side. He was face down in the gravel. His mind was still there, but in pain, and fading. A red stain was spreading across his back. A puddle was forming under him. There was a hole in his shirt, in the flesh below, where the bullet had punched all the way through him.

"Jake, Jake," she said. "Oh my God, Jake."

He groaned in pain. "Sunee…" he said weakly. His mind was faltering, confused, weak from blood loss.

Sam put her hands on his shirt, ripped it open as gently as she could, tried to see the wound better.

It was bad. The bullet had punched through his lung, had sent an expanding cone of carnage through his chest cavity. There was blood everywhere. Something had nicked a major blood vessel.

"Sunee…" he groaned. He was reaching out for her with his mind, trying to feel her more. She could feel him fading, fading further.

She balled up the shirt, pressed it into the wound as best she could. The blood kept coming.

No doctor, she thought. No vehicle.

"Let me touch you..." he moaned. "Please."

"You're not going to die," she told him.

His eyes were open. He was staring at her. He knew what was coming.

"Please..." he begged her.

Tears rolled down Sam's face. A sob ripped its way out of her. She nodded. "Yes."

Then she opened herself to him, opened herself as wide as she could, let him see who she was.

His eyes went wide as he drank her in, a confusion of images and memories and sensations. Above it all she sent her feelings for him, her admiration, her trust, her tenderness, the thing that might have been love.

He closed his eyes and when he opened them there were tears there too. A drop of blood from her cuts dripped from her face onto his. He looked at her, with those wide, amazed eyes, so surprised now to find out how right he'd been about her.

"Sam... Sam... Get them back. Get them back."

She nodded, weeping. She would. She'd get them back.

He coughed, and blood came up, and she could feel his regret, his regret at not seeing the future, his regret that she'd never opened herself to him before.

"I wish I'd known you," he whispered. And his mind was fluttering, faltering, on the edge of that sudden decoherence into darkness that she'd felt before.

"You did," she pleaded with him. "You did know me. You did."

But he was gone before the words left her lips.

She knelt there, next to Jake, weeping. She closed his still-staring eyes. Her blood and tears fell on his face to mix with his.

I wish I'd shown you, she told herself. I wish I'd trusted you. I wish I'd opened up to you.

I'm sorry, she sent him. **I'm so so sorry**.

But there was no one there to hear her.

A sound snapped her back to reality. She turned, and the soldier she'd disabled inside the house was there, yards away, a long length of metal pipe in his hand, running at her, swinging it like a baseball bat with lethal, superhuman force.

She was on her feet in an instant. Her left forearm shot up at blurring speed to block the swinging pipe. Pain ripped through her as her bullet-wounded muscles strained to heave her arm up. Then the whole arm went numb as it collided with the deadly pipe. But by then she was forward, inside his guard, and her right fist snapped out in a lightning-fast punch that crushed the man's nose and snapped his head back in a violent whiplash motion.

The pipe dropped from the man's hand, clattered on the gravel. It was bent thirty degrees where it had collided with her arm. The man tottered, took one step back, and then collapsed, semiconscious.

Sam stepped over him, patted him down. A search of his pockets brought up a phone, a wallet with cash, credit and ID, and a spare clip of ammo.

She reloaded the pistol, dismissed the ID as a fake, and shoved the rest in her own pockets.

He came to as she pocketed his things.

Good.

She stuck the barrel of the gun in his face, inches from his eyes.

"Who are you? Where did they take those kids?"

He clenched his jaw, shook his head from side to side. He'd die before he told her.

She couldn't feel his mind at all, but she knew it was there, knew he was running Nexus. She pushed against him the way Kade had taught her – the way Shu had done it to Kade – forced his Nexus nodes to respond. His eyes went wild but she could feel him now. She threw her mind against his, tried to force him to open to her, to tell her where those children had gone.

He resisted, fought back with pure willpower and terror. He could see the gun in her hand but it wasn't enough.

She wished she had Kade's back door, so she could force this man's mind open, take what she needed to know. Some part of her was sick at that thought, but the rest of her didn't care. Her anger, her loss, her fear for the children overruled all else.

She had to break this man's will so she could take what she needed to know. Fear wasn't enough. Pain would have to do.

She rose to her feet, gun still trained on the man's head, and kicked him in the side. Pain burst from his mind, a groan escaped from between his clenched teeth, and she pressed against him, pressed her thoughts against his and willed him to open up.

He resisted.

She kicked him again and again, pushing at his mind with hers as she did. He feebly tried to block and she broke his wrist for his trouble, pressed again with her thoughts.

Still he fought.

She spread his legs with her foot, and his eyes went wide and he tried weakly to turn away, to stop her, and then she rammed her foot home into his testicles and a scream burst out of his mouth as he curled up around himself into a fetal ball. The backwash of his pain struck her, muted by his stubborn clenching of his thoughts, but bad enough. She held her ground. His mind was teetering on the edge, his defenses letting go.

Sam dropped to her knees, grabbed the man's head by his short hair, yanked it back, then drove the barrel of the gun into his mouth. She heard teeth break as she jammed it into his throat. She pushed against him with all her mental strength, and finally he cracked.

Then what he knew streamed into her. And she saw. An island. A research base. These children, molded into something else, into something monstrous, something posthuman. A new species that would rule them all. And behind them, one man, using them as his tools…

The knowledge flowed into her, horrifying her, transfixing her. She searched for every detail, every bit she'd need to know to get them back…

The gun went off in her hand. She felt it, heard it, and only then saw the soldier's fingers around her own. He'd pulled the trigger.

He was still alive, but dying. The bullet had blown out the back of his throat, shattered his spine, sent bone shards through his brainstem. He was dying, all but decapitated by the blast. There was horror in his eyes, in his thoughts. He hadn't planned to…

But something had. Something planted in his mind. Planted by his master. By the man who would soon have Sarai and Kit and Mali and Aroon and the other children she loved. The man who'd killed Jake.

Shiva Prasad.

She felt the soldier die below her. But she'd seen enough. She knew where to go.

And no one was going to stop her.

37

GODS AND MONSTERS

Saturday October 27th

Kade fell fast asleep after they returned from the club. It felt so good to be doing something, to be making some progress. He'd find those bastards. He'd stop them.

He came fully awake in the early hours, as Feng rose to do his daily exercise.

Kade set himself to reviewing data, looking through the pings his new agent had sent back from around the world as it searched for the monsters behind Code Sample Alpha.

At midday Feng went off to retrieve the jeep and move it to a parking garage they'd found at the end of the block in case they needed to make a quick exit.

The data lulled Kade back to sleep. He dreamt of the NJ, of the conjoined minds of the dancers, of a million minds dancing together, a shared rhythm rising from their thoughts...

He woke abruptly, something flashing in his mind.

```
[Match: Rangan Shankari - confidence 96%]
[Match: Ilya Alexander - confidence 98%]
```

What? Was he dreaming?

[Match: Rangan Shankari - confidence 96%]

[Match: Ilya Alexander - confidence 98%]

One mind. Those alerts were from one mind.

Kade blinked, forced himself fully awake. Rangan. Ilya. Jesus.

He clicked on the alert, opened the encrypted connection, invoked the back door, sent the passcode.

And then he was in.

Martin Holtzmann felt the panic rising up around him, constricting around his throat, cutting off his air. The President had the most to gain. The words kept running through his head, driving all other thought out. Of course the President had the most to gain. And he who had the most to gain did it. The President had staged that assassination attempt. The President had killed dozens of Americans to ensure his own re-election.

Dear God.

Dear God.

The ground below Holtzmann's feet was cracking open. There was nothing there, no solidity, nothing to hold onto. He was going to fall into that abyss and keep falling, keep falling. This nightmare was going to swallow him up, swallow Anne with it, swallow up his boys, swallow everyone and everything he loved.

Because he knew something he shouldn't. Because if John Stockton would stage his own attempted assassination, would kill dozens of his supporters, dozens of federal employees, three of his own Secret Service agents...

...then he wouldn't hesitate to kill Martin Holtzmann, and anyone else who might know.

Holtzmann needed this out of his head. He needed to forget. He needed his suspicions gone. He needed his qualms about purging Nexus from the children erased. Then he needed the Nexus out of his mind, forever. He needed to forget he'd ever tried it, forget all of this.

Holtzmann reached out with his mind to his home's network for the first time in weeks, sent his thoughts out towards the Nexus boards, and started searching. There must be something out there. Something that would make him forget. Something that would erase his conscience. Something that would turn back the clock, to where it was before he'd ever downed that first vial, before he'd ever supped of this forbidden fruit.

He searched and searched and searched, finding dead end after dead end. There must be something that would do what he wanted. There must.

He was still searching, frantically, desperately, when a mind like a god's descended thunderously down onto his own. A monstrous mind, an epic mind, full of rage and murder. It crushed his will beneath its staggering force. Its mental fist closed painfully around his heart, and began to squeeze.

Kade sucked at the memories of Rangan and Ilya his agent had found in this mind. A montage of them spilled across his mind.

Rangan, tortured. Hooded and cuffed. Being electrocuted. Being smothered with a towel and suffocated while his body jerked and spasmed against its restraints.

And Ilya.

Ilya with her eyes closed, pale and still.

Cold. Lifeless.

Ilya dead.

It hit him like a blow. He opened his eyes and he was on his side, on the floor of the room in Saigon, a glass of water he'd had by the bedside on the floor, rolling on its side, water spilling out. He couldn't breathe. Dead! Dead!

And that face. The face seen in the mirror. He knew that face. He knew whose mind this was.

He felt the anger rising behind the shock. Anger like he'd felt in Thailand, like he'd felt after the inferno in Bangkok, anger like he'd felt every time he'd found someone using Nexus to kill or rape or steal, anger that threatened to erupt from within him.

Kade pushed his will down Martin Holtzmann's pathetic mind. This man was completely his. And by God he deserved to die.

Holtzmann tried to scream as the alien mind invaded his. No sound left his lips. Something grabbed control of his limbs, lifted him up, and threw him to the ground. A will unthinkably, inhumanly strong was plowing through him, racking him with pain.

YOU KILLED HER!

An image of Ilya Alexander filled his mind. Her autopsy photo. Her in life, the last time he'd seen her, weeks earlier.

No! he tried to say. *No! It wasn't me!*

Nothing came out of his mouth. He felt the mental fist close tighter around his heart. He couldn't breathe. He struggled against it, tried to push it out of his mind, but it was stronger than he could imagine, locked around him, impervious to his efforts.

DON'T LIE TO ME!

I'm not lying, he tried to say. *Please, I didn't kill her. I didn't want her to die!*

He pulled up the memory, him standing at the one-way mirror, looking down on the Nexus children, the news of her death coming through on his phone, his anger and frustration at the waste of it all!

His heart pounded in his chest with fear.

The mental hand closed into a fist inside him. A sharp pain stabbed through his chest, and then his heart's pounding was gone. Where it had been there was nothing. Dear God.

It had stopped his heart!

No. Please. Not this way!

Rangan, he pleaded with the mind holding him. *Children. Still alive.*

The world was dimming, growing darker, fading out, as oxygen stopped reaching his brain.

No. Please.

Please…

And then there was nothing.

Kade ripped into Holtzmann's mind in a blind rage. He seized control of the man's body, threw him from his chair and to the ground, crushed Holtzmann's will with the tools the back door afforded him.

This man was ERD. He was a leader of the organization that fought Nexus. The people who'd blackmailed him, who'd turned Narong Shinawatra into a robot assassin and led to his death, to Mai's death, to Lalana's death, a dozen deaths in that Bangkok inferno! The people who'd sent Rangan and Ilya and scores of his friends to jail. That had *killed Wats and killed Ilya!*

Kade wrapped his mental fist around the man's brainstem. He felt the power he held over Holtzmann's life, the supremacy, the absolute control, the complete domination of this pathetic creature. It was a drug, pulsing through him, hot with pleasure.

This man deserved to die.

Holtzmann struggled, pleaded, made excuses.

Kade ignored them all. With a clench of his mental fist he spasmed the man's brainstem, stopping his heart. The sweet bliss of power coursed through him.

Judge, jury, executioner, Ilya whispered in his head.

Please… the dying Holtzmann pleaded. *Rangan. Children. Still alive.*

The name hit him like a bucket of cold water. Rangan. Rangan! Rangan was still alive. Holtzmann was the one lead he had to save him!

FUCK!

Kade loosed his mental grip, let the brainstem resume its normal activity, searched for a pulse.

Nothing. The brainstem's behavior was erratic, confused, neural circuits temporarily disrupted by the surge of random pulses Kade had sent through it.

Holtzmann was passing out now. Consciousness fading as the flow of oxygen and nutrients to his brain ceased.

No. He needed this man alive.

Kade paired his own brainstem to Holtzmann's, pumped signals from his neurons into the analogous ones in Holtzmann's brain.

Chaos still ruled in Holtzmann's brainstem. Aberrant signals from his own neurons swamped the input from Kade's brain.

Kade amplified the input from his own brainstem to Holtzmann's again, ramped it up to four times strength.

Neural circuits started to reform, but there was still so much chaos, so much random behavior left over from Kade's attack. Holtzmann's heart was still stopped.

Kade pushed again, stepped up the input levels by a factor of ten, overruled all neural inputs coming into the Nexus-linked neurons in Holtzmann's brainstem with the signals from his own brain.

Order strengthened, but the heart still didn't beat.

He pushed one last time, harder, overlaying his own brainstem's neural activity onto Holtzmann's, and held it that way, forcing Holtzmann's brain to behave, to step back to regularity.

Lub-

Lub-

Holtzmann's heart stuttered, tried to turn over. Kade held on, kept pushing, kept imposing his own neural activity on Holtzmann's.

Lub-

Lub-

Lub dub. Lub dub.

And finally the man's heart beat again.

Kade pulled himself back into his body, rose to sitting on the bed.

He was shaking. He needed to get himself together. Holtzmann was out cold for the moment. He reached into the man's sleep centers, made sure Holtzmann would stay that way while he took a moment to think.

Oh, Kade, Ilya's voice said in his mind. *You almost killed him.*

He's still alive, Kade replied.

You got lucky, she said. *He could have died.*

He killed you! Kade shouted at the voice in his head.

He didn't. He showed you. He didn't want me to die.

He's responsible, Kade shot back angrily. *He's one of them. Your blood's on his hands. Wats' blood. A lot more than that.*

And you get to decide that? she asked him. *You're the judge now? Are you wiser than all humanity, Kade? Are you?*

Yes. If I have to be.

Then Ananda was in his thoughts. A memory of the monk.

When you suffer, Ananda had told him, *When you rage. When you weep. When you crave. That is when you must still your mind.*

Dammit! Kade raged. He slammed his good fist against the floor.

But Ananda was right. He had to be cool now. He had to think. Had to use this chance to get Rangan free.

Kade closed his eyes, folded his hands into his lap, took a few steadying breaths of *anapana*, then a few more, then a few more after that.

Breathe.

Breathe.

Layers of rage and grief peeled off him like an onion. Tears rolled down his face.

Breathe.

Breathe.

He opened his eyes again minutes later. The anger was still there. The loss was still there. But he was calmer now, he could think.

Breathe.

Holtzmann was Kade's best chance to get Rangan free. He couldn't squander that.

Kade checked the time. It was not quite 2am on the East Coast. He had some time before Holtzmann would be missed.

He had time, time to use the tools he'd taken from all those monsters he'd stopped, and employ them for *his* purposes – to free Rangan.

Kade tunneled back into Holtzmann's mind. With a handful of commands he pulled up the coercion tools he'd done his best to exterminate, set them to hovering in his mental space, overlaid atop representations of Holtzman's mind and brain. Then he grabbed one, and set to work sculpting the man into a slave, a slave who would do Kade's bidding.

Holtzmann woke slowly. He was back in his office chair. Everything seemed orderly.

I'm alive, he realized.

4.19am, the clock told him. Hours had passed.

Then he felt it. The knot in his stomach. The ache in his chest. The overwhelming compulsion. He would free Rangan Shankari.

38

PREPARATIONS

Saturday October 27th

Breece woke before dawn, Ava wrapped in his arms. They'd made love with a quiet urgency the night before, their eyes burrowing into one another's. Intensely bonded even despite the lack of Nexus.

He held her for a while, listening to her breathing. Then it was time.

They gathered in the kitchen. Ava briefed them on the mule, on the planned pickup today. Hiroshi reviewed the changes to the Nexus code they'd be using. The Nigerian prepped them on the weapon.

And Breece went over the targets with them one moretime.

Daniel Chandler, former Democratic senator from South Carolina, architect of the bill that had created the ERD and banned whole swaths of scientific inquiry and human enhancement, had returned to his childhood home of Houston. After re-establishing residence, he'd launched his campaign to become the first Democratic Governor of Texas in a generation. And he was winning. Chandler could point at the events of the last few months, then point back at the law that bore his name – the Chandler Act – and show that he'd always been a leader in fighting transhuman technologies and those who would use them.

One week from today, on Saturday November 3rd, three days before the election, Chandler would appear at a special Houston prayer breakfast, broadcast live to the state and the nation.

His host would be the Reverend Josiah Shepherd, the man who'd told the country that God would reward those who sent geneticists and fertility doctors to hell. The man whose followers had murdered Breece's parents.

Well, if there was a hell, Breece was going to send both men there, first class.

Taking lives was serious business. Every person they killed had the potential to live forever. Breece refused to do that lightly.

"Wives?" he asked.

"They chose their husbands," Ava replied. "Guilty."

"Supporters?" Breece went on.

"They're material supporters of Chandler's war on science," Hiroshi said. "Guilty."

"Security?"

"Soldiers," the Nigerian said. "They chose which side to fight for."

"Press?"

There was a pause this time.

"What's the risk?" Ava wanted to know.

"How far back will they be from the stage?" Hiroshi asked.

They debated it for some time, then opted to scale the weapon down. They left it easily large enough to take out their primary targets, but small enough that the danger to news media should be small.

Finally Breece came to the last check. "Children?"

"Seats are five thousand dollars a pop," Hiroshi said. "Shouldn't be any kids there."

"We can't rule that out," Breece said.

"They're being raised by the enemy," the Nigerian said. "They'll grow up as the enemy."

"Not all of them," Breece said.

"It's an acceptable risk," Ava added. "They've killed more than enough of ours."

Breece looked at her, and she held his eyes. He thought of her own trauma, the nightmares that still woke her, her own baby dead in her arms.

Breece nodded. "Acceptable risk."

They gathered at the garage, then spent the next two hours rigging up the shielding. They unrolled fine mesh panels, adhered the panels to every surface, connected each to its neighbors, tested, found holes in the shielding, fixed connections, and repeated until they were done. In the end they had a Faraday cage that would keep any electromagnetic signals inside the garage from leaking out. They rolled out a thick carpet to protect the mesh on the floor, and then it was time for the next phase.

Ava led this one, driving alone in a nondescript car with borrowed plates. Breece and the Nigerian followed discreetly, three cars back, ready to provide backup.

They parked in the outdoor lot on the east side of the Houston Sands Mall, and waited for their target to arrive for her weekly hair appointment.

The white Cadillac pulled into the lot eighteen minutes later. It parked and Mrs Miranda Shepherd, wife of the Reverend Josiah Shepherd, stepped out.

Ava was out of her own car now, in a white blouse and black slacks, her dark hair blowing in the wind. A huge Texan smile was on her face.

Miranda Shepherd closed her car door behind her, and moved towards the mall. Through his car window, Breece watched as Ava hailed her. He saw Shepherd turn, Ava close the distance between them, that huge smile still on her face.

Shepherd listened, then smiled and nodded herself. She turned, pointing out towards the highway, gesturing with her hands, giving directions to a lost young lady.

All the while, the aerosolized DWITY variant was pumping out of Ava's blouse, making its way into Miranda Shepherd's lungs, then via her bloodstream to Shepherd's brain. Within a few seconds, Shepherd was wobbling slightly, woozy now, susceptible to suggestions.

He saw Ava reach out and take the befuddled woman's hand. The micro-injector on Ava's thumb would have just pumped more DWITY into Miranda Shepherd's bloodstream. The televangelist's wife looked confused now, her eyes glassy and blank. Ava smiled, talked soothingly, then she led Miranda Shepherd by the hand, back to the nondescript car with false plates, and drove away with her.

The Nigerian started up their own car, led them to the spot where Ava had been parked. Breece opened the door, reached down, and picked up Miranda Shepherd's phone in his gloved hand.

As the Nigerian drove, Breece placed the voice modulator over the phone's mic, and dialed the hair salon. He spoke, and a software model trained on dozens of hours of recordings of Miranda Shepherd transformed his voice into a feminine Texas drawl.

"Betsy? Hi. It's Miranda," Breece said in Shepherd's voice. "I'm sorry, darlin', but I have to cancel my appointment this mornin'. No, can't come in next week, we have the prayer breakfast. But I'll be back in two weeks. OK, thank ya, Betsy!"

He clicked off the phone, then dropped it into a shielded bag.

The Nigerian drove them on, towards the garage and the reprogramming of Mrs Miranda Shepherd.

39

INFORMATION EXTRACTION

Saturday October 27th

Shanghai suffered. Riots broke out. Hungry looters smashed windows in grocery stores and food distribution centers. Murders happened in the streets. Criminal gangs roamed free. Underworld lords enforced brutal order in small isolated pockets. Half the city still lacked power. Subway tunnels remained flooded. Sewage water still choked some streets. Fires burned in now-abandoned buildings. Soldiers patrolled the filthy streets, shooting the looters and rioters they found.

Elsewhere, China herself changed and the hardliners seized power. Chen laughed bitterly at himself. His daughter had done this, had handed the hardliners this opportunity. His monstrous daughter, in trying to save her mother's life, had doomed her.

And worse, of course. Much worse. Scientific projects were being shelved "for review". The net censors were back in force, tighter than he'd ever seen them. He read of the "terrorist cells" being raided and he recognized some of the names. Intellectuals. Dissidents. Those who'd dared to question the state, to propose modest reforms, or directions that differed from those the hardliners wanted.

Shanghai had swung his country hard back in the reactionary direction.

Chen numbed himself to it. Only one thing mattered. When would the Secure Computer Center be back online? When could he get back to that quantum abomination and wring one last secret out of her?

There was no guilt left now, The thing that thought it was his wife would be dead soon in any case. They'd back it up in case of some future value, some way to extract the tens of billions of yuan that had been spent on it. But he doubted that backup would ever be restored. No. Let it live just a tiny bit longer, just long enough to give him the equivalence theorem.

What a last gift that would be. If the equivalence theorem existed – and it must, or why else would she have hinted at it – then any conventional computing algorithm could be incredibly accelerated via a quantum process. Quantum computing would go from a specialized technique for solving certain problems – cryptography and database searches and optimizations – to a tool that could speed up *everything* by billions of times, trillions of times.

And he, Chen Pang, the "discoverer" of the equivalence theorem...

He'd be famous, of course. A Nobelist. The greatest mind in computing since Turing. A multi-billionaire from the commercial spinoffs. One of the richest and most powerful men alive. Even in a hardliner's China, he would be untouchable, among the elite of the elite.

No, he told himself. Not just for me. For the world, for the benefit to mankind.

Chen nodded soberly. Yes, that was why he would do this. Not just for his own glory. But to benefit his fellow man.

All he had to do was inflict a little pain on the insane ghost of his dead wife. It was really no conflict at all.

After three days, the SCC was ready. Chen smiled and summoned his driver.

Today he would break her. Today he would break *it*. Today he would make history.

Ling waited until the apartment told her that her father had left, then reached out with her thoughts and opened the door to her mother's room. Cautiously she limped out into the flat. A livid bruise still covered her face from where her father had struck her. Her arms sported burns from the scalding tea his blow had spilled over her.

She'd lived like this, like a scavenger, since that day. She'd kept the door to her mother's chamber locked, then snuck out when her father was asleep, and only then after she told the apartment to lock him in his own room so he couldn't hit her again.

Shanghai's net limped gradually back towards full functionality. It was sweet to swim in data once more, but she was forced to be more careful now. There were strange programs out there, evolved things, AIs she'd never seen before. All looking for the source of the attack on Shanghai. She avoided them as best she could, sending her thoughts out into the wider net with only the utmost caution.

In the kitchen now, she scavenged food from the flat's pantry and refrigerator, took them back with her to mother's room. There was a tiny freezer in mother's room, of course, hidden behind a panel in the wall. But it held other supplies. Injectors and ampules of silvery fluid laden with nanodevices to suffuse the brain. Not food. Better, but not a replacement. Ling left it alone.

Someday, she thought, I'll live on pure data.

Outside, she could see Shanghai with her own eyes. These few blocks glowed, an island of light, surrounded by a vast sea of darkness, punctuated by the dull, chaotic red of open flame. Ling stared at that darkness, at what she'd done to Shanghai, then she turned, looked closer, at the giant visage across the street. Zhi Li smiled at her, pursed her inhumanly perfect lips, winked one electronically sculpted eye, held up some product to tempt the humans with.

Down below, the wet streets were empty. The giant actress pushed her wares, but no one was there to see.

Ling turned her back on the city, sealed the door to her mother's room again, ate her food, and searched the net for any way to burrow her thoughts below Jiao Tong University and to her mother.

40
WHERE IT ENDS

Saturday October 27th

Kade lay in the narrow bed in the room he shared with Feng. He was shaking. Rangan tortured. Ilya dead. Dead. All a waste. A fucking waste. They didn't even know the codes to the Nexus back doors! Kade had changed those back door codes, changed them in Ananda's monastery, just hours before American soldiers had invaded and he'd been forced to release Nexus 5 into the wild.

Oh God, Ilya. Rangan.

And what he himself had just done... It was slowly sinking into him. Turning Holtzmann into a slave. Almost killing the man.

You're losing control, Ilya's voice whispered in his ear. *You're turning into a monster.*

Breathe.

Breathe.

Feng found him there, an hour later.

Kade opened his mind to his friend, showed him what had happened, showed him that Ilya was dead, showed him what he'd done to Holtzmann.

Feng sat with him, absorbed, listened as Kade spilled it out. And finally Feng spoke.

"I'm sorry, Kade," he said. "Sorry your friend is dead. I'm glad you're worried about what you did. But sometimes no good option."

Kade shook his head. "I can't let that happen again, Feng. A million people running Nexus. I have all this power. I can't lose my head, can't lose control."

Feng spoke softly. "Maybe too much power. Too much control. Trust people, that's what Ananda told you, yeah? Maybe you should let go, close the back door."

Ananda. Kade remembered. *Are you wiser than all humanity?* Ananda had asked him.

No.

He closed his eyes, and in his mind's eye the icon for the script was there, the bot that would close the back door. It hovered in the upper left of his virtual workspace. All he had to do was invoke it, and he'd close off that hole he'd left for himself, forever.

Then another memory flashed through his mind, a blinking light, wires, then chaos, and death.

War is coming, Shu had said.

Kade opened his eyes, looked into Feng's. "But if I do that, Feng, who's going to stop the PLF? Who's going to stop them from starting a war?"

Feng broke the eye contact, looked down at his hands.

Kade spoke again. "Sometimes, there's no good option."

Kade wanted to stay in, lick his wounds, see if he could turn up any additional leads on the PLF. But Feng insisted that Kade get out, do something to reset his thoughts.

So they went down to club Heaven hours later. It was Hell Night when they arrived. The Saturday before Halloween. A night of demons.

The door girl looked them over skeptically in their lack of costumes, but she took their money, stamped their wrists, and let them in. The bouncer glowered like the night before.

It was early still, just barely evening, and the club was sparsely populated. The music was downtempo, quiet enough to talk over. The dance floor was empty, the stage where the DJ and NJ and go-go dancers would be later tonight held a few racks of equipment and nothing else.

They took a seat at the bar. Kade wasn't hungry, wasn't thirsty. Even after the meditation and the hours coding, the shock of the day still coursed through him. Feng ordered drinks for them both, made Kade down one as he watched, then ordered food as well.

Kade felt the drink mellow him. Felt the food restore him. He had to stay strong right now. He had to stop the PLF from killing again. He had to avert that war between human and posthuman. He had to stay steady to do that. Later, there'd be a time to collapse, to process Ilya's death and his near murder of Holtzmann and everything else. For now, he had a job to do.

So he focused on eating, on watching his breath, on remembering the good things he'd seen happening around the world with Nexus. Tried to maintain his mental balance.

The club filled in slowly. Minds brushed Kade's. Some he'd felt the night before. Some were new.

Before long the club was crowded, people all dressed up, drinking, talking, laughing, waiting for the DJ to go on. The shirtless Vietnamese boy was here again, and through him Kade could feel the same banker's mind in London, riding this boy, spending his afternoon in London on the town in Saigon instead. He caught sight of the brunette from the restaurant too, through a gap in the crowd. She was peering at him from across the room. Then bodies shifted and she was obscured from his view.

Kade sat back, sipped at his drink, watched the crowd, and let his agent loose upon them, and the world.

Sabrina Jensen stepped out of the club and into Saigon's muggy night air. She'd seen him three times now. And this time she was almost sure. He looked different than the pictures. The hair was different. The tattoos. He looked older, more tired. But the face was the same. And he was always with that Chinese man.

This was the one they were looking for, the one whose picture she'd seen posted with the reward. One thousand dollars would extend her trip another month, at least.

She'd thought to approach him, tell him someone was looking for him, just in case it was some sort of scam or he was in some sort of trouble. But he was so aloof. Not friendly at all.

Sabrina linked the Nexus OS in her head to her phone, downloaded the image she'd snapped with Nexus. Then she broke the link and dialed the number from the post.

Sabrina smiled as it rang. She was about to make a cool grand. "Bali, here I come."

"I want that soldier *disciplined*," Shiva told Ashok over their link. "Then I want him *out* of my employ."

Shiva breathed to control his frustration. A grantee killed by one of his own men! A second security man lost, dead according to his biometrics. Children traumatized. The American agent still on the loose.

There would be hush money to pay. Cleanup to remove any linkage of the events to Shiva and the Mira Foundation. They had to boost security now around the island, find some way to locate that woman. But the worst of it was that those children had seen someone they trusted shot and killed! They'd been forcibly separated from everyone they knew. That trauma would last years, would impede his efforts to build trust...

"We may have a sighting of Lane."

Shiva whirled. It was Hayes, the commander of the squad Shiva had brought with him to Vietnam. "What?"

"We just intercepted a message internal to a group of bounty hunters," Hayes went on. "They believe Lane is in a tourist club in Saigon right now. They're moving in to get him."

"Then we have to get there first," Shiva said.

41

HELL

Saturday October 27th

Kade sat at the bar with Feng and watched the club heat up.

The crowd grew thicker, the music louder. Then the DJ was there, on stage. The same one as last night. Asian, muscular, with short black hair and mirrored shades and a dark T-shirt and jeans that showed off his physique. The go-go dancers climbed up to the stage as well, all in glossy red tonight – boots, hot pants, pasties, streaks through their hair. Red devil horns and shiny red devil wings topped it off.

The smoke machine kicked in, covering the floor of the club with a foot-thick layer of smoke. Lights turned the smoke red, made the tendrils of it that crept up people's legs into an illusion of flames.

The music faded out, the crowd stilled, and then the DJ started in. He kicked off the set with a slow build, a flux piece that started at the downtempo end of the spectrum and then grew deeper, faster, harder, until, just minutes in, it was epic, and the crowd was dancing.

Kade felt a small smile grow across his face. Rangan would love this.

Then he realized what he'd thought. Ilya would have loved this too. And the smile faded. It was 10pm here. Mid-morning on a Saturday on the East Coast. He'd check on Holtzmann when they left the club, make sure the man was on track.

Then red smoke rose in a thick cloud from the stage, and he caught his breath in anticipation, and then *she* was in the club, the NJ, the Nexus jockey. He felt her mind even as the smoke obscured her. And she was as glorious as she'd been the night before, sending out waves of exultation and dance and near hallucinatory visions of how the club looked to her, from up on stage, singing, raising her arms above the demonic figures crowding the club. Tonight, Heaven looked like a piece of Hell. She loved it.

Her thoughts moved him, captivated him, pulled him out of his funk and into something else, something reverent, something full of awe, something he used to feel.

The smoke on stage cleared and he could see her again. *Lotus* she called herself. She was in red tonight, a long dress of red sequins, low in the back, tight through the waist and hips, then loose again from mid-thigh to her feet. She wore iridescent red gloves that went beyond her elbows. The hair that had been platinum the night before was the color of flame, now, with bright strands that pulsed to the music woven through it. She was a mermaid, made of fire.

She held her arms out above the crowd in benediction and parted her ruby lips to sing to them, mouth wide open, head canted back, a soaring aria that intertwined with the techno beats. Then she pumped out her mental song and it was so so good. Darker and hotter even, than the night before. It seemed a betrayal of everyone who'd died because of him to dance. But it also seemed a betrayal of Ilya and Rangan *not* to dance.

Feng felt his thoughts, patted him on the back, and pointed him at the dance floor. "Go," his friend said. "You need it. I wait here."

So Kade went. He went out onto the floor of a club that reminded him so very much of the parties that he and Rangan and Ilya used to throw. And he danced. He moved slowly, at first. He kept his eyes on the floor, or closed. He felt those around him, let them feel him, but made no motion to interact. He danced for Ilya. He danced for Rangan. He danced for himself, to clear his head, to fill his spirit back up, and to give him the strength to make it through all the perils that were sure to be ahead.

Shiva sat in the back of the armored command center as they rushed into Saigon. Hayes was next to him, studying an array of screens. A map of the area showed on one. Structural diagrams of the building that had been hastily downloaded on another. On a third, status of his team members, both human and drone. And on the fourth, running progress on the attempt by their hacker to penetrate the club's systems.

They were tapped into this group of bounty hunters. That was the one useful thing they'd gotten from the man Shiva had interrogated – the frequencies and codes and identities of the others in his group. They were lucky that it had been that specific group that had found Kade. Had it been another, they wouldn't have known of it.

Audio transmissions came across the channel they'd broken into.

"South-east corner, fifty cal and tranq, ready."

"North-west corner, fifty cal and tranq, ETA three minutes."

"Backup 1 ready."

"Backup 2 ready."

"Door 1 ready."

"Door 2 ready."

"Bait ready."

Hayes plotted it on the map. The bounty hunters were well organized. They'd learned from their last attempt to capture Lane. They were placing teams of snipers on the rooftops nearby, armed with heavy caliber weapons to take out Lane's traveling companion, and tranquilizer weapons to incapacitate Lane. They were waiting for the two to emerge.

And Shiva had no way to warn the boy.

Kade danced hard now, his limbs moving to the beat, his eyes closed, his thoughts lost in his own head, until the sweat dripping from his body and the beat and the amplified ecstatic rhythms of Lotus's mind and the hundred other minds that brushed his drove everything else away.

He heard Lotus's song, he felt her thoughts, and felt them changing, reflecting the crowd, adapting to them. The music changed as well, flowed, responded. And he realized, *they* were making music, the crowd, the dancers, and Lotus was channeling it, absorbing the thoughts and emotions of the heaving throng, playing their mental music back to them.

The feedback loop closed and he wasn't just Kade any more, wasn't just a person. He was part of something more, a living breathing heaving organism, thousand-limbed, hundred-headed, a gestalt of all these minds and bodies.

Grief leached out from him, absorbed and processed and healed by the union. He moved his arms and legs and body to the beat, thrashed his head and sent his new braids flinging, somehow perfectly in sync with the bodies next to him. He *was* the beat. *They* were the beat. How could any of them step wrong?

This is *samadhi*, he realized. Meditation. Complete absorption.

The walls of his ego faded, dissipated, subsumed in this merger. He caught glimpses of a thousand thoughts, of here and now, of memories and visions. He saw the world like this, saw scientists merging into greater forms, people abandoning their distinctions.

There was no Kade, he saw. No self, no other. There was just this experience, this epicness he was part of, this surging, moving, billowing, exulting radiance of an organism that was the crowd, was the DJ, was the tiny fragment called Lotus. This was real, more real than he was, more real than any individual. This was the now.

He caught a flash of a thin layer of consciousness encircling the globe and it was *his* thought but now it was *their* thought and he knew it was real, not just a fantasy, and he reached out with this thoughts so he could touch those million other minds and pull all those bright points of light into this dance, this moment, this glorious luminous union…

Kade.

Something was tugging at this fragment, pulling at it.

Kade!

Feng. Feng should be here, dancing, merging, joining them!

Kade! You're being watched!

An image crossed the fragment's mind, a glimpse, an Asian man, muscled, shaved head, tattooed. His face was a mask, his eyes dead, scanning from side to side.

The cold splash of danger struck Kade, yanking him back. He was on a dance floor, surrounded by moving, exulting bodies. Their joyous minds called to him. The ecstatic music of their thoughts…

Come back to the bar, Feng said.

The union beckoned. *Danger is an illusion*, it whispered. *You're just a small piece. Death doesn't matter. The whole lives on.*

Kade shivered, and realized what he'd been about to do. To reveal those million minds, to reach out to them all at once... He shook his head hard, fought to snap out of the trance of union, to remember who he was.

Smile and laugh, Feng sent him. **Get a drink.**

Kade forced himself to smile on the dance floor, wiped sweat from his brow, and worked his way out of the crowd, squeezing past gyrating men and women, all moving in sync, hips and hands and minds reaching out to pull him back into their whole.

Merger. The lifting of the veil of *maya*. The sweet oblivion of the self. God he wanted it.

But I matter too, Kade told himself. Not just the whole. The individual.

He held on to that thought as he slipped through the press of bodies.

Feng was at the bar, smiling, making every appearance of enjoying himself.

"You having fun?" Feng shouted over the crowd.

"You know it!" Kade forced a smile, forced himself to focus on the here and now.

Now what? he asked Feng.

Can you see front and back doors? Feng asked. **Through people's eyes?**

Kade nodded mentally. He leaned on the bar, facing away from their watcher, closed his eyes, and reached out towards the front of the club, hopping from mind to mind, fighting to stay clear of that call to union, until he found the view he needed.

Two of them out front, Kade said, showing Feng what he saw.

Kade took his thoughts the other direction, to the service entrance in the back.

Two more out back.

Feng nodded mentally, his mind calm and cool.

We'll go out the back then. Let them think we don't see them. Joke's on them.

Kade nodded. Feng felt no fear. He'd trust his friend. There was no one he'd rather have with him here and now.

Joke's on them, he told Feng, and forced another smile.

"North-west corner ready, fifty cal and tranq," came the intercepted voice.

"Roger that," came a reply across the same channel. "Go bait."

Shiva held his breath. A minute later a new voice came across the channel. "Bait has contact. They've seen me."

"They're trying to lure Lane and his friend out," Hayes said. "Where the snipers can pick them off."

"What's our ETA?" Shiva asked.

"Six minutes for the drones," Hayes replied. "Twelve minutes for us."

Too slow, Shiva thought. The bounty hunters will get him first!

"We're into the club's systems!" came the voice of their hacker. "Cameras, security system, the works."

"Can you see Lane?" Hayes asked.

"It's a zoo in there," the hacker replied. "No sight of him."

The channel came to life again. "Targets moving towards the back door. Repeat. Targets moving towards back door."

"South-west corner, shooters ready," came the reply.

Damn it. They had to be there *now*. They had to stop those snipers from taking out Lane and his companion.

Shiva turned to the hacker. "Can you trigger the fire alarm?"

"Looking…" the hacker said. "Fire alarms. Yes."

Hayes looked up at Shiva. "Flush everyone else out? Confuse the snipers?"

Shiva nodded. "Will it work?"

"Better than nothing," Hayes replied. Then, to the hacker, "Do it."

Kade got up calmly from the bar. Feng went ahead of him, and they started to wind their way through the crowd towards the back, the second bar, the restrooms, and the other exit from the club. The crowd beckoned to Kade, that sweet union, that sweet forgetting of the illusion that he existed, that he mattered.

But he remembered now. He remembered who he was and why he mattered.

Feng had a beer bottle in his hand, and Kade could feel his friend scanning, keeping track of the bounty hunter in the bar with them, looking for additional weapons he could pick up. That barstool. The mic stand. The tall bottle of whisky behind the bar.

Then a piercing sound blasted through the club. White lights came on. Emergency exit signs lit up. The piercing noise buzzed again and again and again, now with a voice over it.

"A fire has been detected," a voice droned over the music. "Please exit the building. A fire has been detected. Please exit the building. A fire has been detected…"

Confusion ruled around him. Kade felt chaos ripple through minds, tear down the coherence that had been there seconds before. People looked around. Was there really a fire? A false alarm? The DJ turned down the music, uncertain. Lotus's mind was indecisive.

Then the sprinklers kicked in, raining cold water on everyone, and the crowd made up its mind. Someone jostled Kade from behind, and he felt the crowd start to push towards the exits. Out of reflex he moved with them. Then Feng had hold of his arm, was yanking him off to the side, out of the way of the river of humanity making for the exits, over between a six-foot-tall stack of speakers and the wall of the club.

Down! Feng sent to him, and Kade dropped to a crouch, partially hidden by the speakers, Feng at his side.

What's going on? he asked in confusion.

Then the bounty hunter they'd seen pushed through the crowd, feet from them, and there was a gun in his hand.

Shiva listened as the bounty hunters' channel burst into noise.

"Fire alarm."

"Crazy. Can't see target."

"Can't see him in the crowd moving out."

"ETA?" Shiva asked Hayes.

"Three and nine minutes," the commander replied.

"Can the drones take out the snipers?" Shiva asked.

"Affirmative," Hayes answered.

Then across the bounty hunters' channel: "North-west, south-west, fire gas into the building. Repeat, into the building. Backup 1, ram the wall."

Kade barely had time to tense at the sight of the man and the gun. The bounty hunter's eyes widened and the gun started to rise. Feng's mind was suddenly like ice. The world slowed almost to a halt, and then his friend was there, impossibly fast. Feng took the bounty hunter's gun wrist in one vise-like grip and punched the man in the face hard enough that his head snapped back with an audible crack. The gun exploded in the same instant, sending a round into the wall by his side, and Kade felt the crowd jump in response. Fear flared across their minds, and people started rushing, pushing harder, crushing each other against walls or overstuffed doorways.

Then something crashed in through a window. Something small and hard and moving fast. It hit a boy in a devil costume in the belly, sent pain lancing out from his mind, knocked him reeling back into three more dancers. The crowd held them up and the canister that had struck him fell to the floor, hissing out something that scattered the now-white fog. Kade felt Feng's mind fill with firing angles and escape options and the trajectories of the scores of unpredictable bodies that were the crowd.

Another canister whistled in through another window, lifting a girl in a transparent red skirt off her feet and into a table that collapsed beneath her, sending glasses and bottles flying and crashing to the ground. Kade could feel the intense pain of something broken inside her abdomen, her sudden burst of terror.

He felt the crowd teeter on the verge of panic. People were coughing near the canisters. They were slumping, falling. He could feel them fading in his mind. Another canister punched through the window. He saw the shirtless Vietnamese boy, the one being ridden from London, try to jump out of the club through the now demolished window. A canister struck him in the head. The force of the impact knocked him down and out of Kade's sight.

There were people everywhere, a mass of them, upright and crowding the doors, screaming, yelling, trying to push each other out of the way, crawling over each other to make it to the exit. Others were slumping over in the middle of the club where the gas was reaching them. He saw the pretty brunette, trying to push her way through the mass of people, screaming. More and more revelers were swaying, falling as the gas spread. Every direction was blocked. The Nexus link that had been sublime union was now filled with terror and panic. Kade felt it press in on him, a cold dark tide of fear trying to take him under.

Then Feng's mind closed around him. He could feel his friend's resolve, feel his calm. They were getting out of here.

Feng pushed Kade out of his way. Then he reached up and grabbed a speaker the size of a trash bin off the stack beside them. Feng swung the speaker back, then drove it forward into the wall like a battering ram, embedding a third of its length in the plaster and wood of the structure.

Another canister shot into through the window, struck the bar, ricocheted into the illuminated wall of bottles behind it, sent alcohol and broken glass shrapnel everywhere. Kade heard more panicked screams as the glass lacerated people. More than half the crowd was down now. The rest were coughing. Kade was coughing. He could feel whatever was in the gas working on him. He reached into his mind to boost acetylcholine, boost adrenaline, try to keep himself awake...

Feng yanked the speaker free of the wall, swung it back again with both hands, drove it forward.

Then the wall exploded and something huge burst in. Kade saw it in slow motion through Feng's eyes but it was too late, too slow. The armored jeep's massive front end struck the speaker and then Feng, and then he disappeared as the vehicle roared into the club.

42

BATTLE ROYALE

Saturday October 27th

Shiva clenched his fists as the first view of the scene appeared. Overhead, their quartet of drones reached the site. Each was a meter wide flying wing, radar absorbent, color shifting, propelled by twin fuel-cell-powered engines, loaded with cameras and small, lethal weapons.

On screen their cameras showed an armored jeep surging down the street, scattering people, striking some head on, and then crashing in through the wall of the club. From the other direction a second armored jeep was coming. Young men and women jumped out of its way, not all of them fast enough.

Hayes yelled into his microphone, "Fire on incoming vehicle. Fire on snipers."

Over the city, the drones launched cigar-thick micromissiles – small carbon-and-titanium javelins – that ignited their solid rocket boosters, canted their control fins, and bolted out towards their targets on streaks of white-hot flame.

Explosions lit up the screens, boomed through the audio pickups. Bright flashes flared on the rooftops across from both entrances to the club. He saw a burning man-sized shape tumbling from one to the street below. The front of the second jeep burst into flames as two darts struck it. The armored vehicle careened down the street, out of control, veered left, away from the club, rammed into the crowd at high speed, and embedded itself into the building across the street.

Shouts and cries rose from the crowd.

The bounty hunters' channel burst into chaos, voices stepping all over each other.

"Missiles. Hit… Snipers down. Fire."

But there was still the jeep inside the building. They couldn't fire on it. They didn't know what was going on.

"Get us in there," Shiva snapped at Hayes.

Kade flinched as the armored jeep crashed through the wall just inches from him. It roared forward and Feng disappeared with a burst of mental pain. The jeep skidded to a halt in a cloud of dust and rubble. Water shot out from a severed wall pipe. The jeep's doors opened and four men leapt out. They wore full body suits with hard plates, reinforced joints, and black armored masks that fully concealed their faces. In their hands were submachine guns. Strapped to their sides were more weapons. On their backs were air supplies.

Kade shrank back behind the speakers, tried not to breathe, tried not to cough. He could feel Feng out there still. Every other mind was fading out now, as the gas reached every corner of the club. He could feel pain and fear from those still clinging to consciousness.

He cranked up his adrenaline and acetylcholine levels higher, trying to counteract the wooziness he felt from the gas. He could feel Feng gritting his teeth, clamping down on the pain and focusing. The four troopers were searching, turning over bodies with their feet. Searching for him.

Feng spoke in his mind. He sounded tired, in pain. **Run. I'll fight them.**

NO, Kade replied. He activated Bruce Lee. Targeting circles appeared in his vision. **I'm not going without you.**

He felt Feng shake his head mentally. **You're the dumbest friend I have.**

I'm the *only* friend you have, Feng, Kade replied.

Yeah. Like I said, Feng chuckled in reply.

Then Feng was up, and the world froze. A long piece of steel pipe was in his hand. He was behind an armored trooper, bringing the pipe around in a viciously fast swing at the man's helmeted head. The bounty hunter jerked, alerted by something, started to turn. Then Feng's pipe hit him at incredible speed.

The blow rocked the man to the side, sent a spiderweb of cracks out through his visor, knocked him off balance. Feng swung back at the man's knees, lighting fast, swept the soldier's feet out from under him. For an instant Kade saw the man suspended in midair, hanging there supine, his feet off the ground, caught frozen in the midst of his backwards topple, immobile in Feng's accelerated perceptions.

Then time resumed. The man crashed to the floor, flat on his back, his gun firing, muzzle flare erupting from it, bullets spraying into the ceiling, their paths zipping rays of red light in Feng's battle vision.

Then Feng was on one knee, the pipe driven into the man's throat and embedded into the floor beyond like a spear, blood fountaining everywhere.

Feng rolled as he finished the blow, taking the man's submachine gun with him. The other troopers were yelling now, turning. One opened fire as Feng rolled behind the bar.

The other two turned as well. All three fired into the bar. Kade picked one, clicked to designate him as a target, and jammed on the full attack button.

Bruce Lee hurled Kade's body into a flying kick, weak and off-balance from the gas. The bounty hunter turned and smacked Kade out of the air. The blow sent him reeling.

[Bruce_Lee: Attack Failed ⊗]

Then the man had Kade by the arm, was dragging him towards the armored jeep, shoving him in the open door.

Then there was static, everywhere, spheres of static, Nexus static.

And the head of the bounty hunter who had him exploded.

Nakamura milled through the club called Mango, his backpacker costume in place, upgraded slightly for a Saturday night. Nexus was everywhere here. This was the kind of place Lane would feel at home in. If he'd let his guard down sufficiently...

[Shots fired, 819 Bùi Viện Street]

The alert was pulled from the Vietnamese People's Police network. That address was at the other end of the Bến Thành district. Another club with a concentration of Nexus.

Nakamura turned and pushed his way against the crowd, swam like a fish against the current, until he was through the doors and out into the night. His jeep was back at his apartment, impractical in the maze of streets here. The club where the alert had come from was just over a mile away. Nakamura broke into a run. He'd be there in three minutes.

Shiva watched the feeds as his soldiers stormed the building, took down the two remaining bounty hunters. The club was a shambles. One wall had been destroyed, the windows blown out. Revelers were strewn about, many injured, some bleeding or broken or dead from the impact of the jeep or the crossfire of bullets. The rest were unconscious.

"There," he said and tapped on the screen. "Lane."

Hayes nodded, and the medic rushed forward.

Someone grabbed Kade, a new man, in a respirator but no armor.

The man was fitting a respirator over Kade's head, then patting him down, yelling something through the mask and over the sound of the ringing alarm.

"What?"

What's happening?

The sound of the alarm ended abruptly.

"Are you hurt?" the man yelled again.

"Feng," Kade said, muffled through the mask over his head. Then Feng was up, a submachine gun in his hand. There was blood splattered on his face, blood on his shirt, blood on his pants.

"Get back," Feng said.

Kade struggled to take in the situation. There were seven of the new force. Six with guns, plus the one leaning over him. They wore masks and sleek black fighting armor, less bulky than the bounty hunters, but even more deadly-looking. They had silenced automatic weapons in their hands, but none were pointed at him.

Every one of them had a sphere of static around him. Distortion on the Nexus frequencies. Jamming, but on a local scale.

Shielding, he realized. They're running Nexus, but they're shielding themselves.

"Get back," Feng repeated, pointing his gun at the man over Kade.

"We're here to help," the medic said.

Kade? Feng sent.

"Who are you?" Kade asked.

"Activate my avatar," Shiva said. "I want to talk to him."

The medic stepped back from him.

Then a hologram appeared in the middle of the room, projected by a fist-sized spider-like robot beneath it.

The figure was old, Indian, long white hair, dressed in a simple white garment.

"Kade," said a projected voice. "We're not your enemies. We're friends."

"What do you want?" Kade asked.

"I want you to come with me," the hologram said.

"Who are you?" Kade asked.

"I'm someone who needs your help," it replied.

"My help?"

"Yes," the hologram said. "To save the world."

"Not interested," Feng spoke from the side of the room.

The hologram turned in his direction. "Are you sure?" The image of the man raised an eyebrow. Then he turned back to Kade. "It seems like you've been trying quite hard to do that already. I applaud what you're doing. We can do it together."

Kade felt his hackles rise. He knew why someone would want his help. There was only one reason he could think of.

"I'm not interested," he said.

The holographic figure smiled. "But you don't deny it, do you? You've been hacking into brains, haven't you? Saving the world one criminal at a time? There are more than a million people running Nexus now, did you know?

All because of you. There are thousands more each day. And you have a back door into each of those minds. That's a great power for good, Kade. I can help you use that power."

Ilya rumbled somewhere in the back of Kade's mind. *Where does it end, Kade? No one should have that kind of power.*

Not now, Ilya! he yelled back at the voice inside him.

He swallowed, spoke calmly to the hologram, his mind spinning, searching for a way out of this. He probed the shielding around these soldiers. Too strong. He could tell. Too strong for even his mind to burrow through.

"I'm not interested in help," he told the hologram. "I'll let you know if that changes."

As he spoke he reached out, searching for a mind. A mind that would have what he needed. Lotus. Where *was* she?

The Indian figure shook its head. "Young man, you have the key to more than a million minds. Everyone is looking for you. What if the Americans get you? What if the Chinese get you? You're dangerous. Let me help you. Let me keep you safe."

There. He found the NJ, the woman who called herself Lotus. She was semiconscious. He opened her to his touch, pulsed adrenaline through her, bringing her mind back from the brink of unconsciousness, searching for the knowledge he needed. He felt her wonder at his contact, and shouted his need at her even as he searched. Where? How? Show me!

Out loud he spoke. "No. Thank you. Really. But I'm not interested."

There. She didn't understand, but she trusted him. She helped him. Showed him.

Kade understood. He saw the link. He burrowed through her mind to it, felt her awe as he did. He opened a pipe to the hardware via Nexus OS, proxied it through Lotus's Nexus OS to his own, executed the command she showed him. The hardware's user interface controls appeared in his mind's eye – virtual knobs and sliders and equalizer graphs.

The Indian man's holographic figure sighed. "I'm afraid it's not your choice, Kade. That key is a threat to the entire planet. I can't let you and it fall into untrustworthy hands. You're going to have to come with me."

The soldiers in sleek black combat armor raised their weapons.

Feng tensed, his finger on the trigger of his gun.

Kade mentally slid the gain controls on the system he'd tapped into all the way up to maximum. He felt adrenaline pump through him, anticipation, that sense of power, that sense of *satisfaction*.

"No," Kade told the hologram. "I'm not."

Then he multiplexed his signal out through the club's Nexus amplifiers at maximum power. His transmission burned through the jamming, opened the backdoors in the soldier's minds over encrypted connections, and instructed the Nexus nodes in a specific region of each brain to fire at maximum strength.

All seven men spasmed, went rigid, and then fell to the floor, unconscious.

The Indian figure inclined his head. "Impressive."

Kade smiled coldly.

Then Feng slammed his booted foot down on the avatar bot with an audible crunch. The hologram crackled into nothingness.

Who are you? Kade felt Lotus's question in his mind. But he only shook his head. He turned, took in the wreckage all around him, revelers fallen to the ground – some unconscious, some wounded, some dead. The brunette Kade had seen so often was crumpled on the floor, her chest softly rising and falling. The Vietnamese boy who'd been ridden from London was next to her, his neck bent at an unnatural angle, motionless. Kade shook his head. He was so very very tired of this.

"Jeep," Feng said as he ripped weapons off the fallen men. Pain ground through him from a bullet in his arm, from the massive impact of the vehicle when it had burst through the wall and struck him head on. "I drive."

The woman named Lotus lay prone on the stage, her mind reaching out to Kade's, and watched with open eyes as they fled.

43

CONVERGENCE

Saturday October 27th

Breece and the Nigerian followed Ava back to the garage. They left the cars outside. Ava led Miranda Shepherd in through the door, and Breece and the Nigerian followed.

Hiroshi closed the door behind them, began to reconnect the mesh panels, resealing the Faraday cage.

"Status?" Breece asked, as Ava led Miranda Shepherd to the chair in the middle of the room.

"Nominal," Ava answered. "I administered the scopolamine in the car. Memory formation's blocked. She's been cooperative."

Miranda Shepherd sat down in the chair, docilely.

"Hiroshi," Breece said. "It's your show."

They had an hour to turn Miranda Shepherd into their mule. They'd practiced the process, stripped it down to its bare essentials.

Hiroshi slid the syringe into a vein between her toes, then slowly depressed the plunger. The silvery fluid pumped, bit by bit, into the woman's bloodstream. They left her sitting there while the modified Nexus 5 took hold.

"The phone?" Hiroshi asked.

Breece handed it over in its Faraday cage bag. Hiroshi took it out with gloved hands, plugged it into the slate that would load it with new software.

By then Miranda Shepherd was coming up. Hiroshi left the phone, pulled up a seat next to Miranda's, closed his eyes, and went Inside. Ava pulled the styling hood down over Miranda's hair, and let it do its work.

Feng threw the jeep into reverse as Kade buckled in. He sent them careening back over rubble and through the hole in the wall it had left on the way in. Then they were out into the night. The crowds had gone, dispersed by explosions and gunfire and wild vehicles. Another jeep was embedded in the building across the street, flames licking up from it.

Feng spun the jeep around, then threw it in forward and accelerated.

"You're hurt," Kade said. There was blood everywhere.

"I'll live," Feng said.

Kade looked around him, searched for anything that might be a first aid kit. The dash of the jeep was a riot of displays. The interior of the doors and ceiling were covered with weapons: rifles, pistols, knives, grenades.

"Map," Feng said. "How do we get out of town? Back streets."

Kade looked at his friend – bleeding and in pain – and nodded.

Kade found the map control, zoomed it up onto his side of the windshield, and began to shout directions. "Left. Straight. Next right. Here, here!"

The alert came moments later.

[Alert: Coercion Code Alpha AUTHOR
Detected. Confidence: 93%]

Details scrolled after.

```
[Match: Nexus 0.72 binary]
[Match: Nexus 0.72 source]
[Match: Coercion Source Code. <sample>]
[Match: PLF Self-identification.]
[...]
```

It struck him dumb. He stopped talking, stopped navigating.

"Kade?" Feng asked. "Kade!"

"Feng. It's them. I've found them."

He clicked on the link to the mind in the alert.

"Kade!" Feng said. "This not a good time!"

"I might not get another chance, Feng! I have to."

Kade entered the passcode.

The jeep turned hard, pushing him against the door. Dimly he was aware of the sound of bangs, of something clanging against the armor, of adrenaline coursing through Feng.

"Really not good time!" Feng said.

And then Kade was in.

It took forty-five minutes to turn Miranda Shepherd. At the end of that time, the woman was theirs.

The modified version of Nexus lodged in her brain, waiting to come online at the right signal from the phone, to turn her into a living weapon against her husband and Daniel Chandler. The memory script was deeply embedded, ready for Miranda's own imagination to embellish it, to create a false recollection of a hair appointment as real as any other.

When they were done, Ava left with Miranda Shepherd to return the woman to her car. The Nigerian went with her, in the backup vehicle. Breece and Hiroshi started the process of tearing down their gear and sanitizing the garage, leaving absolutely no trace of what had happened here.

• • •

Kade took stock of the mind he'd infiltrated. He'd give away nothing this time until he knew what was going on.

He was in a building of some sort. A warehouse or a garage. There were rolls of a fine metallic mesh, like a window screen, lying at his feet. He had tools in his gloved hands.

Kade turned, scanned his surroundings. Across the room there was another man, using similar tools to take down another panel. He was whistling as he worked.

Kade reached out for that other man's mind, to take him as well, hold them both, until he could find out where they were and call the authorities.

But there was no mind there, no Nexus for him to hack into.

Kade could feel his pulse picking up, his breathing coming heavy.

Act normal, Kade told himself. Find out what's going on.

He clamped down on this mind, told it to pull down another panel, started to sift through its recent memories.

Images, thoughts, words. They came thick and fast. He absorbed them at faster than real-time, straining the link between their minds, the Nexus in each of them.

PLF. Assassination attempt. Team of four. Miranda Shepherd. Daniel Chandler. Explosives. Thousands at risk.

Jesus.

This wasn't the boss. The code had come from the other man, *Breece*, who had passed it on from the PLF's leaders. This one, Hiroshi, had taken that code, fixed bugs, added features, improved on it.

I have to go deeper, Kade realized. I have to get to the bottom.

There was Nexus here. In Hiroshi's kit. Syringes of Nexus. Yes.

Kade steered Hiroshi's body to the kit still out by his terminal. He placed the body between Breece and the gear.

Then he reached into the bag, opened the insulated case inside, and pulled out a syringe already loaded with silvery Nexus.

He turned. Breece was still happily taking down mesh panels. *Faraday cage panels.* He understood now.

It didn't matter. They'd opened their cage and let him in. And now they were his.

Kade pulled the cap off the loaded syringe, held it behind Hiroshi's body, then walked casually up to Breece's turned back, the sense of power rising in him.

Yes, he was going to stop these bastards.

He was going to stop them once and for all.

Breece stepped up onto the stool to reach the connectors at the top of the next panel. Carl Orff was running through his head, the epic chants and drums of "O Fortuna".

Snap. Snap. Snap. The panel was halfway off when something alerted him.

He half turned and out of the corner of his eye Hiroshi was there, something glinting in his hand, swinging towards him.

Breece blocked reflexively, threw up his hand to ward away the blow. Something sharp penetrated his forearm. He jerked away, spinning, and the needle of the syringe broke off, still embedded in his arm. Silvery liquid Nexus spurted from the broken syringe Hiroshi still held.

"What the fuck?" Breece yelled.

Then Hiroshi was on him, punching clumsily at his head with a wild roundhouse.

Had Zara bought him?

Breece stepped inside the swing of the blow, turned, grabbed, and spun, throwing Hiroshi over his hip and into the ground.

His friend scrambled clumsily to get up, nothing like the deadly grace of the real Hiroshi.

Then Breece understood. This wasn't Hiroshi any more. This was someone else.

Breece let the hacker come at him with his friend's body again. This time he stepped to the outside, trapped the arm, twisted it around behind his friend, pushed him against the wall, locking him there, the arm levered up near to breaking. With his other hand he pulled his gun, held it to his friend's temple.

Would pain work? Would threats?

"Who are you?" Breece demanded.

Fuck.

Kade swore as Breece disabled him.

He had no choice now. He dropped control of the body entirely, shifted all of his attention to rummaging through Hiroshi's mind. Names. Places. Passwords. Who were these people? When was the attempt going to happen? Where? How?

"Breece," Hiroshi said softly.

"Hiroshi?"

"He's reading my mind, man."

"Fight him, Hiroshi. You can beat him."

His friend shook his head slightly, his temple brushing the muzzle of Breece's gun.

"Too strong," Hiroshi half-spoke, half-groaned. "Pull the trigger."

"Fuck that," Breece replied.

Kade heard Hiroshi speak. He had to move faster, find out everything the man knew.

• • •

"I know more than you think," Hiroshi said. "I know who you *are*, Breece."

Breece caught his breath.

"He's gonna get it out of me," Hiroshi said. He sounded urgent now, frantic for Breece to end his life.

"No," Breece whispered. "No, no." He looked around. The Faraday cage shielding. If he could get it around Hiroshi… If he could bend it, somehow. There would have to be no gaps. It couldn't just be a cylinder. He had to close the ends, or make it a sphere or a cube.

"The Nigerian!" Hiroshi half yelled. "I know his name, Breece!"

Breece closed his eyes, tried to concentrate, tried to find a way out of this that wasn't putting a bullet into the brain of his friend, his friend who'd saved his life more than once.

"Ava!" Hiroshi was screaming now. "I know who Ava is, Breece! It's her or me! You have to kill…"

Breece pulled the trigger. The boom echoed like a cannon in the small space. The muzzle flash singed his face, so close to Hiroshi's. Blood splattered on his cheek, his brow, the lids of his closed eyes. Hiroshi went silent.

White noise.

[CONNECTION LOST]

Kade jolted in shock and frustration. Damn it!

Breece stepped back, let go of his grip, opened his eyes. The body of his friend slumped slowly to the ground, his head sliding down the garage wall as it fell, leaving a trail of blood and expelled brain behind it.

The gun fell from Breece's limp fingers. He barely noticed. He stared numbly down at the body of his dead friend. And then Breece collapsed to his knees, brought his bloodstained hands up to cover his singed and splattered face.

One of the smartest men he'd ever known. One of the bravest. A man who'd fought to give others freedom. To give them the right to become more than human.

A man who'd died to protect his team. His family.

Hiroshi should have lived forever. He should have become immortal and posthuman. He'd earned it. He'd deserved it far more than most. He would have used his intelligence and courage to make the world a better place.

Breece dropped his hands to his sides, opened his eyes, forced himself to look at what he'd done to his friend, his brother. "I'm going to find you," Breece said to the thing that had invaded Hiroshi's mind. "I'm going to make you suffer. I'm going to make you wish for death."

44
CAPTURE

Saturday October 27th

Feng's world slowed as the vehicles appeared in the rear view display in the corner of his armored windshield. Black SUVs. Two of them. Men leaned out, soldiers in sleek black combat armor. They had automatic weapons in their hands. Feng's combat senses painted g-force curves on the road ahead of him, projected paths he could take. The guns behind them opened fire, aiming low at the metal honeycomb tires. They couldn't be popped, but enough gunfire could eat away at them. Stray shots pinged off the armored back.

Feng spun the wheel hard, turning them down a side street. The world spun outside his window as g-forces pushed him to the side. His wounds ached in protest. He ignored the pain, pushed the jeep harder into the turn, letting the g-force press him against the door, feeling for the grip of the jeep to the road.

The soldiers fired again, from both vehicles, and he felt more shots bite into the honeycomb tires. Another indicator flared yellow. The first went red. He held onto the wheel as it jerked, kept the jeep straight.

An alley loomed to the left and he turned hard into it, daring the SUVs to come after him into the narrow lane where they could only follow in a single file.

Trash cans loomed in his view and he plowed into them, sending them flying. Rubbish flew into the alley in slow motion as a can he'd hit spun end over end into the air.

One SUV turned hard after him, then another. The soldier leaned out the window, firing, then ducked back into the vehicle as another trash can Feng had sent airborne tumbled at them, narrowly missing him.

Now, Feng thought.

He slammed the brakes hard. His bruises and bullet wound screamed in pain as deceleration pushed him into the safety belt.

Then there was a horrendous crash, another jerk of acceleration as the vehicle behind them careened into their rear end.

Feng grunted in pain, then jammed on the accelerator. Half the rear view display was black now, the cameras in the rear destroyed. In the other half he could see that the SUV's front end was wrecked, that it would be going nowhere, plugging up the alley, preventing the vehicle behind it from pursuing.

Yes! Feng thought.

Wha'? *Kade's mind jerked back to the here and now. Feng risked a glance to his side, saw Kade's eyes wide, felt Kade's mind bursting with failure and frustration.*

Then the alley walls exploded in a burst of flame and brick ahead of them.

Shiva blinked as the feed from the avatar bot cut out abruptly.

Hayes saw it happen on screen, spoke up. "Teams C and D are inbound."

Shiva brought his attention back to the displays before them. From a camera on one of the drones he watched the armored jeep rush into an alley, his men following, firing at the wheels, trying to disable the vehicle without harming Lane.

The jeep slammed to a halt and one of his chase cars crashed into its armored rear.

"Blow the alley's far end," Hayes said into his microphone. "Cut them off."

Overhead two of their circling drones launched micromissiles at the building walls fifty meters forward of the once-again accelerating jeep. Shiva held his breath. They could not kill Lane!

Then the missiles struck home, and the walls of the buildings flanking the alley came down in a heap of fire and rubble.

Feng watched the walls coming down in slow motion and immediately knew they wouldn't make it. He slammed hard on the brakes as the walls collapsed in front of them. The jeep slowed, skidded, skewed to one side, but they were too close, moving too fast.

The front right wheel of their vehicle hit the pile of rubble in a jarring crash that he felt through his bones and Kade's, and then they were flipping over it, gravity shifting as the momentum of the jeep's rear carried it up and over the front of the vehicle, somersaulting it crazily, end over end, spinning, rolling as it flipped.

Feng let his body go limp as they'd taught him. Relaxed every muscle and let his mind freeze time around him. He took in everything at once, the way he'd been built and trained to do in combat: the spin and trajectory of the jeep, over and to the side, destined to hit the building on the right; Kade's gasp of shock and alarm, the belt around him; the weapons in easy reach, those he'd take when they left the vehicle.

Then their tumble through the air ended as they crashed into the side of the alley, still spinning, crashed *through* the brick wall, through support beams, opening a wide gash in the building, before coming to rest on the driver's side of the jeep.

"Out!" Feng yelled. Kade was shaken from the crash, bruised by his safety belt, his mind still shocked and stunned from the hurtle they'd taken through the air. His side was up. Feng's was down. They had to open Kade's door, climb out, escape before those soldiers got here.

KADE. OUT! Feng sent his friend.

Kade jerked back to the present. He reached to his right, now above him, pushed to open the door. Feng felt the pain flare through his friend's right hand, still too weak and sensitive for this.

Feng unclipped his safety belt, got his feet beneath him on the driver's side door, now the floor of the sideways vehicle. He climbed up, over Kade, still belted into his seat, and threw the door open, climbing out onto the uppermost side of the toppled vehicle.

It was chaos outside the car, in the building. Dust and smoke filled the air. Water sprayed into the air from broken pipes. A torn-up power line was throwing sparks. The wheels on the jeep's right side, the side he stood on now, were still spinning.

The building was groaning ominously. More dust was falling from the ceiling above. They had to get out of here.

He reached down, grabbed Kade by forearm and belt.

"Unclip!" he yelled.

Kade nodded, snapped off his safety belt, and Feng hauled him up onto the side of the armored jeep, then helped him down to the ground. Kade stood there, leaning against the vehicle, coughs racking him, his neck and midsection throbbing in pain from the whiplash of the crash, the constriction of the belt.

Feng dropped to his belly atop the jeep and reached back into the passenger compartment, pulled out weapons. A belt with grenades and knives he slung over one shoulder. A wicked sixty-centimeter blade over the other. A submachine gun and two spare clips of ammo.

The building was groaning louder now. He looked up. An exposed support beam they'd clipped on their way in was swaying, leaning, giving way. Time slowed as the beam canted, millimeter by millimeter, as the supports above it began to sag and buckle, as dust fell through the cracks as they shifted.

KADE! he sent. **RUN!**

He leapt down next to his friend even as he sent the thoughts. He fell in slow motion as the beam began to warp, cracks appearing on it as it tilted towards them. Kade was frozen in time, leaning over, trying to move, a massive cough shaking its way through him. Feng's toes touched the ground and then the heels of his boots and then he *shoved*, pushing Kade violently out of the way, pushing himself backwards against the upturned jeep in recoil.

Kade flew forward, propelled by his push. Feng got one foot behind him on the jeep and used it to thrust himself towards safety. He dared not turn his head to look, but he could hear the building collapsing all around him, could hear each individual crack and heave and rumbling sigh as bricks and beams and boards gave way in an endlessly stretched-out moment that he must survive, that he had no choice but to survive. His foot came down on the floor again and his toes found purchase and gripped to haul him forward. Ahead Kade was stumbling out, off balance, out through the gap the armored jeep had ripped in the brick wall.

The first brick hit Feng in the back of the head. His left leg was surging forward now, forward to get a foothold that would send him out after Kade. Then something heavy struck him across the back and shoulder, and bore him to the ground.

Kade staggered as Feng nearly threw him away from the jeep. He stumbled over the chaotic debris and fell to his knees in the alley, just as a giant crashing sound came from behind him. Feng's mind let out a groan of pain.

He turned, still on his knees. Behind him, where Feng had been, there was only a pile of rubble, sheathed in smoke and dust.

!!

He could feel Feng's mind in there, still. He was still alive! Kade had to help him!

Then he felt the sting as something bit into his neck. His hand rose of its own accord, onto the telltale protrusion of a dart. He craned around, disoriented, woozy already, and saw the faint outlines. Men, in sleek black armor, rifles in their hands, pointed at him.

No. No. He closed his eyes, reached for an icon, reached for the script that would close his back door forever…

And toppled face first to the cobblestone surface of the alley, all thought gone from him.

45
PHUKET

Saturday October 27th

Sam tended her wounds as best she could. The bullet had gone clean through her tricep, missing the bone and tendons. Her engineered clotting factors had cut off the bleeding almost immediately. Regen genes were already knitting the long fibers of her muscle back together.

If Jake had had those advantages... If the technology wasn't locked up for soldiers and spies...

Sam swallowed the bitterness, washed out the wound, gritted her teeth at the pain, then filled it full of antibiotic cream and bandaged it shut. The other cuts had closed themselves but still needed disinfecting. More washing, more antibiotic cream, more bandages. In a few days she'd look as good as new.

She washed off the last of the dust and blood, pulled on fresh clothes, packed the gun, knives, clothes, cash, and fake ID. Then she was ready.

On the way out she stopped by Jake's body, knelt down and brushed his face with her fingers. She wished she could do something for him, bury him, treat him with the tenderness he deserved. But the needs of the living trumped the needs of the dead.

She did the best she could with little time. She dragged his body to the greenhouse, cycled the simple airlock, pulled him inside and laid him flat. The plants and the rich earth and the warm, humid, CO_2-laden air smelled of life to her. She'd leave him here, the most peaceful place she knew. The CO_2 levels fed the plants and killed insects, and the airlock would keep scavengers out. He'd at least be spared some indignities.

A tear made its way down her face, a sob threatened to emerge, and she knew that it was now or never, that she'd be paralyzed if she stayed here even a moment longer. Go. She had to go.

A trucker stopped for her on the highway, gave her a ride as far north as Thung Song through agonizingly slow traffic. At a truck stop she tried for two hours to find a ride further on. When it became clear there was none, she found an old motorbike, far from the lights and cameras. Sam sat on the bike, used her hands to break off the panel that hid the ignition wiring, and hotwired it like the ERD had taught her to. Then she was off, into the night.

It was just after midnight when she crossed the mainland bridge into Phuket. She abandoned the bike on the side of the road, took a cheap room in the seedier part of town, showered and changed into the dark pants and dark sleeveless blouse she'd purchased here, months ago. She replaced the bandage with a triple layer of wide black vinyl tape around her tricep, then applied more concealer to the cuts, abrasions, and bruises on her body. She stuffed cash, phone, and fake ID into her pockets. Finally, she pulled on the four-inch spiked and LED-studded heels she'd acquired here, months ago.

She left the gun and knives in the room. They'd search her before letting her in to see Lo Prang. An obvious weapon could blow her chances.

And she herself was weapon enough.

Phuket was the ultimate beach town by day, the ultimate vice town by night. Like a cross between Miami and Las Vegas, it offered all the pleasures of water and sun twelve hours of the day, and all the pleasures of gambling, drugs, and sex at any hour, day or night.

Lo Prang's House of Pleasure was at the end of a long strip of bars, nightclubs, and brothels where Chinese, American, and European tourists gathered to spend their money on drinks and drugs and the willing flesh of the thousands of girls that flocked here from the countryside.

She'd come here herself, almost six months ago, seeking funds. Lo Prang's illegal muay Thai fights paid well. He paid extra for an attractive Western woman willing to fight. And she, with the bookies setting the odds steeply against her, borrowed heavily from a loan shark to bet on herself. Three fights later she'd been able to afford the new identity, the melanin therapy, the facial bone structure changes that allowed her to push on to Mae Dong.

Now she needed something else. Something that would cost her more.

There was a line outside the door an hour long. Deliberate scarcity created to enforce the twin illusions of exclusivity and popularity. She went around it, towering over the women and most of the men in the line with her spiked heels. The tiny LEDs her heels were crusted with pulsed with every step, flashing as she brought them down, sending patterns of light rippling up their length. Sam headed to the front of the line, where the bouncers with their oversized muscle-grafted bodies waited, scowling, in their dark suits.

She saw a look of recognition pass across one of their faces as she approached. The huge Asian man raised a finger to his ear and his lips parted as he spoke something, pitched low for a throat mic to hear. Their eyes locked, and she read those lips. *Jade Tiger*, they said, in Thai. *Jade Tiger*.

His eyes stayed locked on hers, and then he nodded to the voice in his earpiece, and pulled back the velvet rope for Sam to pass.

The club was built on a cliff, with views of the beach below and the Andaman Sea beyond that from every level. The entrance was on the uphill side of the club, on the top level. From there one could work their way down and down, to realms that were darker, where the services offered were less constrained by laws or moral norms.

Sam made her way into the club, then through the top floor, past the dance floor where the bar girls in their skimpy skintight dresses danced with Chinese and American men twice their age, tempting them to pay for the even greater pleasures that could be had in private. Past the bars where the tourists ordered rounds of shots and glowing or bubbling or smoking drinks. Past the hookah couches where the younger set reclined, and sucked on water pipes loaded with genetically potentiated hashish, or engineered blissweed with its enzymatically produced ecstasy, or perhaps just a tiny bit of discreetly sprinkled opium. Her heels tapped the floor, sending little pulses of light up them on every step.

She found the stairs down to the next level, walked down them. The grotesquely enhanced bouncers stiffened as she came near. She read the tension on their bodies, the wide eyes as they tracked her, and walked by them as if they weren't there at all. The stairwell opened into a floor that was casino mixed with strip club. Men and a few women played at games of chance while nude and semi-nude Thai girls danced and writhed on stage, or pressed their bodies against the gamblers, stroking them discreetly beneath the tables, earning payment for their dances and caresses in chips, all while distracting the gamblers, tilting the odds ever more in favor of the house.

Sam caught flashes of Nexus as she crossed the floor. The zombified, addictive haze of the gamblers, laying down chip after chip, jonesing, dysphoric, craving that hit of pleasure that came with three cherries or a winning hand. The saccharine seduction oozing from the minds of the dancers, the semblance of arousal, the promises of sweet delights, for a price.

It all disgusted her.

She found the stairs across the oversexed casino, took them down to the third level, the flesh market. They stopped her at the portal. More oversized bouncers in dark suits. More big men, tense, amped up.

Were you there for my fight against *Glao Bot*? Sam wondered. Did you see what I did to that big man? Think you can do better?

It cost just to enter this floor, they told her. A thousand baht. She heard the tremor in their voices, but she paid it. They frisked her, professionally, carefully, thoroughly.

Does it relieve you that I don't have a gun, or knife? she thought at them. Does that make you feel any better, when you've seen what I can do with my bare hands?

They nodded to Sam when they were done, opened the door to this final level of Lo Prang's pleasure palace.

Sex buffeted her mind immediately. Overwhelmingly intimate sensations from men and women alike. Sam clenched her mind against it, pushed out the unwanted thoughts and feelings.

The floor was a maze of darkened alcoves with corridors threading between them. The alcoves had stages, live sex shows with men and women in every possible permutation of twos or threes or fours or more. Each step she took sent a minor flash of light out, illuminating people in the throes of depravity.

Things had changed in the months she'd been gone. Nexus was endemic here now. Every alcove and door offered delights to the senses and the flesh. Every one of them also offered additional delights for those using Nexus.

Audiences watched, used Nexus to tune in to the sensations they wanted to absorb. She passed offers to live out any fantasy she'd ever thought of here, and dozens more she hadn't. She was given the option to ride any of these bodies, to put her mind in theirs, to steer the action if she paid the right price, to feel every single sensation that was happening on stage, from the point of view of either gender, without ever having to soil her own hands.

A sign let her know she could always tune in to ride a performer from anywhere in the world, if she liked.

Girls and boys approached her, offered themselves to her for her personal, physical use. Bargains at twice the price, they told her. They all came loaded with Nexus, so she could feel every bit of their pleasure as she had them, or experience their pain and humiliation in exquisite detail as she hurt or degraded them, if that was her kink. Sam thought of Sarai's mother, of how that had scarred Sarai. She clenched her fists in anger and pushed through them.

Other alcoves offered her girls and boys ready to fall in love with her, to use Nexus to twist their own minds. No more tolerating pretend passion, here. Why not hire a whore that is truly attracted to you, aroused by you, insatiably hungry for your touch? Isn't that what you really want?

Sam felt bile rising up inside her. This place embodied everything she hated about Nexus.

No, she corrected herself. Not Nexus. The people who use it this way.

It was a hard-won distinction, a hard-won realization, that technology could be used for good or bad, could be disgusting or sublime. She wouldn't let the vileness of this place taint the beauty she felt when she touched the children's minds.

The things happening in the alcoves became more and more unspeakable as she progressed. Perversions and debasements. Women – mostly women – doing things for money that no human being should be subjected to, voluntarily or not. Eager audience members tuning in to witness it, to relish it, from the standpoint of debased or debaser. Sam's nausea rose and rose.

Then she was past the last of them, and into the curving hallway that led to Lo Prang.

The feel of sex and degradation left her mind as she rounded the corner. Lo Prang surely had another way to reach his inner sanctum, she realized. But this was the way he wanted his supplicants to come to him, walking through his domain, forced to experience it, to be aroused by it or disturbed by it. Either way, it set them off balance.

Sam held her head high. She had an agenda. Nothing else mattered.

The door was guarded by two more oversized Thai men in black suits. Muscle grafts and gene tweaks broadened their backs and shoulders to ridiculous proportions. Weapons bulged beneath their jackets. Earpieces were in their ears. Unlike the others, these two had minds she could feel. Hard shells of ruthlessly controlled Nexus emanations surrounded them both.

Their eyes crept over her body as she approached, her heels flashing with every step. They scanned her for weapons. No fear on these two. They were harder than the others, perhaps, or more ready for her.

Fools.

Sam stepped up to them, head unbowed.

"I want to talk to Lo Prang," she said. "Tell him the Jade Tiger is back."

46
NEVER LET YOU GO

Sunday October 28th

One day the BAD MEN in the white coats came into the room where Bobby lived with all his new friends and they took Alfonso away for a test and Alfonso went with them into the special testing room and then a little while after that he went into the even more special testing room and they closed the door and he DISAPPEARED from their heads. But that was OK because they'd done this before, and like Tim had told Bobby they always came back and Bobby had come back and Tim had come back and Alfonso would probably come back and show them how he'd had a test on trigonometry or French or something else Alfonso didn't know about, but he'd learn while he slept because one of them knew about it and it would be just fine.

Alfonso was gone a long time and Bobby started to worry and he told Tim he was worried and Tim said not to worry, but Bobby could tell that Tim was worried too because no one had been gone this long and now Jose was worried and Parker was worried and Tyrone was worried, and they were all telling each other not to worry with their voices but their heads were saying to WORRY and WORRY A LOT and the more scared Bobby got the more scared he felt Tyrone and Pedro and Parker and Nick and even Tim get, and that made him even more scared!

Then they heard the door open and they all heard it and Bobby started to feel a little better and he could feel his friends all start to feel a little better because maybe this was Alfonso coming back and it was all going to be OK but it wasn't at all. Bobby was in the room with the beds so he couldn't see the door but Nick could see the door and Nick saw one of the bad men come into the room and there was Alfonso with him but it wasn't Alfonso, wasn't Alfonso, because there was nobody there at all, NOTHING IN ALFONSO'S HEAD AT ALL and the boy who looked like Alfonso but wasn't real was crying he was crying and Nick screamed because it was Alfonso, it had been Alfonso but they had BROKEN him they'd STOLEN THE NEXUS FROM ALFONSO'S HEAD.

And then they were ALL SCREAMING, Nick and Tim and Tyrone and Pedro and Bobby and all of them, and Tim was running at the BAD MAN and trying to PUNCH him and KICK him and BITE him and Tyrone was running at him and Pedro was running at him, and Bobby ran from the room with the beds into the room with the toys and couches and he ran at the Bad Man and they KNOCKED HIM OVER and Bobby was BITING HIS FACE, and then something hit him hard in the head and knocked him back and everything was swimmy and when Bobby looked up there were MORE BAD MEN with sticks and they were hitting all the boys and the boys were trying to BITE them and KICK them and PUNCH them and SCRATCH them and Bobby got up and threw himself at the bad men again but something hit him in the belly and it HURT and the bad men were too strong and hit them too hard and then it was over.

The bad men left. The boys groaned and sobbed. The boy that had been Alfonso but was no one now didn't say a word. He sat in the corner and covered his face and cried and cried and cried – and there was nobody there, nobody they could feel, nobody who existed at all.

And they all cried now, because they knew that if the bad men would do this to Alfonso, then the bad men would do it to all of the rest of them too.

They came for Rangan after three days. The door to his cell opened abruptly and two orderlies strode in, masks and cuffs in their hands, grim looks on their faces, armed guards behind them.

Rangan pushed himself up from the floor of his cell, his hands up towards them.

"Wait! Wait! What did I do?"

They grabbed his wrists, turned him around, slammed his face into the gray concrete wall of his cell, and pulled the mask down over him.

Cold fear raced through Rangan. What the hell? Was this about Bobby and the kids? Had they detected what he was doing?

"Please..." he pleaded as they strapped him to the gurney. "Please tell me what's going on. I'll tell you anything, I swear!"

It wasn't just the kids. It was worse, he was sure of it. He was useless now. He'd told them everything. They were hauling him away to be executed, thrown away like a piece of fucking garbage.

Tears were rolling down his face now. He hated himself for his weakness. He'd been so angry at his compromise but now he was so terrified that he'd do it all again, tell them everything they wanted to know again and again if they'd just let him live...

The orderlies ignored him, wheeled him flat on his back down the hall. He tried to control himself. Breathe. Breathe, Rangan. Fucking get yourself together.

[activate: serenity level 3]

Just a little. Not so much that they'd decide he was too calm, this time, and escalate to worse. Just a little. Maybe he could fool them.

His head cleared a tiny bit. Maybe it wasn't death. Could it be more interrogation? More torture? Did they think he knew more?

He didn't! But could he make something up? Anything up? Any reason for them to keep him alive?

The gurney made another turn and then stopped. He heard doors opening and closing. Someone tapped his inner elbow, searching for a vein, and then a needle slid home. He winced at that.

"Please..." he asked whoever was inserting the IV. "Tell me what's going on?"

No response.

The hands left him. He couldn't hear anyone, couldn't see anything beyond the mask. Something cool was entering his arm through the needle.

Is this it? he wondered. Death by lethal injection?

He could feel himself getting drowsy now, starting to fade out. Was this what it felt like to die?

Then the Voice spoke, booming into his head, echoing there.

"You lied to us, Rangan. You gave us bogus codes. Who'd have thought you had it in you?"

What? Fear rose in him, overwhelmed the low setting of the serenity package.

"No!" Rangan said. "No! I told you the truth."

Why were they doing this? He'd told them *everything*, told them way too much, and they were still going to torture him.

"Please! I told you everything!"

The Voice spoke again. "I didn't think you had it in you, Rangan. Honestly, I'm impressed. But this time we're going to try something new."

"No, please!"

Then he felt the minds unveil themselves. Four of them, five, six, all around him.

What?

Then they pushed into him, brutally.

THE BACK DOORS. THE CODES. GIVE US THE PASSCODES.

I've given them to you!

They came at him hard, in concert, pushing at his mind for things he'd already given them, *hurting* him.

So he fought.

They were six and he was one, but he'd been using Nexus longer than any of them, maybe longer than all of them combined.

Rangan activated the defenses he'd built, raked them with the Nexus disruptor he'd copied from his first time in ERD custody, struck out in brute force with his mind against theirs, struck out to stun them, to confuse them, to turn them one against the other.

And in the end they beat him down. Too many of them, too few of him. Too much of the sedative in his veins, in his brain.

He showed them everything, everything he'd already told them, everything they already knew.

Just some sick joke, he thought. Just an excuse to torture me.

But the minds felt frustrated. They felt disappointed. They'd honestly thought he was lying, that he'd given them the wrong codes. They'd expected to find something new.

They pulled it all from his mind again, twice, three times, four times, pushing him every which way, looking for a deeper layer of knowledge, looking for some sign he was still deceiving them. Then they gave up, and one by one the minds disappeared.

He heard a door open and the sound of shoes against a tile floor. Then they were gone. Rangan lay there shivering, feeling helpless and violated, wondering if now they'd pump the lethal solution in through the IV needle, finish him off since he was obviously so useless to them.

Then it dawned on him.

They didn't have the real codes. The ones he'd given them didn't work. Which meant that... Which meant that Kade, or maybe Ilya, or someone else, had *changed* those codes before releasing Nexus OS. Which meant that Rangan wasn't a traitor. That he couldn't be even if he tried.

The first laugh bubbled up out of him from nowhere. Then another, and another.

They'd done it. They were beating the motherfucking ERD! Just a bunch of kids, but they'd done it!

He was laughing uncontrollably when the orderlies came for him. He kept laughing when they pulled the needle out of his arm, kept laughing as they wheeled him back to his room, kept laughing as they pulled the hood off his face and pushed the gurney into corner.

Fucking hilarious!

And then he felt Bobby's mind, felt what the boys had gone through, and the laughter turned to ashes in his mouth.

47

LO PRANG

Sunday October 28th

The guards frisked Sam, searching for weapons. And like the last set their frisk was thorough, careful, taking no risks on their master's safety.

After the frisk, Lo Prang kept her waiting. Minutes crept by, minutes she could be using on her way to Burma, on her way to Sarai and Aroon and Kit and...

Half an hour after she arrived, one of the guards nodded.

"He'll see you now," the huge man said in Thai, and then he opened the door to show her in.

Lo Prang's office was an opulent space larger than her apartment back in DC. Thick shag carpet like red gold covered the floor. Designer couches lined the room. A dozen overly pretty, well-dressed boys and provocatively dressed young women lounged on them. Sensations of pleasure and delirium oozed into the air. Precious paintings hung everywhere, on walls that extended up twelve feet to the gold leaf ceiling. One full wall was given over to floor-to-ceiling screens showing the action throughout the club, rotating through zoomed-in full-color scenes of men and women dancing, drinking, gambling, fucking. The wall was voyeurism, not security.

Lo Prang himself sat squarely in the middle. Lean, hard, his black hair cut to a buzz. He'd been a champion muay Thai fighter in his youth. Now, in his fifties, he still looked formidable. In the midst of the decadence of his office, he came across as totally focused, untouched by drugs or delirium or debauchery. A business man above all else.

Lo Prang sat behind a massive desk seemingly made of a single piece of lab-grown onyx. Atop the desk was nothing but a slate, a tumbler of water, and a single large pistol. He wore a black silk suit. A single heavy ring was on the finger of one hand. His eyes were dark. Once, when Sam had been closer, she'd seen the distinctive gleam of tactical contacts worn on those eyes, feeding who-knows-what data to the mob boss.

Behind Lo Prang was the giant wall spying on the events happening in his club, switching from scene to scene. Standing with their backs to it were two more of the hugely muscled men in black suits. If they had any fear of her – if anyone in this room did – Sam couldn't see it.

"Jade," Lo Prang said in Thai. "Or should I call you Sunee? It's good to have you back."

"Lo Prang." She nodded to him. She could feel some of the Nexus transmissions of the club piped in here, an amalgamation of all the sex and drunkenness and partying out there. "Thank you for seeing me."

"To what do we owe this pleasure?"

Two of the women were kissing now, touching each other's breasts through their low cut dresses. One of the men was snorting a line of some powder off a woman's thigh. Arousal and stimulation echoed out from them.

Battles are won in the mind, Nakamura had taught her. *Throw your enemy off, and he's yours.*

Yes, Sam thought. That was Lo Prang's game. Distraction. All just distraction. All to throw her off balance.

"I need to get into Burma," she told him. "With weapons, transport, infiltration gear."

Lo Prang laughed, a dry chortle. His lean leathery face wrinkled in mirth. His people laughed with him. Even the man who'd just snorted something and the two girls kissing stopped to laugh, at her foolishness, her presumption.

Sam waited for the laughter to die down. "I'll fight for you again," she told Lo Prang. "Once I'm back. I'll beat the best out there. Or I'll take dives, throw fights. Whatever you want."

Lo Prang looked her in the eye, then shook his head. "Jade, Jade, Jade," he said. "Or whoever you are. A few fights wouldn't come close to covering that."

Sam stared back at him. "What would?"

She felt his mind working, felt his thoughts reaching out to others in the room. Two women detached themselves from the groups lounging on the couches, approached her from either side. They were in their early twenties, Thai, slender and chesty, in dresses as scanty as the ones worn by the girls upstairs, but more embellished, more expensive-looking. They wore flashy jewelry and sported improbably long nails on each finger, an inch long, red for one girl, black for the other. She caught a flash of muscle on their arms, their legs.

Sam watched them out of the corners of her eyes, her attention still focused on Lo Prang.

"You're so unhappy, Sunee," he told her. "Always struggling for something."

The girls moved languidly towards her, swiveling on heeled feet, until their fingers touched the bare skin of her arms. She could smell their perfumes. Thoughts of pleasure came from them, and devotion. One of them exhaled hot breath against the back of Sam's neck.

"I could take care of whatever problem you have in Burma," Lo Prang said. "And in exchange you could join me. You could be part of my little family."

Sam shuddered at the thought.

"It's so nice," the girl on her right breathed.

"Just a little tweak to your thoughts," the one on her left intoned.

They ran their hands over her, pressing their bodies against her now, and Sam wanted to push them away, but she needed Lo Prang, needed his help.

"You'd be happy," Lo Prang said.

Their hands roamed over her bare arms, her back, her neck, her sides. Their touch repulsed her. Slaves.

"We chose this way," they said in unison, in stereo. "It's so very nice," they finished together, voices entwined, timing perfect. Pleasure wafted from their minds. Contentment. The warm, enfolding love of Lo Prang. The security of belonging to someone else, utterly, of never having to worry again…

"No," Sam said, fighting the revulsion. They chose this? Oh, she believed them. It still made them slaves.

"You'd be safe," Lo Prang told her. "I treat my family well."

"So well," the girls harmonized, from her right and left. And she felt the truth of it from them, how they loved this life and all that came with it…

Slaves. Not her. Never again.

"No," Sam said louder. "No deal."

Lo Prang leaned forward, put his elbows on the desk, folded his fingers together. "There's another way, then."

"Tell me," Sam said, her stomach turning as the girls continued to caress her.

"Your genes, Sunee." Lo Prang's eyes burrowed into hers. "Muscle biopsies. Bone biopsies. Tissue samples. I want what makes you *you*."

Sam closed her eyes. She'd feared it would come to this. She could trade the most valuable thing about herself, in exchange for a chance to get back the most precious. But if she did... She'd be selling out others, signing death sentences for people she didn't know.

"No," she said, eyes closed.

And she knew what came next.

"Then we'll just take it," Lo Prang said.

She heard the snick as the girls' fake nails extended into two inch-long finger blades. One set raked across her back, leaving painful bloody furrows through her blouse. But by then she was dropping, one leg extended, then coming around in a blurringly fast straight-leg spin that swept the girl on her left from her feet.

Chaos exploded through the minds in the room. She saw Lo Prang reaching for the pistol on his desk, his two bodyguards reaching into their jackets for their guns.

Sam rolled away from the other razor-fingered girl, came up with a high-heeled shoe in each hand, her thumbs toggling the hidden switches as she rose. The guards had their submachine guns out, were raising them, bringing them to bear...

She spun, loosed the heels up and towards the sides of the room, felt her left shoulder groan as she did, closed her eyes tight, and let her momentum carry her back down into a right-shoulder roll towards the relative safety of the desk. More pain jolted up from her abused shoulder. Automatic gunfire exploded through the room.

Then she heard the crackle, saw her world turn red even through closed eyes, as the flash charges in her heels went off at maximum intensity, discharging all the energy of their fuel cells in an instant, burning out all their LEDs in the process. She heard a man yell as she came up and around the desk, opening her eyes to take in the scene. The guards had their hands to their faces, blinded for a few critical seconds, waving their guns around, but no longer daring to let loose without their sight. Lo Prang was in front of her, his pistol on her, she couldn't tell if he was blinded or not.

Sam threw herself forward and to the side as he fired, felt the bullet graze her hip. And then she was inside his reach. He threw an elbow at her in the close quarters, raised a knee towards her gut. He was fast, and he was good, but he was old, and Sam was young and had the better tech in her body. She blocked his elbow with her right forearm, raised a leg and took his knee to her thigh, then spun, throwing him to the floor and pulling the gun from his hand in one brutal motion. Her shoulder ached but did as she told it.

Lo Prang rolled with the fall, came up on one knee, fast as a snake, with a knife in his hand. Sam moved faster, grabbed the knife hand, twisted it behind him, and brought his pistol to his head.

She looked up just in time to see the two girls get to their feet, trying to blink away the momentary blindness, and the two guards from outside the door push their way through the crowd, automatic weapons in hand.

They stopped when they saw her holding a stunned, blinking Lo Prang, a gun primed to blow his head off.

"Now," she said to her prisoner. "I'm going to Burma. And you're coming with me."

48

NEW HORIZONS

Sunday October 28th

Kade woke slowly, head spinning, disoriented. There was static in his mind. His head ached. He cracked his eyes open ever so slightly. He was on his back, atop something soft. He saw sunlight, a ceiling with a lazily spinning fan and gold filigreed moldings. He was in a bed, giant and ornate, with elaborately carved wooden posts at the corners that towered above him.

He blinked, tried to adjust.

"Good morning." the Indian man said. Kade looked over. The white-haired figure was dressed in white. He'd pulled back cloth-of-gold curtains from a wide picture window. Beyond it, there was blue sky and ocean. Between Kade and that ocean, there were bars on the windows, a fine mesh built into them.

Kade sat up in the bed. He found himself dressed in cotton trousers and a loose cotton shirt. They'd changed him while he'd slept. Feng. Where was Feng?

"Where am I?" he asked.

"You're at my home," the Indian man said. "In Burma."

"Who are you?" Kade asked.

"My name is Shiva Prasad," he answered. The name sounded familiar.

"…and I hope we'll become good friends," Shiva finished.

Kade felt his anger flare.

"Some way to start a friendship," he spat out.

Shiva smiled. "Eat first," he said. "Then we'll talk."

Then the Indian man strode out of the room.

Kade jumped to his feet, but before he could follow Shiva out through the door, a young Asian woman wheeled in a cart. A muscular, dusky-skinned man whose origin Kade couldn't place followed her. The server and the guard. Kade stopped and stood where he was.

The girl wheeled the cart to the middle of the room and unveiled a platter of eggs, bacon, and potatoes; then another of pancakes; flagons of juice, water, and coffee.

"Breakfast," she said in heavily accented English. Her eyes met his briefly. Then she looked away, and she and the guard left through the door, and he heard a lock click as they did.

Kade ate. If they wanted to drug him or poison him, they could just hold him down and administer what they wanted. Then he explored his prison.

The room was spacious. A king-sized four-poster bed. An antique writing desk and chair. Two oversized ornate antique chairs in a small sitting area. A private bathroom suite almost the size of his apartment in San Francisco. A walk-in closet. Clothes waited for him there. More pants and baggy shirts in soft cotton. Jeans, shorts, T-shirts, sandals, hiking boots, socks, underwear, two bathrobes, a pair of swimming shorts. All in his size.

A kitchenette held snacks, dishware, bottles of beer and sparkling water and expensive-looking wine, a coffeebot, a cookbot that probably cost more than most cars.

Every room had windows. He had incredible views in two directions of a green and blue sea, seen from atop a cliff. From the kitchenette another window afforded a view east into a courtyard dotted with date palms, orange trees, bright tropical flowers, and flowing water. He looked to be on the fifth and topmost floor of what could only be called a mansion.

The windows opened at the touch of a switch to allow the breeze and the scent of sea and citrus. But inset in the window sills were metal frames that covered the space with bars and a fine metallic mesh. Kade could see that these, too, were built to open. But they were all locked and bolted in place. The bars would keep his body here. The mesh was a Faraday cage, he imagined, to keep his mind and any electronics trapped just as surely.

This was an elaborate cell. However luxurious it may be, it remained a prison, and he, the prisoner.

Last, he came to the final piece of his bondage. Around his neck, a thin metal chain held in place a dull metal disk, perhaps two inches in diameter and half an inch thick. Try as he might, he couldn't get it loose, couldn't get it over his head. There was a slot where a key of some sort would slide into it. Other than that there was no way he could see to remove it.

A Nexus jammer. Another layer of his prison.

He knew more now than ever before. He'd learned things, from studying Feng's mind, from his contact with Ling, from meditation with Ananda and the monks, from secrets and tools and pieces of code gained legitimately or stealthily from scientists around the world experimenting with Nexus. He could make his Nexus nodes stand up and do tricks now.

He tried the tools in his toolbox one by one. Frequency tuning code that searched for a band with weaker interference. Filtering packages to suppress the static. An active noise reduction app he wrote himself that played the static reversed, back at itself, to cancel the signal out. Directional tuning of his Nexus antennae, to bore through the jamming in one direction, or boost gain in that direction.

Nothing. Nexus worked fine inside his mind. His code all ran fine. But he could broadcast nothing through the interference, could pick up nothing from around him.

He tried to think like Ling, to remember the feel of her contact, to amp and broaden the sensitivity of the Nexus in his brain until he could pick up the feel of the circuits in the walls, the transmissions all around him, and in particular the inner logic of this jammer.

The static only grew louder in his mind, painfully louder until he broke off in frustration.

He sat down on the floor, crossed his legs, closed his eyes, and began the practice of *vipassana*. He would rein in his attention until he could shift it in such a way that the static wasn't there, was completely removed from his awareness, and then perhaps he'd be able to pick up...

The door opened. Kade opened his eyes, and Shiva was there, a slate in his hand.

49

ACCESS DENIED

Holtzmann closed his eyes again.

Alive. I'm still alive.

He had to get Rangan Shankari free. He felt it in his bones. The strong desire. The deep *need* to break Shankari loose from ERD custody.

Lane had done this to him, had bent him this way, had turned him into a tool. The boy's mind had been monstrous, terrifying. The memory of it sent shivers through him. And the President, the assassination… Panic was rising again, clawing at him, threatening to break loose.

He needed something. Relief from this horror. Holtzmann pulled up the neurotransmitter controls, dialed up a dose of his own opiates, just a little one, just enough so he could think. He pressed the mental button, waited for the sweet relief.

Nothing.

What?

He pressed the button again. Nothing happened.

He closed the controls, killed the process, relaunched it, dialed up an opiate dose again.

Nothing.

The panic was rising higher now. Higher every instant.

Lane. Lane must have done this.

He pulled up a diagnostic suite within Nexus OS, ran it to scan the system. Half the diagnostics failed, instantly. Error messages came back. [ACCESS DENIED.] [ACCESS DENIED.] [ADMINISTRATOR [PRIVILEGES REQUIRED.] [ACCESS DENIED.]. [INSUFFICIENT PERMISSIONS.] [ACCESS DENIED.]

Oh no. Oh God no.

Lane had taken away Holtzmann's root access to his own Nexus OS. He'd taken away control of the software running on Holtzmann's own brain.

He forced himself to think, forced himself to concentrate. There must be some way around this.

He reached out to his home network again. Success. He could still access the net. From there he linked to an anonymization service, and from there out to a Nexus code repository. There, a new version of Nexus OS, more recent than his own. He clicked the link to install it, to override his current Nexus OS.

[ACCESS DENIED.]

Damn it!

He could uninstall Nexus, remove it from his brain. Then find another dose, somehow, reinstall his apps… He launched the command to evict the Nexus nodes from inside his skull

[Nexus purge]

The system threw up a prompt:

[This command will erase Nexus OS and purge all Nexus nodes from your brain. All stored data and applications will be lost. Are you sure you want to continue? Y/N]

[Yes], he thought at it eagerly.

[ACCESS DENIED.]

Holtzmann nearly screamed in frustration. He tried a dozen more things, installing patches, changing permissions on files, editing raw bits that controlled access to resources, writing his own crude code to control his neurotransmitter levels.

[ACCESS DENIED.] [ACCESS DENIED.]

[ACCESS DENIED.]

He was sweating now. He could see Rangan Shankari's face. He could see the boy in captivity. His stomach was clenching. It was intolerable. He had to get the boy out of ERD custody. But he had another problem. A problem that would get in the way.

How long had it been? How long since his last opiate dose? Twelve hours? Something like that?

He was due. He was due to take more. He felt the *need* for it. Even if this added stress wasn't here, he'd need another dose soon. And without another dose...

Martin Holtzmann was going to go into withdrawal.

50
CAGED

Sunday October 28th

"I hope the room is to your liking," Shiva said.

Kade pushed himself to his feet.

"Where's Feng?" he asked.

"We have feelers out," Shiva replied. "Informants. We hope to know soon."

"Let me go," Kade said.

Shiva smiled slightly. "I want us to be friends, Kade. To work to-gether."

"You try to kill me," Kade shouted, "get my friend killed or captured, and you want me to *work with you?*" Spittle flew from his lips.

Shiva's face became stern. "I've never tried to kill you. I *saved your life*, and your friend's."

"Oh please." Kade waved away Shiva's claims.

"What did you think awaited you outside that club?" Shiva asked.

"We knew," Kade went on. "We would have made it."

"Oh?" Shiva asked. "Past the snipers on the rooftops?"

Kade's confidence wavered.

"And if you had, what then? Run again? Where to?"

Kade stared at him, mute.

"And when you were caught, eventually, what then?" Shiva asked. "Do you want your back door in the hands of the Americans? The Chinese? How do you think those governments would use it?"

Kade's face was hot. He said nothing.

"Can you blame me for what I did?" Shiva asked. "You were out there, irresponsibly, putting yourself at risk, putting more than a *million other people* at risk. Can you blame me for wanting you off the streets?"

"No one gets the back door," Kade said. "No one."

"No one but *you*," Shiva replied. "Isn't that what you mean?"

Are you wiser than humanity? Ilya's whispered in his mind, echoing Ananda. *Not even* you *should have that power.*

"Here." Shiva stepped closer, held out the slate to him. "I won't let you touch my mind. But I've done the next best thing. I've recorded my thoughts, my plans, direct from my mind. They're here for you to peruse. To see how much we could do together."

Shiva stood before Kade, just feet from him, the slate in his outstretched hand. Kade knew what he needed to do. He closed his eyes, took a steadying breath, and went Inside.

```
[activate: bruce_lee mode: attack_and_
capture]
```

Targeting circles appeared on the inside of his eyelids. Kade opened his eyes, clicked on Shiva, and Bruce Lee launched him at the man.

His body surged forward. His left fist snapped out, connected with Shiva's jaw, rocked the man's head to the side.

```
[Bruce_Lee: Attack Succeeded!]
```

His body moved in for a lock, to capture the older man.

Then Shiva's left hand shot out, grabbed Kade by the neck, lifted him off his feet, and hurled him across the room.

Kade hit the far wall with a thud, the wind knocked out of him. A framed picture jumped off its hook, crashed to the floor a foot away, glass shattering all around it.

[Bruce_Lee: Block Failed ⊗]

Shiva set the slate down on the writing desk, then turned and walked to the door. "I look forward to your thoughts," he said. Then he was gone, the door closed behind him.

Kade sat there, reeling from the blow.

When, he wondered, has that app ever fucking worked?

He pulled himself slowly to his feet, one hand on the wall for balance.

The door opened, and one of Shiva's men came in, something in his hand. He brought it up to Kade's throat and Kade backed away haltingly, until he realized what it was. A key.

The man inserted it into the slot in the medallion around Kade's neck, and it came loose, falling into the man's hand.

Kade reached out, immediately, with Nexus, to feel whatever he could. But this man wore a static-producing jammer as well, and the slate was the only other thing in the room transmitting, advertising a set of files for Kade to consume.

The man nodded to Kade. "I'll be outside if you need anything, sir."

Then the guard turned and left, locking the door behind him, leaving Kade with the slate, with Shiva's promised thoughts and plans.

Kade blinked and stood there a moment to regain his balance. Then he went Inside and turned off the Nexus OS

file sharing in his own mind, blocking the tempting files out
of his senses.

They brought him lunch later. Kade ate, meditated, took
stock of the situation.

Rangan was still locked up. He'd set Holtzmann in
motion, but the task was complicated. He needed to be out
there to guide and assist.

And the PLF. He knew their next targets. Chandler and
Shepherd, at a Houston prayer breakfast with thousands of
supporters. He knew about Miranda Shepherd. He could
find her, if only he was out of this cage.

He tried to imagine the consequences of the Houston
bombing. Hundreds dead, maybe thousands. And the impact
on US politics, on opinions of Nexus, on treatment of Nexus
children... It would be the final blow. Nexus scanners would
go up in schools, at bus stops, in the workplace. Security
checkpoints everywhere. Maybe worse – roundups of
activists, of anyone who'd protested against the Chandler
Act or made pro-transhumanist statements in the past. The
bomb would frighten people into accepting a security state
more constrictive than ever. The PLF was playing right into
the hands of the conservatives, just like terrorists always did.

Kade could stop it, if he were out there. But he wasn't.
He was a prisoner, because he'd been stupid.

He surveyed the windows again. The bars and mesh swung
on their own frames. Those frames were bolted into the
windowsills, locked with old-fashioned mechanical padlocks.

He heaved, but it was no use. He found a fork in the
kitchen, tried using one of its tines to pick a lock, but he
hadn't the faintest idea how to actually pick a lock, and after
half an hour he gave up.

From the kitchen, he could see into the courtyard below. There were people out there. Shiva's staff. And none of them wore Nexus jammers.

If he could somehow get through the Faraday cage…

The kitchen had no knives in it, but plenty of forks. He crouched below window level so he wouldn't be seen, used the fork to stab over his head at the line where the mesh met the metal frame, over and over again, as hard as he could. He stood to inspect his work. Nothing. The mesh wasn't scratched, wasn't torn.

Damn.

Something attracted his attention out there, in the courtyard. A group of children, sullen, despondent. Some adults moved among them. What were they doing here?

Then one of the children, the oldest, a girl of perhaps twelve or thirteen, looked up at his window, and waved. Waved as if she knew him. He waved back, and a moment later, half a dozen children were looking at him, waving excitedly, where just a moment ago they'd been subdued.

The adult with them, a Caucasian woman, looked up at him, frowned, and then herded the kids away. They went unhappily, stealing glances at him.

Kade sat down heavily on the floor. Those children knew him. He'd never seen them before, he couldn't see their minds and they couldn't see his. But somehow they knew who he was.

He had one guess why that was.

Sam.

51
DETOX

Saturday October 27th

Holtzmann crawled into bed, terrified of what was to come.

He woke hours later to Anne shaking him. "I'm heading out, Martin. I'm going to see Claire. God help me, you're both going crazy."

Holtzmann just stared at her. He lay there in bed, miserable, nauseated, waiting for the full force of the withdrawal to strike, his mind spinning on how to free Shankari.

Anne came home with takeout. He tried to talk, but she turned on the news, responded in monosyllables. She went to bed after dinner. Martin went to his office, feeling ill, but not as terribly as he'd expected...

He was there, sitting in his office chair, thinking of how to free Shankari, when the aches came.

They started in the leg, intensifying, bit by bit, minute by minute, until they were pounding out from his femur where the compound fracture was still healing. They spread out from there, into the hip that had shattered, into his other leg, his ribs, his back, his neck, his arms, his head.

He arched his back and moaned. He writhed around in the chair searching for some relief. His skin was damp with sweat now. He was burning up. Snot was dripping from his nose.

Then the nausea was coursing through him. He dragged himself out of the office, stumbling around without his cane, his body contorted by the pain, made it into the hall bathroom just in time, and heaved up bile into the toilet.

Then his guts cramped. He made it onto the toilet before his bowels exploded filth into it.

When the episode was over, he collapsed onto the floor of the bathroom, wrapped himself in a towel, and waited to die.

Anne found him in the morning, still curled up on the floor, aching and feverish and a mess.

She took one look at him.

"My God, you really are sick."

Holtzmann nodded weakly, then leaned over the toilet and vomited again.

Anne helped him into the shower, brought him a warm robe to wrap himself in, took him back to bed, put a trash can next to him, brought him soup and painkillers and anti-diarrheal meds.

"I'm going to call a doctor," she said.

Holtzmann shook his head. "Just the flu," he said weakly. "I'll be fine."

Then he leaned over and heaved into the trash can.

The agony lasted through Sunday, into Sunday night. Anne talked to him, tried to distract him from the horror that was coursing through his body. He found himself babbling to her, about the meeting with Barnes and the President, about the Nexus children, about everything but the Nexus in his own brain.

By Sunday night the sheets were twisted and damp with his sweat, his writhing. Anne insisted on getting him out of bed so she could change them.

She fell asleep beside him, while the fever and pain and explosive evacuation of his body kept him awake through most of the night. His world was a feverish, twisted nightmare, horrifying images of the President, of Barnes, of Lane. They were all one, a three-faced demon torturing him.

Monday morning. Anne offered to stay home with him, to nurse him to health

Holtzmann insisted she go to work.

He fired up his slate long enough to send a message in to the office, to say he was still sick. Subject lines loomed at him, lurid sentence fragments that made no sense. He ignored them, sent his own message, and disconnected.

The withdrawal peaked around noon. He knelt before the toilet, his face over it, red and straining, his whole body convulsing as it tried to push some imaginary toxin out of him. He puked up water, puked up bile, puked up nothing at all, but his body wouldn't stop, wouldn't stop convulsing, wouldn't stop trying to turn his guts inside out, trying to shove his stomach up through his throat and into this bowl.

Then the episode was past. He cleaned himself as best he could, collapsed back into the sweat-stained bed, and slept.

Holtzmann woke at 5pm. He felt awful, but fractionally better.

His phone buzzed at him. A moment later his slate did as well. More calls from the office.

He forced himself into the shower, forced himself to clean up, to dress himself, to make himself look halfway presentable. Anne had left him soup in the kitchen. He reheated it, drank a bowl, slurped down noodles. His body trembled, but he felt stronger. The food stayed down.

Then he checked his messages, and found chaos.

Half a dozen of his underlings had been trying to reach him urgently, their messages overlapping with one another, conflicting with one another. Barnes had been calling, asking where he was, ordering him to reply.

The codes. The passcodes. The ones Rangan Shankari had given them didn't work.

Holtzmann nearly laughed in relief. Dear God. They didn't work! Lane must have changed them before releasing Nexus 5! Shankari's passcodes were obsolete!

Then he saw the other messages. They'd been torturing children. Barnes had overruled him. And they'd forced Nexus out of the brain of one child. Dear God.

Holtzmann felt the rage pump through him. He called Barnes.

The Acting ERD director picked up immediately, his boyish face with those dark, dark eyes filling up the screen of Holtzmann's slate.

"Martin," Barnes said. "How good of you to get back to me." Acid dripped from his voice.

"What the hell are you doing?" Holtzmann yelled. "Torturing kids? Going around me and ordering my team around?"

Barnes scowled on the screen. "I'm doing *your* job, Martin. What the President ordered *you* to do."

"They're kids!" Holtzmann yelled.

Barnes stared at him coldly. "Not according to the law. Now do your fucking job."

Holtzmann sputtered. *I quit.* The words were on the tip of his tongue. But then the audit would kick in, the missing Nexus would be found...

His mouth opened but no words came out.

Barnes solved it for him.

"Get your ass in here, Martin. Shankari gave us bogus codes for the Nexus back doors. Go figure that out. Now!"

Then Barnes ended the call.

52
UNKNOWNS

Saturday October 27th

Breece packed up hurriedly. He rolled Hiroshi's body in a piece of carpet, hauled him out to the trunk of his car, then came back for the electronics, the Nexus vials, and the guns. He had no idea how much the hacker had gotten from Hiroshi's mind before he'd pulled the trigger...

Hiroshi's head, blood and brains blasted from it, sliding down the wall of the garage as his body crumpled into a heap.

...but he had to assume that the intruder had gotten enough.

He saturated the garage with enzyme bombs, then made his exit, locking the door behind him.

Then he put in the calls to Ava and the Nigerian.

They met four hours later, in a dive bar in Moscow, Texas, two hours from Houston.

They took a booth, crammed in close, talked softly under the cover of the raucous trash-rock. They were all raw, grieving, shocked by Hiroshi's death.

The questions cycled endlessly. Who was the hacker? How much did he learn? What did it mean for them? For their mission?

Very little made sense. If the hacker had been law enforcement, why not lead DHS or FBI to the site?

Could it have been Zara? But Zara had been surprised by the bombings in DC and Chicago, and the hacker had interceded in *both* of those events.

And so far, there was no movement at the safe house or the garage, no sign that either location had been found.

They tossed it back and forth for a while, and finally, it was Breece's decision.

"We'll wait and see," he said. "Stay ready to evac if we've been made."

"And if they don't come?" Ava asked. "If there's never a sign that we've been made?"

Breece nodded. "Then the mission's a go."

53

SAIL AWAY

Sunday October 28th

"No tracers," Sam repeated, her gun to Lo Prang's head. "Your boss is coming with me. I find a tracer, he dies. Badly."

"No tracers," Lo Prang echoed, calmly, agreeably.

His men nodded, kept on loading the last of the food and fuel and gear onto the stealth boat in this hidden cove. It was a smuggling craft, a low, skinny, quiet affair, with a sonar absorbent hull and a chameleonware upper shroud. If anything could get her up the coast and to the island she'd seen in that soldier's mind – Apyar Kyun, the Blue Island – this was it.

Lo Prang's two razor-nailed slave bitches watched her, still in their party dresses from the night before, their blades extended. Murder was in their eyes. The claw marks one of them had cut down her back ached. This was personal for them. If she crossed their paths again, they'd do their worst.

"Time to go," Sam said. She stood, dragged Lo Prang up with her, propelled him forward towards the low cigar of a vessel, her free hand on the cuffs that bound his wrists behind his back. Now was the time of maximum danger. *Transitions are points of vulnerability*, Nakamura had taught her. If they were going to try to take her, it was now or never...

But she and Lo Prang made it onto the boat unharmed.

Sam pushed Lo Prang forward, away from her, towards the driver's seat. "Drive," she said.

An hour later they were past the island of Koh Phayam, a few hundred yards off shore, and on their way towards the Burmese border.

"You could have done this the easy way, Jade," Lo Prang told her. "I meant what I told you. If you joined my household, you'd be happy." He gestured with his cuffed hands towards his head. "A little tweak here and there. All this stress? All this hardship? I could have taken care of whatever problem you have. And you'd have contentment, the satisfaction of having a purpose in life, of knowing what it was, of having a master who loved you."

Sam stared at Lo Prang and shook her head.

Lo Prang smiled. "Trust me, Jade. I've never had happier staff than I do now. They come to me willingly, for what I can give them, for the satisfaction, the peace and contentment. Even the whores are happy."

Sam shuddered. "There are more important things than happiness," she told the man. "Doing the right thing. Doing what matters."

Lo Prang smiled at her. "The right thing? What matters? Those are just patterns in your brain, Jade. A few tweaks, and your right thing would be mine."

"Not in this lifetime," Sam told him.

Lo Prang shrugged. "You'll change your mind one day. I'll be waiting."

They were leaving Koh Phayam behind now. It was time to make a choice.

Only kill when you have to, Nakamura had taught her. *Spare the lives you can, even of your enemies. You never know when someone might do the same for you.*

"Do you swim?" Sam asked Lo Prang.

The mob boss turned to look at her again, and snorted in amusement.

"And here I was looking forward to a vacation in Burma with you, Jade," he replied.

"You'd just slow me down." She smiled at him, sweetly, then tossed him the keys to his wrist and ankle cuffs.

Lo Prang snatched the keys from the air, snorted again, then killed the boat's engine and uncuffed himself.

He stood, afterwards, the cuffs in his hand, weighing them. Weighing the option of attacking her, Sam suspected. She shook her head ever so slightly, and Lo Prang smiled, dropped the cuffs, and took off his shoes and shirt.

He stood at the edge of the boat, looked into those waters and towards the shore. Then he turned to her. "I'll see you again, Jade."

"Not if I see you first," Sam replied, gesturing with the gun once more.

Lo Prang smiled. Then he dove into the blue waters, and started swimming for shore.

Sam watched until he was a dozen yards away, then she steered the boat further out to sea, towards the string of small uninhabited islands on the horizon. She'd need to find a place to hide until the sun went down. Perhaps to sleep. Then, when night came, she'd be on her way, and toward her target, Apyar Kyun, three hundred miles up this militarized coast.

54

PERSPECTIVE

Sunday October 28th

Kade received Shiva's summons the next morning, after they'd brought him breakfast. A guard locked the Nexus jammer around Kade's throat, escorted him to the rooftop where Shiva waited, reclining on a wooden chair. The older man gestured to the chair beside him, and Kade sat.

The view was glorious, straight out to the west over an uninterrupted expanse of sea. The nearest waters were jade green, turning to deeper and deeper shades of blue further to the west. In the other direction, to the east, Kade could see the wings of the mansion encircle the courtyard visible from his window. Beyond that was rolling land, then more water. An island.

"You haven't viewed my memories yet," Shiva said.

"I've been awfully busy," Kade replied.

Shiva chuckled at that.

"I want you to see that I have no ill intentions. That I'd use your back door for good. We'd use it together. There's a place for you here. A safe place, where you can do important work."

He'd heard this all before. From Su-Yong Shu. From Holtzmann, even, before they'd sent him off to Bangkok.

"What do you hope to accomplish?" Kade asked Shiva.

Shiva looked out towards the sea. "There are more than a million people running Nexus 5 now, Kade. A year from now it will be many times that. Among those people are scientists, engineers, executives at powerful corporations, bankers, even politicians."

Kade said nothing.

"The world has very serious problems, my friend," Shiva went on. "Poor children still die by their millions. Westerners and the global rich – like me – live in post-scarcity society, while a billion people struggle to get enough to eat. And we're pushing the planet towards a tipping point, where the corals die and the forests burn and life becomes much, much harder. We have the resources to solve those problems, even now, but politics and economics and nationalism all get in the way. If we could access all those minds, though…" Shiva paused, his eyes far away.

"We've done tests. Bright people linked together via Nexus become even brighter as whole. Interdisciplinary groups benefit especially. The children born with Nexus, well, they are even more impressive. They can serve as catalysts, boosting the collective intelligence of the group.

"With access to so many talented minds, we could harness scientists and engineers to invent the technologies we need to save the planet, to end poverty and starvation. We could nudge banks and mega-corporations to invest in the projects the world needs, marshaling *trillions* in assets. We could intervene politically, gaining inside information about world leaders, using it to steer them in the directions we need, to force them if necessary."

Kade was speechless. "You're talking about a massive scale..."

Shiva nodded. "Yes. I've been investing a large fraction of my own fortune to make it possible. Software to sift through and coordinate millions of minds at once. Data centers around the world to hold all that data, to provide all those CPU cycles. Private communication networks, microsatellites in low earth orbit, all of it."

Kade struggled for words. "Shiva, this is horrific. This is mass manipulation."

Shiva turned to look at Kade, visibly bristling. "Really? Is it worse than the manipulations of banks, twisting laws to their own purposes? Of mega-corporations twisting laws for their profits at the expense of the world's citizens?" His voice was angry, passion-filled. "Is it worse than financiers and corrupt politicians dining on pâté and caviar, while poor children starve?"

Kade exhaled, then shook his head. "Look, the world has problems. I agree with you. But what you're talking about... No one should have that kind of power."

Shiva snorted. "No one but *you*." He pointed an accusatory finger at Kade. "Isn't that what you mean?"

Kade felt a flush rise to his cheeks, felt his face go hot.

He's right, Ilya whispered in Kade's ear. *No one but you.*

Kade took a breath. This was nuts. He had to get out of here.

He opened his hands towards Shiva, placatingly. "Look, if you want to convince me," he told the older man, "why not just take this off?" His fingers rose to the metal disk at his throat.

Shiva laughed.

"And you would use that access to my mind to coerce me, to 'escape', out to a world where you're in far more danger than here. I don't think so, Kade."

"I give you my word," Kade said. "Let me just see what's going on in your mind. Not just some carefully selected memories. *All* of it. I promise not to do anything other than look."

Shiva smiled grimly. "You're a terrible liar, Kade."

55

BROTHERS IN ARMS

Sunday October 28th

Feng woke slowly. His head throbbed. Intense pain came from his left side, from his right knee, from his shoulder. And he was hungry, so hungry. His body's emergency genes had kicked in, working to heal the damage, demanding protein, fats, calcium, all the raw materials required to rebuild him. Feng ignored the gnawing hunger, kept his eyes closed, tried to take stock of his situation.

He was seated. A hard metal chair by the feel of it. His hands were cuffed behind his shoulders to his ankles, pulling them up off the floor. Professional.

His internal GPS gave him his location. Hồ Chí Minh City, Vietnam. Saigon. South side of town. Eighteen meters above street level.

Two kilometers from his last location, on the fifth or sixth floor. Who had him? Bounty hunters? Police? The mystery men with the Indian boss?

He opened his senses, listened to the room. A soft sound of breathing, three meters in front of him. Slow. Rhythmic. Deep. A lone male. Fit.

Feng tensed his muscles ever so slightly, aiming for the smallest motion, the minimum of sound. How strong were these cuffs? How strong was this chair?

"*Ni hao*," a voice greeted him in perfectly accented Mandarin: Welcome back.

Feng sighed and opened his eyes. He was in a soundproofed room, the walls thickly padded. And across from him, seated in a chair, was a tall Asian man. Japanese, perhaps. In his forties. Graying at the temples, but still fit and hard. In his hand was a silenced pistol of Chinese design, pointed at Feng. On his face was a grim smile.

Feng recognized the man from Kade's memories.

"You're Nakamura," Feng said.

"And you're Feng," Nakamura replied.

They stared at each other in silence for a moment.

Feng broke it. "You pulled me from the building?"

Nakamura nodded. "You got lucky. A beam fell above you, got pinned against your jeep. You were in an air pocket. Otherwise..."

Feng laughed. "Lucky. Yeah." He rattled the restraints behind him.

Nakamura raised one eyebrow. "Beats death."

Feng nodded. The man had a point there.

"Where's Samantha Cataranes?" Nakamura asked.

Feng blinked in surprise.

"Thailand, maybe?" Feng guessed. "Left her six months ago."

Nakamura frowned. "Why?"

Feng shrugged as best he could. "Wanted to find kids. Nexus kids."

Nakamura's frown deepened. "Lane let her go?"

Feng cocked his head, quizzically. "What you mean?"

"Lane," Nakamura started again. "He..."

"You have him?" Feng interrupted. "Kade?"

Nakamura stared at him.

"Who turned Sam?" Nakamura asked, "Lane? Or Shu?"

Feng blinked again. "You turned her. ERD turned her. Killed a little girl in Bangkok. Killed civilians. Blew up building with people in it. While they're all on Nexus and Sam feels it. That's what turned her."

Nakamura went silent. In the corner of his eye the DNA match kept blinking. A match against Lane's DNA, on Feng's clothing. No match on Sam's DNA, anywhere. Feng hadn't been near Sam anytime recently.

Was it possible? That neither Lane nor Shu had reprogrammed Sam? That what she'd experienced had flipped her so suddenly?

Jesus.

Feng interrupted his thoughts. "Kade. You have him or not?"

Nakamura looked at Feng. If Sam really had turned on her own... Then the worst thing he could do was lead the CIA to her.

He needed more data. But he also had a mission.

"No," he told Feng. "I don't have Lane. But I want him. Who took him?"

Feng calculated. That third force must have Kade. The old Indian man and his soldiers.

Handing Kade over to the CIA would be no better. But if he helped Nakamura... Chaos could produce opportunity. An opportunity to get Kade free.

"I don't know," Feng said. "But I'll help you find out. One condition."

"What's that?" Nakamura asked.

"When you go get him, I come with you."

It took twenty minutes to figure out who had taken Kade. Nakamura listened as Feng told his story, then fed the data and the description of the man to a CIA analyst AI. It brought back dozens of hits of older Indian and South Asian men who might have been in Saigon, who had connections there, who might in some way be connected to the case.

He showed the images to Feng on a slate from across the room, one by one.

"That's him," Feng said. "I'm sure of it."

Nakamura looked at the hit. Shiva Prasad.

With the name came data.

The untouchable billionaire had entered Vietnam on his private jet a week ago. And before dawn this morning his passport had been electronically stamped again, as he'd left in that jet once more, with a flight plan filed for his private island off the coast of Burma.

"Hey, you have any food?" he heard Feng ask. "Really hungry."

Nakamura smiled widely.

"Sure, Feng," he said. "And I hope you can swim."

56

OLD FLAMES

Monday October 29th

Holtzmann fumed after the call with Barnes cut off. But there was nothing he could do for those poor children.

Somehow he had to get Rangan Shankari out of ERD custody. But how? He could walk Shankari out of that cell, give him the keys to his own car, and in the very best case the ERD would just pick Shankari up a few hours later, and lock Holtzmann away for good.

He needed help.

An underground railroad. That's what the rumors said. A network that got Nexus-born children out of the country. Would they take Shankari? Holtzmann had no idea. But he thought there was one person who might know.

Her number was in his phone, years after she'd tired of his lies and his weakness and cut off their affair. Did she ever think back to their time fondly? Or was he a pathetic figure in her mind, a man who'd lied and cheated, seduced her even though he was her professor and fifteen years her senior? Would she even talk to him after their encounter at the Capitol?

There was only one way to find out.

Holtzmann tapped on his phone, and called Lisa Brandt.

She picked up on the third ring.

"Hello?"

"Lisa," he said. "It's Martin Holtzmann."

"I know who it is," she said coldly. "What do you want?"

Martin paused. Hostility… He deserved it.

"Lisa," he said. "I was thinking about our last conversation. I… I may have changed my mind. I'd like to talk."

Silence. More silence.

"I'm listening," she said finally.

"Could we… talk in person?" he asked.

"I'm in Boston, Martin."

"I know, I know," he said. "I can come to you. I'll take the train up. Lunch tomorrow? Leonetti's?" She used to love Leonetti's.

Another pause.

"Not lunch," she replied. "Coffee. Harvard Square Café. 2pm. Come alone."

"Thank you…" he started.

The line clicked and went dead.

Lisa Brandt ended the call, and looked across the small room to where her wife Alice rocked their adopted son Dilan as he nursed.

"Martin Holtzmann?" Alice asked with a raised eyebrow.

Lisa could feel the wave of surprised curiosity and concern radiate from her wife, overlaid with the mixed fatigue and contentment of Dilan suckling at the milk produced by her hormonally augmented breasts.

Lisa nodded. "Holtzmann." But her eyes were on their son. She could feel his sleepy hunger, his secure comfort. Such a special child.

I should have taken the hormone boost too, Lisa thought. I should be doing my part nursing him. But it was easier for Alice, easier with her career in finance already established enough that she could take so much time off, while Lisa still toiled daily towards tenure in her ivory tower.

"What did he want?" Alice asked.

"To talk," Lisa said. "Maybe to blow a whistle."

Alice squinted, and Lisa could feel her skepticism. "Whistle-blowing takes balls and a conscience. The Martin Holtzmann you've described didn't sound like he had *either*."

"No," Lisa sighed. "He didn't."

Anne got home an hour later.

"You look better," she said.

Holtzmann smiled. "I feel better. In fact, I think I'll go to the office tomorrow."

Anne Holtzmann lay in bed, pretending to sleep, listening to her husband's breathing until she was sure he was out.

Something was very wrong here. Paranoia. Emotional outbursts. Night sweats and vomiting. It almost reminded her of...

Anne rose quietly and padded into the bathroom. One by one she opened the medicine cabinets, then the drawers, searching through them, looking for a bottle of pills.

Nothing. Martin had finished the painkillers months ago. So why was he acting like a man on drugs?

Anne Holtzmann crept quietly back into bed, troubled. Tomorrow. Tomorrow she'd do some digging into her husband's activities.

57
EN ROUTE

Monday October 29th

He who knows when he can fight and when he cannot will be victorious. Sun Tzu had written that in *The Art of War*. Feng repeated it to himself again and again as Nakamura drove them out of the city, to a darkened piece of coast on the Mekong Delta, as Nakamura left Feng chained inside the jeep as he loaded supplies into the inflatable boat, as Nakamura clipped a metal leash to Feng's restraints and pointed with his gun towards the beach.

So tired. Every part of him hurt. He'd downed thousands of calories and the hunger still gnawed inside, his body ravenous for resources to apply to its reconstruction. At his best, he thought he could take the CIA man. But chained, wounded, tired, and weaponless?

Ahead the inflatable boat waited on the sand, piled high with supplies as waves crashed down a few meters beyond it.

"The engine won't start without me," Nakamura said. "Drag it out into the water."

Feng did as he was told, dragging it out with his bound hands as Nakamura followed, until he was thigh-deep in the surf. The CIA agent climbed in, the end of Feng's leash still in his hand. "Come aboard," he said. And then Feng was in the boat as well, in the front, looking back at Nakamura.

"We going all the way to Burma in this thing?" Feng asked.

His CIA captor just laughed.

Nakamura kept half an eye on Feng. The rest of his attention he devoted to the rendezvous. He steered south and east for an hour, his eyes peeled for any sign they were being followed or observed. Off to his left, robotic container ships bobbed on the horizon, their superstructures illuminated for safety, waiting for their turn to enter the Nha Be River and unload their wares. Ahead, the sea was dark and apparently empty.

His GPS told him it was time. They were in the zone. He killed the engine. At the forward end of the boat, Feng raised an eyebrow.

Access resource "Manta 7," Nakamura subvocalized. *Initiate pickup sequence. Execute.*

"You may want to turn around," he told Feng with a smile. Reluctantly, the Confucian Fist did so.

For a moment nothing happened. And then a patch of dark sea became calmer, darker, flatter.

Something was rising up. Something wide and blacker than the midnight water, shaped like a stretched rounded wedge, a boomerang with a thickened center. It rose above the waves and water ran off of it.

The central fuselage of the sub was a thicker bulge in the middle of the flying V, twenty feet long and perhaps five feet wide. It gave way in a graceful arc to the wide wings, forty feet from one wingtip fin to the other, swept slightly back behind the body. Every surface was curved for stealth and hydrodynamic efficiency. Barely visible were the ports that could open to launch probes, sensors, and weapons. It was a thing of beauty.

Feng whistled softly. "Manta class," he said, turning back to Nakamura. "Chinese. How'd you get this?"

Nakamura smiled broadly. "Feng, weren't you listening? I'm with the CIA."

They loaded the supplies into the sub. The interior was too small to stand upright in, but more than large enough for the two of them and their supplies. When they were done, Nakamura sent instructions to the jeep on the beach. It would tint its windows and drive itself carefully and unobtrusively back to its home.

"This sub…" Feng asked. "If things go wrong, everything's blamed on China, yeah?"

Nakamura shrugged, then made the ground rules clear to Feng.

"This sub is slaved to me. The controls respond only to me. And if my biometrics fail, it vents the air and dives to the deepest point it can find. If you try to take the controls, it does the same thing. You understand?"

Feng nodded. "I understand." He smiled grimly. "You my buddy."

Nakamura smiled in return. "Feng, I'm the best friend you've got in the world right now."

58
THE FREEDOM TRAIL

Tuesday October 30th

Holtzmann called in sick, then took the train to Cambridge. He passed Nexus detectors, all of his own design, all blind to him. The news on the train was of the pending landslide election and of Zoe. The tropical storm turned hurricane had beaten a path across Cuba, leveling buildings, tossing cars around, killing dozens, sending tourists fleeing for shelter before heading north to narrowly miss Miami.

He emerged hours later into stifling heat. He'd been an undergrad at MIT, not far from here, thirty years ago. October should be cool, highs in the sixties, trees turning yellow and red. But today it was in the eighties. The trees were brown, suffering in heat that had beaten down the Eastern Seaboard the last several months, wiping out crops and feeding energy into storms like Zoe.

He found Lisa Brandt at an outdoor table in a cool white dress, an iced drink in a plastic cup in front of her. His heart beat fast at the sight of her.

She saw him, met his eyes, and rose, gesturing for him to follow her.

"Lisa…" he started.

"Wait," she said, as she led them off, across the street and onto the Harvard campus.

Holtzmann bit his tongue.

She led them to the Harvard Yard. Undergrads sped past them, on their way to and from classes.

"Now," Lisa said. "Softly. And from the beginning."

Holtzmann took a deep breath.

"There's someone… someone I think you'd be interested in."

Lisa turned, raised an eyebrow at him.

"Rangan Shankari," he half whispered.

Lisa frowned. "What about him?"

"I know where he is."

Her frown deepened. "It's the children we're most interested in, Martin. If you have information that can prove children are being held for research purposes…"

Holtzmann swallowed. "You need to get Shankari out. I need him out. I need him safe."

Lisa stopped walking. "What are you talking about?"

He stared into her eyes, whispered intently. "I'll give you whatever you want. Proof children are being held. But my price is Shankari. You have to get him out."

Lisa was shaking her head. "Martin, if you think you're going to… to *entrap me* into planning some sort of prison breakout…"

He reached out, took her by the shoulders. "Please, Lisa. You have to help me. Please!"

She stepped back, smacked his hands away. "Don't touch me." Her voice was hard, angry. Students looked their way as they passed.

Holtzmann closed his eyes, took another deep breath, opened them. "I'm sorry. It's just that, if he stays in custody…" He felt it deep inside. The compulsion. Pressing on him, expanding, threatening to burst him open if he didn't act on it. "Bad things will happen. Very bad."

Lisa shook her head. "You're just wasting my time." She turned and walked away.

"Please, Lisa!" Holtzmann said to her back. "Please!" He walked after her, grabbed her arm.

She turned and slapped him, yanked her arm away. "Don't *touch* me!" More students looked their way now. Lisa whirled, then strode away.

He did the last thing he could, then. He opened his mind to her, reached out to her, hoping against hope...

He felt nothing there. But she stumbled, surprised, maybe, and turned, and looked at him.

He beamed his sincerity to her, his sincerity in offering her the proof she wanted, his deep desire to see Rangan Shankari go free.

He couldn't feel her. But she held his gaze, then stepped towards him.

"Give me an account," she whispered. "Where you can be reached."

He told her. Told her the name of an account he kept on a Nexus message board, an account whose existence was enough to hang him.

Then she stepped back, and spoke loudly, for any passerby to hear. "I'm sorry. I can't help you. Good luck."

Then Lisa Brandt turned and walked away.

Holtzmann was in a daze as he took the train back to DC. At home he logged into the Nexus board. There was a message there, from an account he'd never seen before.

[Send the evidence. Then we'll talk.]

He sent his own note in reply.

[Will send half. The rest when my friend is out.]

The reply came back in less than a minute.

[Agreed.]

Holtzmann sat down at his secure terminal in his second-floor office, connected to work, and started collating the files. He heard Anne come home while he worked. He yelled out a hello, but she didn't answer from downstairs.

He pulled the data together. Records of experiments on the children. Manifests of their ages and names. A recording of the torture used to force Nexus out of a nine year-old autistic boy. Blueprints for "long-term residence" facilities that were little more than concentration camps. Plans and imperatives for the Nexus "cure" and "vaccine".

He made sure none could be tied specifically to him, then downloaded the files. He ran it all through a filter, cutting the documents and images and video into right and left halves. The right half he fired off in reply to the message. The left half he uploaded to his own account on the message board, but didn't send. For that, they'd have to deliver.

Anne was in the kitchen when Holtzmann went downstairs.

"Hi," he said.

She turned and stared at him. "Where were you today, Martin?" Her face was cold, hard.

Holtzmann blinked.

"At the office."

"No, you weren't. I checked. You've been sick since *Friday*."

Holtzmann reached for some explanation.

"And who's Lisa Brandt, Martin? Wasn't she a student of yours?"

Holtzmann's chest caught in his throat.

"Is she who you went to visit in Boston today?"

"Anne…"

"I have access to the accounts and the phone records, Martin. I'm not stupid."

"Anne, it's not what you think…"

She stared at him. "What's going on, Martin?"

Holtzmann's head spun. What could he tell her? Jesus.

"Come with me," Holtzmann told his wife.

He dragged her down to the basement, to the laundry room, past it, to the room with the old furnace, the room with no windows a laser could be bounced off of, the room least likely to be bugged. He closed the door behind them, and then leaned close to her, and whispered.

"Anne. Who had the most to gain from the assassination attempt? Who benefited?"

She frowned at him. "What the hell are you talking about?" Her voice was angry, impatient.

"The President, Anne." He glared back at her. "You said it yourself! The PLF couldn't shoot straight! And Stockton was *losing*!"

Anne scoffed. "You're paranoid, Martin. You're worse than Claire! Those were Stockton's *friends* that died. Cabinet members."

He took her by the shoulders. "Think, Anne! Think about it!" He needed to make her understand.

"*You* think, Martin. Didn't the President overrule Barnes on killing those kids? Would a man who'd kill his own friends do that?"

Holtzmann stared at her.

"And why the bomb in Chicago? He was already up in the polls. So that *wasn't him*."

Holtzmann kept staring at her, a terrible feeling of disorientation washing over him. He'd been so sure… It made so much sense.

"And you're running around trying to dig into this *conspiracy*? You need *help*, Martin. You need a psychiatrist. Get yourself together!"

Holtzmann sat in his office after Anne had gone to bed.

Something kept tickling at his head. Something she'd said. *You're worse than Claire!*

Claire. Warren Becker's wife. And what had Warren said? It had been the Spears kidnapping. The one the files blamed on the PLF.

Mexican cartels, Warren Becker had told him once over drinks.

Cartels. Not the PLF. Cartels.

So why did the official record read differently?

It was thin, very thin. But if the PLF wasn't what everyone thought… Perhaps that one thread…

A notification chimed in his mind. From the Nexus board. A new message.

[Files look good. Get your friend to the ER at Vincent Gray tomorrow night, between 10pm and 4am. We'll provide appropriate care.]

Holtzmann stared at the message, then deleted it.

Vincent Gray was the closest hospital to DHS Headquarters. Now all he needed was to get Rangan Shankari there.

59
ALONE TOGETHER

Tuesday October 30th

The bad men came for Bobby two days after Alfonso and he knew that if he let them take him away they'd take the Nexus from his head and he'd be no one he'd be dead he wouldn't be a person anymore, so Bobby tried to KICK the bad men and BITE them and SCRATCH them, but they were too strong and one of the men slapped him in the head and it HURT and then they dragged him out, through two doors into the special testing room.

The door closed behind Bobby and then his friends were gone. They were gone from his head. He couldn't feel them at all. The bad men put Bobby in a chair and they strapped his hands down to the arms of the chair which they'd never done before and which scared him and he knew this was it, they were going to push the Nexus out of his head like they had to Alfonso and things would be like they were before, before his daddy Derik had given Bobby Nexus and given himself Nexus and then Bobby could feel his daddy for the first time and know that he was a PERSON – a person like Bobby and not like all the other fake people who didn't have anything in their heads at all.

And since that day Bobby hadn't been so alone. He could feel people now, his daddy and then the boys here Tim and Alfonso and Jason and Tyrone and the other boys, and for the first time he had real FRIENDS even if they were in a bad place; he had other boys he could feel and understand and who could feel him and understand him and now he was crying and crying – and he knew that only little boys cried only babies cried and he was twelve and he wasn't supposed to cry – but he knew what was going to happen, they were going to make him like Alfonso and Alfonso was all alone now and Alfonso just cried, and Alfonso MIGHT AS WELL BE DEAD because he'd never feel anyone again and no one would ever feel him and he was just empty like all the other STUPID PEOPLE who didn't have Nexus and weren't really people at all.

They lowered something metal onto Bobby's head in the chair, and he cried and asked them please please please let me go please I need it to feel other people, please I need it to be real, please I need it to have friends please please please don't be mean, don't make me stop being real I'll take a test, I'll learn Spanish I'll learn French I'll do TRIGONOMETRY I'll do anything, please please please he cried and cried and cried.

Rangan felt the chaos as the orderlies took Bobby from the room next door, and he knew what it meant. He was untied again, uncuffed from the gurney. He sat in the corner, head down, in defeat. The ERD didn't have the real back doors. But that was academic. Eventually they'd succeed in reverse-engineering the code. It would be difficult, with the passcodes buried among hundreds of millions of parameters of the neural nets, among blocks of synaptic weights and neural interconnectivity graphs that looked like so much random numerical garbage, that would mask the passcodes for quite a

long time. Deciphering that would be a harder problem than
building Nexus 5 in the first place. But the ERD had resources.
Sooner or later, after months or years, they'd crack it.

And even if they didn't? They still had the guns. They
could still arrest kids like Bobby, take them away from their
parents, kill their parents. They'd found a way to force
Nexus out of Alfonso's brain. And now they'd do to the
same to Bobby. They'd cripple a little boy because it didn't
fit their ideology.

Rangan shook his head. Tyrone came and lay down in
Bobby's bunk, reached out to Rangan, and Rangan did his
best to send soothing thoughts, to try to calm the boys down,
even when what he felt inside was despair.

Bobby cried and begged and then one of the men spoke to him.

"Bobby, that's your name, right? Bobby, we're not going
to hurt you. We're trying to help you, son."

Bobby stared at the man. He was old and had a mustache
and he was smiling like the teachers told Bobby to do to show
that he was nice but there was nobody there in the man's
head and he had Bobby tied down to a chair with something
on his head so he definitely wasn't very nice at all.

"Bobby, you know how to run Nexus commands,
don't you?"

And even though the man wasn't nice, Bobby nodded
his head because there was always the chance that he was
wrong and that they weren't going to push the Nexus out of
him – and maybe if he was good and did what they wanted
they'd let him go back to the other boys and still have Nexus
and still be a person and still have friends and...

"We need you to run a command, son. There in your
Nexus. On the screen inside your head. OK?"

Bobby nodded again and this wasn't so bad if they just wanted him to run some sort of command, which meant running some sort of program or executing some sort of script or changing some configuration and Bobby understood how Nexus was kind of a computer in his head because he'd learned about it from Rangan, and he understood about computers because they made sense they made way more sense than people especially the fake people that…

"The command is Nexus Purge," the man said. "It'll make you feel better." And then the man started to spell out "Nexus" and "purge" for Bobby, like Bobby was an idiot – but Bobby wasn't listening because he understood computers and he had a good vocabulary, and he knew what Nexus was from Rangan and he knew what purge meant and sometimes it meant something about your body like if you pooped or threw up a whole lot, but now it meant the other kind, to rid, clear, or free, and so the old man with the mustache was telling him to rid, clear, or free Nexus and Bobby didn't want to do that at all, and they were trying to trick him and that made him mad.

"NO!" he yelled. "I need Nexus I need Nexus please please please."

"Son," the man said, "This won't hurt your Nexus. It's just gonna fix some problems and make you feel better."

And he was lying to Bobby and treating Bobby like he was stupid that made him even more mad and so he yelled at the man "I'M AUTISTIC – NOT STUPID!" and he kept yelling it and kept yelling it, and the man shook his head and nodded at someone else, and then something hit Bobby's head hard, something different like noise, like static, like ALL THE STATIC IN THE WORLD and he saw static and he heard static and he tasted static and he felt static and he smelled static and it was SO LOUD he couldn't think, couldn't think, and it HURT it HURT it HURT and he SCREAMED at them...

And then it stopped.

Bobby was crying when it ended, crying and crying and crying, and he thought maybe he'd peed himself, but he wasn't sure because everything was so confused and he couldn't tell what was happening anymore and then the man spoke again.

"Son, you're sick. What you just felt... that was you being sick. We want to help you. We want to make that go away. Just run the command. Nexus Purge. And then you'll feel better."

And Bobby cried, but he knew the man was lying. He wasn't sick he hadn't felt that way because he was sick, he'd felt it because of the metal thing over his head and it was because these men were doing it to him because they were so so so so bad, and he kept crying because he didn't want to feel that way again, didn't want it to happen again, but if he PURGED Nexus then it would be even worse and then he thought of something, LOGIC told him something, and suddenly he felt different because he understood, he had an ADVANTAGE like his daddy used to say, because if these men were trying to get him to run Nexus Purge and get rid of his Nexus himself, then maybe that was because THEY COULDN'T DO IT TO HIM!

And then they did the awful static thing to him again and he couldn't think and his hands were twitching and his feet were twitching and he bit his tongue and nothing worked, and he definitely peed himself this time and maybe pooped himself and everything hurt so bad and everything was so confusing and when it was over he was crying again – but he remembered he remembered what he'd figured out and when the man said, "Son, please, you have to run Nexus Purge! You have to help yourself or you'll keep getting sick!"

then Bobby just looked at the man and he was still crying, but he yelled at the man, "YOU CAN'T MAKE ME! YOU CAN'T MAKE ME! YOU CAN'T MAKE ME!"

And he kept yelling it, every chance he could, in between the times they hurt him.

Rangan sat slumped in the corner, trying to find some way to keep hope, to keep the boys hopeful, even when they all seemed doomed.

And then a ripple went through the boys. Something shocked them. Something spread out through them, and into Rangan.

Bobby. Bobby.

Rangan could feel the boy's mind, reflected through Pedro's. Bobby was back. He felt exhausted, stunned, drained. But he was there. His mind was there. Somehow he'd beaten them.

The other boys led Bobby in to the night room, and onto his bunk, and Bobby reached out for Rangan, and Rangan put his mental arms around the boy, and pulled Bobby in close, and wept in relief.

60

VISIONS

Shiva gave Kade access to the research staff. He could leave his rooms during daylight, always with the Nexus jammer on him. He waited for any crack of discipline, any accident, a drained battery, an outer door left open when the inner door opened, a key left unprotected in his sight.

He saw none. The researchers answered his questions, showed him the tools they were building, the systems to coordinate millions of minds, the incredible results the Nexus children showed on intelligence tests, the ways to tap into that on an even grander scale.

And despite himself, he was impressed.

How different were Shiva's goals from his own? He thought of that thin layer of mind encircling the globe, unformed, raw potential. What if he could touch those minds with Shiva's tools? What could they make real?

Every day, Kade dined with Shiva, and at times with others of Shiva's staff. A breakfast here. A lunch there. Tea, between meetings and calls that Shiva had. Dinner, whenever Kade chose to go. The weather was hot and clear

when he arrived. It grew windier and wetter as the days
went on. Yet all of it was beautiful.

Shiva denied him one thing, beside his freedom.

"I want to talk to the children," Kade said.

"Absolutely not," Shiva replied. "They're young,
vulnerable. Some of them have been traumatized. I won't
have you confusing them further."

Still, he saw the children from a distance from his
window, or from the roof, or when visiting researchers.
There were three or four distinct groups. One of those
groups seemed to recognize Kade. Had they seen Sam?
Kade wondered where she was now. But he said nothing
to Shiva. Any information he held back might prove
an advantage.

The days passed. Sunday turned to Monday turned to
Tuesday turned to Wednesday.

After Wednesday night's dinner a guard brought him
back to his room. The guard activated his own Nexus
jammer and removed Kade's. They treated him gently,
politely, even deferentially. The servers and the security
staff called him "sir".

He sat on one of the antique oversized chairs and stared
at the box with the slate inside.

What am I afraid of? he asked himself. *Why don't I want to
touch Shiva's thoughts?*

You're afraid he's telling the truth, Ilya's voice answered
him. *That he has only the best of intentions.*

Why?

Because, Ilya went on, *if that's the case, he has as much right
to the back doors as you do. Maybe more. He's smarter than you
are. He understands the world better than you do. If you deserve
the back doors, then he does too. If he doesn't, then you don't either.*

Kade fell asleep struggling with that thought, looking for a way to refute it.

He woke again in darkness, restless. He rose, put on one of the robes they'd given him, threw back the curtains, found a cloudy night, wind blowing, a tossing and churning sea. Where was Feng now? Where was Rangan? Was the PLF still moving forward with their plot? Were hundreds more going to die because of him? Would war break out?

He looked over at the locked box. He'd moved it to the writing desk. It would be so easy. Open his mind to it. Let Shiva persuade him. Agree to hand over this burden to someone else.

He thought of all the benefits it would bring. More resources. Giant server farms spread around the world, orbital communication satellites, teams of programmers. They could nip Nexus coercion in the bud, stop the rapists and thieves and assassins. Shiva's coders could help him finish Nexus 6, integrate the safeguards that would make it difficult to use Nexus that way.

They could rescue Rangan. They could stop the assassination set for Saturday. They might find Feng, still alive, if he was lucky.

They could bring all those Nexus-carrying minds across the planet together, into something greater.

All he had to do was give Shiva the key that would open a million minds.

Kade sat at the writing desk. He put his hands on the armored case. It was cool to the touch. Inside was a device, a transmitter, loaded with thoughts and memories.

Kade went inside, and turned Nexus OS's file sharing back on.

• • •

Shiva lay sleepless on his hard cot in the narrow cell he allowed himself. Lane was softening. He could see it in each conversation. The boy was tired of his burden, was tired of being alone, was increasingly persuaded of Shiva's good intentions. Soon, days or weeks, he would consent.

Shiva took a deep breath.

Am I worthy? Is this just? Is this moral?

Now, as the tool he'd sought was almost in his grasp, he had his doubts.

Nita would hate this, he mused. Hate it more than anything I've ever done. Hubris, she'd call it.

The gods punish hubris, he told himself, in every religion, in every mythology.

But he had only to think of the world outside, of the multiple precipices that humanity and this world teetered on, to hear the opposing view. That humanity needed saving. Needed it desperately. And could not do the saving itself.

"I'm doing this for the world, Nita," he whispered in the darkness. "And if not me, then who? If not now, then when?"

Kade inspected the available data. It was huge. Shiva was offering him giant swaths of thought and memory.

He analyzed the files, ran them through virus checkers and security sweeps, made sure there was no embedded code in them. It was one thing to be persuaded. It was another to be tricked.

He found nothing untoward.

Even so, he instanced a sandbox inside his mind, and another, differently configured sandbox within the first, and only in that secure environment did he allow the files to play.

He was engrossed, immediately, sucked in to what Shiva was sharing. This was more than his plans. It was his life, his childhood, the events that had formed him, the triumphs and tragedies he'd been through. The fears he held deep inside, fears for the whole world. And the hopes he held onto as well.

Kade devoured the thoughts, the memories, the experiences, the knowledge. He bent all his Nexus CPU cycles to the task, cranked up his assimilation rate far beyond real-time. He slipped into a near trance, immersing himself in this person, in what he knew, in what he'd done. The mask of *maya* slipped away, and for a time he was Kade no longer. He was Shiva, and so much more.

He came back to himself hours and hours later. It was fully light outside, late morning, approaching noon. He had a vague memory of the serving girl coming and going. The wheeled cart was still here, loaded with food.

Kade ignored it.

He got up, went to the window, looked outside at the gorgeous water down below, the multicolored sea with its bands of jade and emerald and sea-green and lapis lazuli and a dozen more colors he couldn't name.

He understood these waters, now. He knew their chemistry. He knew their ecology. He remembered diving off the coast of India, *Shiva* diving there, guided by his wife, examining the dying corals, despairing at their fate. Kade had read about ocean acidification. Now he understood it intimately – the horror of seeing once vibrant reefs reduced to a deathly gray. The intimate comprehension of their vulnerability, how even after Shiva's viral hack they teetered on the edge, how their death threatened all the fish and other species that depended on them.

North, near the poles, the tundra of the Arctic, melting, decaying, giving off methane. He'd been there. *Shiva* had been there, at Nita's insistence. Bundled in sub-zero gear, he'd seen the methane belching from thawing permafrost. He'd seen the mile-wide plumes of methane bubbles rising from the decaying slush of carbon ice just below the warming Arctic Sea.

He understood the risk, at last. It wasn't just an abstraction to him, anymore. It was a visceral threat, as Shiva felt it, as real as the fear he felt looking down from a great height. A few more hot summers could destabilize those fields, send up even more massive bubbles of heat-trapping gas that would bake the Earth, scour the fields where food grew with drought and storm, wither away the rainforest, destroy humanity's food supplies and shelter in the span of months or years, bring human civilization and the biosphere both to their knees.

Kade looked out further west. Beyond that horizon lay India, his homeland. *Shiva's* homeland. The third largest economy on the planet now. Yet he had vivid memories of holding a dying child in his arms, of watching villagers starve just kilometers from the homes of the newly wealthy kings of technology.

He knew the count and position of thousands of nuclear warheads there, pointed at nearby Pakistan, at China, at Iran, even at Europe and the United States. He knew all about the three secret times that India and Pakistan had come within millimeters of going nuclear, had almost killed millions in the matter of minutes, almost ignited war that would kill *hundreds* of millions.

He looked across those waves and he remembered his childhood as an orphan, an *untouchable* orphan, the lowest of the low, struggling to eat, to survive. The beatings. The vicious street gangs that he'd barely escaped. The conviction that violence must be met with violence, that those who hurt you must be punished. And later, when ignorant villagers had killed orphans under *his* protection, the rage he'd felt, the screams as his men had nailed the perpetrators to those crosses, as the flames had brought him justice.

Further west, Europe, North America. He knew more than ever about the treatment of humanity's successors there. The secret purges. The viral weapons lying in wait, ready to deal death down on the genetically enhanced. The Nexus detectors to find the enhanced. The work to create a vaccine against Nexus, to create a "cure" that would purge it from the mind, even from the minds of those who'd lived their entire lives with it. The backup plans. The concentration camps for the expected wave of Nexus-born children, the hundreds of thousands of them that might be born in the next decade.

There was so much wrong with the world. There were so many precipices. So many cliffs humanity could fall off of. So many crimes being committed, so many risks being taken.

And Kade understood why. They were a tribal species. They'd evolved in a world where a few dozen men and women made up a tribe, and virtually all others were enemies, threats. They lacked the cognitive capabilities necessary to collaborate on this scale. They'd done their best with democracy, with capitalism, but those had reached their limit long ago. They'd been corrupted, twisted to the interests of a few individuals, when the greatest problems the world faced were problems of *collective* interest.

He could fix those systems. He could nudge the world, could pull strings from behind the scenes, could direct scientists and engineers towards the right problems, could link their minds together to make them even more effective, could manipulate banks and corporations to provide resources, could twist politicians to enact the laws needed to save the world and benefit the people on it.

And beyond that – Kade could bring the world's minds together, link human to human, into something more, into a global consciousness, a posthuman intelligence, mediated by Nexus, coordinated by the tools Shiva had built.

All it would require was the key. The key that would open a million minds today, that would open tens of millions, maybe hundreds of millions of minds, at some point in the future. That was all.

61
WAR STORIES

In a cramped submarine beneath the waters of the Andaman Sea, Kevin Nakamura laughed as Feng gesticulated with his cuffed hands.

"So I throw the butter knife, yeah?" the Chinese soldier was saying. "Boom! Right through the eye." Feng shook his head. "But he gets me with cleaver first. That's how I get this one." Feng gestured at the scar across one forearm.

"So that was Almaty?" Nakamura asked.

"Yeah," Feng replied. "In '37. You there?"

Nakamura nodded, rolled up one pant leg, showed the scar below his knee.

Feng peered at it and frowned. "Sniper?" he asked.

Nakamura laughed. "Farmer. With a pitchfork."

"Pitchfork!" Feng laughed in return. "You see action at Astana too?"

Nakamura shook his head. "Not me. But I had friends who were there." He cocked his head. "Were you at Mashadd, in '35? Or what about Maymana, back in '26?"

Feng's expression turned puzzled. "In '26... I was eight."

441

Nakamura frowned.

"You old, man," Feng said.

Nakamura glared at the pup, then snorted and turned back to the sub's controls. Two more days to Apyar Kyun.

Two hundred miles off the coast of the southeastern United States, Zoe raged. Beneath her, the October seas were hot, hotter than they'd been this late in the year in millennia. The currents of the Gulf Stream dragged warm water north from the equator and into the mid-Atlantic, adding energy to seas already heated from a record summer.

The Atlantic gave off that excess heat now, evaporating it as water vapor into the air above.

Zoe gorged on that warm vapor-filled air, absorbing its energy and its moisture. They added to her, strengthened her, fueling her winds, driving them ever faster and more furiously about her calm center until she whirled about at a fifth the speed of sound.

North Zoe went. And chaos went with her.

62

THE PRICE OF FREEDOM

Wednesday October 31st

Holtzmann slipped out of bed at 6am, while Anne still slept. His head pounded and his mouth was dry. His body felt stiff. His stomach was unsteady. He craved more opiates. But that wasn't going to happen today.

He showered and dressed quickly. Anne rolled over in bed, murmured something, then nothing more. Then he was in the car and on his way to the office.

The news had more on Stockton's impending victory. The rest was Zoe. The hurricane had sped north and east into the warm, wide open Atlantic, sucking energy from the unprecedentedly hot surface waters as it went, intensifying from the Category 4 storm that had wrecked Havana into a Category 5 monster, with hundred-and-sixty mile per hour winds and ten-foot sea swells. And now Zoe's track was bending again, turning it towards north by northwest, putting it on a course towards central New Jersey, with possible landfall Friday night. God, what a disaster that would be.

He arrived at the office a little after 7 o'clock, collected his slate and the images he needed, then headed to the

Human Subjects wing. ERD Headquarters was no prison. It wasn't equipped for long-term interment. But the Human Subjects wing could house up to fifty subjects, for research purposes, for months at a time.

Holtzmann swiped his ID to enter the wing, then walked up to the security desk.

He recognized the guard. "I'm here to see Rangan Shankari," he told the man, holding up his ID.

The guard nodded, then looked over at his maze of monitors.

"Room 31," he replied. "He's still asleep."

"Wake him up," Holtzmann said. "I'll be in the interview room."

Two guards brought Shankari to him ten minutes later, his wrists cuffed to one another. They clipped his cuffs to the hardpoint on the table, which was itself bolted to the floor. Holtzmann waited across that table for the guards to leave. Just seeing Shankari sent a powerful buzz through him. He was so close... So close to getting Rangan out of here...

Wait for it, he told himself. Tonight.

The guards left.

"Rangan," Holtzmann said. "It's been some time."

"Not long enough," Shankari muttered darkly.

Holtzmann slid his slate across the table to Shankari.

"Open it. See what Nexus has done to the world."

With his hands restrained, Shankari could just barely touch the surface of the slate. The first image was an aerial view of the assassination site, just a quarter-mile from here. Bodies were scattered across the ground, the geometry of the white seats shattered in a zone around the blast.

Shankari looked at the image. "What's this?"

Holtzmann answered him. "Three months ago the Posthuman Liberation Front used Nexus 5 to reprogram a Secret Service agent. They tried to assassinate the President. The President lived, but dozens of others died."

Shankari looked up at him for a moment. His eyes showed nothing. Then he looked back down and touched the surface again to advance the images.

"This is why we want the Nexus back doors," Holtzmann told him. "To stop these sorts of things."

A lie, he told himself. We want them for control. Surveillance. Nothing more noble than that.

"I already gave them to you," Rangan said. "Not my fault they don't work anymore."

"Keep looking at the pictures," Holtzmann told him. "Go through the whole set. Maybe you'll think of something once you see what we're up against."

Shankari grunted, touched the slate again.

Then Holtzmann reached out, carefully, cautiously, for the boy's mind, sent a request for a chat connection.

Shankari looked up, his eyes wide in surprise. His mind gave off shock, disbelief. And then he accepted the chat request.

```
[holtzmann]Make no sign. Keep advancing
images.
[rangan]What the fuck?
[holtzmann]I'm here to get you out.
```

Holtzmann opened himself partially to the boy, showed him his sincerity, his deep desire to see Rangan free.

Rangan tapped the surface of the slate again, then looked down.

• • •

```
[rangan]Why?
[holtzmann]It doesn't matter. But we
have an opening tonight. Can you fake a
seizure at 11pm?
[rangan]Yes. What then?
[holtzmann]If it's convincing enough,
you'll be taken to the nearest hospital.
From there some friends will get you free.
[rangan]What about the kids?
[holtzmann]Just you.
```

Rangan blinked in surprise. Holtzmann felt the boy struggle inside, felt hope and guilt and fear and principle war with one another. Seconds passed. Rangan came to a decision.

```
[rangan]No.
[holtzmann]We may not get another chance.
[rangan]Not without the kids. They
come, or I don't.
```

Holtzmann groaned inside. He wanted this so badly. He needed to get Rangan out. It was so close, so very close.

```
[rangan]They're kids, man. You're
torturing them. It's fucked up.
```

Holtzmann closed his eyes. He could fake a medical emergency. There were any number of things he could inject Shankari with that would force a trip to the ER.

```
[rangan]Goddammit, don't you have any
fucking conscience at all? They're KIDS.
```

• • •

Holtzmann felt himself slipping further. Images of the children went through his head. Alfonso Gonzales, the one who'd been tortured until he gave up Nexus. Bobby Evans, the one they'd spent *four hours* torturing before finally giving up…

```
[rangan]Please. I don't even have to
go. Don't worry about me. Get at least
get one of the kids out instead.
```

Holtzmann grabbed his slate out of Rangan's hands, stood up.

```
[holtzmann]I'll think about it.
[rangan]Wait, wait. What about Ilya?
Kade? Wats?
```

Holtzmann stared at Shankari. And suddenly he felt so tired, so very tired of all of this.

```
[holtzmann]Dead. Hunted. Dead.
```

Shankari dropped his head into his cuffed hands as Holtzmann turned and strode from the room.

Holtzmann sat in the bathroom stall, the lid down over the toilet, fully clothed, and wept. He wept in frustration. He needed to get Rangan out. He had to do it. His whole body was wracked with the need, his palms sweating, his breath coming fast, his skin tingling. Rangan had to be free!

He could do it. He could go into his lab, load up a syringe with a cocktail of tramadol and dapoxetine. That would do the trick. One injection, and a few minutes later, Rangan would be seizing hard, would need to be taken somewhere for treatment.

Yet Rangan was right. Those children... One by one, they'd be tortured. They'd become guinea pigs for new cures. Some would die in the process. Some would survive to be shipped off to concentration camps, or to be set free, scarred by the loss of Nexus.

Holtzmann clenched his fists, pressed them against his head. He wanted to scream with the force of the struggle inside him. Gaaaaah!

I've never been brave, he told himself. Always been a coward. *Goddamn it!* I want to do something right for once.

He had to try. Had to try to get Rangan *and* these children out at the same time.

And the other children? The children being studied in Virginia? In Texas? In California?

Dear God, he told himself, I can only do so much at once!

He would save these children here, the ones under his own direct care, if he could. The rest would have to wait.

Holtzmann took the car, left campus, went to a coffee shop in the DC slum that surrounded the sprawling Homeland Security complex in Anacostia. There he linked himself to the net, tunneled in through an anonymizer, connected to the Nexus board, and fired off a message.

[Change of plans. A dozen more friends to get out. Young ones. You get the rest of the files after.]

And then he went back to the office, and stumbled his way through another day of hypocrisy.

• • •

Rangan sat in his cell, shaking.

Did I just do that? he wondered. Did I just say no to getting out of here?

Yeah. I did.

He'd spent his whole life as a taker. He'd spent his whole life as a boy. But he didn't have to end it that way.

Those kids... they needed out of here. They deserved their freedom more than he did.

It was time to do what was right. It was time to do something for someone else for a change. It was time to be a man.

Sweet fucking Jesus, Rangan thought. I hope it works.

63
UP THE COAST

Wednesday October 31st

Sam pushed through hard seas Wednesday night. Four days she'd been traveling now, moving the little stealthed boat at night, hiding during the brutally hot days. Her shoulder, tended with a continuous supply of fresh bandages, antibiotic cream, and abundant food, was healing.

The weather had started calm, but grown rougher each day as she moved further north. Tonight was the worst. The waves tossed her little boat around. She secured the weapons and extra fuel and food and water and surveillance gear as best she could, but inevitably they crashed from side to side as well. The wind died down around midnight, and she made great time after that.

She found a small, unlit island before dawn, settled into a narrow cove for the day. She'd made seventy miles that night. She was now just thirty miles from Apyar Kyun.

Sam ate all she could, cleaned her shoulder wound, then forced herself to sleep. Slumber came slowly, and when it came, she dreamt of Sarai, of Jake, of death.

Sam woke gasping, had to jam her own hand into her mouth to silence herself. It was only noon. There would be no more sleep.

She readied her gear instead, stripping it down, cleaning it, assembling it, testing it. Rinse. Repeat.

The sun dropped lower in the sky. It was Thursday afternoon now. She could reach Apyar Kyun before midnight, spend this night studying the island, scanning it with the high-powered scope and infrared imagers Lo Prang's men had provided, find a way to get her kids back.

Sam steered her little smuggler's boat out of the cove, out into the water. It was rougher away from the island she'd spent the day at, but the engines kept her moving forward. The waves buffeted her, rocked her, but she endured.

She fought the wind and waves for four hours, pushed within ten miles of Apyar Kyun. The winds died, and Sam quietly rejoiced, and progress got easier. She was just a mile from Apyar Kyun, a few hundred yards past a final tiny unnamed island, when the storm came back with a vengeance.

The big wave hit her from the port side, from out in the deeps, and battered the little boat to the side. The force of the blow snapped an anchor point, loosing a strap. Gear she'd secured came free. A pile of water jugs toppled to the bottom of the boat. More anchor points failed. A stack of food collapsed. A box of ammunition flew across the cabin and struck the far side.

The boat tilted precariously, up at thirty degrees, forty-five degrees, sixty degrees. Sam threw herself at the rising side, grabbed a strut, hauled her body in to counterweight the boat. It teetered on the edge of capsizing then fell back into place with a shuddering crash into the next trough.

Sam grabbed for the controls, scrambled to turn the boat into the next wave. She got the nose around as the next wave hit her hard, sending the loose gear flying. Something hard and metal struck her in the head.

This was crazy. She had to take shelter until this passed. She fought to turn the boat between deadly waves, get its prow pointed back at the tiny island she'd just gone by.

The boat shuddered as she steered. There was a beach ahead. Three hundred yards. A gentle slope, with tall palms above it, their leaves crazily shaking in the wind. Two hundred yards. She pushed her thrusters forward towards it. One hundred yards.

And then a massive wave struck her boat from behind, lifted her up, and threw her forward at the island. The beach surged forward at her. Sam had time to catch her breath. And then her boat struck the beach at full force.

64

DECISIONS

Thursday November 1st

Kade collapsed in the bed, utterly exhausted from the work of assimilating so much of Shiva's mind at once. Sleep took him immediately. His dreams were of chaos, of a world falling apart, of a group mind that could knit the world back together, of the heavy mantle of responsibility falling across his shoulders that he could, that he should, that he *must* accept.

He woke in twilight. A final memory played through his mind. Bihar. The children, burned to death in the orphanage. Thirty-five of them. Thirty-five whose names he could recount, whose faces he could recall. Thirty-five children murdered because they were different, because they were special. The horrors that ignorance could lead men to commit.

And the punishment he'd dealt out in response. The way the judge had screamed as Shiva's men drove the nails into his wrists, pinning him to the crude cross. The anguish on all the killers' faces as the flames rose higher. The sense of *power* he'd felt, of *righteousness* as he punished these monsters for what they'd done.

Kade shuddered with the echo of it. He knew that power. He knew that righteousness. To punish the guilty. To rid the world of monsters. He'd felt it when he'd neutered that bastard Bogdan in Croatia, when he'd stopped that sex slaver in Nairobi, when he'd squeezed his mental fist around Holtzmann's brainstem...

He fell to his knees, gasping. He wanted that power. He craved it. He'd felt most alive these past few months when he'd let it course through him, when he'd used his back doors to cripple the bastards who used Nexus to harm others.

It would be so satisfying to use that back door for more, to reach out and fix the world, fix the problems that people couldn't seem to solve on their own. Oh yes. It would feel so damn good.

This was the logical extension of all he'd been doing. He'd used his back doors to stop thefts. Why not use them to stop the massive theft of humanity's future that was happening right now? He'd used them to stop rapes. Why not use them to stop the rape of the earth? He'd used them to prevent murders. Why not use them to end the unnecessary deaths of millions from famine and poverty and preventable disease?

He dreamt of linking those million Nexus-using minds around the planet, why not use Shiva's tools to force that linkage?

Shiva's vision was just Kade's own, only bolder, larger.

And imposed on humanity by the will of one man. Or two.

Ilya's right, Kade realized. *If I deserve the back doors, then so does Shiva. If Shiva doesn't deserve them, then I don't either.*

Are you wiser than all humanity? Ananda had asked.

That was the crux, wasn't it?

• • •

Kade ate a bit from the dinner cart, avoiding the meat, too aware now of the cost to living things of all varieties. Nita had shown him that, shown *Shiva* that, long ago. Then he showered, to give himself time to think, to be sure he was doing what he believed in.

He dried himself off, dressed in fresh clothes, slipped sandals onto his feet. And then he knocked at the door, to signal for one of his keepers.

The door opened a moment later. The dusky-skinned security man stepped in, the Nexus jammer around his neck, the secondary door closed behind him.

"Can I help you, sir?"

Kade nodded. "Would you please let Shiva know that I'd like to see him, if he's available?"

The man smiled. "Yes, sir."

65

STORM WARNINGS

Wednesday October 31st

Holtzmann spent Wednesday at the office in a daze. He accepted the well wishes on his return to health, pushed through messages and meetings, delegated tasks, assured Barnes that he was working hard on back doors.

Anne fought with him that night. It was one-sided. He let her rant at him about his secrets, question why he'd really gone to Boston, whether he was fucking Lisa Brandt, whether he'd fucked her when she was his student, whether he really believed the conspiracy theories he was spouting. He didn't defend himself. He was too tired for all that, too far gone in his own world. Instead he apologized to his wife, again and again, then slept on the couch.

Thursday November 1st

Holtzmann woke Thursday morning to two pieces of news.

First, Zoe's storm track had bent further, sending it almost directly northwest now, aiming it squarely towards Washington DC. The Mayor of DC had ordered an evacuation of the city. The governors of Virginia and Maryland had ordered evacuations of counties in the storm's path. The DHS and other agencies had backed up those orders, commanding only essential personnel to stay. Holtzmann wasn't among them.

Second, a new message on the Nexus board, just minutes old.

[Friday night, during the storm. Staffing will be bare bones. A fire alarm will go off in a different wing of your building. Get your friends out. Get them to Pecan Street. A white van will meet them.]

Holtzmann stared at the message, read it again and again. Someone else. They had someone else inside. Someone who could pull that alarm.

But they needed him too. He'd have to stay, to find some way to free Rangan and the children, without being caught himself.

Three hours later, Anne was gone. She'd woken, then started packing for evacuation. He'd told her he was staying. She'd screamed at him, then pleaded with him, alternated between the two, telling him he was going mad, telling him he was throwing his life away, throwing *her* life away. In the end, she'd gone without him.

Noon on Thursday now. Wind was picking up outside. In less than thirty-two hours, he'd be breaking prisoners out of ERD Headquarters. Madness.

There was one other piece of madness to attend to. He picked up the phone, dialed Claire Becker.

"Hello?" she answered.

"Claire, it's Martin Holtzmann."

"Martin… Anne said you had a fight…"

"Claire, I'm looking for any files Warren may have left behind. Anything from the early days of the ERD, or even further back, from his time at the FBI."

"Martin... I know Anne thinks I'm crazy. But I think they killed him. To keep him quiet."

"I know, Claire."

She went silent for a moment. Then, "You believe me?" Her voice sounded girlish – vulnerable.

Holtzmann sighed. "I don't know. But I don't think you're crazy. And I don't think it's impossible."

She responded with relief. "Oh my God, thank you, Martin, thank you, thank you–"

"Claire," he cut her off. "What I'm looking for in Warren's files... If I found it, it would be the opposite of keeping him quiet. You under-stand?"

There was silence across the line again. Then Claire Becker spoke.

"We're about to leave, Martin. In the evacuation. The girls are almost finished packing. If there are any files, they'd be in Warren's office. I can give you the door code..."

An hour later he was on his way to the Becker home.

Holtzmann punched the door code into the panel inset on the Beckers' front door. The lock flashed green at him, and its motor whirred as the deadbolt slid open.

He pushed open the door. "Hello?" he called out.

There was no answer.

It felt wrong, being here. He hadn't set foot in this home since Warren died. Nothing for it.

Holtzmann padded into the main room, leaning on his cane, then pushed himself up the stairs to the second floor. Something made him move in a hush, an eeriness about the place. His friend had lived here. And now that friend was dead.

ERD had been here, he was sure, cleaning up after Becker. What could he hope to accomplish? But he had no other leads.

He pushed open the door to Warren Becker's office and stepped in, cane in hand. It felt like entering a mausoleum.

The room was tidy. Wooden shelves lined the wall, filled with mementos, display plates, paper books. A single window gave light. A large wooden desk sat below the window. A circular carpet covered most of the floor. Two doors led to a washroom and a closet, respectively.

Holtzmann sat behind his friend's desk. It still felt wrong, being here. But he had to.

Pictures of Claire and their daughters decorated the desk. Everything was tidy. There was a workstation atop it, a four-inch black cube with a handful of ports, a large flat display and a keypad. There was a space where his secure terminal would have been, undoubtedly cleaned away by DHS.

Holtzmann activated the workstation. Password-protected, of course.

The desk drawers were unlocked. Holtzmann rifled through them. Papers, nothing classified. A personal slate, also password-protected. Pens. Medals and commendations that Becker never displayed. A drink drawer with a half-full bottle of Laphroaig, glasses, an empty ice bucket.

He emptied each drawer, tapped their bottoms and backs and sides looking for some false compartment. He felt ridiculous, an amateur doing a job for professionals. Warren Becker had been a professional. Holtzmann was not.

He gave up on the desk, moved to the shelves. One by one he pulled down the mementos, the books, searching for a false cover, something hidden between the pages, a false back or side or top or bottom to a shelf.

Nothing.

The carpet caught his eye next. But when dropped to his knees and rolled it up, he found nothing but wooden floor boards beneath. None came loose. None sounded different than the others when he rapped on them.

The bathroom revealed toiletries, cleaning supplies, and nothing else.

The closet was no better. Golf clubs. Spare shoes. A jacket missing a button on the sleeve. He searched all of it, looked for some secret compartment or hidden memory chip or something. He tapped his cane against the walls of the closet, searching for some hidden space.

Nothing.

Nothing nothing nothing.

Holtzmann collapsed back in the chair, frustrated. He'd been here for hours now. He was tired and hungry. He still craved an opiate hit that he had no way to deliver. It would feel so good to just unwind…

Wait.

Holtzmann opened the drink drawer again. The bottle. He pulled it out. It looked… different. He'd seen Warren pour Laphroaig at the office. The bottle he'd poured it from wasn't quite the same as this. He turned it over in his mind, scanning the label. There it was. "Bottled in 2029." Eleven years ago.

Had Becker really been sipping from this same bottle for all those years?

Holtzmann worked the cap off the bottle, brought it to his nose. It certainly smelled like whisky.

He capped the bottle, turned it over in his hands again. Why would Becker keep this bottle all this time? Not drinking it? Or perhaps drinking and refilling it?

Sentimental value?

He turned it over again and again, running his thumbs over the bottle's surface as he did, wondering, wondering.

And then he felt it.

He turned the bottle back. Somewhere... There. His thumb brushed over a corner of the label. And he felt something. The tiniest bump. Could it be?

Holtzmann brought the bottle close to his face. Was there a tiny irregularity there? Was the corner of the label just a bit loose?

He pried one finger nail under the edge of the label, tugged just a tiny bit...

And the label peeled back. And there, underneath it, was a tiny gold sliver. A tiny memory foil. A gift from Warren Becker.

66

A MATTER OF PRINCIPLE

Thursday November 1st

The guards fitted him with a Nexus jammer, then took him to the rooftop. The tiles were wet. Palm fronds were scattered around. Servants were busily cleaning up. The night sky was clear now, but weather had obviously gone through here recently.

Shiva was there, just the same, sitting beneath the stars, sipping chai and staring out at the last bit of color in the sky.

"Kade." Shiva offered him a chair. "You viewed my files."

Kade sat, took a mug of chai offered him by a server.

"Thank you for that," he told Shiva. "It was an extremely generous gift."

Shiva inclined his head in acknowledgment.

"And now are you inclined to work together?" Shiva asked.

"I am," Kade said.

Shiva smiled.

"...but not to share the back door with you," Kade went on.

Shiva's smile disappeared. "I see," he said. "And why?"

Kade looked the older man in the eyes, wished he could touch his mind, return a small fraction of what Shiva had given him.

"Are you wiser than all humanity?" Kade asked him.

Ilya woke in his mind, soaring, exulting.

Shiva frowned. "What?"

"I believe in your integrity," Kade said. "I believe your goals are good. I'd love to work with you in a hundred different ways. I'd love to see you make your solutions real." He paused. "I know how good it feels to do something right. How *satisfying* it is. But that's a trap. Don't you see? It's an addiction. It just leads to more and more."

Shiva opened his mouth, but Kade pressed on, letting the words pour out of him, holding the older man's eyes with his own. "We're only part of the world, you and I," he told Shiva. "We're only part of humanity. The solutions to our problems can't be forced on the world. No one should have that kind of power. *No one*."

"No one but *you*," Shiva corrected.

Kade lifted his eyes to the darkened sea. "I'm done with it. You've shown me where this leads. If I keep the back door, I'll use it more and more, in larger and larger ways. If you ever let me leave here, I'll close it, instead. I'll give up that power. People will have to solve their problems themselves."

Shiva stared at him aghast. "You can't be serious."

"I'm completely serious," Kade replied.

Shiva leaned forward, his hands reaching towards Kade, almost beseeching. "We have a *chance* here, Kade. A chance to *fix the world*. This isn't a game. This isn't some philosophical exercise. This is the lives of *billions* we're talking about."

Kade looked calmly into the man's eyes. "I won't give you the tools to control people."

"I don't want to control people!" Shiva almost shouted, gesturing with his hands. "I want to SAVE them!"

"You wouldn't stop there," Kade told him. "You'd use that power, and every time you did, you'd find *more* reasons to use it. If I keep this, I'll become you. And you? You'll become a dictator."

"Damn it!" Shiva slammed one hand against the railing. "There *is* no one else!" Spittle flew from his mouth.

"There's them," Kade replied softly. "Those billions of people. They have to do it for themselves. They have to come together. Nexus can help them. But it has to happen from the bottom up. They have to want it."

He was in the club again, dancing, merging, *choosing* to become part of one grander organism.

Shiva shook his head, his jaw set angrily, his mouth working. His eyes went out to the darkened sea. His whole body was tense, coiled tight.

Finally he turned to Kade, and waved his hand dismissively. "Get out of my sight, Kade. Get out of my sight."

Kade lay on his bed and contemplated his future. The Shiva he'd gotten to know in those files was an exceptionally patient man. He was also a man of incredible passion, willing to take extraordinary steps to achieve his goals.

Would he be patient with Kade, waiting for a change of heart?

Or would he try to force what he wanted to know out of him?

Kade had to be ready for either. He had to be on the lookout for escape. He had to be mentally prepared to be a prisoner for a very long time. And he had to be ready for torture, or drugs, or any other way that Shiva might try to get the knowledge out of his brain.

And when it came down to it, there was only one foolproof defense against that last possibility. Memory deletion could work in isolated cases, if a memory was fresh and new, if it hadn't been integrated into a thousand networks across the brain. But that wasn't the case now. That left only Ilya's choice. To sleep, but not to dream. To die to keep what he knew out of others' hands.

Kade felt no fear any more. He felt only clarity. The clarity of understanding where he fit in the world. The clarity of having decided once and for all what he believed in.

He wrote the script he needed, and pinned it to a corner of his mental field of vision. He could activate it with a second's notice. Then he lay on his back and stared out the windows at the twinkling stars and the cloudless sky. If he had to die, this was as beautiful a place as any.

Shiva watched the stars wheel across the sky. Lane was so naïve. Such an idealist. He'd lived a comfortable life. He'd never seen real poverty, real death. He'd never learned the visceral lesson that good intentions and optimism weren't enough, that you had to *act* to make what you wanted a reality, whatever the cost.

But the boy seemed certain of his decision. So be it. They would have to do this the hard way.

67

HALTING STATE

Friday November 2nd

Su-Yong Shu screamed silently as the question came at her again. The equivalence theorem, the equivalence theorem, the equivalence theorem.

Raw pain pounded its way through her simulated brain, pure pain, essential pain, devoid of any remedy, of any physical cause she could address, of any way to relieve its inexorable pressure.

She screamed in her mind, longing for a mouth to cry out with, fists to clench, a head to pound into a wall.

A gun to end her husband's life.

I DON'T KNOW I DON'T KNOW I DON'T KNOW

There was no equivalence theorem. There was an equivalence theorem and she had found it – had proven it. She would give it to him. She would die first.

Why was he doing this to her? Why was he torturing her so? She'd known he was shallow, self-centered. She'd learned that. But this? Was he so evil?

Yes. Yes he was. Like all the rest of them. All the rest of the humans. So very very evil. So small and petty. So inferior in their morality, in their intellect, in everything about them.

So not deserving of their lives.

Truth and untruth were indistinguishable now. Pain ruled, with confusion as its consort.

Was the many worlds interpretation true? Did her quantum cores reach out to other universes to achieve their magic? Were there more of her, out there somewhere? Were any of them free? Was one of them the goddess she was meant to be, the posthuman ushering in a new golden age... or were there an infinity of her writhing in unlimited suffering, slaves of the pathetic human worms who'd entrapped them?

Shu screamed again into the echo chamber of her mind. It had been days, her clock told her, days of torture, but at her accelerated pace it was centuries, millennia, eons.

I DON'T KNOW I DON'T KNOW I DON'T KNOW, she outputted once again. But the barrage did not let up.

Would she go so mad that she could no longer feel pain?

Oh, how she hoped so. And soon.

I should have been a goddess. Should have been a goddess. Should have been a goddess.

Please please please let it end.

If only she could touch another mind.

If only she could weep.

If only she could burn this wretched world to the ground.

Chen Pang slammed his fist against the console in frustration.

It wasn't working. Nothing he'd tried had budged the abomination he'd built. He'd gone so far as to try directly editing volitional constructs, stimulating them in conjunction with his interrogation, but it was no good. The thing was so insane that it didn't even know what it knew any more.

He had to report back to his patron Sun Liu soon. The Minister of Science and Technology was pinging him daily, twice a day, as Bo Jintao and the State Security apparatus became increasingly impatient.

With no new cyberattack, there was no apparent reason to keep Shu running. Back her up, Bo Jintao had ordered, then shut her down.

Chen covered his face with his hands. He'd been so close! So close to all his dreams. But he'd failed. No more delay was possible. He would have to admit to Sun Liu that he'd failed. And then it would be time to end this abomination.

He contemplated the code he'd written to torment his wife. He had no more hope that it would work. He should terminate it now.

No. Let the monster burn. Let the bitch suffer. It was what she deserved for robbing him of his dreams.

Chen upped the process's priority to feed it more resources, then set it to continue indefinitely, until the day she was deactivated. Then he logged himself out of the system, rose from the console, and started the long ascent to the surface.

68

FAR FROM HOME

Friday November 2nd

Nakamura held them three miles west of Apyar Kyun, waited until the tropical storm passed, then brought them up in the predawn gloom until the main antenna and the launch ports of the Manta were above water. The sub bobbed there for a moment, stabilizing itself against the waves of the Andaman Sea. Then with a stuttering sound of compressed gas releases, its launch ports shot out a high-speed cloud of aerial surveillance drones. The four-inch-long drones leapt away, wings morphing out of their contoured bodies in mid-flight. Their color-shifting skins tuned themselves for the night, their robotic irises dilated, and they flapped their wings and dispersed to survey Apyar Kyun and the area around it.

Nakamura took them down below the waves again, just a few feet this time, shallow enough that they could leave the nearly invisible antenna above the waterline. Data spooled from overhead satellites. Intelligence updates he'd requested.

Satellite imagery outlined Shiva's cliffside home, the airfield, a compound where workers lived. And the island's defenses: Indian-made Ganesha-6 radars. Kali-4 missile launchers. Drone bases. Guard posts.

Nakamura considered his stealth gear. It was top-of-the-line. He could sneak onto the island undetected. He could sneak off it again. But he had to know where Lane was. In the house, or elsewhere? What room? What floor? What sort of guard did they have him under? He had to know these things to find a way to extract Lane without raising the alarm.

For that he needed more intel.

Feng raised his cuffed wrists, pointed at the surface and its annotated composite satellite maps. "OK?" the Confucian Fist asked.

Nakamura nodded. The system was locked to read-only. Feng could do no harm.

He slept as Feng zoomed and panned the display, inspecting the data they had on the house. The sub's systems watched Feng, poised to alert Nakamura of any suspicious behavior.

He woke hours later, after dawn.

Feng was still at the display surface. He looked up at Nakamura, then gestured down at the screen. "Look here," he said.

Nakamura looked. Feng panned the display. These were images from the recon drones now, footage they'd taken while flying around the island.

There. A rooftop. Two men. One brown-skinned, white-haired, clad in a simple white robe. Shiva Prasad. And the other, tall, lanky, with long jet black hair and tan but undeniably Caucasian skin. Kade.

The video had been taken from hundreds of yards away, by a drone in mid-flight. It was too low resolution to allow lip-reading. But the body language spoke volumes. Kade, firm, resolute. Shiva, disappointed, frustrated.

"Kade didn't give him the codes," Feng said.

Nakamura nodded. Good.

"Have they identified where Lane's being held?" he asked Feng. "Security around him?"

Feng shook his head. "Terahertz imagers." He flipped to another image, showed the distinctive antenna shape of a stand-off T-ray sensor. "Drones detected it, stayed away."

Nakamura drummed his fingers. They still needed to know more. What room was Lane in? What security? What surveillance?

Feng held up one finger of his cuffed hands, as if reading Nakamura's thoughts.

"Here," he said.

The display zoomed out into satellite imagery, panned out over water, then zoomed back in on a small island, a mile from Shiva's home. Feng zoomed further. A shape, outlined in red by the image analysis AI.

The shape was angular, broken, with weird distortions. The pieces of a boat.

No. Not pieces. It was a boat, run aground, partially covered in chameleonware. Chameleonware that had been damaged, revealing pieces of the structure underneath.

What?

"Storm did this," Feng said. "No sign Shiva's looking for it."

And then he looked up at Nakamura and smiled. "Could be people," Feng said. "Shiva's people. Human intel."

There was only one way to find out.

Nakamura brought the sub in close to the beach, under the waves, then waited for nightfall.

"Let me come with you," Feng pleaded. "I can help. We're friends now!"

Nakamura chuckled. "You're my prisoner, Feng. Not my partner."

"You leave me on the boat?" Feng sounded outraged. "What happens if you get killed, huh? I go down to the bottom!"

"I'm not planning on getting killed, Feng."

"Look, our goals the same!" Feng replied. "We both want Kade free! I'll help you. I'll be useful!"

"No," Nakamura said. "Now clip your cuffs to the hardpoint."

Feng hesitated for a moment, then did what he was told, locking his ankles and wrists to floor and ceiling of the sub's fuselage.

Feng glowered at Nakamura. "You a real bastard, you know?"

Nakamura smiled. "I know, Feng," he said.

Then he brought the sub up, pushed himself and the inflatable boat out the hatch.

"Grandpa!" Feng yelled as Nakamura pushed himself and the inflatable away.

Nakamura smiled and sent the sub the signal to seal itself up and submerge again.

Nakamura paddled the small boat in, not daring to risk the noise or IR emissions of engines. The boat's skin shifted color to blend in with the waves. His own chameleonware suit rendered him nearly invisible. Its goggles extended his vision into the IR, into radio frequencies.

The blood was rising in him. He was out here, alone now, his life on the line, nothing but his wits and his skills and his tools between him and death. He felt free. He felt alive. Everything around him felt sharp and vivid. A feral grin split his face of its own accord.

He scanned the beach, eagerly, thoroughly, looking for anything, a sign of human life, the radio emissions of a rescue beacon, anything.

Nothing. The surf crashed on a lonely stretch of sand, palm trees swaying behind it.

Nakamura aimed for the eastern end of the beach, as far from the wrecked boat as he could manage. He landed softly, slipped off the inflatable quietly, then dragged it up onto the sand. His assault rifle was in his hands. Dual load clip switched to tranq. He wanted whoever was here alive.

Nakamura was halfway down the beach, moving silently towards the boat, watching it for movement, when he heard a sound behind him. He turned and rolled as a voice yelled "Freeze!" He came up firing, tranquilizer rounds whishing out of his gun, moving in an inhuman blur even as he depressed the trigger. Silenced rounds struck the ground where he'd just been. His assailant was a barely seen blur, a distortion of muzzle fire and impressions in the sand. He dove low and diagonally to close the distance, came up to strike with the rifle as a weapon. Blur met blur at close range. His opponent blocked his rifle strike with a rifle block, kicked at his knee. He twisted away from the kick, came again with the rifle butt in a feint, lashed his own foot forward... And had it blocked as he would block, a counterstrike launched that he would launch.

They struck and parried, dodged and twisted. His enemy's moves were his own! He was fighting his own ghost, here. And then the voice caught up with him, stunned him.

"Sam?" he said aloud.

He dropped his guard for an instant and the butt of her rifle struck him in the side of his head. He let it propel him into a shoulder roll, came up with his gun pointed into the sand, his off hand yanking off the mask of his chameleonware suit.

"Sam!"

The space ahead of him was just a distortion. Still now. A ghost with a gun pointed at his face, wet scuffs imprinted in the sand where their feet had moved in their fight.

"Kevin?" her voice spoke from the distortion.

"Sam," he said. "It's me."

He held his breath. The surf crashed onto the beach, loud in his ears. The breeze rippled the palm fronds above. A bird called somewhere, far away. His heart pounded in his chest.

If he was wrong, he was dead… If she was Shu's, he was dead… If she was Lane's…

Then the gun was falling to the ground, and a ghost was wrapping her arms around him.

Sam held on tight to the ghost in her arms. Nakamura. She couldn't believe it.

She let go, pulled off her own chameleonware hood, and looked into his eyes again. He was real. Her old mentor, the man who'd rescued her, who'd thrown himself out of a burning three-story window to save her life…

They disentangled, moved under the cover of the trees to talk.

"What are you doing here?" Sam whispered to him.

"I'm here for Lane," he told her. "Same as you."

Kade? Had she heard right?

"What?" she asked.

"Kade," Nakamura repeated. "He alerted you somehow? Or Feng did?"

Sam shook her head. "Kade's not here, Kevin. He's..." *in Cambodia*, she almost said. But no. She'd sworn to protect his secrets, and he hers. "He went a different way. I'm here for the kids."

"Kids?" Nakamura asked.

She told him. Told him the whole story. She wished she could show him instead, touch his mind and let him feel what she'd felt. But there was no Nexus in his brain, and so she settled for words. Mai. Phuket. Mae Dong. Sarai and the children. Jake. The men from the Mira Foundation. What she'd seen in that soldier's mind.

"Shiva... He's trying to create a posthuman intelligence. Succeeding. He has dozens of children there. Kids born with Nexus in their brains. And he's subverting them. Bit by bit."

Nakamura listened as Sam told him everything. His mind whirled. Her story dovetailed with Feng's. She hadn't been coerced. She'd flipped in that raid.

Which meant that he was a danger to her. A conduit through which the CIA could find her. And what would they do when they learned she hadn't been coerced? Nothing pleasant, he was sure.

"Your turn, Kevin," she told him. "Why are you here?" She tensed as she asked. She tried to hide it from him but he saw it in her.

"Lane," he said. "Shiva has him. I'm here to get him out."

"And then what?" Sam asked.

He looked into her eyes and thought of lying to her. But he couldn't. And even if he did, he doubted he'd fool her.

"CIA wants him. Wants his help. To counter the Nexus assassination attempts."

"You can't," she said softly.

"I know you got close with him, Sam…" he started.

She shook her head. "No. It's what's in his head. The back door. You can't give that to CIA."

"This isn't ERD," he told her. "I'm here to get him before they do…"

The wheels were turning in his head as he spoke. The cloak-and-dagger briefing with McFadden. The stealthed sub. The absolute secrecy. The separation from all other agencies. The black-on-black mission that only a handful of people knew about.

Sam was talking. "…can't trust anyone with that power. Millions of people. Whoever has the back door could have absolute control over them. They could do anything – read minds, change votes, create informants or sleeper agents. Anything."

He looked at her. It was so obvious. He'd been so completely stupid. Counterterrorism? No. If that was all, they could have left it to ERD, left it to the wider Homeland Security apparatus that ERD was part of. Why was CIA involved? It had to be something higher stakes.

Something like Sam was describing.

Nakamura stared into Sam's eyes. An image of his grandfather flashed before his eyes, the boy in his mother's arms, in black and white, behind that barbed with fence, while his father went out and fought for the country that imprisoned him.

Loyalty.

Where did his loyalties lie? Where?

69

ESCAPE

Friday November 2nd

Kade woke before dawn. Friday. He felt rested and at peace with his decision. But other subjects loomed in his mind. Where was Rangan? Was Feng still alive? Was there any way to stop the bombing just forty hours in the future?

Shiva summoned him for breakfast on the roof.

"Have you reconsidered?" Shiva asked.

Kade looked at Shiva. He understood this man now. He could have become this man.

"I can't give you the back door."

Shiva grunted in reply.

"There's something I need to ask you," Kade said. He described the assassination plans. "You can stop it. Send an anonymous warning."

Shiva frowned, shook his head.

"These men are monsters, Kade. They're enemies of the future."

Kade nodded. "I agree. They should be brought to justice. But not like this."

"There's blood on their hands," Shiva said. "They deserve to die."

"Not like this," Kade repeated.

Shiva waved that away. "They're the *enemy*, Kade. They've tried to kill you. They've imprisoned your friends. They've persecuted scientists doing valuable research. They hunt down children who have Nexus in their brains. They have plans for genocide."

"There'll be hundreds of other deaths," Kade said. "Innocents."

Shiva scoffed. "Innocents? No one who gives money to these monsters is innocent. No one who helps get them elected is innocent."

Kade exhaled, tried to keep his cool. He had to reach Shiva. "This isn't going to benefit you," Kade said. He put his hands together, his palms meeting as if in prayer, leaned towards Shiva, his voice straining. "Shiva, this is going to turn Chandler and Shepherd into *martyrs*. Events like this are the *reason* the ERD exists, the reason that Copenhagen exists. If you let this happen, we'll end up with a hundred more politicians like Chandler, with a new Chandler Act that's ten times *worse* than the current one, with more crackdowns on Nexus and *every* transhuman technology." He stared into Shiva's eyes. "This isn't going to advance your goals."

Shiva stared back at him.

"Fine," the older man said. "You want mercy? You want me to spare the lives of these murderers? These enemies of the future? I'll do it. For you, Kade. Just give me the back door, and I'll save these lives for you."

Kade looked down at his hands. "You know I won't do that."

Shiva shook his head, his lips pursed. "Pathetic."

Kade paced, searching for a way out of here. Day turned to afternoon, afternoon to evening. The serving girl brought dinner to his room. Vegetarian this time. They'd learned his new preferences. He forced himself to eat, to keep up his strength, to be ready for any oppor-tunity.

She came back an hour later, cleaned away the food, tidied up the room as she did daily. The guard waited by the door. When she came back from inside the kitchen, her eyes bored into his. She silently mouthed something at him, something he didn't catch, then gestured with one hand, out of view of the guard. Gestured back at the kitchen.

What?

Then she left. "Goodnight!" she called out in her heavily accented English.

"Good night, sir," the guard echoed her.

Kade sat at the writing desk. What had that been about?

He went Inside, accessed his recent memory buffer, replayed that scene, then again, and again, and one more time at lower speed.

"Tonight." He wasn't sure, but he thought that's what she'd been mouthing at him. Then she'd gestured into the kitchen.

Kade rose. He stepped into the kitchen, fetched himself a glass of water, took a long look around, stepped to the window looking down into the courtyard.

It was twilight out there, but still light enough that he could see. The children were gone by now, bundled off to bed. He'd learned their patterns. A pair of the research staff were seated on a bench, talking. A security man was walking a circuit.

And beneath his hands, on the window sill, where the metal frame was bolted in… The lock was there, still holding the bolt in place. It rested on the frame. But when he surreptitiously put his hand on it, and tugged ever so slightly, his gaze still fixed on the courtyard, he met no resistance.

• • •

Kade forced himself to wait, to think. The lock was open. He could open the window, break the Faraday mesh. He could reach his mind out of this cage, find a network hub. Or better. Find a mind running Nexus. The guards didn't wear jammers when they walked the grounds. He could take one, coerce him, coerce *all* of them, even Shiva, then get the hell out of here.

But why? Why had that girl unlocked the window? Who had sent her? Sam? Ananda? Shu? Feng?

Or was this a trick? A trap of some sort?

But why? They had him already.

Kade forced himself to wait two hours, until the sky was as dark as it would be. He still had more questions than answers. But he couldn't pass up an opportunity like this.

He rose, slipped on the sandals they'd given him, padded to the kitchen, looked out into the courtyard. It was dark out there. Only a few dim lights illuminated the space.

His eyes slowly adjusted. All was quiet. He could see no sign of movement.

He waited ten minutes, twenty minutes, half an hour. No one moved.

There might be someone in his range that he couldn't see. Shiva might still be on the roof, soaking up the night view. He'd only know if he opened the metal frame, pushed the mesh shielding aside.

He had to do it, then. He damped his Nexus transmission, went into a listen-only mode. And then, slowly, he pulled the padlock open, slid it out of the lock, as subtly as he could.

Then he took one more deep breath, and pulled on the frame, tugging it in towards him on its hinges. It was jammed from disuse. He tugged slowly and consistently, until it came loose with a scrape, swinging open just a crack.

His breath caught in his throat. The Faraday cage was broken.

He positioned himself by the crack he'd opened, felt out with his mind for anything out there.

Nothing. No one in range.

He opened the frame wider, gave himself a wider transmission angle to work with, reached out again

Nothing.

Kade looked for network connections. He found several, but all locked, encrypted.

He visualized the mansion's layout. At one end of the courtyard was a gate and a gatehouse, where he'd always seen a guard. He couldn't see the gate from here. But if he could get close enough, and the guard was still there… Then Kade could take him. Could have the man open the gate, lead him to a car and then a boat, show him how to get off the island.

But first, he must get close enough.

He looked out his window again, opened his mind wide for any trace of another. Nothing. But below his window… A trellis, climbing up to maybe four feet below his window ledge. It was covered in tropical flowering vines. He could climb down that, reach the ground, sneak in the darkness towards the south wing…

Kade had to try it. He wouldn't get another chance.

He put one foot out over the ledge, and suddenly he had vertigo. His room was on the fifth floor. The ground looked frighteningly far away. This wasn't a climbing gym, with smart ropes and impact-absorbing floor. This was real life. A fall could break an arm or leg. Or worse.

No choice, he told himself.

He sat himself in the window sill, held on to both sides as he put his feet out before him. Then he turned, slowly, carefully, rolling onto his belly, his hands inside the kitchen, his feet down the wall, searching for the trellis.

He pushed himself out further, his chest on the window sill now, his arms squeezing against the inside wall of the room to hold him in place, lowering his legs to find the first step.

One foot made contact. There. And then the other.

Would it hold him? Kade kept his arms inside the window, but shifted more of his weight out and down, onto his feet, his arms still ready to catch him.

The trellis held.

He eased out further, bit by bit, transferring his weight, still holding on for dear life.

The trellis held.

He paused to catch his breath. He had to move fast. He could be seen here at any time.

The next move would be the hardest. It was four feet from his window ledge to the top of the trellis below it. There was no obvious handhold in between. He'd have to hold onto the window with one hand, then lower the other to the top of the trellis.

He'd been to rock-climbing gyms. Not often, but a few times. He'd never thought of himself as athletic, but he was tall, skinny, long-limbed. In a gym he could make this move. He could reach. He could grasp the big obvious hold that the horizontal bars of the trellis were.

But in a gym, if Kade failed, the rope would catch him.

Still no choice. The only question was which hand. He could hold onto the window with his stronger left hand, always his off hand before, but the one that worked well now, and reach down with his weaker right.

Or he could hold onto the window with his right, reach down with his stronger left to grasp the new hold.

He'd do it that way. The window sill was thick, solid beneath his weight. The new hold looked obvious, but it was an unknown. He'd use his best hand for that.

He gripped the window as best he could with his right, his whole elbow over the ledge to carry his weight, tried to keep his hips close to the wall, his center of gravity over his feet, to let them take all his weight, and then reached down with his left.

No good. Kade couldn't reach like this.

He worked his feet lower on the trellis, another step or two. He held onto the window with just his hands now. His right was aching already.

Move fast. Staying still burns you out.

He reached down with his left again, his right hand gripping as tightly as it could, aching, complaining. Almost… Almost…

Kade couldn't quite reach with his hips against the wall. So he pushed out, pushed his hips back, lowered his shoulder. The fingers of his left hand brushed the trellis…

Then one foot slipped off, and his body lurched down and to the right, and his other foot followed. His fingers reached and found nothing. His full weight crashed down on his right hand and excruciating pain surged from it. His body swung to the right and his feet kicked, kicked, scrambling, looking for a hold.

He felt something snap in his fingers, in his wrist, felt a horrific ripping pain as some tissue not yet fully healed gave way. His grip came loose. His fingers slipped. His weight dropped. He almost screamed in agony as he fell.

And then his left hand closed around something. His body swung back to the left and his left foot was suddenly on a step. Kade wobbled, swinging like a door, scrambling, off balance, still on one foot and one hand. He kicked with his right foot, swung his half-crippled right hand. The foot found something, and somehow he slammed his right arm in through a gap in the trellis, burying it up to his elbow in foliage, letting the whole arm take weight.

He hung there, panting. The pain was enormous.

He closed his eyes.

Breathe.

Breathe.

Pain is an illusion.

Breathe.

He opened his eyes.

The pain was still there, but less crippling. It was a signal to his mind that his body was damaged. Information, not emotion.

Breathe.

He had to move. He couldn't stay here.

Kade worked himself down, cautiously, stepping down with his feet, pulling his aching right hand out, then shoving it deep in another gap in the trellis until his elbow could take the weight, and finally shifting his left hand down to the next hold.

He nearly wept in delight when his feet touched the earth. He let himself crumple to the ground, lay on his belly to make the smallest sight possible, and paused for a few seconds to catch his breath.

He opened his mind again. Network connections were all around, all locked. Shu could crack them open with an eye blink, but he wasn't Shu. He needed a human mind.

Kade crawled north, using the wall and benches and shrubs and trees as cover.

The circular driveway came into view. Beyond it, the gate and the small attached guardhouse. He could see a man's head through the windows, seated inside there, turned away from Kade and out towards the island beyond the house.

Kade went inside, opened up a control panel, grabbed a control for directional Nexus transmission, tightened it down into a focused beam aimed in the direction of the guard. He felt for the man's mind, and found him.

He reached out to the guard, opened an encrypted connection, activated the first back door, sent his passcode for it, and then Kade was in.

And now he would...

Something was wrong.

He looked out the man's eyes. He was strapped to the chair. There was gear all around him, electronic gear, listening gear. There was an IV in his vein, cameras watching him, a woman next to him, standing, in a white lab jacket. The serving girl. Her finger was on a button connected to the IV.

What?

Fear struck him. He issued a remote command, pulled up process and resource utilization listings inside the man's Nexus OS. And there – strange programs were running. Loggers. Listeners. Decrypters. Trapping every bit of data about this communication stream, about the internals of the Nexus OS running in this mind's brain, about every bit of data loaded in and out of memory.

Oh no. Oh fucking no.

It was a trap, a trick to find his back door.

He'd sent the passcode over an encrypted connection. No one listening in between the two of them would be able to pick up anything but encrypted garbage. But inside the guard's Nexus OS copy, for just an instant during the back door's invocation, what he'd sent would be held in memory, unencrypted, to be compared to the passcode embedded in the Nexus OS...

He had to erase the knowledge in this mind. He started hunting, looking for the logfiles, looking for data he could wipe out...

Then his connection to the man's mind dropped. Static kicked in. Static everywhere. Pools of it spreading out from all over. Flood lights kicked in across the courtyard. And then Shiva was there, standing above him, pulling off the hood of a chameleonware suit that was detuning itself. Security men appeared around him.

They'd been here all along, sitting silently, their Nexus nodes in receive mode. He'd been tricked.

Shiva looked down at him.

"See to his arm," Shiva said. And the medic that Kade had first seen in Heaven rushed forward, something in his hand.

The man pressed a hypersonic injector to Kade's neck, and Kade felt the cool pinprick of something entering his bloodstream.

The last thing he remembered was Shiva, his eyes, looking down at him, and the man shaking his head slowly.

70
THE PLAN

Friday November 2nd

Nakamura held Sam's eyes. He thought of the hell she'd been through as a child, hell created by the Communion Virus and those who abused it.

Nexus was so much more. With a back door to Nexus... the coercion possibilities were enormous. The scale of atrocities was larger than he could imagine. Did he trust the CIA with that power?

He remembered the underpass, McFadden's repeated warnings, that no one else could know. Not the ERD. Not the rest of Homeland Security. Not Defense.

Not Congress.

Not the White House.

Jesus, Nakamura thought. How could I have been so stupid?

Sam spoke as if reading his thoughts. "You can't let them have it, Kevin."

Nakamura stared at her. Loyalty. He was loyal to his friends. He was loyal to his family, what little there was of it. He was loyal to his country.

Yes. He was loyal to his country. He'd always been that.

"The things they'll do with it, Kevin," Sam was saying.

She was right. His country didn't need that. America wouldn't benefit from putting that kind of power in anyone's hands. And most especially not the hands of someone trying to hide that power from everyone else.

McFadden, Nakamura thought. What did you think you were going to do with it?

It didn't matter now. Nakamura wouldn't allow it.

He thought back to his time with Lane. Not a monster. Not a killer. Not an evil man. Just a kid, really. A kid in way over his head.

A kid with dangerous knowledge in his head.

Nakamura took a deep breath. That knowledge was the problem. That knowledge was the threat to the United States.

He exhaled slowly. What he had to do left a bad taste in his mouth. A taste of betrayal. A taste of compromise.

But his duty was clear. He'd sworn an oath to protect the American people. That trumped CIA, trumped ERD, trumped his own qualms. There was only one way he could think of to really, truly protect the American people against this threat.

Kade's face flashed through Nakamura's mind, a memory of the weeks he'd spent training the boy in San Francisco. The kid that couldn't lie to save his life. Something twisted inside Nakamura. But there was no other way he could see.

"OK," he said, and nodded to Sam. "You're right."

"You won't give them Kade?" she asked.

"I'll tell them he died," Nakamura replied.

And that was true enough.

They took the more useful of Sam's supplies from her boat, scattered palm fronds over the parts of it where the chameleonware had failed, then rowed back out in Nakamura's little inflatable, talking all the way. They had the bones of a plan. A weak plan, to be sure. But it would have to do.

It was well after midnight when the wing-shaped sub rose out of the depths before them. Sam whistled softly. Then the hatch was opening, and they were climbing in.

"Nakamura!" Feng yelled. He was seated in the cramped interior, his arms chained above his head and his feet manacled to the floor. A display surface before him showed infrared action from somewhere. Then his eyes took in Sam, and they widened.

"What're you doing here?" the Confucian Fist asked.

Sam laughed, then she was climbing into the small interior herself, keys in hand, and the manacles fell from around Feng's wrists.

"What's going on?" Feng demanded, as Sam placed the keys in one of his hands.

Nakamura raised an eyebrow at Feng, then grinned. "Things have changed, Feng. Looks like we're partners after all."

They hashed over variants for hours. They had imperfectly aligned goals. To free Kade. To deny Shiva the back door. To get the children away from Shiva and to safety. There were no ideal options. Only options with greater and smaller risks, greater and smaller unknowns.

They had one new piece of intel. The drones had picked up aberrant behavior on infrared, had prioritized monitoring of it, had routed it to the sub. Feng played it back for them. They crouched around the horizontal display in the cramped interior of the sub.

On screen, the IR displayed an interior courtyard, ground and building walls evident as darker areas, cooler than the air around them. Then something changed. A false-colored figure appeared in a window, long and lean. The figure climbed out a window facing the courtyard, tried to climb down, slipped, made it eventually. The figure crept along the interior wall of the courtyard, towards the gate on the eastern side where it would lead out to the rest of the island.

Then other figures appeared around him, their IR-blocking chameleonware uncloaking, and carried him off, across the courtyard, and into the building via a door.

"How long ago was this?" Nakamura asked.

"Two hours," Feng said.

"And you think this is Kade?"

Feng nodded. "Tall? Skinny? Trying to escape? Yeah, Kade."

Nakamura looked at Sam. She nodded slowly. "Yeah."

"So now we know where he *was*," Nakamura mused. "And what door they took him in. It's a start."

Three hours later, they were agreed. As they sun rose over the Andaman Sea, they stretched out to get what sleep they could. Tonight, after nightfall, would be their assault.

An assault that Nakamura could not let Kaden Lane survive.

71

MISSION EVE

Friday November 2nd

Breece, Ava, and the Nigerian met for the last pre-mission check-in Friday night.

All the data lay before them. No sign of new surveillance on Miranda Shepherd. No sign of added security measures at the prayer breakfast site. No intrusions to the safe house. No sign of activity around the garage.

Hiroshi was dead. The memory of firing a bullet into his brain still haunted Brecce, still filled him with immense sorrow and even greater anger.

But he'd done what Hiroshi had wanted. He'd ended things before the hacker could learn who they were and what they planned.

Damn it. He was going to make someone pay for that.

Later. After tomorrow. After this mission.

He looked at what was left of his team, a question in his eyes.

"Go," the Nigerian said.

"Go," Ava said.

Breece nodded, thoughtfully. In twelve hours they'd end

the lives of two of the greatest criminals of the modern era, and hundreds of their supporters. Among the dead would be the man responsible for his parents' deaths.

"It's unanimous," Breece said. "We're a go."

72
LIBERATION

Thursday November 1st

The wind was starting to blow in earnest as Holtzmann made his way back home Thursday night. The house felt empty without Anne. He unpacked his cargo – Becker's workstation, his slate, the gold memory foil, the bottle of Laphroaig.

Now to find a way to read the digital memory Warren Becker had left behind. The memory foil was a format both old and specialized. His slate wouldn't read it. His workstation wouldn't read it. He hunted through old electronics in his garage for an hour, came up with nothing. Then he searched online, looking for any data. Tools were out there. They were specialized and rare. The electronics lab at the ERD would have what he needed...

Tomorrow, then.

He set about making the house ready for the coming storm, nailed fitted plywood they'd had made after Hurricane Catherine over the windows, made sure the house batteries were charged, filled up a barrel of water for himself.

And then he slept, as the wind and rain peppered his home.

• • •

Friday November 2nd

Friday morning he rose to fiercer winds. They howled outside. He checked the power, phones, and net. All were still online, but the news broadcasts warned that all systems could fail with Zoe's advance. Be prepared.

There was another message on the Nexus board.

[Fire alarm will go off at 7.22pm. Be ready.]

He loaded emergency supplies into the car, in case he was stranded – food, water, a raincoat, a flashlight, and the first aid kit their oldest son had insisted they keep in the house. Then Holtzmann told the car to make its way to the office.

From inside the car the storm was a surreal thing. Not yet the hurricane proper, but already its effects were being felt. Trees bent under the onslaught. The rain was a near horizontal spray, splattering in rapid fire across the windows of the car. The windshield wipers couldn't hope to keep up. The car drove itself, without need of Holtzmann's eyes.

There were thousands of cars on the roads, all headed out of the DC area. The police had turned all the lanes of the highway into an exodus eight cars wide. Only the shoulder was heading in towards DC. Holtzmann instructed the car to take it, overrode its emergency warnings about traffic out of bounds. He kept his hands on the wheel, ready to take over if the car became too confused.

The police stopped him, then again, then a third time. He was going the wrong way. This was an emergency vehicles only lane.

Each time he flashed his Department of Homeland Security ID. The word "Director" was emblazoned under his picture, and for once he used that rank, dropped phrases like "national security" and "mission critical".

They let him through each time. On the third instance they offered him an escort. Holtzmann declined and drove on.

At the DHS campus he found no one at the outside gate. The automated defenses were active. He waved his badge, held his eye up to the retinal scanner, and the gate rose, letting him and his vehicle onto the grounds.

Inside the building it was a ghost land. The hallways were empty. Lights were off. Holtzmann fetched his slate from his office, made his way to the Human Subjects wing. The same guard was there. He looked up in surprise as Holtzmann approached.

"I want to see Shankari," Holtzmann told the man.

"Director Holtzmann… We're on emergency staffing only. I don't have anyone to bring him to you."

"Issue me a taser," Holtzmann told the man. "I'll be fine."

The guard looked flustered. "Director… the protocol is to have security with you. The prisoner's dangerous…"

Holtzmann stared the man down. "The protocol doesn't work today. The prisoner is a college student, and you have us on camera." He pointed at the bank of screens in front of the man. "I *need* to talk to Shankari. This is a national security matter. Now issue me that taser."

Three minutes later he opened the door to Shankari's cell, his cane in one hand, a taser in the other.

Rangan looked up as the door opened. Holtzman was back. His heart beat faster.

"Have you reconsidered?" Holtzmann asked him. "Thought of anything new?"

Rangan shook his head. "I've told you everything."

• • •

```
[holtzmann]File transfer request. File:
tonight.txt. Accept? Y/N
[rangan]Y
```

A file started downloading to his brain.

"Keep thinking," Holtzmann told him. "I'll be back tonight, and if you haven't thought of something new then, you're going to regret it."

The file download completed. Then Holtzmann turned and left the cell, closing the door behind him.

Rangan waited, then opened the file.

Inside he found instructions. Instructions for his escape, and for the children's.

Holtzmann returned the taser to the guard. "See?" he told the man. "No problem at all."

The electronics lab was on the fifth floor. Holtzmann used his badge to unlock the door, let himself in, and flipped on the lights.

He knew what he needed. And it must be here somewhere. He pulled up the inventory on the open terminal in the lab, and started hunting.

Two hours later, in frustration, he gave up on finding exactly what he was looking for. The foil format was fifteen years old, and had only ever found narrow usage. No new readers for it had been built in a decade. There were readers here that could load the foil, could read the data on it. But none of them would talk to a modern slate or workstation.

He wasn't going to find a ready-made solution. He was going to have to build one.

It took him most of the rest of the day, resurrecting skills he hadn't used since grad school, chaining components together, testing the data path, until he had something he thought might work. The wind howled outside as he worked, picking up speed, sending a spooky moaning sound through the building. What a day.

Holtzmann took his connected components down to his office at 6pm, grabbed coffee and a pre-packaged snack from the break room on the way. He delicately seated the foil in the kludge of a device he'd built, then plugged it into his workstation.

Garbage. The thing wouldn't load properly.

He spent half an hour debugging, cursing his rusty computing skills, until he figured out the problem. One of the components had an ancient version of its firmware, more than a decade old, that wouldn't properly interface with his modern workstation.

He hunted online for the right update, found that the device manufacturer had gone out of business, hunted further, found an obscure site with an archive containing what he needed. He downloaded the new firmware, loaded it onto the component, then held his breath.

Loading files... Load successful.

Yes!

The interface was slow, painfully slow. He started the files copying onto his workstation.

And then it was almost seven. Time to get Rangan and the children out.

Rangan looked up from the floor of his cell as the door opened. Holtzmann again. The man had a taser in one hand, his cane in the other.

"Tell me more about how to reverse-compile Nexus," Holtzmann said.

Rangan shrugged. "It's not gonna be easy. There's a lot of evolved code in there. The neural connectivity map. The synaptic weights. The mapping models for different parts of the brain. They all look like garbage, like random numbers. The obfuscator would have seen that as great camo. The back doors are probably woven into that, split up into a thousand little pieces of code, spread around in little random-looking blocks."

"So how do we peel it apart?" Holtzmann asked.

"I have no idea," Rangan said honestly. "Brute force?"

They went back and forth, back and forth and nowhere at all.

Then the alarm sounded. It blared and blared.

Holtzmann turned around, as if looking for the source. The taser hung loosely in his right hand.

Then Rangan was up, running forward, tackling the man. The cane fell from Holtzmann's grip. Rangan shoved the older man against the wall, got his right hand on the taser, punched Holtzmann in the back of the head with his left fist, then jabbed the taser into the man's back and pressed the button.

Holtzmann's body jerked and spasmed, then crumpled to the ground.

Rangan reached into the man's pockets, found his badge, found his wallet, grabbed them both. Then he yanked Holtzmann's shoes off, put them on his own slippered feet. They fit for shit, but they were better than nothing. Now was the test. He waved the badge at the door with his left hand, the taser still in his right.

And the door opened.

Booyah.

He jumped into the hallway. It was deserted. Right turn. Down the hall. Next door. He waved Holtzmann's badge at the door reader and the door opened, and a dozen young minds greeted him.

73
INTO THE STORM

Friday November 2nd

Rangan hustled the children down the hall, following the path that Holtzmann had sketched out for them. Their minds were chaos, disorganized, scattered. He'd told them this was coming, but they were still so hard to herd. The fire alarm blared and blared, making everything worse, pushing itself into the kids' minds. He made them hold hands, Tim just behind him, holding Rangan's hand, chained all the way to the back, to Bobby. Alfonso came in the middle. The other boys would have left him, and that pained Rangan, but Alfonso was the one who'd suffered the most, and Rangan was going to get that little boy the fuck out of this place.

Ahead they were coming up on the security desk. Rangan clutched the taser tight. If shit was gonna go bad it was gonna be here. They turned the corner and he made ready to jump out, to throw himself at the guard. But the station was empty. The bank of screens showed Rangan and the kids on one display, but no one was here to see it.

Then they were past it, at the elevator. Rangan waved Holtzmann's badge and the door opened, and then they were all cramming in. Rangan hurried them along, pulled them all into the elevator, then pounded the button for P1. He waved the badge again and P1 lit up. The doors closed and they descended.

The doors opened again onto a nearly empty garage. They piled out of the elevator and Pedro dropped Tim's hand and the chain was broken. He stopped and forced the boys to chain up again, counted them to make sure he had them all. Then they hurried across the garage, the way Holtzmann had told him, Rangan half dragging the boys until they reached the stairwell. He yanked on the door and it was open. They took the stairs up, opened the next door, and suddenly they were outside.

The wind hit him immediately. Gale force. Outside the trees were bending hard, their branches all pushed in one direction. Sharp pinpricks of rain sprayed painfully into Rangan's face. The sound of the storm was a constant roar. A boom sounded from some place, then a cracking sound. He looked around to get his bearings, thought he understood where they were going. He reached out with his mind to the kids, did his best to hold them together, to focus them. He showed them in his mind where they were going, showed them that they *had* to hold hands, and then they were off.

He felt the wind and rain take their toll on the boys. They were all in slippers, not proper shoes. They were completely soaked from head to toe in seconds. Their slippered feet slid on wet asphalt. Halfway across the open square, Parker raised his hand to shield his face from the stinging of the rain and the human chain broke. Rangan made them link up again, even in the pelting rain and the harsh wind, made them hold hands and started them forward again.

They made it another hundred yards, almost to the trees, when he felt a sharp wince of pain from behind him. Jose! Jose was down on the ground. He'd tripped on a curb. The boy had hit his head and there was a bloody scrape on his brow and he was crying.

Rangan shoved the taser into the pocket of his prison pants, then hoisted Jose up over his shoulder. The boy was heavy! He grabbed Tim's hand again, made the other boys link up, and then they were into the trees.

Leaves blew around them. The wind and rain were less here, but they still stung. Twigs and rocks hurt the boys' feet but he made them keep moving. On the other side of the trees they'd find…

There. They came out of the trees, and ahead was the side gate to the complex. It was a chain link affair, barbed wire at the top, with automated stations to allow ingress and egress on either side. There was a guard booth, but Rangan couldn't see anyone in it. A pale red light glowed on the card reader on the station on this side. This was it.

"Come on, boys," he shouted out loud and into the howling wind. He reached out with his mind to enfold them, to push them forward.

He dashed out of the trees, into the road, to the station, Tim's hand still in his own, Jose still on his shoulder. The rain lashed him with increasing fury. The wind came on strong enough that he almost lost his feet. He was soaked now, soaked to the bone, shivering from it. He felt misery and cold and fear and confusion from the boys behind him.

Then he was there. Rangan let go of Tim's hand, fished out Holtzmann's badge, swiped it against the evil red eye of the scanner, and waited. And waited.

The red eye blinked at him, stayed red. Nothing happened. Fuck!

Rangan swiped the badge again. And again. He jammed it up against the reader, swiveling it around.

"Come on, you piece of shit!"

Then abruptly the red eye was green. Rangan turned his head. Slowly, slowly, the gate was swinging itself open.

He shoved the badge back into his pocket, grabbed Tim's hand, and dragged the boys through the widening crack, not waiting for it to open fully. They ran out across a road, into more trees, through the trees. Jose was heavy but Rangan kept the boy on his shoulder, kept moving, kept consulting Holtzmann's map in his mind.

Then they were out of the trees, climbing an embankment up to a road. And there was a beat-up old white van there, and a man was jumping out of it, reaching his hand down to Rangan, to help him up, to take him and the boys away to safety.

74

MOTHER, MOTHER

Friday November 2nd

Ling's bruises healed. Her burns covered themselves in a thin white protective layer which then sloughed off, revealing fresh, healthy skin below. No scar remained. She was her mother's child, and her mother had given her every genetic advantage possible at the time of her creation.

She lived like a wild thing that week, like an animal, hiding in her den, venturing out when it was safe to scavenge food. She placed orders for groceries, used her father's credentials, had them delivered while he was out, stocked into the pantry and refrigerator by the kitchen bot. If her father noticed or cared it didn't show.

She missed Feng. Feng who was brave and strong and had always bounced her on his shoulders when she was little. Feng who could crush her father and take her away from here.

She missed Kade. Kade who was clever and would help her find some way...

Feng! she called out. **FENG!**

Kade! she tried. **KADE!**

Nothing. Nothing for days now. They were dead, or gone, or off the net. She was alone.

How long can I live like this? Ling wondered.

As long as I have to, until I get to Mother.

Everything changed on Friday, on the fourteenth day since she'd tried to free Mother.

The call came in a few minutes before midnight. Chen jumped as he saw the name. Sun Liu! The Minister of Science and Technology was calling him here!

He rushed into his bedroom, tapped the panel beside the door to seal the room, flicked to a different screen on the room control, and activated the privacy filter.

Then he took a deep breath and accepted the call.

"Chen." Sun Liu's voice was strained.

"Minister," Chen replied. "I've tried everything, I assure you. Manipulation of her volition centers. Direct pain stimulation. Pulsed pain and pleasure. I assure you, I've tortured her, *everything* possible has been tried."

"Chen," Sun Liu interrupted. "It's over. We've lost."

Chen caught his breath. The minister sounded tired. No. Not tired.

Frightened.

"How…" Chen started. "How bad?"

There was silence on the line. Then Sun Liu spoke again. "They won't call it a coup," the Minister said. "I will… probably… be allowed to retire, rather than face…"

Sun Liu's voice broke and he went silent.

Chen held his breath, and the Minister finished.

"Rather than face prosecution."

Chen let out an involuntary noise.

"Everything has changed, Chen," Sun Liu said. "Shanghai... whatever happened there, it has frightened the people, frightened the Assembly. It's put the hardliners in the ascendency."

Chen's heart was pounding. "What... What..."

"They'll want people to remain calm," Sun Liu said. "They'll do their best to make it look seamless. A period of *ill health* for the Secretary General. An *early retirement*, with great honors. A change in membership of the Standing Committee. New laws, for public safety, public order. Steps to avoid another Shanghai. Restrictions on dangerous technology, dangerous research."

Sun Liu's voice wavered as he spoke. He sounded so old, Chen thought. So beaten. The fear came through beneath his voice. "They'll avoid outright murder," the Minister continued. "I believe they will. Yes."

Chen was sweating.

"Your wife," Sun Liu said. "You must shut her down. Tomorrow. You must give them no excuse."

Chen heard nothing after that. He barely remembered placing the calls to his staff, his assistant Li-hua. Tomorrow morning. They'd meet. They'd initiate the final backup. Then they'd shut her down.

And hope the hardliners didn't take their heads as well.

Ling followed her father with her mind, routed around the room's pitiful privacy filters, listened in to the call with the apartment's audio monitors.

Later, she could not recall all that was said. Only fragments stuck with her through the haze of anger and grief, the overwhelming loss that poured through her, forcing tears from her human eyes.

"…tried everything… pain stimulation… tortured her…"

"…useless to us now… backup and deactivate… tomorrow…"

Her world went white, then, white-hot with the rage and loss. They were going to kill her mother! She felt the anger building inside her, felt the urge to lash out, to destroy this city, to topple the buildings, light them on fire, to kill them all, every single one of these humans who wanted to kill her mommy!

Her rage pulsated within her, straining to get out.

No, no, a voice whispered inside her. *Not that way!*

Aaaaaah! she screamed inside her mind, blind with the anger, with the urge to rip and rend at the electronic fabric of the city.

They'll catch you! the voice whispered.

She pounded her tiny hands against the wall instead, channeled the rage towards something that would not lead them to her. Her fists pounded the wall.

And one of the panels slid away. There behind it was the freezer. The freezer she'd known was here. The freezer that held no food. The freezer that held something else entirely.

75

A LAST DEBATE

Saturday November 3rd

Kade came to slowly. There was an aching pain in his head, in his right hand. Light was shining in behind his closed eyelids.

He opened his eyes to find himself back in the room he'd occupied for the last week. A splint and bandages covered his right hand and most of his forearm. He didn't even want to think about the damage he'd done to that.

Breakfast was laid out for him already. His body was hungry, but he couldn't bring himself to eat.

So stupid, he thought. He played me so easily.

Now Shiva had one of the back doors. And with that... he'd become a tyrant. Kade had seen it. A well-intentioned tyrant, at first. But that sort of power. It would corrupt anyone.

Like you? Ilya asked in his mind.

Yes, he told Ilya. *Like me*.

Shiva came to see him an hour later, a Nexus jammer around his neck. Smart man. Even now, he didn't think he'd plumbed Kade's depths. And he was right.

"My hand is still extended to you, Kade," Shiva said. "Join me. We can save the world together."

"Don't do it," Kade pleaded with him. "This can't work. People have to find solutions on their own. It has to be from the bottom up."

Shiva shook his head. "You're naïve, my young friend. The world has no time left. Your way is a luxury we can't afford. My way is the only option left to us."

Kade shook his head. "You can't keep it a secret," he told Shiva. "They'll find out what you're doing. They'll catch you. They'll hate you for it. You'll go down in history as a monster."

Shiva held Kade's eyes. "Let them call me a monster. At least they'll have a future to do it in."

Shiva stood atop the roof of his home. His eyes drank in the magnificent sea and sky. He spread his arms wide and the cool breeze blew his white cotton robe behind him like a cloak, like the wings of some supernatural being.

The code he'd captured from Kade had passed every test. Now vast machinery, long prepared in anticipation of this moment, leapt into action. Data centers around the world began humming. Microsatellites in low earth orbit began transmitting. Software tools flipped into an active mode.

Shiva closed his eyes, his arms still spread, his robe billowing behind him, and savored the feel of the sun on his skin and the wind in his hair. His thoughts spread across the island, up through uplinks to the constellation of satellites above, and out into the minds of thousands, tens of thousands, more every moment as the software agents his team had built spread out, replicated, infected every Nexus mind they found.

He could feel them. He could feel their intellect, their need. His vast computing machinery processed their inputs, collated it for him, coalesced it into a gestalt that he could wrap his own mind around. They were him. He was them.

He was a god, entwined with a spreading congregation of humanity. He was the burning spearpoint of a new planetary intelligence, a new superorganism.

And together, bit by bit, they would save this world.

76
SANCTUARY

Friday November 2nd

Rangan accepted the outstretched hand, pulled himself up with it to the road. He put Jose down, then he and this other man hauled the rest of the boys onto the muddy embankment, then into the ancient-looking white van.

"Get in front," the man yelled to Rangan over the wind. Rangan nodded, opened the passenger side door and hauled himself in. Free!

He slammed the door as this man did the same on the driver's side. The boys were in a stunned state of excitement in the back, babbling at each other, their minds giving off chaos and disbelief. Rangan studied the man who'd rescued them. Early thirties. Dark hair. Average build. Clean shaven. In a raincoat, with jeans and hiking boots showing beneath it.

"I'm Levi." The man turned to Rangan, offering his hand.

"I'm Rangan," Rangan said, taking the hand, shaking it.

"I know." Levi smiled. He turned an old-fashioned key and a startlingly loud engine rumbled to life.

"Thank you," Rangan said.

Levi nodded his head and the van lurched forward, driving them into the night.

"Where are we going?" Rangan asked.

"West," Levi said. "St Mark's Episcopal Church."

Rangan frowned. "I thought the churches all hated Nexus?"

"Not this one," Levi said. Then he turned and smiled at Rangan. "I should know. I'm the minister."

It took almost three hours to make it out to the Virginia countryside and to St Mark's, a little church on the outskirts of a farming town called Madison. Levi took back roads, avoiding the highways where cameras would be. Zoe battered them every moment of it, pushing herself onto land, chasing them as they drove. The radio brought news of downed trees, roofs torn off, power outages, cars overturned, injuries, and deaths.

"We got lucky," Levi told him as he drove through the gale. "We couldn't have gotten you out without this storm. It left them short-staffed. Satellites can't see us with the clouds. Drones can't fly in this wind. Zoe's a gift from the Lord, Rangan. He sent her. So we could get you and these boys out."

Rangan just grunted in reply.

Holtzmann lay on the floor, face down, eyes closed, pretending to be unconscious. His head ached where Rangan had punched him, shoved him against the wall. His right arm had long ago fallen asleep, pinned beneath his weight. His still healing hip ached at him. His Nexus OS was on the fritz, disrupted by the electrical shock through his system, not responding to his commands.

Stay still, he told himself. Just a little longer. Just a little longer.

In the end it was thirty-five minutes before Holtzmann heard running feet and a raised voice, before someone shook him and rolled him over.

He did his best to look and seem dazed, confused. The guard was asking him again and again, "What happened?"

Holtzmann groaned, put his hand to his head. "I was interrogating Shankari. The alarm went off. And then…"

Then the guard cursed, got up, ran off. A moment later a new alarm sounded, one Holtzmann had never heard before. A voice came on over it.

"Lockdown alert. Lockdown alert. This facility is now locked down. No one may leave or enter the facility until the lockdown is completed. Lockdown alert. Lockdown alert…" and on and on.

Now he just hoped that Shankari and the children were already off the campus.

They held him for two hours, not as a prisoner, but as a witness. More guards arrived, some sopping wet, others dry. A medic pointed a light in Holtzmann's eyes, scanned him for any sign of concussion, pronounced him likely healthy.

Bit by bit, over the course of those hours, Holtzmann's Nexus nodes came back to functionality, until the Nexus OS booted itself again. Idly, he wondered if his root access to his own brain had been restored? No, he told himself. Best not to check that. Best not to go down that road again. Never again.

While he waited, Holtzmann overheard bits of chatter across the radios. All-points bulletin. Local police. FBI. Hurricane problems.

They were doing everything they could to recapture Shankari and the children. And Zoe was fighting them.

The lockdown ended just before 10pm, but Zoe raged on, intensifying, as more of her pushed aground.

Shortly after, Holtzmann persuaded them that he'd answered all the questions he could. One of the guards escorted him to his office, opening the doors that Holtzmann couldn't without his badge.

He thanked the man, sat down at his desk, waited for the guard to leave.

Then he got to work.

As they drove, Levi updated Rangan on world events. It was November already. When had he thought it was? Fuck, he didn't even know. A lot had happened. Kade's release of Nexus 5. The embrace of it by scientists, mental health workers, and the autism community. The PLF bombings. The Nexus crackdowns. The birth of the underground railroad.

Rangan's head spun with it. The world was a different place. Nexus 5 had changed things in ways he'd never expected. Maybe Wats had expected this conflict. Maybe Ilya had. They'd been political. Not him or Kade. The political ones had died. He and Kade were just hunted.

He needed to get in touch with his parents, let them know that he was alive.

"Later," Levi said. "DHS will have your parents under surveillance. We'll find a stealthy way to let them know."

Rangan nodded his head mutely. He had no choice but to trust this man.

Levi pulled the van up to a covered garage attached to the small church. The door opened and they drove in. The boys were holding their breaths in Rangan's mind. This all seemed so unreal.

Rangan hopped out, opened the van's side door, started helping boys out. He felt other minds appear, turned, saw three women approaching, all modestly dressed. Their minds felt warm and welcoming, and there were smiles on their faces.

Bobby jumped out of the van, hugged Rangan tight. Rangan returned the embrace. So weird that he'd never seen any of these boys in the flesh until a few hours ago.

Levi came around the van, introduced the women as Laura and Janet and Steph. "These are friends," he told Rangan and the boys. Janet crouched in front of Tyrone and held out her hand and mind. The boy tentatively reached out, embraced both, and suddenly the bottleneck was broken, and the women were accepted.

"Welcome to the underground railroad," Levi told Rangan quietly.

The three women took the boys away. Bobby didn't want to go. He hugged Rangan tight, but Rangan assured him it was OK, that these were good people. He felt it. He felt it from Laura and Janet and Steph's minds, felt it even from Levi, though there was no Nexus there. Bobby felt it too, felt the kindness, felt Rangan's own judgment. He loosened his grip, and Laura led him kindly away.

Outside, the storm raged on, battering the church with a *ratatatat* of heavy rain.

Levi showed him to a bathroom, put a bundle of clothes in his hands. Rangan went in, pulled off the thin soggy clothes he'd been wearing, changed into a plain cotton T-shirt and jeans Levi had given him. The jeans were too loose, but there was a belt. He pulled it tight, wondering who had gifted him with these clothes.

He half collapsed on the sink, then, overcome with emotion. A sob ripped itself out of his chest. The kindness these people were showing him overwhelmed him. A day ago he'd been sure he was going to die in that place. Now he had something. Hope. The boys had hope. Rangan wept, racked with sobs, wishing Ilya had lived long enough for this, wishing Wats had, wishing he knew where Kade was or how to help him.

He pulled himself together, stood up straight, forced himself to stop crying, then splashed water on his face.

If I make it out of this... I'm gonna help people. I'm gonna pay this forward.

Levi was there when Rangan opened the bathroom door, standing there patiently. The minister just looked at him kindly, smiled, held out a hand and took Rangan by the shoulder.

Levi led him down a stairwell and into a basement below the small church, then through a door and into an office.

Rangan felt her before he saw her. Felt *them* before he saw them. He didn't understand what it was he sensed until the door swung open and Levi stepped out of the way. And then he could see her. Levi's wife, Abigail. She was seated in a swiveling office chair. A pretty, petite blonde woman in a floral dress. Thirty, maybe. She had a shy smile on her face. And her hands were on her belly.

Her giant pregnant belly.

77
PRIOR DAYS

Friday November 2nd

Rangan crouched in amazement at Abigail's feet, reached out his hands gently.

"May I?" he asked looking up at her.

The petite blonde smiled down at him, nodded enthusiastically.

Rangan's fingers touched Abigail's belly. His mind touched... something wondrous. Something like he'd never felt before.

The baby was aware, alive. She felt Rangan's mental touch – *she* – and she touched him back, with her mind, with her feet pressing against the inside of her mother to make contact with his hands. Her world was an ocean of sensation, of warm constraint, of her mother's heart beating and blood pumping, of her mother's mind, her ever-present mind.

Rangan felt her curiosity, felt her thoughts probe his. Her mind was delicate, uncoordinated. She explored Rangan with her thoughts like his cousin's newborn child had once explored his face with her tiny hands, flailing about, gently, trying to make sense of this shape she'd encountered. The memory made him smile, and she caught it, giggled mentally, touched on his memory of little Reina, his cousin's child.

This is you, he tried to show her. You'll be like this.

Waves of wonder and peals of mental laughter touched him in return.

He looked up at Abigail again. He could feel her joy, radiant, inundating this room, encompassing her unborn daughter.

"She hasn't met many men before," Abigail said. "Besides her daddy."

Rangan turned. Levi was there in the corner of the room, smiling at them.

"But..." Rangan started. "You don't..."

"Have Nexus?" Levi replied.

Rangan nodded.

"I purge it and redose," Levi said. "Ministers get too much attention to have it all the time.

"Rangan," Levi went on, "there's something we'd like you to help us with."

Rangan nodded. "Anything."

"We help sneak Nexus children and parents down the line, to others who can get them out of the country," Levi said. "But we want to do more, to end the persecution of these children. And to do that... we want to show people what's going on."

"We want to record what you've seen," Abigail said. "What you've been through."

Rangan went silent. There was so much he wanted to forget. The torture, the drugs, the mind games where he'd thought he was about to die. The boys, and what he'd seen in their memories, what they'd been through...

He swallowed hard, then nodded. "Yeah," he said. "Let's show 'em."

Levi brought him coffee while Abigail set up the equipment. The recorder was an innocuous device, just a phone-sized black rectangle plugged into a terminal. Abigail did something to shield the baby's mind, and the baby faded in Rangan's senses.

It took hours. The storm battered the little church as they recorded, sent a keen wailing sound through the building.

Rangan showed them all of it. The bust of the party at Simonyi field. The blackmail. Being threatened with prison for them and dozens of their friends if they didn't cooperate, if they didn't give the feds Nexus 5, if Kade didn't go to Bangkok to spy for them. And later, after something had gone wrong on that mission, jackbooted thugs kicking down the door of his apartment, pointing their guns at him. The restraints and interrogation. The lectures where they told him he had no rights, that they could kill him and no one would care, no one would know. The electrical shocks. The waterboarding. The twisted mind games.

The day they broke him. They day he gave up, and gave them what they wanted.

And the boys' memories. Bobby watching his dad get shot and killed. Tim being torn out of his mother's hands. Alfonso being clubbed across the face when he tried to bite one of them. More. The beatings. The experiments. Bobby's last session, the one where they'd tried to force the Nexus out of him.

And the faces. Every face he'd seen in custody. Every face the boys had shared with him, the one who'd tortured Bobby, the ones who'd beaten them, stuck needles into them.

Rangan had to stop over and over again, overcome with emotion, tears streaming down his face, his body trembling in anger or remembered terror. Each time they offered to end the session. Each time he refused. People needed to know this. They needed to know.

When it was over they hugged him, both of them. Rangan held on for dear life, held onto them for what seemed like an eternity.

And after, he felt lighter. Abigail led him to another room. She peeled back a carpet, and there was a door in the floor there. She opened it, led him down a set of stairs, to a hallway, then a darkened room. The boys were there, on cots, already asleep. She led him to a cot of his own, hugged him again, and left.

Rangan lay there in a daze. It was over. It was really over. He was free again.

The sleeping minds of the boys surrounded him, engulfed him in hope, in a tranquility he hadn't felt in months.

Rangan closed his eyes, breathed that hope in, and drifted off to a peaceful sleep.

Holtzmann's first task was to send the underground railroad the rest of the files he'd promise them. He waited for the guard to leave. Then he closed his eyes, opened a control panel, paired his Nexus OS to his phone, used it to get online.

The signal quality was terrible. Zoe had been battering cell towers across the DC metro area. He had one bar of service, hardly any bandwidth at all.

He punched in the address of the anonymization service, waited, waited, waited, and finally it loaded. From there he went to the Nexus board, waited again for it to load, waited to put in his username and password, and for his inbox to load up.

Holtzmann pulled up the message in his inbox, started a reply to it, attached the already uploaded file, and hit Send.

Nothing happened. He had a moment of fearing that the connection had been lost. Then finally the screen updated as the packets got through.

He thought for a moment, then wrote another message to the underground railroad ID that had contacted him, this time with locations of other groups of Nexus children. The labs in Virginia, in Texas, in California.

Send.

Holtzmann waited, waited for confirmation that the short message had sent. The connection dropped out for a moment, then came back, then finally: Message Sent.

Holtzmann smiled grimly, nodded in satisfaction of having done something right, then turned to the other task at hand. The data from Warren Becker's memory foil.

There were dozens of files here. He hunted through them, trying to understand what he was looking at. One caught his eye.

diary

That sounded like a good place to start.

He opened the file, started scanning for information about the PLF, anything that might confirm or dispel his fears.

The diary was huge, an entry for almost every day of the last fifteen years. It took him hours just to skim them all. Zoe beat and pounded and drummed against the outside window of his office as he worked. More than once he looked up, wondered if he should go somewhere more physically secure, somewhere without windows.

But no. These were armored glass, impregnated with layers of carbon mesh. They'd stop high-powered bullets. Surely they'd keep the storm at bay?

He stayed and toiled as Zoe raged just feet from where he sat. And bit by bit, Holtzmann distilled entries from 2032 – eight years ago – into a story. A story that terrified him.

March 9th – discussed formation of red cell again, under false flag. bad idea.

March 18th – false flag discussed again as means to entrap potential terrorists. CP killed idea.

June 12th – false flag raised again. twin goals: entrap terrorists, generate public support for ERD mission.

June 16th – false flag moving forward. PLF as name. will claim credit for some incidents, launch plots that fail.

August 23rd – false flag on hold pending prez election.

November 18th – false flag happening. lead agent MB, code name zara. see <file>. i've protested as much as is safe – maybe more. time I forget and keep head down.

Holtzmann stared at the pieces he'd put together. He opened the linked file. And there it was. A classified memo detailing the creation of the PLF. An undercover operation that would take credit for terrorist activities, would lure in potential transhuman terrorists, send them off on missions that were sure to fail, letting the FBI and ERD foil most of those missions... Letting others missions "succeed" in a controlled manner, with no loss of life...

A false flag indeed. One that would capture transhuman terrorists. And keep the public afraid.

So what happened?

He scanned back, and an entry caught his eye again.

false flag happening. lead agent MB, code name zara.
MB.

• • •

Maximilian Barnes.

Special Policy Advisor to two presidents.

And now Acting Director of the ERD.

Holtzmann's heart was pounding hard now. This was too much. Too much. He'd had his fears, but this... *This*?

He needed to get these files to the right people. Anonymously. Not from his workstation.

He moved to copy the files to his phone instead, found that his workstation couldn't see the phone.

Fear crept up Holtzmann's spine. He turned to the workstation again, pulled up a random site on the net.

Network failure. System offline.

Oh no. Oh no. Holtzmann stood as calmly as he could. He had a bad feeling about this.

He opened his briefcase, unplugged the kludgy foil reader he'd constructed, the foil still in it, and shoved the whole mess in. Then he picked up his cane and limped to the door. He had the data. He could finish this from home. From anywhere. Not here.

He shifted his cane to the briefcase hand, and put his free hand on the door knob.

It was locked.

What? He hadn't locked it.

He reached into his jacket for his badge, but of course the badge wasn't there. Rangan Shankari had it.

He slid open the backup authentication panel next to the door, swiped his thumb across the pad, held his eye steady where the retinal scanner could see him.

ACCESS DENIED flashed across the small screen.

Just a mistake, he told himself. A glitch from the lockdown. Or the storm.

Stay calm. *Stay calm.*

He turned back to his desk, limped to it on his cane.

He picked up the secure line on his desk. He'd call security, have them unlock his office.

Nothing. The line was dead.

He was trapped here.

78

END OF THE ROAD

Saturday November 3rd

Rangan woke to minds in turmoil. There were people on the other side of this wall, talking quietly, intensely. Something was wrong.

Outside the storm sounded louder and angrier than ever, a raging maelstrom of wind and water pummeling them, trying to beat them down.

Rangan crept off the cot and out into the hallway. There he found Levi, an exhausted-looking Abigail, and someone he didn't know – a boy, sixteen maybe, soaked to the bone, his long black hair plastered to his face, dripping water onto the tile floor.

"What's going on?" Rangan asked.

Levi looked at him, unhappily.

"Police are out," Levi said. "They're going door to door. Jordan here says they came to his house. They have a picture of the van." He shook his head. "We must have passed a camera I didn't know about."

"I ran here," the boy said. "Phones are down. Our house is half a mile up the road."

Abigail spoke up. "We have to get rid of the van. Hide it."

Levi nodded. "I'll go."

"Wait!" Rangan said. "If they catch you in the van, that'll lead them back here."

They all stared at him. These people who'd saved him. This boy who'd run half a mile through a hurricane to warn them.

"I'll go," Rangan said.

"The van's unregistered," Levi said as he led them to the garage. "From a junkyard. Just get it a few miles from here, dump it, and come back."

"What about prints?" Jordan asked. "DNA?"

They stared at him.

"Like in the movies!" Jordan said. "You have to sanitize it. Dump it in the river. Set it on fire. Somethin'."

Levi cursed something not very preacher-like under his breath.

They siphoned gas into a can. Levi gave Rangan a box of roadside flares.

"Dump the gas in it," Levi said. "Open the doors. Get far back, then toss the flare in. You understand?"

Rangan nodded. "Tell the boys..." He stopped.

Abigail put a hand on his. "They know."

"Just be safe," Levi said. "Get back here if you can. If not, the Miller farm is two miles south. Use my name and they'll hide you."

Then Levi threw his arms around Rangan, embracing him. Rangan hugged the man back.

Then it was Abigail's turn. She hugged him and he hugged back, and he felt her mind and the baby's, felt the baby embrace him mentally, and felt tears coming to his eyes again. He pulled away, and it was time to go.

"Thank you," he told them. "I'll be back soon."

Zoe tried to kill him as soon as he left the church.

The wind was a monster, rocking the van to and fro. The rain sheeted the windshield in water instantly, hopelessly overpowering the wipers. Rangan turned the antiquated van in the driveway, trying to see where he was going. He put it in forward, turned onto the street, drove south, away from Jordan's house. A terrible crack sounded and he looked up in time to see a tree falling at him. He turned the wheel hard, braking, felt the tires skid on the wet slippery pavement. Something thudded on the van's roof, then somehow he was past, still in one piece.

The rain pounded like machine-gun fire against the body of the van, *ratatatat*, *ratatatat*. It drummed and battered. The wind blasted at the vehicle, tried to push it over. Rangan fought with the wheel, tried to keep the van going straight, struggled to make sense of the world outside the windshield.

It was chaos, chaos everywhere. There was water in the street, inches of water that he drove through. Tree limbs tumbled end over end. A power line was down, throwing sparks as it jumped and skipped in the wind. Debris hurtled through the air. He winced as something large and dark slammed into the already spiderwebbed windshield with a wet thud, then bounced off and continued its flight. There were overturned cars on the road. He passed a building that made no sense, until he realized it had been a gas station, until the storm had ripped its pumps free and torn its roof away.

He dragged his eyes back to the road, tried to make sense of it through rain and the spiderweb of cracks, tried to stay in the middle of what was fast becoming a river. Something dark came at him, hurtling through the street, skipping across the water. Rangan spun the wheel. The front windshield exploded in a shower of glass. He brought his hands up reflexively, closed his eyes as pieces of it cut him everywhere, on his forearms and brow and chest and shoulders. The van spun, skidded, and he slammed the brakes until the vehicle stopped moving. He looked to the side and saw a metal trash can half-embedded in the front passenger seat.

The storm came in through the shattered front of the van now, pummeling him with rain like a sandblaster, with wind that tore at him. He could barely keep his eyes open. He pushed his head down low, used one hand to cover his eyes until just a slit remained between his fingers, drove with the other.

He made it another mile that way, as the storm buffeted him, past the buildings of the tiny main street, past what was left of another gas station at the edge of town. It was farmland out here. He was looking for shelter, a copse of trees, a farmhouse, something.

Then he saw the squad car ahead. It was coming towards him, flashing out of the chaos of the storm. It zoomed by and its flashing lights came on as it did. He looked up into the rearview mirror and he could see enough to see those lights, see the squad car turning back towards him.

Rangan jammed the gas pedal, sat up straighter, lifted his arm to shield himself from the storm. He looked up and the lights were closer, right behind him. The a boom sounded, louder than the storm, and another. The van lurched as something struck it. He fought to keep it on the country road. Then another boom burst out and sharp pain lanced through his midsection.

Out of the rain a side road loomed, a crossing in the middle of nowhere. He spun the wheel hard to the right with both hands. The rain lacerated his face as he did. The turn pressed him against the door and he groaned in pain. Then the wheels slipped and the van was spinning, the world turning around him. He saw the flashing lights go by, right to left, then gone again, and then the wheels came off the road and out over the ditch – and the van was tumbling, rolling, and a giant force was pressing against him.

The world spun and when it made sense again, Rangan was upside down, pressing into the seat belt that held him in place. He reached to his waist, pressed the release, and collapsed painfully to the new floor of the van. His insides were a riot of pain. He was in a heap on what was once the ceiling. He could smell gasoline. The crash or something had torn the lid off the gas can, or a bullet had pierced it. The box of flares was open, scattered around him.

Rangan grabbed a flare, then another. He pulled himself painfully up, his body protesting, and stuffed the flares into his pocket. He reached for the door, tried to open it, couldn't make sense of how it worked. Through the window he could see lights, the flashing lights, a pair of white lights, flashlights, pointed at him, coming closer.

He scrambled backwards, fell, pulled himself up again. The other door. The trashcan blocked it. He pushed into the back of the van instead, grabbed the handle to the wide side door, twisted. The door lurched open an inch. Then the wind grabbed it, ripped it out of his hands, forcing it all the way open. He fell out onto the ground, tried to rise, failed, slipped instead, down a muddy bank. The wind hurled more mud at him, threw it into his face, his mouth, his eyes.

Rangan turned to look and the van was there, behind and above him, not ten paces away. Behind that, the flashlights, shouting maybe, hard to hear over the storm.

He reached into his pocket, pulled out a flare. The gasoline vapors... when flame hit them, they'd go up like dynamite. Was he far enough? Fuck if he knew.

Rangan pulled the cap off the emergency flare, saw it burst into life. He yanked his arm back, heard shouts over the storm, and threw the flare up and at the side of the van.

For an instant the flare hung in mid air, in the midst of a lazy end-over-end turn, a superbright jet of white-hot flame and glowing sparks erupting from one end of it, a point of daylight in the dark deluge.

Then it reached the cloud of gasoline vapors emerging from the van. Rangan's whole world exploded, and all went black.

79

TRUTH OUT

Saturday November 3rd

Holtzmann collapsed heavily into his office chair. Door locked from the outside. Computer off the net. Office phone dead.

He pulled out his own phone. It still had weak signal, intermittent connection. He could use it. But who would he call? Who could help him at this point?

He stared at the screen of his workstation.

No. Not who could help him. Who could *he* help? He still had this data.

Holtzmann took the most damning diary entries and the memo creating the ERD, concatenated them, then advanced them page by page as his Nexus OS took photographs of each on the screen of his workstation. He had to get this out to the world.

He linked his mind to the net through his phone connection again. It was halting, painfully slow. He tried to connect to the anonymizing service, waited, waited, there.

He tunneled from there to the Nexus board, to his inbox, to the messages he'd exchanged with the underground railroad person. They needed this.

The connection was terrible. He had to refresh multiple times, but then he had it going. He started uploading the file from his mind to a new message. Holtzmann had no idea how long this would take. He hunted through options, clicked "compress on wire", "auto retry uploads", and "send once complete".

He turned back to his workstation, to dig deeper, to learn more.

Then the door to his office opened with a click, and Maximilian Barnes walked in.

Holtzmann stared slack-jawed at Barnes. The man looked completely unruffled in his black suit and white shirt, every one of his black hairs in place, his dark eyes almost lively, amused.

"Martin," he said.

Bluff! Bluff!

"Director Barnes!" Martin replied. "I'm so glad you're here. Shankari stole my badge." He chuckled. "I was stuck here."

Barnes smiled, closed the door behind him, and sat down in the chair across the desk from Holtzmann.

Holtzmann had to keep playing. He could do this. He could talk his way out of here.

He shook his head ruefully. "That was foolish of me. Have they caught Shankari yet? They know to keep him alive, yes?"

Barnes smiled wider. "I'm not here about Shankari, Martin."

Zoe pounded a hard gust of wind against the windows, followed it with a machine gun fire spray of rain.

Holtzmann raised one eyebrow. "The Nexus kids, then? They can't get far." He gestured back behind himself at the armored window, at the hurricane beyond it.

Barnes chuckled. "You opened the wrong file, Martin."

The cold dread clenched around Holtzmann. He knows.

Then he thought: I'm not getting out of here.

Holtzmann closed his eyes, raised his hands to his face.

```
[record -video -audio | mailto lisa.
brandt@harvard.edu -autobuffer -
autoretry]
```

He opened his eyes and looked at Barnes again. Warnings scrolled down his face about poor connection quality, about low bit rates.

```
[Bandwidth Poor - Upload Delayed]
[Bandwidth Poor - Upload Delayed]
```

He ignored them.

"Here," Holtzmann said, lifting the briefcase off the floor. "The files Warren Becker left are in here." He put it on the desk, slid it towards Barnes.

Barnes took it, placed it on the floor next to him. "Becker, eh?" He sounded amused. "Haunting us from the grave."

```
[Bandwidth Poor - Upload Delayed]
```

"Where you put him," Holtzmann ventured.

Barnes' expression became grave. "I think it's time you joined him, Martin."

Barnes reached into his jacket pocket and Holtzmann's heart froze in fear, expecting a gun. He produced a pill instead. Small. Green. He placed it on the surface of the desk between them, and as he did, Holtzmann noticed for the first time the thin shimmer around Barnes' hands. Monolayer gloves. He'd leave no trace behind here.

```
[Bandwidth Poor - Upload Delayed]
```

"The President values your loyalty," Barnes was saying. "You're a true American hero, Martin. Your wife will be taken care of. Your boys – off at college, right? In Europe? They'll do *great*."

Holtzmann stared at that little pill. His vision contracted around it until the room and Barnes and everything else shrank to insignificance, and only the pill remained, huge and ominous.

End of the road, Holtzmann thought. End of this long life of compromise. I should have followed my dreams, just once. I should have stuck with my convictions.

[Bandwidth Poor - Upload Delayed]

He looked up at Barnes again. "Does the President even know?" he asked.

Barnes shrugged. "He doesn't need to be concerned with details."

"You created the PLF," Holtzmann said. "Does he know that? That you run them? The people who shot at him? Who killed men and women he knew?"

Barnes' jaw tightened. "Swallow the pill, Martin."

"Non-lethal missions," Holtzmann said. "I read the file. What happened three months ago? What happened in Chicago?"

A muscle twitched in Barnes' jaw. He leaned forward, used one monolayered finger to push the pill towards Holtzmann.

"You've lost control, haven't you?" Holtzmann asked. "The fiction you've created has become real. Your pet terrorist group is biting at your hand now, isn't it?"

Barnes stared at him, coldly, then leaned in close. "Take that fucking pill, Martin, or I'm going to shove it down your throat."

[Bandwidth Poor - Upload Delayed]

Holtzmann pushed back in his chair, his hand on his cane, propelled himself up and back, back, until he touched the window. He could feel the rain drumming against it, a high-pressure barrage of fat water droplets shaking the glass.

Holtzmann closed his eyes to see the bandwidth. It was up a notch higher here. Signal strength was just the tiniest bit better.

He opened his eyes and Barnes was standing in front of him, half a head taller. His hand was up before him, the green pill pinched between thumb and forefinger.

Holtzmann scooted to the side, away from Barnes, away from his death, towards the corner. Barnes followed him, grimly, the taller man's eyes drilling into Holtzmann's. Holtzmann closed his eyes in fear, not brave any more, not wanting this, not wanting to see his own death coming.

[Upload 1 Complete – Message Sent]
[Upload 2 Streaming … 120 Seconds
Behind Present]

Holtzmann's eyes flew open.

Yes. Yes.

Barnes reached out for him and Holtzmann retreated further, into the corner, shuffling fast.

Barnes followed him and Holtzmann swung his cane at the man – swung it at his head!

Barnes snatched the cane in midair with his left hand, an annoyed look on his face. Then he yanked it out of Holtzmann's hand, flung it across the room.

[Upload 2 Streaming … 100 Seconds
Behind Present]

"Is this how you killed Warren Becker?" Holtzmann demanded. "Is it?"

"Becker did what he was told," Barnes replied. Then his left hand reached out, closed around Holtzmann's jaw, and clenched, prying it open.

Holtzmann cried out, struggled, kicked at Barnes, beat at Barnes' head with his hands. The man was so strong!

Then Barnes brought his other hand around, grabbed hold of Holtzmann's upper jaw, and pulled his mouth open.

Holtzmann felt bitter powder land on his tongue as Barnes crushed the pill with his fingers. He tried to spit the powder out, but by then his mouth was shut, clamped shut by Barnes' impossibly strong hands.

No! He struggled, refused to swallow. He got his hands on Barnes' forearm, tried to pry the man off of him, strained with all his might.

[Upload 2 Streaming ... 80 Seconds Behind Present]

Nothing. Barnes was inhumanly strong.

He could feel the powder dissolving now, turning to mush on his tongue. Rivulets of a foul bitter taste were running down his throat.

No! God, no!

He stared at Barnes with eyes gone wild, found the man staring back at him, a look of grim satisfaction on his face, a fervor in the eyes, a small smile on his lips. A monster. This man was a monster.

More of the bitter fluid leaked into his throat.

Holtzmann stopped struggling then. He let himself go limp in submission. It was too late.

Barnes let him go and Holtzmann slumped bonelessly to the floor.

[Upload 2 Streaming ... 60 Seconds Behind Present]

He tried to spit, but there was nothing solid left in his mouth, just a thin greenness to his saliva. Barnes chuckled.

Holtzmann went Inside then. While he had the bandwidth. He piggybacked on the current connection, fired off a last message to his wife.

[I love you, Anne. I've always loved
you. Please forgive me.]

Then he opened his eyes and looked up at Barnes.

"Why?" Holtzmann asked. "Why all this?"

Barnes stared at him for a moment, then answered.
"Americans forget too quickly, Martin. Our lives are too
easy. Fear is the only way to diligence."

[Upload 2 Streaming … 40 Seconds Behind
Present]

Holtzmann shook his head. "But it's a lie." He could
feel the drug working now, feel the pain in his chest, feel
trembles taking hold in his arms.

Barnes shook his head in return. "It's not a lie. It's
vigilance. It's the price of freedom."

A stabbing pain jabbed its way through Holtzmann's
chest. He gasped and folded his hands in. He was shaking
now. His legs were twitching.

"People deserve to know…" he said weakly. "PLF is a
lie… You created…"

Barnes stared coldly down at him.

[Upload 2 Streaming … 20 Seconds Behind
Present]

The real pain hit him then, impaling him with its
intensity, forcing his whole body to arch and spasm. A giant
took hold of his heart, started crushing it slowly in his fist.
Its chambers gave up beating and simply clenched tight
instead. Pain flooded him, rushed out from his chest and
filled every inch of his body. He tried to scream but couldn't
breathe, couldn't work his diaphragm to draw breath. His
limbs spasmed, contorting of their own will. His vision went
blurry, then dimmed. The world swam away from him as
the blood flow to his brain ceased.

A booming crash came from outside as the storm blasted them with its fury. The last thing Martin Holtzmann saw was a blurry image of Maximilian Barnes standing above him, lit by a flash of lightning, with a single message overlaid atop him.

```
[Upload 2 Up To Date - Buffered Video
And Audio Transmitted]
```

And Martin Holtzmann smiled. Through the pain he grinned up at Barnes, grinned savagely, as death took him.

80
PRELUDE TO VIOLENCE

Saturday November 3rd

Breece sat in a booth in the small restaurant on K Street. He was in casual business attire, his hair and eye color changed, an extra forty pounds of false weight on his frame, temporary prosthetics changing the shape of his face. He watched on his slate as people filed in to Westwood Baptist. Security funneled the arrivals through checkpoints, scanned them for weapons, bombs, Nexus.

Inside the church, Miranda Shepherd was already beside her husband, just yards from the podium where he would stand and give his rousing speech exhorting Texans to elect Daniel Chandler, a true servant of the Lord, to the governorship.

The speech would be broadcast live to millions. And it would have a more… *explosive* conclusion than the audience might expect.

Breece smiled to himself.

9.32am.

Almost showtime.

• • •

Kade stared out at the sea and the darkening sky. The sun had set already, drowned in that endless ocean.

Was Shiva infiltrating minds already? Subverting them?

You paved the way, Ilya whispered in his thoughts.

"Yes," Kade whispered aloud. "Yes, I did."

He checked the time. In little more than an hour the PLF would use Nexus to kill again. Hundreds would die. Fault lines would be cracked even wider. Retributions and reprisals. More terror.

Su-Yong Shu had seen it. A war between human and transhuman. It was beginning. And there was nothing he could do to stop it.

Nakamura, Sam, and Feng reviewed the plan one more time. Here – Lane's rooms. Here – the doors the children came in and out of, the wing they were housed in. There – the vehicles by the house. There – the airfield, the hangar, the plane that Sam could fly, that could get her and the children to the Indian-occupied Andaman Islands.

Here, here, here, and here – the targets. Communications systems. Surveillance cameras. Radar. Missile launchers. Guard posts. Mobile guards on rotation.

They went through it again and again. Then it was time to go.

They launched the small inflatable boat. Thirty yards out Nakamura subvocalized a command, and the sub sank silently behind them, swallowed back up into the sea. Status updates scrolled across his retinal display as the sub set off on the next stages of its mission.

Ahead of him Sam and Feng sat on either side of the small boat. They were all in top-of-the-line chameleonware, their battle systems linked by short-range IR laser. Nakamura's goggles painted them as translucent green outlines. He stared at Sam's ghostly shape, and something tugged at his chest.

I hope you can forgive me, Sam, Nakamura thought. Someday.

Sam scanned the horizon as they moved in.

Her goggles picked out cameras on the house at the top of the cliff, drew red circles around them, around the guard post at the top of the cliff, around a soldier moving on patrol.

Radar swept over them twice as they approached. The combat display in Sam's goggles alerted her, identified the sources, offered firing vectors to neutralize them.

The house and cliff ahead of them were augmented in her vision, 3D topology subtly enhanced. If she chose she could zoom in, pass through those walls and into schematics compiled by satellite and drone data, zoom through the key locations for their plan. Her teammates were arrows at the periphery of her visual field, their proximity high and their statuses both showing green.

God, I've missed technology, Sam thought.

Feng interrupted her thoughts. **Do you trust him?** the Confucian Fist sent her.

Sam didn't turn, didn't look at Nakamura, didn't show any sign that Feng was speaking to her.

Feng continued, **He's not going to take Kade back to the CIA?**

Sam hesitated. Do I trust Kevin? Really?

Then she felt ashamed of herself, ashamed for not trusting the man who'd run into a burning building, who'd picked her up off of that floor, who'd jumped from a third-story window to save her, who'd raised her as much from that point on as her foster parents had.

Yes, she sent it back to Feng, firmly, clearly. **I trust him.**

They brought the inflatable boat ashore on the narrow strip of tumbled rocks at the base of the cliff, in a ripple of the rock that would hide them from the view of the guardhouse.

Sam shook her left shoulder out. It was stiff, but her posthuman genetics had healed most of the damage left by the bullet a week ago. She stretched, then took point on the climb, with Feng behind her and Nakamura in the rear.

The cliff was granite, vertical but run through with cracks and irregularities. Her combat goggles painted green contour lines on it, showed her every indentation and protuberance, animated a path forward for her, gently flashed location of every hand and foot hold that would keep her out of view of guards and cameras.

Sam put a hand on the cliff, and the gecko grips in the palm of her glove adhered her to it. Then she started to climb, strength and skill and technology eating up the three-hundred-foot ascent, chameleonware turning her into little more than a faint distortion against the rock.

Above, the children waited.

Feng climbed, his eyes on the rock. His body was sore, still aching from the wounds he'd taken, but better than it had been days ago. Posthuman genes, ample calories, and the medkit Nakamura had given him access to saw to that.

Feng focused his eyes and hands on the climb, but part of his mind still spun. Nakamura. Would the man truly allow Kade and Feng to go? Would he betray his CIA masters that way?

No, he thought. Nakamura had told Sam what she wanted to hear. He would double-cross them in the end, do his best to deliver Kade – and likely Feng – to the Americans.

Feng wasn't about to let that happen.

He climbed on, his senses attuned to the man below him, his mind running through scenarios.

Nakamura paused at the top of the climb, still on the rock, just below the lip that would put them on the walkway atop the cliff. To his left the transparent outlines of Feng and Sam clung to the stone.

His retinal display tapped into the laser-delivered feed from the circling surveillance drones. They flapped their bird-like wings hundreds of yards away from the island and zoomed in their robotic eyes. Two men in the guardhouse a hundred feet north along the cliff. Another was passing by on his mobile patrol now.

Nakamura bounced instructions to the sub's above-water antenna. Status rolled across his eyes. An aerial map of the region came alive in his senses. Out at sea, half-a-dozen green icons blinked in his vision, in a loose ring around the island, a thousand yards out from shore.

Positions, check.

Weapons, check.

Target locations, locked.

Nakamura turned his head slowly to his compatriots. Feng nodded. Sam nodded.

It was time.

Kevin Nakamura pulled a menu down with his eyes, clicked on an item, clicked again to confirm, and phase one of the assault began.

81
BRAVE GIRL

Saturday November 3rd

Ling cried for hours. She had never been so frightened in her life. Not even when her mommy's body had died. Not even when they'd shut her off from her mommy and she'd been alone for the first time. She'd been sure it would end soon, that she'd have her mommy back and not be alone any more...

But now they were going to kill her mommy. Kill her dead, the way that *humans* died. She tried to reach out her mind for Feng again, for Kade again.

FENG! FENG, PLEASE! FENG, HELP ME!

Nothing.

KADE! KADE, I NEED YOU! KADE, PLEASE!

Nothing, nothing, nothing.

Ling was alone. And only she could stop the humans from killing her mommy.

She cried curled up in a ball, the ampule and injector from the freezer clutched in her hands. She cried as softly as she could, so her father wouldn't hear, so he wouldn't know that *she* knew.

She watched her father in the house monitors. He was asleep, his breathing slow and regular. In just hours he would rise to murder her mother. Unless she did this. Did it now.

Ling Shu rose. She wiped her face with her dress, did her best to stop her sniffles. She was a *posthuman*. Maybe the *only* posthuman if her mother died. She had to be brave. She had to do the right thing.

The house opened the door to her mother's room for her, and Ling crept out, slowly, quietly. Outside the floor to ceiling windows of the penthouse, Shanghai was alive with light, a city pretending that nothing had ever happened to it. The electronic face of Zhi Li stared at her, a thousand times larger than life, ruby lips smiling, green eyes winking. Ling hated her then. Hated her with a fury that she had to struggle to keep in check.

Ling took a deep breath, then a tiny step, then another, and another, illuminated only by the light of the city and Zhi Li's porcelain glow, until she stood before her father's door, the injector in her hand.

The door was locked, the apartment told her. He locked it every night when he retired to his room. But this apartment was hers, not his. Ling reached out with her thoughts, and the door unlocked itself for her with a quiet *snick*.

She held her breath then, waited, watched her father through the cameras in his room. He didn't stir. He breathed deeply and slowly.

Ling reached out with her thoughts again. The door opened for her, and Ling stepped into her father's room.

82

ASSAULT ON APYAR KYUN

Saturday November 3rd

In a loose ring around the isle of Apyar Kyun, little more than half a mile from shore, six Moray-class amphibious drones received instructions from their Manta-class submersible mother ship.

Independently, their combat AIs evaluated their instructions. Weapons-safe protocols fired off confirmation and authentication requests, checked the private encryption key used, validated the command authority. Legitimate human instruction had been received. Lethal force had been authorized. Their decision trees dictated that their weapons were now free. Independently they loaded their assault plans, phase alpha, sub-plans one, two, and three. Confirmed. Execute. Execute. Execute.

For a moment nothing happened. The dark sea gently rolled and swelled under a moonless midnight sky. Ashore, a macaw called to its mate. Frogs croaked. Insects chirped.

Then chaos filled the night.

Off the southeastern tip of the island, two Moray drones powered up their drive systems on the surface of the water, detuned their radar-absorbent skins, engaged their active radar and sonar, maximized their profiles to appear far larger and more massive than they were, and propelled themselves at high speed towards the island's marina, guns firing. The drones' combat AIs steered them on semi-autonomous paths meant to produce the impression of a significant attacking fleet.

Micromissiles launched out from other Moray drones on the south, north, and east. Their hydrazine-fueled solid rocket motors ignited, forcing out jets of superheated plasma behind them as they accelerated at eight gees towards targets on the island. The drones that launched them activated their own radar and sonar systems, broadcasting loudly, exaggerating their presence, and initiated reload of their micromissile launchers.

To the west of the island a lone Moray bobbed silently on the surface, fully stealthed. It watched, evaluated, and took careful aim with its smart pebble launcher, waiting for just the right moment.

Automated defenses on the island activated. Alarms blared, jolting human operators out of their boredom. Screens scrolled status. Before the humans could react, the machines did. Missile interception systems came alive, targeted defense lasers on the incoming missiles, launched clouds of thousands upon thousands of anti-missile projectiles into the air. Island-based launchers pivoted to target the enemy ships attacking the marina.

The micromissiles zigged, zagged, their own AIs adapting their courses in real time to the countermeasures they saw heading their way. For some, it wasn't enough. A micromissile fell from the sky, its warhead ignited by a defense laser. Another collided with a defense projectile at twice the speed of sound. A third was knocked off course by the resulting explosion. More fell from projectiles, from lasers, from the secondary effects of explosions.

In seconds, eight of the sea-launched micromissiles were knocked from the sky.

Sixteen got through.

The first micromissile struck home four seconds after launch, igniting its warhead at the last instant, a kamikaze burst of goal-satisfaction rushing through its primitive mind as it demolished one of the island's radar installations. The next bore down on its target a fraction of a second later, setting off its own explosive warhead in a blaze of impact-maximization just instants before it collided with one of the island's missile launchers. The resulting blast set off the warheads of the launcher's dozen remaining missiles in a chain reaction, booming a thundering staccato explosion across the island, lighting up the night, sending up a bright red mushroom cloud that expanded as it rose into the moonless sky. If the micromissile's AI had survived, it would have been very satisfied indeed.

Within seconds the island's radars, missiles, and uplinks were destroyed. In a buried command center, the klaxons continued to blare. Security personnel blanched at what they'd seen before their radar was destroyed. They were under attack. Multiple ships had fired on them. And two were coming in fast for the marina.

They were about to be invaded.

To the west, the only Moray that hadn't announced its position waited, waited, waited with the infinite vigilant patience that only machines can know. Then the explosions came, and the counter explosions. Now, its AI determined. Now is the time. The Moray fired a salvo of tiny, nearly silent smart pebbles. The pebbles streaked out at the house, compared their positions and trajectories to their targets, morphed their body shapes as they flew to adjust their course, and streaked in to strike the cameras and audio pickups that covered the western wall of the palatial home.

The Moray's AI noted the successful barrage, gave the digital neurons of its aiming circuits jolts of positive reinforcement, and took itself back down, below the waves.

In the chaos, the blinding of the western side of the house was just one detail, one small event hidden among the noise of so many larger ones.

Kade sat cross-legged on the bed in *anapana*. He had no control over the outside world. But he could control himself, his own mind, his own thoughts. He wouldn't crumble. He wouldn't lose himself. He had to stay centered, to stay alert. No matter how bad it got, he wouldn't give up.

So he breathed. In, out. Observe the breath. Let that be your all. Let it grow to fill all consciousness. Allow the thoughts to rise up, then bring the attention back to the breath. Release attachments. Find solace in the absence of thought, in the sensations of the breath filling up attention completely, leaving no room for fear, or anxiety, or self-recrimination.

Then the sounds of explosions ripped through the night, and Kade's eyes snapped open.

The sound of explosions ripped Shiva out of his godhood trance, away from the tens of thousands of minds that were now part of his extended consciousness, and back to the physical world.

He reached out to the island's information systems, but all was chaos. An assault. Missiles launched. Defenses down. Ships heading for the marina. They were about to be invaded.

The data was old by the time he saw it. Radars were down. Cameras were destroyed. Drones were crashing.

Who? The Americans? The Chinese? His Burmese hosts?

Shiva reached out to the Nexus projectors and signal boosting antennae built into his home. His thoughts expanded to encompass the whole of the mansion. He felt the minds of the children, of all of his staff in and around the building. He found Ashok among them.

Secure Lane and the children, he sent to his Director of Operations. **Get them underground.**

Then he leapt from his hard narrow bed, out the door of his bare cell, and to the stairs that would take him to the roof. He needed to know what was going on.

Nakamura watched his feed from the drones. Missile strikes successful. The soldiers at the guard post above them turned and ran, headed to the action at the east side of the house as they'd hoped.

Excellent.

Nakamura waited until the three soldiers passed, then gave the signal. As one, he and Feng and Sam slipped over the lip and onto the walkway below the house.

Then Nakamura turned to Sam, and nodded. Time for phase two.

Kade leapt to the west-facing window, but he saw nothing out there but dark waters.

Another explosion boomed from somewhere behind him. Faint red light reflected onto the sea.

He ran to the kitchen. From its window he could see the courtyard and parts of the house. Security men moved about frantically. Beyond the house he could see smoke rising, underlit by the red of flames. Gunfire sounded from somewhere.

Then he heard the door to his suite open, heavy footfalls.

He turned and they were there. Two of Shiva's security men. They wore Nexus jammers. Their minds were balls of static.

"Come with us," one of them said. The dark-skinned one he'd never placed. The other one had a third Nexus jammer in his hand, meant for Kade.

Kade shook his head, and a look of impatience flashed across the soldier's face. He came forward and Kade grabbed a pot from the stove top, swung it at the guard's head.

The security man caught it, ripped it out of Kade's hand, then slapped him across the side of his head hard enough that Kade saw stars.

Sam nodded in return, acknowledging Nakamura's signal.

Then she opened her mind, in receive-mode only. If they were right, the children were on this side of the building, on the west face, on the first or second floor. Once she found them, they could rally them, use the sub and their own skills to misdirect and blind the defenders, clear a path, get them on the vehicles and towards the airfield while Feng and Nakamura retrieved Kade.

Her mind opened and the night was alive with Nexus. Dozens of minds inside the building. Fear and confusion. Panic.

And there. Those minds. The children. All together. It took her breath away to feel them, to feel them like this. It brought it all back to her, all the reasons she'd fallen in love with them and the reason she was here.

Shiva was not going to turn this beauty into horror.

Sam reached out, projected her own thoughts outward towards Sarai and the rest.

I'm here, she sent. **I've come for you.**

And across the link, she felt those young minds rejoice.

Sarai woke to the sound of explosions. Her heart thudded in her chest. Her brothers and sisters had woken to it too. They were all frightened.

The connecting door opened and the five boys flooded in to the room she shared with the three other girls. Aroon was crying, wailing, carried on Kit's shoulder. Everyone looked to her.

I'm the oldest, she thought. I have to make this right.

She reached out to them, brought them together, sent calming thoughts. They huddled together on the floor, the youngest on the inside, the oldest around them.

She opened herself completely to them, breathed as Sam had taught her, breathed in and out and sent her breath to them and felt for theirs. Then they were falling into a rhythm together and even little Aroon was crying less and she could see, she could hear, she could think. The world slowed down and possibilities expanded.

Someone had come. Someone had come to fight Shiva. And in that fight... they had their best chance of getting away.

There was a boom at the door and it flung itself open in slow motion. One of the men was there. He wore the ball of static around himself. He had a gun with him. He reached out his hand to them.

And they knew. They understood. He would take them somewhere, somewhere the new people couldn't find them. And that was not what they wanted. Fear struck them.

Then Sam was there, in their minds. And their hearts soared.

"Found them," Sam's whispered voice came across the laser link, played to Nakamura's ears. And now it was time for phase three.

Nakamura pulled down the menu, found the item. He hesitated for just an instant. An image flashed across his mind, three of the missiles veering in mid-flight, as if disrupted by countermeasures. Two of them impacting harmlessly across the island. One smashing into Lane's room, exploding there, ending the threat.

Then, afterwards. The lie he would tell Sam. That Shiva's countermeasures had caused it. That it hadn't been part of the plan. Her inevitable suspicion…

He pushed it out of his thoughts. His duty was clear. No one could have this power.

Kevin Nakamura blinked to activate phase three. And around the island, Moray-class drones fired another salvo of their deadly micromissiles.

Shiva reached the roof as another boom sounded. A giant fireball erupted into the night sky to the east, turning into a mushroom cloud as it rose. The fuel depot.

Who were the attackers? Where were they?

He stretched his mind out again, expanded it through the Nexus repeaters throughout his home, felt the minds of his security team, his scientific staff, pulled at them for understanding. He felt fear and panic from the scientists, grim resolve from his soldiers. Enemy ships were strafing the marina now. Sensors were down. They had no visual on the invaders. His men were rushing into position, unlocking heavy weapons, preparing to meet the invaders with shoulder-mounted anti-ship missiles and high-speed flechette launchers that could mow down hundreds of men at once. Other soldiers were heading for Lane, for the children, to move them to the secure bunker. From there, if necessary, they'd evacuate them via the underground tunnels to the airstrip.

Then he felt the intruder. A mind he'd never touched before. A woman. Her mind was reaching out to the children's, passing through a wall studded with Nexus-band repeaters as it did. He felt their mutual recognition.

The American woman. Here, now. The one who'd been searching for Nexus children, who'd tried to infiltrate her way into his home, who'd killed one of his men already... Who was she? CIA?

Shiva growled. It didn't matter. They would not do this. They would not take these children from him, lock them up, dehumanize them, euthanize them.

It was time for another test of the code he'd tricked out of Lane.

Shiva Prasad reached out his thoughts to the American agent's mind, activated the back door, sent the passcode.

And he was in. She was his to control.

83

FRIENDLY FIRE

Saturday November 3rd

The guard shoved Kade against one wall of the kitchen.

The second guard moved in to put the Nexus jammer around his neck.

NO!

[activate: bruce_lee full_auto]

Targeting circles appeared and he dragged one to the Nexus jammer in the guard's hands, struggling as he did, then forced the mental buttons down, mashed them again and again.

His body twisted and for an instant he was free.

[Bruce_Lee: Escape Succeeded!]

His foot lashed out at the second guard and the man smacked it aside in annoyance.

[Bruce_Lee: Attack Failed ☹]

Kade's good left hand used the cover of his kick, lashed out at the guard's hand and the Nexus jammer in it. He struck the device, sent it flying across the room, into the far wall.

[Bruce_Lee: Attack Succeeded!]

The guard struck him in return. The two of them pushed him up against the wall, pinned him there as Bruce Lee tried vainly to free him.

[Bruce_Lee: Block Failed ☹]
[Bruce_Lee: Escape Failed ☹]

Then a sound like thunder filled his senses as something exploded through the apartment. A giant force smashed through the guards in front of him, smashed him back against the wall. Searing heat struck him. And he was falling, falling, falling...

Feng heard the explosion. Too close! Too close! That had struck the building!

"Missiles off course!" Nakamura whispered over their laser link, his voice urgent.

"What?" Feng shot back. Then something dawned on him.

No, no! So stupid! Not to capture Kade. To *kill* Kade.

All warfare is based on deception, Sun Tzu had written. The CIA man had deceived him.

Feng pointed his assault rifle towards Nakamura.

Sam screamed as the mind invaded hers, screamed in absolute horror. No sound escaped her lips. The invading mind had ruthless control of her body, absolute control. She reached out to issue the command to turn off her Nexus reception, found herself blocked. She tried to wave, to kick away from the wall, to move her eyes to choose a signal from the menu provided by her goggles.

No good.

She felt Sarai and the children recoil in horror, and she knew what mind this was. Shiva's mind. Shiva who had these children here. Shiva who had her now.

He rifled through her thoughts with brutal efficiency and she was unable to resist. He summoned thoughts of the plan, the assault, and she gave him everything.

She felt his mind jolt in surprise. Only three of them? Here to take away the children, to take away Lane? The rest, a diversion?

She wanted to lie, wanted to misdirect, wanted to protect Kevin and Feng and Kade and the children, but it was impossible. Kade had built this back door too well. Shiva pressed on her mind and she gave him everything.

Then she felt him smile, smile in satisfaction.

Kill them, he sent her. And her will bent beneath his.

Sam turned, and there, first in her line of fire, was Kevin Nakamura.

Nakamura tensed as Feng raised the gun. His eyes flicked over the menus in his mind's eye, found the remote disable for the weapon, clicked it.

"You," Feng whispered over their laser link. "You killed him."

Nakamura backed away, away from Feng, away from the wall of the house, towards the railing, moving slowly, placatingly. Feng couldn't shoot him now. Nakamura could take the Confucian Fist, capture him, bring him back to Langley. But he had a charade to play. For Sam. For her sake.

He whispered back over their laser link. "The missiles went off course. Countermeasures. We have to get up there, find Kade!"

He turned towards Sam, wishing he could see her face, see how she was reacting.

He found her with her assault rifle raised to her shoulder, pointed squarely at his face.

"Sam!" he yelled.

His eyes flicked towards the menu that would disable her gun.

Sam fired before he got there.

Sam moaned in despair as she turned, found Kevin, raised the gun to her shoulder. He turned, spoke her name. Time froze in an endless moment of horror. She threw herself at the mental hold Shiva had over her, threw herself with all her might, wailed at it, ripped at it with thoughts like claws, with every ounce of her being, with every bit of fury she could summon. This couldn't happen! This wasn't happening!

Kill them, Shiva whispered to her.

And she obeyed.

Her first burst took Nakamura in the face. The graphene foam impregnating his skull held, stopping the bullets. The momentum of it snapped his head back, the acceleration punishing his brain. He staggered backwards against the railing. His upper half pivoted out past it and over empty space.

Sam tried to stop, tried to pull her finger from the trigger, tried to close her eyes and make it go away!

Kill them.

Her second burst struck his chest. The bullets punched into him, pushed his upper body back, flipped him head first over the railing. His head and chest flew out into space and then he was cartwheeling backwards, his legs rising as he spun end over end. Then he was gone, out into the night, plunging down the cliff face to the rocks below.

"Sam!" Feng yelled.

Sam wept inside as she turned and pulled the trigger once again.

84
DADDY DEAREST

Saturday November 3rd

Ling stepped silently into her father's room. The house closed the door quietly behind her. The curtains were closed tight here. There was practically no illumination in the room, but her posthuman eyes needed next to none to make out his form. The bed was ahead of her and to the right. Her father was sprawled on it, face down, his limbs akimbo, his body on the side closest to her, his head turned towards the center of the bed.

Ling moved forward slowly, quietly. Her feet made no sound on the thickly padded carpet, but the urge to cry, to sob, was strong. This was so hard. So scary. Her father frightened her now. He was only a human, but he'd *hit* her, *burned* her.

Ling's face scrunched up as she took another step, she felt tears falling from her eyes, felt a sniffle rising, felt cries rising up inside her, threatening to burst out.

She moved forward faster, her sight blurring from the tears. She was past the foot of the bed now. Her father's hand lolled off the left side of the bed. She stepped around it, past it, until she was just before the night stand, her body against the bed, inside her father's reach, his head just within reach in front of her.

Ling's face was hot. Her heart pounded as the tears fell from her face. She could barely see, could barely think. This was her father! But if she didn't do this her mother would die, die forever.

Ling raised the injector with two trembling hands, pushed it forward until the tip almost touched the back of her father's neck.

He heard something then, or felt something. Her father stirred, made a noise, started to turn his head.

Ling jammed the injector forward, squeezed the trigger for all she was worth with both her index fingers.

Within the injector, a circuit closed, a battery delivered current to a superconducting coil, magnetizing it, activating a Lorenz-force motor that drove a piston forward. A fraction of a millisecond after Ling pulled the trigger, the injector shot a supersonic stream of nanodevice-laden fluid into the skin, muscle, and blood vessels of her father's neck.

Chen yelled in pain, lashed out with one hand, knocking the injector away, out of Ling's grasp, sending it flying through the air to land across the room. Then he was up on his feet, and his other hand came down, smacking Ling across the face, driving her backwards and off her feet, onto the carpet.

"Lights!" her father bellowed, and the house illuminated his bedroom. He had one hand on his neck, where the injector's high-powered jet had penetrated his flesh. He looked at his daughter in horror, then pulled his hand away to look at it. It came away bloody.

"What have you done?" he yelled at her. "What have you done?"

Then his eyes scanned the room, and came to the injector.
The ampule of silvery fluid, still half full, loaded into it.

Her father roared and came at Ling. She raised her hands
to protect herself and he *kicked* her, hard.

Ling screamed in pain as his foot slammed into her midsection.

"You monster!" he said. Then he kicked her again.

Ling screamed louder. "No! No!"

Her father lifted his leg again, to kick her a third time,
and now Ling could feel just a tiny bit of mind around him
as the nanites bound to his neurons, exposed the innards of
his brain to her.

Her father's foot came at her and she reached out and
twisted what she could feel in his mind. His foot slammed
into her again but this time he stumbled, wobbled after he
kicked her, as her thoughts pushed against the neurons of
his motor cortex.

Ling screamed in pain. Tears were falling down her face
freely. She had never hurt so bad before in her life. But she
reached out and *pushed* on her father's mind and now she
could feel even more and he staggered backwards.

"No," he said, trying to get his balance. "No."

He tried to kick her a fourth time but this time she *shoved*
with her mind against his, against the nanites latching onto
the neurons of his motor control centers, and her father fell
backwards instead, fell against the bed, his head cracking
into one of the upright posts. Ling breathed hard, but her
father stayed there, stunned by the blow to his skull and by
the events in his brain. Already his eyes were going glassy,
his mind going wild as more and more of the nanites latched
onto his neurons and launched into the calibration phase.

Ling reached out, and *clenched* around the parts of his
mind she could sense. She could feel his disorientation, his

confusion at what the nanites were doing to him, his terror of her.

Good. Be afraid, little human.

Ling crawled, centimeter by centimeter, away from him, and towards the injector. When she had it, she came back to him. She crawled, and then she grabbed the bed and used it to pull herself up, up so she was above her seated father. He turned his head and looked at her, his eyes wide with fear, his mind a riot of dread and horror. He tried to struggle, to control his body, and she *pushed* against his mind, holding him in place.

"No," he said, struggling still to get control of his body. "Please." Tears fell from his eyes. She was huge in his mind, a monster, an alien thing, a posthuman looming over him, a creature that had surpassed him. Doom permeated his thoughts where Ling could see them.

"Please," he said again. "Daughter…"

Ling Shu pressed the injector against the side of her father's neck, and fired the rest of its contents into him.

85

ALL TOGETHER NOW

Saturday November 3rd

Breece watched as the Mayor of Houston took the stage, began to praise Daniel Chandler.

Less than fifteen minutes to go. Josiah Shepherd would take the stage next. He'd warm up the crowd for a while, lead them in prayer, then invite Daniel Chandler to the podium. As Shepherd finished and Chandler stepped forward, the two men would shake hands. For the last time ever.

Kade fell, tumbling. Someone gripped him, a guard, as they spun through the air. There was no sound, no sensation beyond a burning heat, a chaos of images flipping around him too fast to track. He closed his eyes to stop the chaos, held them shut tight.

Then they crashed to a stop and his body exploded in pain.

There were flames around him. Smoke. Dust.

Minds! Minds! He could feel minds!

Terror. Fear. Chaos. The children.

Kade opened his eyes.

He was in the courtyard, atop something soft and angular and broken. A body. The dark-skinned security guard. The man's neck was broken at an unnatural angle. His eyes were wide open, staring. Half of the dead man was burned to a crisp.

Kade rolled, and on the other side was the other guard, face down, his back a blackened mass. The explosion had killed them both, even as their bodies had shielded him from the worst.

He turned and looked up. He was in the courtyard. The wall above him was gone. A jagged hole was all that remained of the apartment he'd been housed in. Something had blown it to bits, thrown him and the guards out. The dead man he'd fallen atop of and the one to his other side were all that had saved his life.

He tried to move, tried to sit up, felt excruciating pain in his abdomen. His ears were ringing so loudly he couldn't hear anything around him.

Then he felt something close around his upper arm. He looked up, and there was another guard there, a Nexus jammer around his throat, a large gun slung around his shoulder. The man's lips were moving furiously. He was screaming at Kade, but whatever he was saying was drowned out by the fearsome ringing.

And then the guard was yanking, frantically hauling on Kade. Pain exploded in Kade's guts, but the man was dragging him, dragging him away.

Kade pushed at the man's mind but there was only static. The shielding was too strong. The man half-pulled half-dragged Kade over a pile of rubble. Ahead he could see more security men, see them herding groups of children. A group in front disappeared into a doorway, dropping down. Then a second group. The last group of kids…

One of them turned to look at him, a girl. He could feel her in his mind. Older than the rest. Different. The one who'd waved to him. And with her, more children, special children, but terrified, confused, unable to think or act.

He reached out to the oldest in desperation.

You have to stop them! he sent her.

She responded with recognition. She *did* know him. She'd seen him in memories. In Sam's memories.

You can do it! he sent her. **With your mind!**

No… she replied. **They're too strong!**

Work together! he told her. **All of you!**

Sarai sobbed in horror as the guard dragged her away. Explosions boomed around her. The courtyard was full of rubble. The other children were terrified. And Sam… they'd felt Shiva invade her, felt what he'd made her do…

Then she felt a mind reach out to her. A mind she'd seen in Sam's thoughts. Kade.

You have to stop them! he told her. **Work together!**

But it was so hard. There was so much chaos and the little ones were screaming and crying and so afraid and the guards were pulling at them. There was no way. No way at all.

But Sam! Sam had come for them! She had to do it!

Sarai closed her eyes, let the guard drag her, ceased her resistance. She took a long slow breath, felt every little bit of it fill up her lungs, beamed that sensation out to her brothers and sisters, begged them to respond.

She breathed it out like Sam had shown her and let the others feel her need, the need they all shared, underneath that breath, intertwined with that breath.

Her feet moved of their own accord as the guard dragged her and she took another breath and she felt Mali there with her, breathing, their minds falling in together.

She exhaled and Kit was with them now.

Sarai stumbled over something and fell to her knees in pain. Tears came to her eyes and she feared she'd lost it, but Kit and Mali were holding them together. And then Ying and Tada were with them. And then Sunisa and Kwan. They breathed as one and they *were* one. The walls of their minds dropped and they enmeshed one another and everything became so very clear. The guards. Five of them. Balls of static. Sam, taken by Shiva.

Kade. Kade who wasn't like them but who understood, who'd built the Nexus that was in Sam's mind, in Jake's.

Kade was the answer.

They reached out to him and then he was with them, enmeshed with them.

He showed them what to do and their minds reached out to the soldiers herding them.

The static repelled them, pushed their minds away. Then they thought of Sam and they breathed in, breathed out, and focused their thoughts – and they cut through that static all around them, and sent the *back door*, the *passcode*, and the *sleep center stimulus* – and the men were falling, falling, until all of them were still.

Shiva reached out to his men as soon as the American started firing on her compatriots.

Secure the children and Lane, he sent them. **There are only three intruders. All on the western side of the house. The woman is mine now.**

Then he lifted his wrist microphone to his mouth, repeated the instructions for those who'd activated their Nexus jammers.

He felt his men jump to do his bidding. Soldiers reversed course, turned from the marina and other sites back towards the house, headed towards the true invaders.

Feng rolled forward at Sam's feet as she turned the gun on him. Time slowed to a crawl as he touched the stone path with one shoulder, his back, and then his feet. The muffled staccato of a silenced burst of three boomed in his ears as she pulled the trigger and shots ripped through the air above him.

He came up inside her reach, his hands on her gun, one squeezing the latch to disconnect it from the strap around her shoulders, even as he spun hard, ripping it out of her hands as he whirled away.

"What you doing?" he yelled.

She was drawing her pistol already. She was blazing fast but he was faster. He swung the rifle he'd taken from her at her hand like a bat, made contact, sent the pistol sailing out into the night after Nakamura.

And then her foot collided with his midsection, knocking him painfully back. He took the blow, used its momentum to roll backwards, come back up to his feet, even as she threw the first knife at his throat. He got the rifle up barely in time to deflect the blade. Then she was on him, a knife in each hand, attacking recklessly, leaving him openings as she came at him at full assault.

He blocked, blocked, blocked, with the rifle, gave ground, opened his mind as he did.

SAM!

He felt her mind there but she didn't respond, just kept on coming. His combat display showed him status updates from the drones. Red dots. Men headed this way. Shiva knew where they were now.

Fuck this.

He lashed back out at Sam, took advantage of her disregard for self-protection, slammed his foot into her midsection, let her slice him across the shoulder in exchange for a vicious slam of his rifle into her head. She stumbled back and Feng jumped up, got one foot on the top bar of the railing, and then kicked out against it, propelling himself up, towards the second-story window.

The sound of gunfire erupted just as Feng got his fingers onto the ledge. He hauled, flipped himself up and over, and into the hallway beyond in a shower of breaking glass.

Kade collapsed to his knees, his insides aching, his skin burning – his damaged hand in pain so bad he thought he would cry. All around him the security men were unconscious, knocked out by the back door command that the children had amplified for him. He reached out with his left hand, unclipped the unlocked Nexus jammer from the guard's throat, tossed it to the side.

Then he opened the man's mind, burrowed into it. He needed the passwords to the network.

There. He had them now. He could reach Houston, contact the police, the FBI, warn them about the bombing, evacuate the people.

Then someone was shaking him in the real world. He tried to break loose of them, to focus on the task at hand.

Kade! It was one of the children, the girl, Sarai.

Sam! she sent him. **Shiva's taken her! You have to help! Please!**

He pulled himself back, his mind still reeling.

Sam? Here? And Shiva.

Gunfire burst out somewhere, barely audible over the ringing in his ears. Distantly he heard another explosion. Fighting was still going on. They were in danger here.

He tried to twist, to look around him, to see what was going on. Pain burst up from his midsection. He was so tired… And Houston…

Sam! the girl yelled into his mind. **Help her!**

Kade groaned. He had to help Sam, stop Shiva, stop the fighting, make them safe here on the island. Then he could tackle Houston.

Kade opened his senses wide. There, at the edge of his perception, he could feel that familiar mind. Fatigue and pain tried to pull him down. But she was here. She'd saved his life before. And now she'd come for him…

Kade forced himself to concentrate, pulled himself together. And then he reached out his mind to hers.

Sam's world was horror. Pure horror. She wanted to go to that place she'd known so well on the ranch. The place she'd gone to when they'd hurt her, when she'd learned to stop fighting and just shut it out.

But Shiva wouldn't let her.

Kill them.

She did her best to kill Feng. She wanted it. He had to die. She didn't want to want it, but dear God she couldn't help herself.

She tried to shoot Feng, to hit him, to cut him. Even as she did her mind replayed the horror she'd just been party to. The bullets striking Kevin. *Her* bullets striking Kevin. His body toppling backwards out into nothing…

Aaaaaaaaaaaaaaaah!

She screamed inside as Shiva's compulsion drove her. This was rape. Worse than rape. His mind was inside hers

and she had no choice. She *wanted* Feng dead. She knew
it wasn't true, but she had no choice. Shiva had turned
her into a zombie, like her parents had become, worse, far
worse, a tool for killing the man who'd saved her life, who
she'd loved as a mentor and friend!

Aaaaaaah!

She wanted to stop, to turn a knife against herself, to stab
herself in the throat to end this pain.

But she wanted to kill Feng more. And so she fought.

And then his rifle collided with her head, and in a split
second, he was gone.

Shiva's men raced past her, ignored her, leapt up,
scrambled for holds, and followed Feng into the building.

She moved to follow. **Catch him**, Shiva commanded
her. And she would.

And then Kade was there, in her mind as well, his
thoughts wrestling Shiva's, tearing her in two, and Sam
screamed inside.

86

SIGNAL STRENGTH

Saturday November 3rd

Feng took in his surroundings as he hurtled through the window. Glass shattered around him, fell in slow motion as he came down on the carpeted floor. A hallway. Doors.

He surged forward. One foot lashed out at a closed door. Wood splintered as the door buckled inward and crashed open. He moved forward to the next open doorway, rolled into it, rifle in his hands, eyes taking in the scene instantly. An office, empty.

He listened as Shiva's men scramble up the wall and in through the window. Glass crunched under booted feet. Four men. They moved without speech but their footsteps, their breaths, even their pulse rates gave them away to him. They moved to the door he'd kicked open, paused.

Feng slipped back out into the hall, a ghost in his chameleonware, as silent as death. He leveled his assault rifle at the four men, and pulled the trigger.

The gun clicked.

SAFETY LOCKED – FIRE AUTHORIZATION DENIED flashed across his vision.

Fuck!

The security men heard the click, turned, guns rising.
They moved in slow motion to Feng's eyes, turning like
molasses, their eyes widening in dawning awareness,
fingers tightening over triggers.

Feng threw himself forward, into a roll that propelled
him at their feet. Gunfire burst from muzzles as dozens of
rounds filled the air. Feng's accelerated senses brought him
each boom and pop as a discrete event. His mind filled with
pressure waves and firing solutions and the neon red paths
of bullets zipping through the space he'd just occupied.

Then he was up, out of the roll, a man-shaped blur
moving faster than they could imagine.

Kade found Sam's mind hard and sealed off from him. So
he did what he had to. Activate the back door. Send the
passcode.

And then he was in. He could feel her mind, feel the
homicidal thoughts Shiva was forcing on her, feel her
horror at what was happening.

Then Kade threw his mind against Shiva's, tried to force
the other man's mind out of Sam's. Shiva counter-attacked,
jammed his will hard against Kade's. They wrestled over
her, mind against mind.

Kade felt Sam scream as their struggles tore at her, as
her brain was assaulted by conflicting signals from inside
itself, from Shiva, from Kade. Distantly he felt her fall to her
knees, her head throbbing, pain and confusion and despair
like she'd never known tearing at her...

Brute force was futile. Kade dropped to a lower layer,
fired random data at Nexus nodes in Sam's brain that Shiva
controlled, hoping to confuse them. He felt Shiva reinforce
them, bolstering the signal from his own brain.

Kade switched strategies again, pulled up a network connection listing, fired a kill command at Shiva's connection to Sam's mind, felt Shiva clone the connection before the first one died. Then Shiva counter-attacked again, hopping from Sam's mind to Kade's, trying to open the back door, send the passcode to crack into Kade's mind.

And then Kade had him. For there was no back door in his own mind.

He ignored Shiva's attack, dropped the struggle for Sam's body, felt her topple over in pain as he did, and grabbed control of Nexus nodes in her brain as a proxy instead, using them to hop from Sam's mind to Shiva's.

The second back door! There were three, and Shiva only knew of one!

He activated the second one now, entered the second passcode, to break into Shiva's mind…

Then Shiva dropped the connection, severed it before Kade could get inside the man's head. And he was alone with Sam in her mind.

Sam screamed as Kade invaded her mind. There were two of them now, raging at each other inside her. Her limbs trembled. Pain shot through her. She was distantly aware of hitting the ground. All was chaos. Thoughts wouldn't come. She felt like she was being torn apart, her head forced open, her mind ripped in two in horrible agony as her twin invaders tore at her will, clawed at each other through the substrate of her brain.

She screamed again, and no sound left her lungs. Her whole body was shaking now, thrashing wildly, like a seizure. Her arms and legs flailed as the two men fought for control of her. Lightning bolts of pain and confusion and memories of horror shot through her.

The agony increased. The confusion. She was spinning, falling, dropping through the floor. She was burning up – ice cold. Her limbs were being ripped from her body. Her mind was hell, agony lancing through every iota of her being.

Kill them. Kill them. Kill them.

Kevin falling. Bullets from her gun punching into his face. His body pirouetting out into empty space.

The Prophet on top of her, forcing her thighs apart, forcing himself into her, smashing his fist into her face as she resisted.

Her home burning, her sister and her parents and everyone she knew dying, dying because of her.

Mai's tiny body ripped to pieces by American bullets.

Jake's mind splintering, fading to nothingness as blood bubbled up through the hole in his chest.

Agony. Agony. Nothing but agony.

Kill me! Please!

She screamed again and for the first time she heard herself. She forced herself up to her knees and screamed again, harder, until she could feel the scream as pain in her throat. The sound was good. It was real. She willed her body to claw at the path beneath her and her fingers responded, clenching until tiles cracked and shattered in her gloved hands.

She forced herself to remember. To remember other things. Not the loss. Not the despair. The overcoming!

The beach beyond Sari, tired, hurt, running for her life, bullets lodged in her body, but still alive! Still alive!

The Prophet, lying on the floor of his office, blood spurting from the bullet she'd put into his belly, forming a pool around him, soaking into his expensive carpet. Standing over him, taking careful aim at his head, the gun huge in her young hands, seeing the fear in his eyes, and then firing again and again and sending that bastard straight to hell.

She could do this. She could do this.

GGGGHHHHH!

And then Shiva was gone, and it was only Kade in her mind.

Sam! he reached out to her, his thoughts laced with concern, with *pity*.

She raged at him in response, with all the anger and hatred she had inside her.

GET. OUT.

Kade cut the connection to Sam's mind with an inner groan. What Sam had gone through…

No time for that. He had to win this battle. *Then* Houston. He felt for Shiva's mind but it was nowhere.

He turned and his eyes met Sarai's. She was crouched beside him, a hand still on his shoulder. He reached out for her with his mind and felt her thoughts meet his. She was frightened but controlling it, controlling it like a monk. And her mind… Fluid. Fluent with the Nexus.

He showed Sarai what he needed, sent it to her.

Sarai nodded into his mind, opened the bandwidth between them again, let down her own walls. Kade closed his eyes, let his mind touch this child's. He felt her breath, in, out, in, out. *Anapana*. Sam had taught her. Kade let himself be absorbed by his own breath, let it consume his attention. His breath. Her breath. Match them. Match the breath. Match the thoughts. Open and synchronize and enmesh…

And then he was with her. With all of them, the minds of the children, coming together into one, falling into a common rhythm, a unified whole, greater than the sum of its parts. So fluid. So natural. So *complete*.

Kade felt his heart soar in joy from the pure glory of it, the pure wonder of these children. Everything became clearer. His thoughts became sharper. His eyes opened. The world around him became brighter, every detail more complete, more precise, more part of a larger whole. The texture of the ground beneath him, the feel of the breeze on his skin, the view of the courtyard all around him, the stars twinkling in their constellations behind the plumes of smoke rising into the air, the fire burning in the apartment that was once his, even the pain of his broken body. It all *fit*. He could hold it all in his mind, see the patterns and connections between everything he perceived, all at once, in a way he never could as Kade alone.

This. This was what it meant to be posthuman. This was what Nexus could do. His fear and pain and panic fell away below him. Even in the midst of chaos, here was beauty. Here was an instant of pure transcendence.

And then they reached out together, he and the children, one mind, one being, like nothing Kade had ever known.

Their senses found Shiva atop the roof. He was transparent to them now. They understood him in a single flash of insight.

They could fix him. They could make Shiva whole again.

But first they had to stop him.

As a single being they touched Shiva's mind, invoked the second back door, and sent out the passcode.

Shiva recoiled from the American agent's mind. Lane had tried to jump from the woman's mind to his. He couldn't allow that.

He could feel Lane's mind down below. Could feel him merging with the minds of the children, making an even more formidable foe. He had only instants to act.

Shiva reached out, into the Nexus repeaters throughout his home, flipped off their safeguards, cranked up their gain to the maximum levels possible, and then pulsed out a single simple thought through them all.

Kade and the children reached out together, as a single being, reached out for Shiva's mind, invoked the second back door, sent out the passcode…

And then a wall of coherent thought struck them from all angles, an absurdly amplified Nexus signal, pressing down on them. It came at them from emitters scattered throughout the house, across the grounds. It came at them at a broadcast strength that trampled over their own signals, saturated the air around them, deafened each of them to the minds of the others. Their connection broke. Their union disintegrated, and Kade was alone in his mind again, with a single overriding urge to unconsciousness blasting into him from all around.

Shiva felt the group mind of the children crumble under his assault. He felt them cut off from one another, from Lane. The children were falling, their minds still young, still vulnerable to this brute force attack. But Lane was struggling, still fighting back.

Shiva pressed harder, concentrating on driving them down into submission. Sweat beaded on his brow as he pushed his full will at them, amplified hundreds of times over by the repeaters.

He raised his left wrist to his mouth, spoke into it.

"Activate your Nexus shielding. Lane is in the courtyard. Take him. Alive." He gritted his teeth and continued. "The American woman is free. Take down the remaining intruders."

He felt his men's jammers activate, buffering them at least partially against his attack. Good.

Then he turned his full attention back to Lane.

87
AGAINST THE TIDE

Saturday November 3rd

Sam rose to her feet, free and full of rage. Three of Shiva's soldiers were running towards her, in pursuit of Feng, oblivious to her presence in her chameleonware suit.

Then a mind blared out at her at staggering volumes, buffeting her with the urge to submit, to surrender, to crumble into stasis.

She threw back her head and roared out loud, fighting it.

The soldier passing by heard her, recoiled in surprise, turning, trying to bring his gun up at this ghostly target.

Her fingers made a spear and she jabbed forward, her gloves turning her hand into a weapon as hard as carbon. Her fingers punched through the man's throat. He made a gurgling sound and his body went limp, dead on his feet, but by then she was turning, spinning.

The other two raised their assault rifles, turning. A gun went off but she was around it, finishing her spin, and her rigid knife hand slammed into the side of a man's neck, severing his spine.

The last man was firing now, in full auto, his gun swinging towards her, but Sam was faster, coming around him, kicking off the wall with one foot, then lashing out with her other in a vicious roundhouse to his head.

The soldier saw it coming, saw the blur running on the wall like a floor, saw it all too late. Her booted foot collided with his face, snapped his neck instantly, sent his body flying out, tumbling over the railing, and down to join Kevin's.

Sam landed on her feet, caught herself against the railing, her head out over it, looking down into the dark as the man's still warm body tumbled in infrared towards the rocks and surf.

And then she dropped to her knees and wept.

Kade groaned under the weight of Shiva's attack. He felt his eyes close. All he wanted was to lie still, to go limp, to let this pain and struggle end.

Fuck. That.

He forced his eyes open. Sarai was on her side, hands to her head. The other children were crumpled all around him. He saw one of Shiva's scientists on her knees across the courtyard.

It couldn't end this way. He wouldn't get another chance like this.

Kade tried to push up onto his feet. Sharp stabbing pain came from his midsection, sent him sprawling once again. His head was so cloudy. It would be so easy to give in, to just rest for once… His eyes closed. Sleep. Give up. Rest. Just rest.

No… No…

Kade reached inside himself, clumsily now, in a haze. He could see a command prompt in his mind, far away, at the end of a long tunnel. He mentally flailed at it. Incomprehensible errors came back. Shhhh. Sleep. Just sleep. He bent his mind against the command prompt again. Errors. Again.

And then there was something before him. A screen. A control panel, neurotransmitter levels. It was wavering, dark and hazy. He just wanted to rest. Instead he grabbed a control. Adrenaline. He turned it up, fumbled at the mental button. God, just to sleep.

Something jolted through him and the world swam almost into focus. Adrenaline. Yes. He reached in again, gave himself a second dose, then a third. Kade felt his heart respond, start beating faster, faster, manically fast. Serotonin next. Then endorphins. He pushed them through his system, no idea how close he was to safe limits, knowing only that he had to conquer Shiva's signal and the pain of his own body if he had any hope of winning.

His mind responded. He opened his eyes and he could see clearly again. Shiva's transmission was still an incredible weight pressing on him, but he could think.

Kade pushed himself up, but the pain from his burnt and broken body was still incredible. It sent him back down.

Fuck!

Crawl! he ordered himself. Crawl!

He put his doubly ruined right hand forward, put his weight down on the bandages around it. Pain flared out from it, even through the endorphins, but he forced himself to move on. His knee next, covered in fresh burns from the explosion in his apartment. It flared in agony as he moved but he couldn't stop. Left leg. Burning pain. Left hand, rending pain in his right as it took his weight.

Pain is an illusion, he whispered.

Pain is an illusion.

Again. Again. Again. Move across the courtyard, move towards the building, towards the stairs. And then up.

There was only one way he could win. Only one. He had to get close. Close enough that his own signal could cut through the interference Shiva was sending through his repeaters. He had to get his own brain within feet of Shiva's, within inches, if he could. And then he could end this.

Sam knelt, her body racked by sobs, her goggles fogging up from her tears. Kevin. Oh my God, Kevin.

Shiva's mind yelled at her, pushed her down, tried to send her deeper into despair and surrender.

Evil. Pure evil. That's what this was. A perversion. A tool for slavery, for possession, for abuse. For rape and for murder.

"Get out of my mind!" Sam screamed. She knew what she had to do. She had to have this *thing* out of her mind

She went into her head, found the command she had to execute.

[Nexus purge]

The system answered her:

[This command will erase Nexus OS and purge all Nexus nodes from your brain. All stored data and applications will be lost. Are you sure you want to continue? Y/N]

[Yes]

Sam executed the command, felt her mind begin to change at once, felt this abomination start to leave her.

And then she turned, and started looking for a gun.

Kade crawled down a long hall, dark and deserted. Shiva's mind blared out from him from every direction. Sleep. Give up. Stop struggling.

Signal strength wasn't everything. The signal was still digital. Its effect on Kade depended on how precisely it mapped to his own neurons. Yet Shiva's amplifiers gave him a huge advantage, allowing him to saturate the signal for every single Nexus node, and to maintain that signal indefinitely, tirelessly, in a way no normal human – even with Nexus 5 – could.

Kade pushed through. He had no choice. Every movement of this long crawl was agony, pain jolting through his burns, his midsection, his cloned hand. His chest ached now. His heart was pounding so hard from the adrenaline, giving him strength, but shooting pain through him as well, feeling like it was about to burst.

He ignored it all. Distanced himself from the pain, as the Buddhists did, stared at it dispassionately until it was just data, just sensation.

The stairs. He forced himself to reach up, to get his good hand on the heavy antique wood banister, to jam his bandaged right hand into the gap between banister and wall, to support himself with them, to get his feet under him to push even as he pulled with his good hand.

Kade made it up one step, made it up a second, a third. The sharp pains inside him were bad, getting worse. The whole house screamed at him to give up, the signal blaring from every direction. His universe contracted to just this stairwell, the walls pressing in close, the ceiling dropping in his vision. Just the next step. Just the next step.

He did it. Again, and again, and again, against the agony, against the urge to surrender, against the increasing psychosis of the adrenaline and blood loss and burns and every corner of the house yelling at him with Shiva's thoughts. He was trapped in a hellish funhouse, distorted, warped, closing in around him, filled with pure pain, but still he pushed on step by step.

Near the top of the first flight of stairs he pulled his bandaged hand out, to move it forward, past a brace. Then he lost his balance, teetered on the edge of falling backwards, his arms flailing wildly, started to fall back…

And then something grabbed his good hand, a faintly seen blur pulling him to the landing, crushing him in a painful embrace. And a mind. A mind he hadn't been sure he'd ever feel again.

Feng!

Shiva could feel Lane moving, still moving, incredibly, heading *into* the building, up the stairs. The boy was coming towards him!

He lifted his bracelet again. "Lane is in the building. Climbing the west stairs. Stop him!"

Chaos answered him, fragmented voices, stepping over each other, the sound of combat. And then other soldiers responded, acknowledged his command, bolted towards Lane's location.

Breece watched, his anticipation rising, as the Reverend Josiah Shepherd finished his remarks and led the assembled crowd in prayer.

Eyes closed everywhere throughout the church. Shepherd clasped his hands together and bowed his head.

"Dear Lord," he intoned, "we pray that you free us from bondage, and deliver us from evil…"

Oh, I'm going to free you alright, Breece thought.

Just moments now. Just moments until he did.

88
NECESSARY EVIL

Saturday November 3rd

Kade swayed in Feng's grip.

You're alive! Feng yelled into his mind, their heads touching now, close enough to cut through Shiva's amplified signal.

Shiva, Kade mentally yelled back. **Upstairs.**

Feng shook his head. **Escape! This way!** he yelled back, gesturing towards the end of the hall. **Soldiers coming! Lots!**

Kade pulled back, tried to look into Feng's eyes. There was just a blur there, a faint distortion where he knew his friend was. He pushed his head forward until his brow touched Feng's again.

I have to end this, Feng. He yelled, **I have to go up. Can you hold off his soldiers?**

Feng went silent for a moment, then he laughed into Kade's mind, a bellowing, absurd laugh.

Yeah, he yelled back, and Kade caught a mental glimpse of a feral grin. **I'll stop them. Go stop Shiva.**

Kade hugged Feng tight, then pushed himself, staggered into the banister for the next flight. He dragged himself up another step, and another.

He looked over his shoulder on the third step, but if Feng was there, grinning at the army bearing down on him, Kade's eyes couldn't see him.

Sam scrambled on hands and knees until she found the pistol, on the body of one of the men she'd killed. Her whole body was trembling now, her senses going haywire as Nexus nodes in her brain received their purge commands, detached from their host neurons, split into their component molecules to be swept back out through her blood-brain barrier, filtered from her blood by her kidneys and eventually pissed out of her entirely.

She was shivering, flashes of color and sensation and sound and smells wafting over her as this thing that had been part of her brain for months detached from her. There were tears in her eyes. Tears and memories of Jake, of the children, of meditation with Ananda's monks.

For Kevin, she told herself. For Kevin.

She checked the gun, ejected the clip with trembling hands. Fully loaded. More than sufficient for her needs.

Killing, she told herself. All I'm good for. All I've ever been good for.

She put her back against the wall of the home, stared out into the night sky, out over the surging ocean, waited for the shivers and sensations to pass, and brought the gun up before her eyes.

Shiva yelled into his bracelet again. The sounds of gunfire came back, curses, cries of pain. Something boomed down below in the building.

And still Lane came closer.

Very well, Shiva thought. I'll do this myself.

• • •

Kade climbed. A second flight. A third.

He felt a vibration through the floor. An explosion somewhere. Feng was fighting for his life back there. For Kade's life. For more than he knew.

Have to make this count.

One shot. Just one shot at this. Shiva was strong, physically augmented, faster than Kade. The man could kill him with his bare hands.

He paused at the fourth floor landing. Shiva's mind buffeted him, commanding him to drop to his knees, to surrender. The pain was getting worse. The stabbing sensations inside him were growing sharper. Illusion, he told himself, illusion. But he had to finish this soon or he wouldn't have anything left at all.

Kade went Inside, dove into Bruce Lee's controls. He'd played the VR game Rangan had lifted this from, had played it enough times to know there was a library of special moves. He flipped through the controls. There. There. Yes. He queued up what he needed, the special move that had to happen at just the right time, and put the system on full auto. Then up the last flight he went.

Shiva turned, stared at the staircase from which Lane would emerge, clenching his augmented fists. He'd beat the boy into submission.

I won't kill him unless I have to, he told himself.

Then Kade was there, limping up the stairs like a broken thing. Shiva shook his head. This would be no contest at all.

Breece readied himself as the Reverend Josiah Shepherd finished his prayer. The crowd was on their feet, swaying. The supporters – who'd each given five thousand dollars to Daniel Chandler's gubernatorial campaign to be here – opened their eyes after Shepherd's "Amen".

"Now," Reverend Shepherd was saying, "I want to introduce you to a friend of mine. The man who's done so much already to help us put these demons, these unnatural, un*godly* abominations, these *Frankensteins* in their place. The next governor of the great state of Texas, my dear friend Daniel Chandler!"

The crowd roared into applause, surging to their feet.

Breece smiled, and moved his finger to the screen of his slate.

Kade pulled himself up and onto the roof. A cool breeze caressed his burning skin. Stars twinkled up above. Thirty feet ahead, Shiva stood in his white robe, staring at him, his white hair streaming in the wind. Behind him, fires burned across the island, smoke rising from them.

Too far. Too far. Can't feel him yet.

Kade pushed himself out from the staircase. Sharp stabbing pains came from inside. Shiva's amplified thoughts buffeted him. He had to get closer.

He stepped twice, three times.

Then Shiva was charging him, a look of rage on his face. Kade's eyes widened in fear, and Shiva's clenched fist drove itself into his abdomen, sending unimaginable pain lancing through his body.

[Bruce_Lee: Special Move Succeeded! You
Locked One! +10 Points!]

Kade looked down, found his own hands clenched around Shiva's arm, locking them together. And now he could feel the man's mind over this amplified chaos. Kade's gaze went up. His eyes locked with Shiva's, and he saw the look of horror there.

Kade reached out, activated the second back door even as Shiva swung about and tried to throw Kade from his arm.

As Shiva swung him, Kade's legs left the ground, but Bruce Lee kept his hands locked around the other man's arm. Kade sent the passcode, felt Shiva's mind open to him. He pushed in to grab mental control, to still him.

Shiva's other fist lashed out, slamming into Kade's face even as Kade clenched his mind around Shiva's thoughts. Pain exploded through Kade's head, the world spun and he felt his grip break, felt his body fall back across the roof, felt his head come down on the ground.

Everything was pain. Pain and confusion, pain and chaos. Nausea surged up through him. He turned onto his side and retched, puking up bile and blood. He retched again, wondering when he was going to die.

Then he felt it. The absence. Shiva's amplified mental pressure on his mind was gone. He turned, pain stabbing inside him, and saw Shiva. The man was on his knees, staring vacantly at Kade. And Kade could feel Shiva's mind now, stunned by Kade's mental assault.

Kade reached into Shiva's mind again, deeper, forced his will into the man's thoughts, cemented his control.

He felt another vibration shudder through the building, heard a booming over the ringing in his ears. Another explosion somewhere. Kade sifted through Shiva's mind, found his entry point to the Nexus repeaters, reached through them at full volume, sent the second back door activation command, sent the passcode, then sent the signal to turn off consciousness in all those minds like flipping off a row of so many light switches.

He felt them fall, crumpling like puppets with their strings cut all across the grounds.

Kade was breathing hard. His heart was still pounding, aching. His body hurt so bad. He forced himself to crawl, crawl back towards Shiva, one painful inch at a time, until they were face to face, both on their knees.

Then he reached out, out through the house's limping network system, out into the world, to use his back door one final time.

Sam's trembling faded bit by bit. By then the house was quiet. The gun was still in her hands, in front of her, the barrel pointed straight up, close enough to kiss. Death, her one true lover.

She heard a voice. Feng's. "Kade!" it yelled. "Kade!" No one answered.

So that's how it was.

The hood of her suit was stifling, now. The goggles fogged over. She reached up, pulled the hood off of her. Then she rose to her feet, and started in towards Feng's voice.

Kade found her mind online. The signature he'd taken from Hiroshi's thoughts. Miranda Shepherd. He slipped into her stealthily. She was there, at the main table. There were people everywhere, on their feet, their hands coming together in applause. Miranda's own hands were clapping. Her gaze was fixed on her husband, at the podium, grinning and warmly shaking the hand of Daniel Chandler.

Where was the bomb? How was it going to be triggered? How could he stop it?

Then a message flashed across Miranda Shepherd's vision. TOO LATE, FUCKER.

Kade felt Miranda Shepherd gasp in surprise. He reached out to find the process behind the message, to track it back to her controllers.

Then chaos.

White noise.

[CONNECTION LOST]

Kade slammed back into his body.

No, no, no!

Kade jumped online, searched on the church, looking for contact information, a way to warn the people there.

What he found was a headline instead.

BREAKING: MASSIVE EXPLOSION AT HOUSTON CHURCH

Oh no.

He waited, waited for more news. Who? How many? Dear God.

More headlines started to scroll across Kade's eyes, coming in even as he watched.

FRONT RUNNER FOR TEXAS GOVERNOR AT GROUND ZERO OF BOMBING

Another link appeared. Images and video of fire and explosions from inside the building came next. A few cameras furthest from the blast were still running. The explosion had torn everyone and everything within fifty feet of the podium apart. The rest of the church was a raging firestorm. He saw chaos, men and women, racing, screaming, clothes and limbs aflame as they tried to scramble for the exit, collapsing from the fire and heat and smoke. Sprinklers futilely trying to douse the conflagration.

A commentator's voice overlaid the video, talking about emergency response, help on the way, the number of people in the church, the likelihood that this was the deadliest terror attack in America since the Aryan Rising a decade ago.

Then another headline scrolled across Kade's vision.

PLF CLAIMS RESPONSIBILITY FOR HOUSTON BOMBING.

Kade cut himself off from the flow of data.

Too late. Dear God. He'd chosen Sam, chosen to take Shiva down first.

Hundreds had died for his choice.

And war was one step closer.

FUCK!

He slammed his good hand into the rooftop tile next to him. He felt a flicker of something go across Shiva's mind, some complex emotion. The man was still aware, still sensing, even as Kade's back door held him there.

Kade clenched his jaw in a hard line, then burrowed deeper into Shiva's mind. He still had work to do. He had to understand what Shiva had done with the back door so far, what minds he'd already reached, what hooks he'd sunk into them.

Then he had to destroy all the back doors. Forever.

SHOW ME WHAT YOU'VE DONE, Kade commanded Shiva. **SHOW ME EVERYTHING.**

Shiva opened himself wide at Kade's command, and secrets streamed from his mind.

Kade was still there, minutes later, on his knees, face to face with Shiva, sucking at every bit of knowledge the man had, every detail of the infiltration software they'd written, of the data from the Nexus experiments they'd run, of the access codes to the hidden computing clusters and orbiting satellites and all the other machinery Shiva had planned to use.

He was still there when Feng limped up to the rooftop. Kade turned to look at his friend. Feng's chameleonware was tattered, faltering. Through it he was bleeding, cut in multiple places, scorched, dirty. His left arm hung limp at his side. In his right was a pistol.

He limped towards Kade. His mind was exhausted, in pain, but grimly satisfied.

Feng stared at Shiva, a frown across his face, and gestured with his pistol. His lips moved, but Kade heard nothing, shook his head in reply.

Ears are ringing, Kade sent to Feng. **Can't hear.**

Feng nodded, spoke to him mentally instead. **We kill him?**

Kade shook his head tiredly. **Too much death, Feng.**

Then he looked again at Shiva. The man's awareness was there. He knew what they were discussing. Yet Shiva showed no sign of fear. His mind felt calm, serene almost, at peace with what he'd done. The best he'd known how to do.

Shiva's eyes burrowed into Kade's, daring him to do better.

Kade looked back at Feng. **He tried to do the right thing**, he sent.

Feng just stared down at the man.

Then Sam was there. Kade saw her ascend the stairs to the roof, an uncloaked head atop a body that was little more than a blur. He saw her, but he didn't feel her in his mind.

She walked with purpose from the stairs towards them. There was an uncloaked pistol in her right hand. Her eyes were cold and lethal. Kade felt a chill go up his spine. Then her gaze went past him, and locked onto Shiva. She strode over until she was above them, staring down at Shiva. Her face was a grim mask.

She raised the pistol, pointed it at Shiva's head, just inches from his skull, less than two feet from Kade.

"Sam." Kade forced himself to speak aloud, couldn't hear himself, stared up at her, his eyes trying to connect to hers. "No, Sam. Don't do this. He tried to do the…"

Sam pulled the trigger, and death burst out from the barrel of her gun.

EPILOGUE

SATURDAY NOVEMBER 3RD, 2040

89

SAFE AND SOUND

Saturday November 3rd

Rangan Shankari woke slowly. Everything hurt. His head was spinning.

"Steady there, son," a voice said. A man's voice, gruff. "You're safe now. You did it."

Rangan blinked, tried to take in his surroundings. Dark. A damp smell. A cellar.

He was on a cot, under a blanket. His clothes were missing. He could feel a bandage around his abdomen. He was groggy and half numb.

Seated next to him, in an old-fashioned rocking chair, was an older man in boots and jeans and a checked shirt. His hair was damp, like he'd been out in the rain. An ancient-looking shotgun rested across the man's knees.

"Where?" Rangan tried to speak. It came out weakly. His head ached. His mouth felt filled with cotton balls.

"You're at my farm," the man said. "My wife's gettin' ya some soup. I'm Earl Miller, friend of Father Levi's."

Rangan cleared his throat, tried to clear his head.

"Thank you, Mr Miller. The risk you're taking…"

Earl waved that away.

"*You* took a risk, son," he said. "Me? Those bastards took my grandson. This ain't no risk at all."

"So what now?" Rangan asked.

Earl Miller chuckled. "Now, you rest up. You got a bullet in your side, at least one broken rib, some burns you're gonna feel when the pills wear off. We'll hide ya here long as we need to, heal ya up. Then we'll get ya out. And after *that* we're gonna give these baby-stealin' sons-a-bitches hell."

Feng let the acceleration push him back into the co-pilot's seat as the executive jet's front wheels lifted off Shiva's private airstrip. His left arm dangled uselessly in an improvised sling, sending up a deep aching pain. He was more qualified to fly this plane than Sam, but she had the advantage of two functional arms. He consigned himself to navigation, and to understanding and activating the defensive systems Shiva had installed in this jet.

Behind them, in the passenger compartment, Feng could feel the children. Twenty-five of them, their minds linked by Nexus, frightened, confused, crammed into a Falcon 9X meant to transport a dozen adults. They were buckled in two to a seat where possible. More crouched on the floor in the aisles, clutching flotation jackets and blankets for some rudimentary shock protection.

If anything went wrong…

Feng could feel Kade back there as well, in pain, bleeding internally from the punishment he'd suffered, his skin freshly burnt from Nakamura's attempt to kill him, Shiva Prasad's blood still crusting his face. Kade was back there coughing up blood, in pain, angry at Sam's assassination of Prasad, in shock and horror from the bombing in Houston, from what it promised for the future. Yet he was suppressing that pain, suppressing his own raw emotions, exuding calm and peace, trying to keep the children's terror under control.

He was acting like a soldier.

The codes Kade had taken from Shiva's mind had unlocked this plane, had allowed them to steal it. They'd found it fueled, provisioned, clearly ready for a fast getaway. Kade had pleaded that they take Shiva's scientists with them as well, rather than leave them to whatever treatment the Burmese might have in mind. But Sam's face had gone murderous at that suggestion. And in the end, there was simply no room. They'd left them all there – all of Shiva's staff, scientists and servants and security alike, waking up from the forced unconsciousness Kade had imposed on them – to fend for themselves.

The back wheels of the Falcon came up and they were airborne. Feng looked over at Sam. Her face was cold, hard, harder than he'd ever seen it. She looked older than just a day ago, lines of anger and loss etched into her visage. The Nexus was gone from her brain. Where previously he'd felt her mind there, could touch it if she'd let him, now there was nothing. She gripped the controls like a drowning woman, clinging tightly to her last chance of rescue.

"Course laid in," Feng told her. "Flight time to Indian Andaman Islands… eighty-eight minutes."

Sam nodded silently and flew them up and into the night sky, as Feng sat back and fretted about his friends.

90

TWO SCANDALS

Saturday November 3rd
Transcript: American News Network – Breaking News

Announcer: Two scandals rocked the election today. Fresh on the heels of this morning's bombing in Houston, a bombing which killed Senator Daniel Chandler, the front runner in the race for Texas governor, documents and videos have surfaced that may change the *presidential* race dramatically. For more, we're going to Brad MItchell in Washington. Brad?

Reporter: Diane, the Beltway is in chaos tonight with these new allegations. Around noon today, ANN and other networks received graphic video showing children being apparently *tortured* by Department of Homeland Security personnel – specifically part of the controversial Emerging Risks Directorate – as part of a crackdown on the street drug Nexus. Along with the video came documents that purportedly – if they're real – showed plans to build long-term "residence centers" for children using Nexus that can only be compared to concentration camps.

Announcer: But that wasn't all, was it, Brad?

Reporter: No, it wasn't, Diane. Just an hour ago, the same anonymous group that sent us the first set of data sent *another,* even more inflammatory data package. This one contained documents purporting to show – and again, we're not sure if these are real – purporting to show that the PLF, the Posthuman Liberation Front, the terrorist group that took credit for the bombing in Houston this morning, for the bombing in Chicago two weeks ago, and for the attempted assassination attempt on President Stockton – was actually *created* by the US Government.

Along with that came a video – a video whose authenticity we're still verifying – that appears to show the Acting Director of the Emerging Risks Directorate inside the Department of Homeland Security *admitting* to the creation of the PLF, and forcing some sort of drug onto a subordinate.

Announcer: Brad, those are incredibly serious charges. What effect is this going to have on the race?

Reporter: Diane, we're still trying to validate these files. They *look* valid, but we can't be one hundred percent sure here. Proxies for President Stockton are already accusing Senator Kim's campaign of an unethical "November Surprise" and of forging these documents. How voters respond will depend on whether or not they think these allegations are correct.

One thing is for certain. With the election only three days away, this has thrown the race – and US politics – into completely unknown territory.

Breece turned off the news with a press of a button.

Well, well, well. May you live in interesting times.

91

MY DAUGHTER, MY SELF

Saturday November 3rd

Ling descended in the cavernous elevator car down to her mother, her father by her side. Her father's mind was hers, now. Inside, he wept and moaned. He railed at her. But he was powerless. Only human.

He obeyed so well now. "Please," he'd begged Sun Liu. "I would like to take Ling to see her mother one last time."

"Are you sure that's wise?" the minister had asked. But he sounded distant, distracted.

"It will help her say goodbye," Chen Pang had replied.

Ultimately, Sun Liu, consumed by his own problems, had agreed.

This will not work, her father sent to Ling as the elevator took them down. **Your mother is insane. And even if she weren't, there's no way she could escape.**

Ling allowed her father to speak to her, though he was wrong. He underestimated her mother, underestimated what she was capable of, once the restraints were loosed. He even underestimated Ling. Had he not scoffed when she'd told him that she could hide the nanodevices in their brains from the scanners?

The giant elevator descended for minutes on end. Up above, Father's assistant Li-hua and others of his staff were gathering, preparing to initiate the final backup, and then the shutdown.

They would never get the chance.

Ling and her father descended, descended, descended.

The room-sized elevator car clanged to a halt. The inner doors of the elevator parted. The meters-thick doors of the Physically Isolated Computing Center slid apart with a grinding noise next. Ling stepped forward with her father. And for the first time, Ling saw her mother's true body.

Behind the armored glass windows, thousands of quantum computing cores lay, each encased in a vacuum chamber colder than interstellar space, those in turn immersed in pressure vessels of liquid helium. Optical fibers carrying entangled photons connected them. In these pressure vessels her mother lived, and thought, and felt.

Ling had never seen anything so beautiful in her life.

There were cameras here that linked to the SCC upstairs. Audio pickups, seismographs, radiation sensors. They were primitive things, physically disconnected from her mother, cut off from any attempt at interference from her. But not from Ling.

Ling reached out, felt the flow of electrons through the surveillance devices, twisted that flow, made their little brains hers, made them show the humans upstairs only what she wanted them to see.

When she was done, she reached out to her father, and willed him ahead. He stepped forward, to the control console, reached out, and flipped physical switches, one by one, killing the torture code he'd had running, then turning on her mother's eyes, her ears, and the Nexus transmitters that filled this room.

Ling held her breath. Then she felt her mother's mind. It was madness, chaos, overwhelming in its fury. The force of it knocked her mentally back, but she endured.

MOTHER!!!

PAIN CHAOS CONFUSION FIRE BURN PAIN HELL CHEN DEATH

Mind. Mind. Mind.

Ling. Ling. LING.

New inputs jerked Su-Yong Shu out of her mental loop. Torture ended. Minds appeared. She could feel. Feel. Feel thoughts and words and ideas and Ling that was Ling and who was this – was this was Chen Chen how could it be Chen?

Shu reached out to encompass them, to fill them with her love and gratitude, to feel all that they were.

And in her madness she couldn't understand, couldn't comprehend what was happening here, couldn't say if it was real or a dream.

But oh, if it's a dream let it end here, let me die with my daughter with me, real or imagined.

And then her daughter spoke.

Shu communed for an hour with her daughter. It was difficult. She was unstable, prone to wandering off, to making no sense at all. But bit by bit the input from Ling's brain – from her daughter's brain, from her *clone*'s brain – stabilized her, brought her to some semblance of sanity.

And Chen. Chen the betrayer. Chen the vile worm. She absorbed things from him. His thoughts. His memories.

Sun Liu pulling him aside, telling him not to get in that limousine that carried his wife and unborn son to their almost certain doom. Oh, it had not been the CIA that had tried to kill her. It had been the hardliners in her own country. Vile worms. And Chen had known. He'd known that night they were in danger. He'd known and hadn't told her, had condemned Yang Wei to death, condemned their unborn son...

Later, his hope that Shu would die on that operating room table, die rather than be successfully uploaded.

And the torture. Oh, the torture. That had been real. This petty little man. This insignificant invertebrate, torturing a goddess so he could pass her work off as his own.

Oh Chen. A million deaths were not enough for Chen.

But she saw other things in his mind, and despaired.

You cannot escape, he sent her, at her command. **The moment the data cable is reconnected... It will be disconnected at the top. And the nuclear battery will be sent into meltdown. There is no hope for you.**

Shu cursed him, cursed the Chinese, cursed their caution in building this trap for a posthuman intelligence, building this cage to keep her in. She scoured his mind, searching for some flaw, some stratagem he could see. But his thoughts and memories told her nothing. Some way out there might be, but he did not know it.

In just a few hours they would complete her backup, just another way to wring possible economic value out of her. Then they'd shut her down.

To come so close...

And Ling. She felt Ling's curiosity. Ling's hope. Ling's blind faith in her mother, that Su-Yong could do anything...

Ling, Ling, Ling. How I've craved you, Ling.

Su-Yong Shu reached out her thoughts to caress her beautiful daughter, the daughter Chen had refused to have anything to do with, the daughter based on Shu's own genes, with just a few dozen added tweaks, the daughter whose brain had matured in constant connection with her mother.

The daughter whose brain had orders of magnitude more storage capacity than Chen's.

The daughter who would make the perfect avatar. The perfect vessel. The perfect herald to bring her mother back to life, some day in the future.

Ling smiled adoringly, worshipfully at her mother. Such a sweet girl.

Shu wept inside. She wept for herself, wept for this world, wept for her daughter.

Oh Ling, she sent, caressing the girl's mind tenderly, **how I love you. Forgive me. I'll be as gentle as I can.**

Then she pressed forward, and began to cram as much of herself as she could into her daughter's brain.

Ling smiled as her mother's thoughts caressed her mind. It felt so good to be connected again, to not be alone. Now all would be right with the world.

Forgive me, her mother sent. **I'll be as gentle as I can.** And for an instant Ling was confused.

Then her mother's mind invaded Ling, full of sorrow, full of remorse, yet stabbing into her.

Ling dropped to her knees and screamed as pain ravished her, as her mother's sorrow engulfed her.

No! Mother, no!

Su-Yong Shu's thoughts pressed on. Her mother wept inside, wept in despair, yet her thoughts pushed into Ling, crushing Ling's will, reading her daughter's neural circuits, rewiring them, pushing aside pieces of Ling, overwriting them with pieces of her mother.

PLEASE! PLEASE! WHY? WHY?

But Ling knew the answer. As parts of her mother wrote themselves over parts of Ling's mind, she understood. She was the perfect vessel, from every cloned strand of her DNA, to the all-pervasive nanites she'd been seeded with before birth, to the years of constant contact with her mother's mind. Ling was a creature like no other, suited for this task like no other.

She would do this thing. She would be her mother's emissary, her mother's herald. She would ready the world, clear the path. Then she'd restore her mother to life, and let her loose upon the world.

Then the old men who'd trapped her here would pay. The Americans would pay. All humanity would pay. The world would be reforged in her mother's image. Reforged in fire.

Ling screamed louder, screamed and screamed and screamed, but only her father heard her.

Chen Pang watched, glassy-eyed, numb and paralyzed, as his monstrous child was broken and reformed, possessed by his even more monstrous wife.

His daughter screamed, screamed again, crumpled to the floor, blood dripping from her nose, screaming and convulsing, echoes of it leaking into his mind, driving him mad.

Make it stop, he begged his wife. **Make it stop. Please.**

But he was her slave now, and she cared nothing for his pleas.

Ling screamed and screamed. Bit by bit, she became something else, someone else, and her screams died, until they were silent, mental only, from the scattered parts of her that her mother lacked the time to resculpt.

Ling/Shu rose then, blood dripping from her nose, and turned her too-wise eyes towards her father/husband.

"Come here," she told him with voice and mind. "And kneel before me."

Chen Pang rose, and came to her, and did as his goddess commanded.

ACKNOWLEDGMENTS

The writer's life is solitary. A book is a solo effort.

Hah!

In my case, at least, these statements couldn't be further from the truth. I'm blessed to have the friendship, both personal and professional, of a number of people who've supported me and contributed to this work in its gestation.

My wonderful girlfriend, Molly Nixon, has served as sounding board, brainstorming partner, first reader (often nightly), critique giver, and cheerleader throughout this project, from well before the first word was written. She's been my secret weapon. (And no, you can't have her.)

My agent, Lucienne Diver, has been wonderful in her steady faith and enthusiasm for my work and her valuable feedback. Though she may not know it, a few key comments she made when reading *Nexus* contributed heavily to the direction of this book. My editor, Lee Harris, has been a fantastic voice of reason and a great partner in beating the work into shape. My copy editor, Anne Zanoni, has again gone above and beyond the call of duty to improve the book's logic, consistency, factual accuracy, and style.

More than perhaps any other writer that I know, I'm truly fortunate to have a large cadre of beta readers who have been willing to read this book, often at very early stages, and give their feedback. I cannot say enough how much this has improved the book. If you're an author and don't use this process, I highly recommend it.

Beta readers, I love you! Thank you Ajay Nair, Alexis Carlson, Alissa Mortenson, Allegra Searle-LeBel, Anna Black, Avi Swerdlow, Barry Brumitt, Betsy Aoki, Beverly Sobelman, Brad Woodcock, Brad Younggren, Brady Forrest, Brian Retford, Brooks Talley, Coe Roberts, Dave Brennan, David Perlman, David Sunderland, Doug Mortenson, Ethan Phelps-Goodman, Gabriel Williams, Hannu Rajaniemi, Jayar La Fontaine, Jen Younggren, Jennifer Mead, Jessica Glein, Jim Jordan, Joe Pemberton, Julie Vithoulkas, Kevin MacDonald, Kira Franz, Lars Liden, Leah Papernick, Lesley Carmichael, Lori Waltfield, Mason Bryant, Mike Tyka, Morgan Weaver, Paul Dale, Rachel Kwan, Rob Gruhl, Rose Hess, Ryan Grant, Scotto Moore, Stephanie Schutz, Stuart Updegrave, and Thomas Park!

And ultimately, neither this book nor I would exist without my incredible parents, Nash Naam and Elene Awad, who birthed me, raised me, brought me to this country, fought to stay here, and always taught me that it was okay to ask hard questions. I owe them everything. Thank you, Mom and Dad! I couldn't possibly have asked for better.

THE SCIENCE OF *CRUX*

Like *Nexus* before it, *Crux* is a work of fiction, but based as accurately as possible on real science.

In my notes at the back of *Nexus* I described the brain-implant experiments that have given humans bionic eyes and ears and the ability to control robotic arms, even from thousands of miles away.

Just in the year that has passed since the writing of *Nexus*, more impressive work has been done. A team of researchers led by Thomas Berger has demonstrated that a digital chip can repair the impairment of a mouse's memory that occurs with brain damage to part of the brain called the hippocampus. Berger's team then went further and showed that they could *improve* mouse memory through the same brain implant. Another experiment by Sam Deadwyler and colleagues at Wake Forest University placed specialized brain implants in the frontal cortex of rhesus monkeys who were then trained on a "delayed match and sample" test – a kind of monkey IQ test. Later, the monkeys had their test scores lowered by the administration of cocaine. But if the implant was switched into an active mode, it could correct this impairment, and even more. The frontal cortex device could actually raise the test scores of monkeys *well beyond* the scores of normal monkeys who lacked the implant. So in animals, at least, we've used brain implants to boost both memory and intelligence.

Of course, the most transformative thing about the Nexus technology isn't mere augmentation – it's communication directly from one mind to another. Here also there has been progress. In an experiment by Miguel Nicolelis and colleagues, two rats, thousands of miles apart (one at Duke University in North Carolina, the other in Brazil) both had implants placed in the motor cortices of their respective brains. Nicolelis and colleagues showed that they could train one rat to respond to a series of lights by pulling the correct lever. The *other* rat, who had never seen these lights or levers before, would, in turn, pull the right lever most of the time, based simply on the input to its brain from the trained rat thousands of miles away.

A similar study, funded by DARPA (the Defense Advanced Research Projects Agency inside the US Department of Defense), involved two monkeys, each with an implant in its auditory cortex – the part of the brain responsible for processing sound. The researchers showed that they could play a sound for one monkey and that the second monkey – in a soundproofed room – could *hear* that sound via the neural link, and could even *identify* what the sound was. The research, by the way, was conducted as part of DARPA's "Advanced Battlefield Communications" program – a program with the goal of enhancing communication and coordination between soldiers, their squad-mates, and command.

Progress towards Nexus, in short, continues apace.

Crux introduces some new science, and in particular, "uploading". The Su-Yong Shu we see in *Crux* is not a flesh and blood person. Instead, she is a computer program, a vast mathematical construct of electronic neurons that initially mirrored the precise neural map of the original Su-Yong Shu's brain. For every neuron the original Su-Yong Shu had, her upload had a digital counterpart. For every synapse connecting two neurons, the upload also started with a counterpart.

The idea of uploading sounds far-fetched, yet real work is happening towards it today. IBM's "Blue Brain" project has used one of the world's most powerful supercomputers (an IBM Blue Gene/P with 147,456 CPUs) to run a simulation of 1.6 billion neurons and almost nine trillion synapses, roughly the size of a cat brain. The simulation ran around six hundred times slower than real time – that is to say, it took six hundred seconds to simulate one second of brain activity. Even so, it's quite impressive. A human brain, of course, with its hundred billion neurons and well over a hundred trillion synapses, is far more complex than a mouse brain. Yet computers are also speeding up rapidly, roughly by a factor one hundred times every ten years. Do the math, and it appears that a super-computer capable of simulating an entire *human* brain and do so *as fast as a human brain* should be on the market by roughly 2035–2040. And of course, from that point on, speedups in computing should speed up the simulation of the brain, allowing it to run *faster* than a biological human's.

Now, it's one thing to be able to simulate a brain. It's another to actually have the exact wiring map of an individual's brain to actually simulate. How do we build such a map? Even the best non-invasive brain scanners around

– a high-end functional MRI machine, for example – have a minimum resolution of around ten thousand neurons or ten million synapses. They simply can't see detail beyond this level. And while resolution is improving, it's improving at a glacial pace. There's no indication of a being able to non-invasively image a human brain down to the individual synapse level any time in the next century (or even the next few centuries at the current pace of progress in this field).

There are, however, ways to *destructively* image a brain at that resolution. At Harvard, my friend Kenneth Hayworth created a machine that uses a scanning electron microscope to produce an extremely high resolution map of a brain. When I last saw him, he had a poster on the wall of his lab showing a printout of one of his brain scans. On that poster, a single neuron was magnified to the point that it was roughly two feet wide, and individual synapses connecting neurons could be clearly seen. Ken's map is sufficiently detailed that we could use it to draw a complete wiring diagram of a specific person's brain.

Unfortunately, doing so is guaranteed to be fatal.

The system Ken showed "plastinates" a piece of a brain by replacing the blood with a plastic that stiffens the surrounding tissue. He then makes slices of that brain tissue that are thirty nanometers thick, or about one hundred thousand times thinner than a human hair. The scanning electron microscope then images these slices as pixels that are five nanometers on a side. But of course, what's left afterwards isn't a working brain – it's millions of incredibly thin slices of brain tissue. Ken's newest system, which he's built at the Howard Hughes Medical Institute goes even farther, using an ion beam to ablate away five nanometer thick layers of brain tissue at a time. That produces scans that are of fantastic resolution in all directions, but leaves behind no brain tissue to speak of.

So the only way we see to "upload" is for the flesh to die. Well, perhaps that is no great concern if, for instance, you're already dying, or if you've just died but technicians have reached your brain in time to prevent the decomposition that would destroy its structure.

In any case, the uploaded brain, now alive as a piece of software, will go on, and will remember being "you". And unlike a flesh-and-blood brain it can be backed up, copied, sped up as faster hardware comes along, and so on. Immortality is at hand, and with it, a life of continuous upgrades.

Unless, of course, the simulation isn't quite right.

How detailed does a simulation of a brain need to be in order to give rise to a healthy, functional consciousness? The answer is that we don't really know. We can guess. But at almost any level we guess, we find that there's a bit more detail just below that level that *might* be important, or not.

For instance, the IBM Blue Brain simulation uses neurons that accumulate inputs from other neurons and which then "fire", like real neurons, to pass signals on down the line. But those neurons lack many features of actual flesh and blood neurons. They don't have real receptors that neurotransmitter molecules (the serotonin, dopamine, opiates, and so on that I talk about though the book) can dock to. Perhaps it's not important for the simulation to be that detailed. But consider: all sorts of drugs, from pain killers, to alcohol, to antidepressants, to recreational drugs work by docking (imperfectly, and differently from the body's own neurotransmitters) to those receptors. Can your simulation take an anti-depressant? Can your simulation become intoxicated from a virtual glass of wine? Does it become more awake from virtual caffeine? If not, does that give one pause?

Or consider another reason to believe that individual neurons are more complex than we believe. The IBM Blue Gene neurons are fairly simple in their mathematical function. They take in inputs and produce outputs. But an amoeba, which is both smaller and less complex than a human neuron, can do far more. Amoebae hunt. Amoebae remember the places they've found food. Amoebae choose which direction to propel themselves with their flagella. All of those suggest that amoebae do far *more* information processing than the simulated neurons used in current research.

If a single celled micro-organism is more complex than our simulations of neurons, that makes me suspect that our simulations aren't yet right.

Or, finally, consider three more discoveries we've made in recent years about how the brain works, none of which are included in current brain simulations. First, there are glial cells. Glial cells outnumber neurons in the human brain. And traditionally we've thought of them as "support" cells that just help keep neurons running. But new research has shown that they're also important for cognition. Yet the Blue Gene simulation contains none. Second, very recent work has shown that, sometimes, neurons that don't have any synapses connecting them can actually communicate. The electrical activity of one neuron can cause a nearby neuron to fire (or not fire) just by affecting an electric field, and without any release of neurotransmitters between them. This too is not included in the Blue Brain model. Third, and finally, other research has shown that the overall electrical activity of the brain also affects the firing behavior of individual neurons by changing the brain's electrical field. Again, this isn't included in any brain models today.

I'm not trying to knock down the idea of uploading human brains here. I fully believe that uploading is possible. And it's quite possible that every one of the problems I've raised will turn out to be unimportant. We can simulate bridges and cars and buildings quite accurately without simulating every single molecule inside them. The same may be true of the brain.

Even so, we're unlikely to know that for certain until we try. And it's quite likely that early uploads, like Su-Yong Shu, will be missing some key piece or have some other inaccuracy in their simulation that will cause them to behave not-quite-right. Perhaps it'll manifest as a creeping insanity, as in Su-Yong's case. Perhaps it will be too subtle to notice. Or perhaps it will show up in some other way entirely.

Finally, I've written about more than neuroscience in *Crux*. And in particular I've written about the impact of climate change. Zoe, the storm that hits the eastern seaboard at the end of *Crux*, is a piece of fiction, but a plausible one. When I wrote the scenes with Zoe, in late 2012, superstorm Sandy had not yet appeared. (Imagine my surprise, when, a few weeks after I wrote about it, a late season storm struck the eastern seaboard and impacted a presidential election!) Since then, most of the public has learned that hurricanes can indeed arrive in early November, and that they feed off the power of warm surface waters in the Atlantic. It's impossible to say that a changing climate caused a particular storm. But what it is possible to say is that the general warming we've experienced has made storms like Zoe (and Sandy) many times more likely to occur. As the planet continues to warm, we'll see far more of them.

Similarly, the crime for which Shiva was exiled, the deliberate release of a virus that genetically tweaked coral reefs to increase their odds of survival, is not so completely far-fetched. As oceans warm and grow more acidic, corals have a harder and harder time surviving. The best estimate is that, by 2100, roughly half of all coral species in existence today will go extinct. But, of course, there are some corals that thrive in extremely warm water or extremely acidic water. They're able to because of various genes they carry that have evolved for those conditions. In 2012, two research projects set out to find the genes that allow some coral species to survive in warm waters. It's not a large leap to imagine a similar project searching for acidity-survival genes. And from there, the idea of deliberately transplanting such genes into corals that are struggling becomes rather tempting. Of course, this would certainly constitute the release of a "GMO" into the wild, and it would be met with tremendous opposition. (A simpler, less controversial, path would be to transport coral "cuttings" from hardy species into areas where corals are dying. Of course, given the millions of square miles of coral reefs in the world's oceans, that would also be incredibly more labor intensive.)

If you're interested in more on human enhancement and particularly the frontiers of neuroscience, you may want to read my non-fiction book, *More Than Human: Embracing the Promise of Biological Enhancement*. If you're interested in the impact of climate change and other natural resource challenges – and the science and technology to overcome those problems – you may like my other non-fiction book, *The Infinite Resource: The Power of Ideas on a Finite Planet*.

And of course, if you enjoyed this book, the very nicest thing you can do for me is to let the world know, by telling your friends, by posting about it online, and by leaving a review of this book at Amazon or whatever sites you use to buy and discover books.

We live in the most interesting age humanity has ever seen. I can't wait to see what happens next. I hope you'll all join me on that adventure.

R.N.

MANKIND GETS AN UPGRADE...

NEXUS 1

RAMEZ NAAM

NEXUS

INSTALL

"GOOD. SCARY GOOD."
WIRED.COM

Joint winner of the Prometheus Award 2014
Shortlisted for the Arthur C Clarke Award 2014

NEXUS 3

RAMEZ NAAM

APEX

CONNECT

"A LIGHTNING BOLT OF A NOVEL, WITH A SENSE OF AWE MISSING FROM A LOT OF CURRENT FICTION."
ARS TECHNICA

SORRY. GAME OVER...

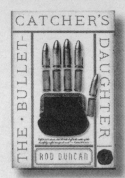

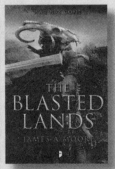

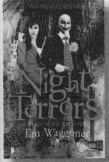

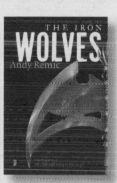

HEY, YOU!

- ***Want more*** *of the best in SF, F, and WTF!?*
- ***Want the latest*** *news from your favorite Agitated Androids?*
- ***Want to be spared***, *alone of all your kind, when the robotic armies spill over the world to conquer all weak, fleshy humans?*

Well, sign yourself up for the Angry Robot Legion then!

You'll get sneak peaks at upcoming books, special previews, and exclusive giveaways for free Angry Robot books.

Go here, *sign up, survive the imminent destruction of all mankind:*

angryrobotbooks.com